Himaya

Julie Kabouya

Copyright © 2020 by Julie Kabouya

All rights reserved.

No portion of this book may be reproduced in any form without written permission from the publisher or author, except as permitted by U.S. copyright law.

For my three pumpkins

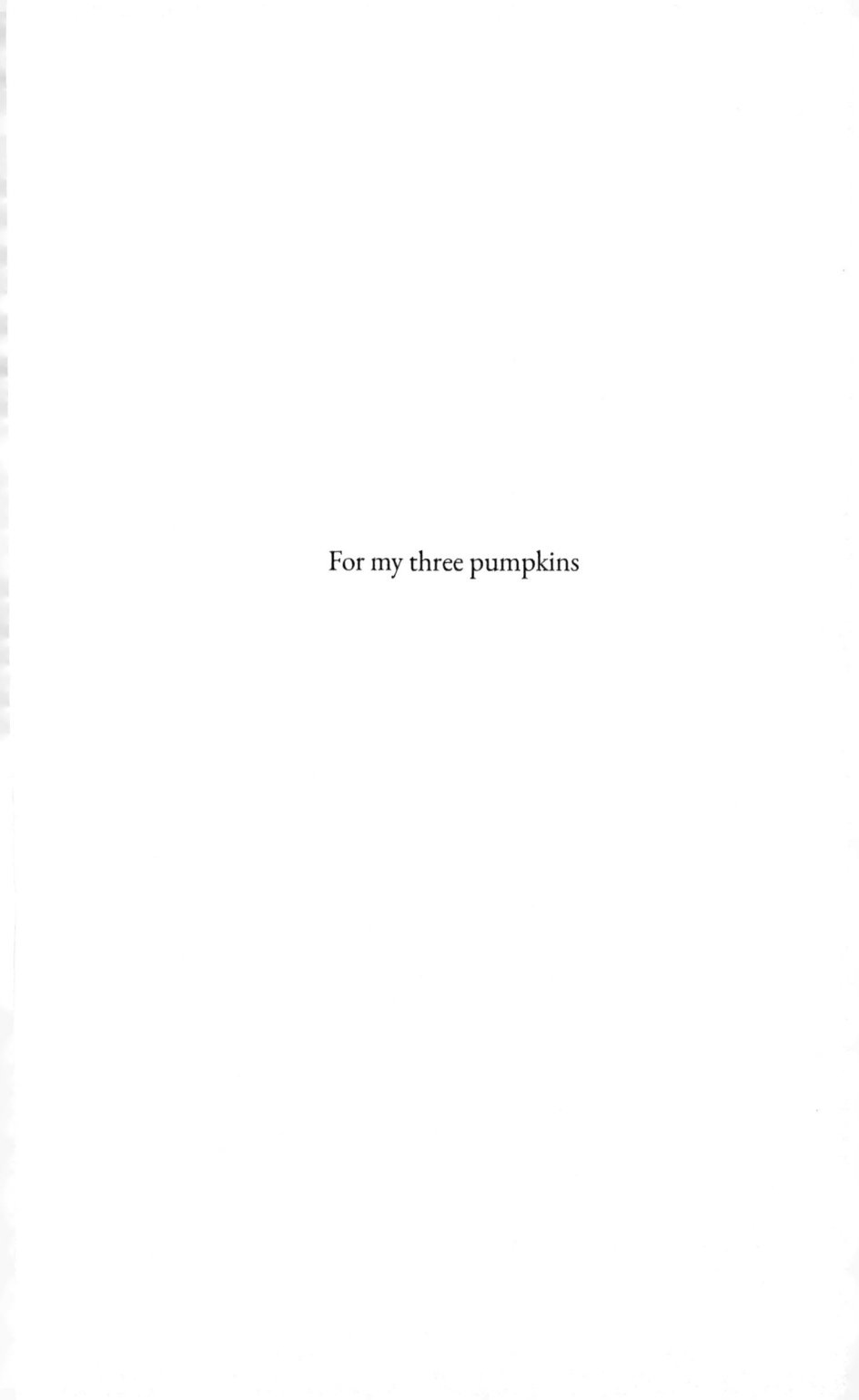

One

June 1993. South Wales.

    The decrepit Honda Civic rattled as it struggled to keep up with her suppressed right foot. She had to make it there and back without raising suspicion- anxious how she would feel and at what cost. Forgetting to indicate she swerved sharp left into the small, gravelled car park, her eyes wet with emotion. A forbidden endeavour which was long overdue. It was either that or disintegrate from apathy. Pulling on the handbrake she was alone, every move she made felt like a disturbance in the muted surroundings of ancient woodland. The Scots Pines and Cedars gave her a majestic welcome, their canopies stretched endlessly as she gazed upwards, making her feel insignificant and fragile. She noticed her sacred space was no longer a secret - Trust ownership announced its crude invasion.

She hesitated at the stile before pushing her long, white linen skirt between her legs and lurching over it, scuffing up the dirt from tripping a little on the other side. The entrance sparked excitement - enchanted whispers rushed forth tingling her skin. She hesitated, wanting to enjoy the tantalising moment a little longer, preparing herself before going in - she tucked her short, mousy brown hair behind her funny-shaped ears, exposing her petite features. They were convinced she wasn't human - she was, of course, but with a twist. Lillian the odd girl who felt she didn't belong here, bullied throughout her school life - often referred to as a tangled ball of Christmas lights. Weird things happen when she's emotional, especially during full moons. Having an aura that attracted the crazy ones and made total strangers open up to her.

'Oh my God. I've missed you,' she uttered - inhaling deeply, her breaths shuddering. The smell of pine and leaf rot filled her nostrils and lungs, releasing the tension. Grounding her, pulling her in like a lasso - she was ready, tiptoeing over the threshold, her eyes alight.

Vast in either direction, the harmonious network was cloaked in grey and truffle tones with hints of green; illuminated by penetrating sunrays. She chose her tree, wrapping her arms around it - the bark warm from the day's heat. Bending her neck back as far as it would go, she mentally wound through the branches, receiving their silent wisdom in divine rushes - they had missed her too. Lillian projected her core to the higher realms, her sobs overflowing from an impatience and surrender to a greater will, uniting with her organic telephone line. Everything on the outside faded into oblivion - she wanted to linger but time was pressing, letting go reluctantly. It felt good to be back and release the anxieties she held deep within. The trees were the only source to rid her of the negative energy that had become such a main part of her making.

Taking one last look, she patted the animal-like bark with acknowledgement, before moving on. She touched everything she passed, manipulating foliage and twigs into abstract shapes. Lillian was in her element walking the dirt path, it was still as she remembered. Taking off her sandals, contentment lit up her face when she wriggled her toes in the soil. The reunion and inter-relationship with her surroundings slotted all her chakras into place.

Walking deeper in a dream-like state, swinging her arm, the soothing rhythmic calls of wood pigeons and cuckoo opened her receptors, and the magic resurfaced. It had been waiting, replenishing - her presence unleashed it from the dead. Dancing around her, pulling out the negative, weaving through her limbs. Every hair on her body stood on end. She glowed, her colour pulsating from every pore - giggling from the euphoric sensation.

She barely looked down as she continued, trusting the invisible guides - the height of the deities held her admiration, getting lost in the hypnotic movement of tousled canopies.

The path began to widen, their proximity thinning, slowing her pace and leading her to a circular clearing. The scent of felled wood and pine needles filled the space. Her heart sank at the devastation that seemed to be expanding, which violated the atmosphere. Wigwams had been erected from discarded branches by forestry schools and night-time antics. She hopped onto a fallen pine trying her luck at jumping from one stump to another, seeing how far her short legs would stretch. Resting in the middle, she scanned the darker places, which were alive with a nothing, before raising her head and holding her arms out to the side. The surrounding space pulled her off-balance, but she was willing to fall amongst the deadletting the vibe cleanse her from toxicity and judgements. Breathing new life into a stifled soul and coating it like melted chocolate.

The reality of going back home on time sparked rebellion. Just five more minutes, maybe ten. Stepping off she wanted to explore one of the dens, a makeshift womb. Touching the structure and admiring our primitive need to make shelters, she ducked low enough, so she didn't destroy anything, and sat on a log. Huddled over she kept her feet close together to avoid the discarded syringes that lay in the ashes of a doused fire. She sifted through debris with her shoe, screwing up her face as she uncovered unsavoury items and then something caught her eye amongst the ashen, brittle covering. Lillian picked it up, and brushed it off, studying it, holding it up to the light. The onyx rune intrigued her, turning it between her fingers

- the symbol of Eiwaz Death scarred the jet-black shine. She discretely put it in her straw handbag, the one she only used in summer.

A snap of twigs to the right startled her, raising her heartbeat. She looked out, 'I know you're here,' she whispered, the response static. It watched, disguised against the barks - manoeuvring between them, afraid to enter the light. They needed her help, her special gift.

'Why don't you come out and see me?' It respectfully resisted. The passing of years had changed her, she looked different, vivacious. But her soul remained the same with a constitution that forced it to bow in submission. It retreated for now, waiting to be called when the time had come.

Two

The blackbirds flew over like spitfires into surrounding Oaks, chirping their signals of retreat. Lillian checked her watch - they were on time. Following the innate rhythm we all have but have lost connection with. She unbuckled it, rubbing away the sweat from her wrist and admiring her tanned skin against the white mark. It was another beautiful evening, alfresco dining had been an everyday thing and there hadn't been rain in weeks, possibly months. No one could remember the last time they wore normal shoes.

Having made it back home from the woods with minutes to spare, she sat alone on the patio listening to her latest album, drowning her elevated emotions with Portuguese Mateus. The din of bass could be heard over several gardens; it usually happened after the quarrelling. Lillian wasn't allowed to be Lillian, a persecution from her school days filtering through to adulthood.

'When you gonna turn that bluddy music off! It's making me depressed!' Jeffrey Cunningham shouted from the kitchen, aggressively interrupting her wallowing. A troubled, thick-set man from the West-Midlands, with large hands and dark features - eight years her senior. His three-bed semi-detached house was on the highest point of a newly built cul-de-sac.

Half brick, half painted render. Mahogany framed windows and doors. Drive, small front garden, your typical 2.4 children housing estate, surrounded by trees. They had the best views, and everyone could see and hear what went on in that house. Their side, along with nine other houses, backed onto a large cemetery. You could see it, through the wire fence at the foot of the garden, took getting used to. The summer months screened most of it, but in winter when the trees were bare, they could see the headstones in regimented lines. A repetitive joke amongst everyone, but they didn't know anything. She'd seen things that would spark a new fear of death in all of them.

The garden offered daily solace for her, a merciful nourishment. It wasn't that big, just a square plot that lacked character-surrounded by low, stone walls. Lillian made the best of it with curvy borders filled with her Peace Roses. So well kept, they resembled exquisite puddings on sticks - stirring the peptides with custard-coloured petals and decadent scents. The neighbours admired them from bedroom windows whilst eavesdropping on the arguments. She needed more nachos and different music to compliment her mood. Her stomach rumbled from the smell of fading barbeques laying thick in the dusk heat. Nearly all the neighbours were having one, wishing they were turning burgers and having stimulating conversation.

'I think you've had enough of that you're drinkin'! You're gettin' drunk!' Jeffrey yelled over her music.

'I've only had one glass!' Lillian shouted back, 'well, two now' she muttered, emptying the last measure into her glass, discretely scanning the other plots to see if she could catch someone's eye, for a bit of small talk. But they were all hiding, talking about them.

'That music gets louder every bluddy week! I'm switichin' it off inna minnit!' Lillian rolled her eyes, nonchalantly wafting the dopey wasps away from the tomato salad. It was a constant battle with the creatures, they were savages, relentless in their pursuit. Sundown was the only respite from them of late. Then, her song came on, the one she was waiting for—the one that got her out of the seat to dance with her demons. She took her glass with her, swooning heavily at the loss of romance which the lyrics had temporarily given back; her passive aggressive, with Vibrato.

The revisit to the woods had prompted a deeper rebellion. The quiet girl in her teens, two doors down—was spying on her through ornate railings. She often watched Lillian, relating to her caged spirit and bouts of anarchy. The woman that everyone's husband took a second look at, including her father—shacked up with a bloke who reminded her of the school's headmaster. The girl liked the loud music but not the shouting. Lillian listened to the same bands as she liked, especially that new Boy Band everyone was going crazy over. When the track faded into its end, Lillian knew she was being watched, turning her head in the culprit's direction.

She waved and smiled at the girl, feeling sorry for her- that house was too quiet, and she never got a good feeling from it. The windows were dark and dirty, no curtains or decorative material adorning them. Their souls must be unrested, she thought, living like that. Living with Jeffrey was quite the opposite, with his obsessive disorders. She pondered on which she preferred, somewhere in the middle would suffice. The girl swiftly ducked out of sight without returning the greeting.

Lillian drank what she left in the glass, wincing at the warm, flat liquid - going back to her seat. The sky turned from a peachy pink haze into a soft indigo as dusk fell, which meant it was time to star gaze. Venus made its brief appearance, she was always pleased to see it when conditions allowed and religiously bid it a farewell before dark descended. She pulled the red and black tartan blanket up to her chin and held it there with her fists. The heat of the day made the astral circus a little hazy, it was better in winter. She had spent many a clear, crisp night outside wrapped in her duvet or Jeffrey's coat. The sight of them filled her with wonderment; drawn into their hidden message - it had so much to say if you listened carefully. Jeffrey held no regard for her fascination, it was annoying and pointless, all this romantic stuff just cost money and it wasn't real.

Getting into a comfortable position, she put her legs up on the other chair, wriggling from side to side she accidently knocked the table - the new bottle of Mateus fell and spread out over the surface, hitting the patio loudly and sounding like a peeing horse. She gasped and fumbled to correct the situation, cursing repeatedly in panic trying to catch the drips with her hands and blanket before Jeffrey would notice. He predictably came out tutting and huffing - his bat-like hearing tuned into Lillian's mishaps. It irritated him. But his menacing supervision made her worse.

'Bluddy 'ell Lilly! It will stain the slabs! I worked bluddy 'ard on these! When are you ever gonna be'ayve like an adult?!' he said, his accent deep, direct and unforgiving. Lillian took some kitchen roll and mopped up the liquid with him, burning to the tips of her fingers. His frequent interrogation struck her veins like hot rods of steel.

'It's Mateus, it won't stain,' she said feebly. Lillian was used to being criticised about her every move, Jeffrey wouldn't let a day pass without it. It kept her in place and where she should be - beneath him.

'Stop squirming! I know what I'm talking about!' he prodded his chest. His awkward stance and purposeful walk portrayed his need to be as far away from people as possible, and everyone adhered to that. When he scuttled back into his domain and her heart began to resume its normal rhythm, she spotted the first stars straining to penetrate. It was her signal that the real treasures were on their way.

'The light from the stars took millions of years to get to us' Lillian called out, to sweeten Jeffrey's bitterness.

'Patrick Moore said it on the Sky at Night, and I found this incredible book on it, at the library. It was old and...' Jeffrey snorted in arrogance, 'and how the bluddy 'ell did they come up with that idea?! Measured it, did they?! They need to get bluddy man's job, like mine! You wanna stop watching that rubbish and reading them stupid books! That's why yer out there like a bluddy fool every night!' Lillian was non-responsive and picked the food out of her teeth, scanning the sky as it consumed the day respectfully.

'They do measure it, from the sun,' she murmured solemnly, a little hurt from her passions getting constantly burned. Jeffrey stormed off into the dining room and turned her music off, telling it to shut up as he took control of the power - the spillage was the last straw and he put the Eagles on instead.

'Right. Shall I put the Kettle on?' he said, Lillian pulling a mocking face. She hated that album especially that track about the hotel Jeffrey forever played over and over. But she still sang along to it. 'You havin' that hippy tea or Joe Blog's?' he waited for her response as he stood by the kettle, admiring the blinding white worktops, brushing away specks of insignificance. Lillian could sense the aggression in his voice which made her ponder over her choice.

'Umm.... isn't it too hot for tea? And can you get my cardigan, please? The blanket is wet.'

'Get it yerself!'

'I'll have peppermint tea please, if there's any left,' Lillian answered. The acid from the salad and cheap fizz was causing havoc with her digestion.

'Did you put my cardigan away?' she asked, convinced she'd left it on the back of the chair. 'I ain't touched yer bluddy cardigan!' She searched the house for it, coming back to the kitchen, and there it was on the back of the chair.

'What?! Are you messing around with me?' He turned and looked at her, 'what d'ya mean?'

'My cardigan, wasn't here, and now it is,' he continued washing up.

'I ain't touched it, I said. There's summat funny going on 'ere. I keep losing me keys an awl! Summat to do with you probably!' She put the cardigan on, blinking with confusion and returning to her spot. Maybe she had finally lost the plot. One of her aunts had early dementia and perhaps that's where she was heading -a knock on effect from having to keep the hell inside.

'This tea you drink. It's no bluddy miracle. All this new fandango stuff they're bringing out, this organit what's it called.' Jeffrey thought he'd give the sink another wipe over and spraying his favourite cleaner three times, 'it's all a ploy to make the fat cats bluddy money, nothing wrong with a proppa cuppa.' The smell of the bleach comforted him and represented the same stringency as his demeanour. He took the tea bags from the cupboard, putting the boxes back exactly where they came from, twitching slightly at the perfection of alignment. Lillian half listened while drawing hearts on the garden table with some of the spilt liquid - clutching the cardigan around her waist.

'Organic, not organit. I do drink proper tea, just not before bed. I'll be awake all-night thinking about work,' she defended. Lillian was awake most nights, mulling over when the shift was coming. When her cliché knight in shining armour would charge in and take her away from the iron grip of Jeffrey Cunningham. She often imagined it- the knight ringing the doorbell with his lance still on his horse, looking for *'Miz Lillian'*. But the dream soon dispersed as the vision of Jeffrey came to fruition, shooing him off and giving him a piece of mind about horse hooves and manure on his new drive. He brought the tea out and threw a tea towel in her direction. They sat together, poles apart, like two strangers on a park bench.

'It doesn't change y'know, from last week. It's the same bluddy stars in the same bluddy place. I don't know what yer bluddy lookin' for every week! Yer barmy!' he said, running his critical eye over the garden. It wasn't his domain, gardening, but the intuitive way Lillian planted things gave him a nervous tick. Preferring the elderly man's garden at number twenty-six with all his plants the same size and in neat rows, like little soldiers.

'They're not in the same place all year, the Earth's rotation changes their position. But they do move, some more than others, it's called *proper motion*,' Lillian responded and held her mug up to her mouth waiting for a backlash, while the steam gave her a mini facial. Jeffrey was silent and he had no comeback because Lillian's response was out of his depth, so had nothing further to say on the matter. She longed for him to just humour her and go along with her fixation. Being romantic on her own wasn't any fun and it left her yearning for fulfilment in that department.

Jeffrey got up abruptly and threw the remains of his tea on the lawn, his chores were pressing him and anyway, he was getting bored sitting with Lillian as she looked up to the heavens.

'I don't know how you find the time to fill yer 'ed with all that bluddy stuff! We're all here by chance. We die and end up in the dirt and they don't, that's it,' he said as he stomped back in. His lack of belief disturbed her; shut off to his own wonders and the ones around him. He claimed intelligence but struggled to be innovative, maybe he was too scared to.

Comfortable where she was, transfixed by the night sky – she was shifted out of her seat, standing and pointing at a shooting star.

'Oh God! Look!' privileged it had made an appearance just for her. Was that the sign she'd been waiting for? It was a flash of hope, that's what it was. Reminding her not to give up, which strengthened her law of attraction she desperately tried to uphold.

'Why do you believe they are perfectly aligned like that, by pure chance?' her question directed at him. Jeffrey heard her but ignored it, he wanted to continue the conversation about the 'organit' epidemic and how the neighbours opposite buy new cars like hot cakes.

'I have to work tomorra. What yer doin' with yerself?' she barely heard him over the clatter of crockery.

'Going to Mum's for dinner,' that's where she spent most weekends and found every excuse to go there. Her parents' house was always a welcome solace. Leaving her home was one of the hardest decisions she ever made, being an only child - a place where she could be Lillian without being ridiculed or mocked about it. Lucky for her he was a bit of a workhorse; a sought-after fabrication welder working for British Aerospace on the edge of the city docks. Recently promoted to site foreman, which just fuelled his obstinate behaviour.

'Well, make sure you tidy up before you go,' he said, running the hot water tap, squeezing a generous amount of detergent in the sink. Lillian clenched her fists and held back her emotion, pouring her heart out silently to the black sky instead. A familiar 'meow' swiftly diverted her rage, one that filled her with joy. Oliver jumped on her lap; a flamboyant ginger Persian that turned up at Jeffrey's house when she moved in. He was all she needed for comfort in a harsh environment, becoming her shadow and spiritual companion and good deviation from reality. Oliver made himself comfortable, purring loudly as he kneaded her lap. He was a special feline, big and cumbersome but held an indigenous wisdom in those deep amber eyes of his.

'Where have you been? Where do you go when you leave me? You're getting fat, too.' Oliver squinted with pleasure as she kissed him repeatedly and spoke in her special cat voice. 'You'll get stuck in the cat flap, you silly old thing,' she rubbed his torso. He loved her but hated Jeffrey, scratching him whenever he was within reach and sabotaging his possessions and clean clothes.

'It doesn't know how to use the bluddy cat flap, let alone get through it! He's just 'ere for his bluddy stomach! I warned you not to let him in. You should have taken him to the vets, like I said, 'ave him put to sleep. Bluddy nuisance, that's all!' Jeffrey huffed as he wiped down the garden table, rubbing hard over Lillian's side.

'Come on. Put that bluddy animal down and do some wiping up,' pointing with his thumb over his shoulder. Lillian did as she was told. The romance of the stars had lost its lustre from his criticism anyway. She left her peppermint tea and needed some Dutch courage, carrying Oliver in with her. The shooting star had prompted a touchy subject - one she wasn't allowed to mention, ever.

Three

His reaction was as she anticipated, he didn't want her looking for another job and was frustrated at her persistence about it. Lillian felt the shift arrive within as she climbed the stairs with heavy legs and rejected affection, bringing her to tears. She would speak to the recruitment agency Monday morning and no backing out this time. Although backing out sat better with her fear of change. She tried to smooth things over but his anger was untameable and he became threatening. Her excuse to have an early night and read her book was the quick exit she needed away from those large hands. The pent up resentment behind them would be a fatal weapon one day, and she wasn't hanging around to find out if that was tonight.

 Jeffrey stood with his hands on his hips watching her leave, suspiciously. Something was up, it had manifested since the star gazing malarkey. The cat watched his person leave feeling her pain and wanting to resolve it. But he didn't follow because he knew the rules, no cats upstairs. Jeffrey clapped his hands to shoo Oliver out the way making the cat's ears fold back as the sound bounced off the walls. Oliver made a mad, scuffled dash to the lounge to get a seat, the one with Jeffrey's newspaper on it. The cat turned in circles a little disturbed by the crunching and tearing - he liked newspaper, it generated heat but not as much as a duvet. Jeffrey came in to close the patio doors and windows so he didn't have to listen to the frivolities outside; bursts of laughter and the rumble of a repetitive bass. 'Bluddy idiots' he mumbled, looking out to the garden as he locked the doors, making sure everything was in its place before he settled.

Lillian hadn't put her chair back in the right place but he didn't want to go back out again – even though it niggled him. He sat down heavily in his armchair and let out a groan as the weight of his worries pushed him down - not best pleased with her disobedience. Pointing the remote control at his Baird TV and pressing down hard because the batteries were running out, it eventually clicked into action. He began flicking through all five channels in annoyance. They were the only house in the street without satellite, it bemused him how anyone had time to watch all those stations. Snooker was on, he liked the relaxing green felt table and gentle 'clicks' of the ricochet making his eyes heavy and doze, sporadic applause prompting a heckle. Oliver finally got himself in a suitable position, his feet tucked under his chest and boring holes in Jeffrey with his infallible stare, on alert for a quick escape.

Jeffrey yawned loudly fighting off the need to nap, looking to the floor either side of his chair and then underneath it.

'Where's me bluddy newspaper?!'

Lillian leaned against the bedroom door, her shaking hands held out in front of her, having just dipped her toes in hot water - but she was determined to immerse a little deeper. The bedroom often became the place where she wallowed in self-pity, plotting her escape or Jeffrey's death.

Decorated in a delicately flowered wallpaper in lilacs and blues-with a rose border that ran around the centre of the walls, with curtains to match. The furniture made of heavy walnut wood and the bed dressed in white cotton during the summer months.

Picking up discarded clothes and shoes- she stopped to peer through the net curtain. The hue of orange streetlights changed the perception of the neighbourhood. Being in the semi-rurals was the only thing she liked about the strange situation. The two young men who lived opposite, keeping everyone guessing about their relationship, were staggering back from the local pub singing Bohemian Rhapsody at the top of their voices. The widower's dog was wondering about as usual, sniffing in the gutter and stopping to put his scent on just about everything.

There wasn't much else going on, most of them had gone to bed - concentrating on the darker parts of Coed-y-Ffrind Close, waiting for the shadows to move.

She needed the danger back to liven up her mundane life, it was all too safe and too 'normal' and it was time to do something about it. Lillian kept the façade in place with a smile that hid her screams, dying from emotional starvation and third eye stimulation. The resentment seeped through her pores, dousing her spark - building in her chest like a tightening vice. Her greatest tool for making her spiritual connections.

Being engaged to Jeffrey was a decent thing to her, an honour and a forever notion - but she was unhappy and clinging to a mistake, a burst bubble and shattered dream. It became a saving-face entrapment, the ring mark had almost gone, barely visible. She told Jeffrey and everyone else that it was too big for her now. When the situation improved a little, usually when Jeffrey was in a good mood, which wasn't that often - she tried it on again, but it itched and that was her sign to leave it in the drawer. No dates had been set, it was a rain check commitment. There were no romantic moments or going down on one knee. Jeffrey just handed her the ring at breakfast one morning. 'Spose I'd better give ya this,' was all he said.

Jeffrey came with small print and a carnival of red flags, the type she ignored for fear of losing the affection she needed to breathe. The confident, self-sufficient man she fell in love with had turned out to be a bitter disappointment. Behind the bravado was just disguised cries for attention and entitlement - turning out to be just another rescue case, attracted to her vulnerabilities, good nature and willingness to please. His oppressive tendencies eventually crushing her identity. Her fear of dysfunction was all that stopped her from moving forward, unsure of herself. He filled her personal space with his toxic behaviours, stifling her ability to think for herself. What kept her hanging on?

She curled into a ball under the cotton sheet, listening to the outside noises, feeling envious of the other lives she could hear. The last of the neighbours bid farewell to their married friends, slamming taxi doors and drunken exchanges ringing out and bouncing off the night. Her eyes searched in the dark, her constitution jagged and on edge. Sleep had left her from an empty stomach and wired head. All the remedies for lost sleep hadn't worked, even though there had been many appointments with alternative therapists and counsellors, she kept hidden from her family. Shuffling to the bedside to switch on the light, covering her eyes - she opened the top drawer of the dressing table where she hid her silver antique hand mirror, with an embossed Damask pattern on the back. A treasured gift from her mother handed down through generations. The glass was eroded around the edges, leaving only a small, misshapen reflection. Its purpose was for scrying - a wireless artefact for clairvoyant messages. But Lillian had found an alternative use for it - she could go further than that, receiving intricate detail when it came to foretelling; becoming as precious to her as one's smart phone is today.

Wiping it clean with her pyjama top she held it up; glimpsing Lilly, which was always hard to swallow. It was time to reopen the psychic links that had been abandoned because there was no waiting for something to fall in her lap. The revisit to the woods sparked her abilities into life, but the return of love would make it easier to get out. She didn't want any trouble, just an easy transition - one she could slip into like nothing ever happened. Lillian called for the messages to appear, the same way she asked the trees, focussing on her reflection. They came through in pink and gold, changing to dark purples and indigo as the information strengthened. Once the connections were made, the deliverance affected her vision, causing rapid eye watering.

Just as the whisperings became audible, the contact was interrupted when Jeffrey burst through the door, jolting her out of the moment.

'Where's me paper?!' she quickly pushed the mirror under the pillow, blowing her nose as she stood up and faced him.

'Uh... I don't know, it was on the other armchair last time I looked.'

'Huh! And what yer bluddy crying for now?! Ay?' he asked, but Lillian just sniffed and shook her head. He narrowed his eyes and lunged forward, lifting the pillows, tossing them aside. But he found nothing.

'I'm bluddy watchin' you, just remember that!' he said, waggling his fore finger.

'You ain't getting another job, and that's that. And if I catch you doin' any of yer funny stuff ere...' he paused, making direct eye contact – prompting a hard swallow from Lillian.

'I'm not doing that anymore,' she lied. He tutted and left the bedroom in a huff, unconvinced. She waited for the lounge door to slam then reached under the pillow to retrieve the mirror, sneering wickedly as she wrapped it back up in the scarf. It would keep. But the brief contact had already unpicked a stitch.

'You can come out now!' she whispered in her cat voice. Oliver jumped on the bed with an equally smug look. She let out a cunning laugh at their little plan, stroking his thick fur and taking great comfort from him.

'I don't know what I'd do without you.' His love was unconditional, his soul light and pure. They connected, spiritually. If only she had that in the form of a man, a psychic one, someone who loves trees. The thought of it made her swoon and her heart ache - it seemed all so unreachable.

She applied her scented oil from the bedside to soothe her bruised soul and promote sleep. But it was primarily used to contain her hysteria; lavender, patchouli and geranium - its potency dispersed the black webs that held her in resilience.

Oliver clawed at the cotton sheet trying to plump it up, purring and choking between swallows while Lillian lay on her side. He had to be near her, making himself comfortable by her head and absorbing her soothing energy like a basking reptile. She fell into a deep sleep from the sound of his purrs, and exuberance of hope.

Four

Lillian woke startled, falling from the dream void but it was the best sleep she'd had in a while. She checked for Oliver; he was curled up on the bottom of the bed looking like a Cossack.

Laying back down, she stared at the ceiling for a few minutes, making out faces in the artex. There was the head of a polar bear she always saw first, smiling when it morphed before her eyes.

'Still here I see,' she said to it. Then her eyes relaxed to let the other images come forth–an angry man with large ears, a Viking and the leopard leaping over a moon. It was past nine and the melodic hum of the neighbourhood busying themselves with car valeting and mowing, was an indication it was Sunday. The children's laughter and screeches echoed as they rode their bikes around the close.

Lillian rubbed her face, stretching as she went downstairs to call her parents.

Twiddling with the curly cord while she waited for her mother to pick up.

'*Hello sweetheart,*' Rose answered, already knowing it was her.

'Morning Mum. What did you get up to last night?' Lillian always asked.

'*Oh, nothing much, we sat outside. Your father and I got eaten alive by mosquitoes! But it was too hot to go inside, it's getting unbearable, don't you think?!*' Lillian looked at her painted toenails, wishing she had been with them.

'I can't sleep or do anything much else in this heat either.'

Rose hummed in agreement whilst checking her hands.

'I'm coming today. I have some chores to finish before I do,' Lillian said with a yawn. Rose rolled her eyes.

'*Don't overdo it. See you later darling, about two-ish?*' The call ended. Rose pondered where she stood, redressing her hair in the mirror that hung above the telephone, it had been there for 30 years like most of the things in the house. A medium built, feisty lady in her late fifties. Married to her only husband Martin, for as long as she could remember. Lillian was their only child after the death of her first, which they never spoke about as a family. The deep loss remained silent in her bones and passing butterflies.

She tied her apron a little tighter, brushing it straight to set things right. Time to prepare Sunday lunch, refusing to let her loss become her imprisonment. Her daughter made up for that, tenfold.

Lillian sat on the last but one stair curling her toes in the carpet, thinking about last night. The house bright and cheerful once Jeffrey had left and it was calling out for the comforting noise of a kettle. She ate breakfast in blissful solitude on the patio accompanied by Oliver and bird song, it was in the late twenties again. Jeffrey's little instruction notes were left in each room for her to follow. Classical FM played in the background; Lillian needed something without lyric. All the songs were about love and devotion, she'd had enough of it, and they were all lies. The echo of piano keys inspired her creativity, intensifying her need for romance -feeding, stealing and giving. Each room she cleaned Oliver made sure he was around helping, sitting on or amongst things.

Alone with her thoughts, which became a tormenting place - how was she going to keep everything hidden from Jeffrey? Perhaps she should just do as she was told and leave it at that. The people she had distanced herself from was what she usually thought of. Jeffrey didn't want her mixing with people with an ounce of intuition or intelligence and that included her best friend. She felt agitated with herself, at her misplaced loyalty, afraid to challenge it because she needed the praise from him. Nothing was ever quite in its place until Jeffrey was pleased- only then, could she function properly.

Slamming the cupboard door on the vacuum, glad to see the back of it, she was looking forward to her mother's cooking. Oliver laid on the tiled kitchen floor where it was cooler, flinching the tip of his tail while Lillian stomped about. All that work was far too exhausting for a cat. She cast one last nervous eye over the house.

'Be good! Don't get stuck in the cat flap!' Trudging to her Honda Civic called Brutus; a 1982 wreck of a thing - stood in its usual place at the end of the drive, making the place look untidy with its multi-coloured body panels and rust spots. Jeffrey towed it all the way back from Bristol with a bent wheel and something squeaking underneath the chassis. He patched it up at work, making it roadworthy by the skin of its teeth–Lillian became attached to the little car, feeling sorry for it, but now it was just an eyesore.

She had to open all the doors and wind down the windows to let the air get in because it still smelt like wet socks from the winter leaks. The faux leather seats in burnt toffee nearly melted in the heat, burning her back when she sat down. The one thing she loved about the car was the CD player, a present from her father- to make her journeys a little more bearable. She looked through her collection but put the radio on instead, searching through the stations for some summer tunes. Lillian pulled the choke out; just one click, two in the frost. Despite its appearances it was a good runner and refused to give up, proving that looks weren't everything.

Putting on her sunglasses she checked herself in the rear-view mirror, before reversing out down the long driveway, with Sheena Easton blasting out of the speakers; she liked that one, about being a modern girl. Most of the neighbours were out maintaining their fakery. They were fond of Lillian, she always had a friendly smile and behaved like the perfect neighbour, frowning upon her recent bouts of rebellion. She hated most of them, with their small minds and pointless pursuits. Her moral compass never got involved with the usual gossip, which made them compete for her attention. Raising her hand to acknowledge them, harbouring condemning whispers in her heart. She sang at the top of her voice as she left the Close. Lillian took immense pleasure from being in control of something for once. Brutus was her escape, her independence. The tank was full, and she wanted to drive until the roads ended. She could have done it with a newer model but that was something else she added to her new list, in black.

The colours from the mirror contact the night before, filled the Honda with their incandescent lights, dancing around her, chattering and whiz-popping.

'Stop messing with me! Be patient!'

Five

Lillian's tense muscles relaxed as she got closer to her family home, arriving in a different zone, one that washed all the bad guys away–a return to the womb. Places she passed that hadn't changed since she was a child, ones that held all the pieces together- the landmarks of her life. The same people living in the same houses, the only difference was, they were growing old and losing their minds.

Her family home was right at the red-letter box and just a short way into the council estate. It was decent enough, everyone had looked after their property. Some painted, some not. Her house was the cream one on the left, with white PVC windows and mature shrubs in front. Elevated by five steps, set in Welsh flag-stone walls, which she sat in the middle of as a child, concealed from passers-by. Her grubby doll by her side, which Rose had made from old bed covers. The family dog, a long-haired mongrel, sat on the wall and kept guard.

It was her best friend, a four-legged sister. They practically did everything together. She didn't need any friends, they were all mean and fickle and made fun of her ears. The dog understood her, without judgement. Its passing was the end of most things and the beginning of others. She was in the back garden now, under the Rhododendron where she used to sit. Lillian acknowledged her place on every visit.

She parked behind her father's car, filled with joy as she looked forward to going in, like a freshly tumble-dried duvet on a cold day. 'Yoo-hoo!' she called out as she opened the front door, wiping her feet on the coconut mat. The Carpenters were playing, accompanying the smell of roast dinner. The entrance hall had changed over the years, it was fresh now, minimal, beiges and whites. A brass wind chime still hung above the door, the one she always blew on just to hear it tinkle. There had been a new arrival to the family; Benny the Dachshund. Running and skidding on the laminate floor to get to her, nearly wetting itself from excitement. Barking and sneezing all at once. Lillian rubbed his constricted little body as he turned in awkward circles. Benny methodically sniffed her feet and up her legs detecting the scent of a feline, like it was a new smell to him every time.

'Hello sweetheart!' her mother called out from the kitchen, 'come and help me with the gravy, please!' Her father, Martin, was reading his paper at the garden table with a large parasol open overhead. She walked through the main reception room, neat and tastefully done out. Rose had changed the wallpaper again; big ghost heads of silver Alliums, set on a truffle background. Lillian stopped and admired it, running her fingers over the raised pattern. Her mother was amongst the steam of boiling pots and an overworked oven, getting plates ready. She kissed and hugged her first, then joined her father; the man she idolised. She should have followed his example of what a good man looked like.

'Hey there, bluebell! You're looking very cool.' Lillian sat down with him and poured herself some lemonade, with Benny sat under her seat.

'I don't feel cool–I've been sweating cough drops all morning, cleaning!' she guzzled the drink and belched loudly when she finished, 'sorry, pardon me. I needed that like you can't believe it.' Her father chuckled at the apple of his eye, his beautiful tom boy that burped like a bloke and wore a pink tutu in the dirt.

'Cleaning? In this weather? – Purgatory,' he said, sipping his scotch and soda with the ice cubes chinking the glass, adding to its pleasure. He only ever had one glass on a Sunday, every Sunday, looking tired of late. Retired from his lifelong job as a civil engineer, not sure what to do with himself anymore. When he worked, he couldn't wait to leave, now he wanted to go back.

'Yes, well, I didn't do all of it, unfortunately. I'll finish it later.'

'Are you helping me with the gravy or what?' Rose called from the kitchen, 'oh yes, sorry mum, I just needed a drink and your lemonade hits the spot.' She stirred her mother's signature gravy, fanning herself with the other hand. Rose thought Barbeques and salad were inappropriate for a Sunday.

'I'm calling the agency tomorrow, mum.'

Rose emptied ladles of vegetables. 'Oh? What made you decide that?' Lillian was lost in the gravy's bubbles that busied themselves around the edge of the saucepan.

'It came to me while I was staring into space. I need to shed this skin, before it suffocates me.' Rose didn't take much notice, she'd heard it before.

'Good for you sweetheart, good for you. I have every confidence in you.'

Martin folded his paper and placed it on the garden table, pushing himself up from his chair, wincing while his back and knees reluctantly adjusted themselves. His navy-blue cardigan was falling apart in places, but there was no way he was letting go of it, it kept him sane. He joined his girls in the kitchen, 'what's happening?' he asked as he walked in. Lillian smiled at her father's grounding presence. He held good height, but his gusto had left him. Still a looker at sixty-nine, although his trousers were sagging at the back a bit, reminding Lillian of a baby elephant when he walked. He was also losing his hearing, much to Rose's frustration.

'Lilly's calling the recruitment agency tomorrow! Try and get herself a new job! And why are you wearing that damn cardigan? Let me give it to animal rescue!' Rose answered, raising and emphasising her voice.

'Ah, jolly good. Don't work for someone who gives their managers hefty bonuses to keep them sweet. They have no sense and a big overdraft,' he said and kissed the top of Lillian's head. 'What's the name of that place you work in?' he asked,

'Pulse,' Lillian answered.

'That's right. Well, they haven't exactly got their finger on it, have they?' He added, clapping his hands and rubbing them together as he watched Rose dish up. Her father's subtle yet sharp witted attitude on life amused and comforted her. Many people thought he never knew what was going on; well-spoken with an apparent lack of savvy, just nodding and smiling during conversations. But he was the silent observant, absorbing, making up his own mind.

'Isn't it too hot for a roast?' he said, as he began to carve.

'It's never too much of anything for a roast, and you're a fine one to talk with that cardigan! You must be on fire in there!' Rose responded, keeping a close eye on the thickness of the beef slices.

'You leave my cardigan out of it. I've had this since 1979!' Lillian wiped the sweat from her brow with the back of her hand, 'yes, you can tell' - they all laughed.

'I've lost a few pounds standing here!' she said, getting overwhelmed.

'Nonsense. It's good for the complexion. Right, is that gravy ready?' Rose interrupted and got them both organised.

They ate under the parasol and talked about times and moments gone by, sometimes talking about the same ones as the last get together. Martin always had plenty of stories from his days as a boy. Like the one where he rolled car tyres down the hill, watching them crash through back gates, running like hell when he heard the smashing of greenhouse panes. But that didn't matter, she'd listen to them all over again, knowing one day-they would stop. Her mother was a part-time care nurse, a very popular employee and one with the most experience. She had a special way with the needy and they always asked for her specifically when passing over was imminent. Rose wasn't so open with her experiences, she preferred to keep them to herself. They had a humble but sufficient lifestyle, still living in their two-bedroom terrace since the early 60s- subbing Lillian on the quiet.

She aspired to her parents' marriage, it was a constant reminder of her less than desirable situation. She had been inconsistent with a lot of things throughout her life, so she had succumbed herself to settle for it. Her body was changing, and she wanted children. What was her purpose otherwise? Rattling around in a three-bedroom house, maintaining it for a nutbag?

Zoning out as her parent's conversation got onto to life's trivia and first world problems– watching a bee trying to push open the snap dragons with its front legs, putting in some extra buzz in for thrust. Her mother had bought some new terracotta pots, all filled with gaudy-coloured annuals. The lawn was mowed within an inch of its life - Martin liked it that way, it saved doing it every five minutes. A cherry tree had taken over in recent years, but it added character to the garden, dappling the shade and providing a welcome respite for Benny. He was begging beside her for any small piece of something, except potatoes, he didn't like those. She had a special way with children and animals–they noticed her before anyone else. Lillian secretly dropped morsels of beef on the floor for him, stroking his close-cut fur; silky and tactile, with a shine on it that would put L'Oréal to shame. He was a bit of a princess though, for a German badger hunter that is.

The dog barked for more, snapping her out of her daydream.

'Benny! Naughty boy!' Rose said, 'he won't eat his own food when you're here, Lilly, I wonder why?' giving her daughter a look of blame.

'Sorry. He's just got that helpless look about him. Must be boring eating the same old stuff every day,' Lillian replied as she played with her food. Her thoughts preoccupied.

'What's up, Lilly?' her mother asked, watching her separating the runner beans on her plate.

'Uh? Oh, nothing, well, I'm nervous about calling the agency tomorrow.'

'Lilly, you have just as must chance as anyone else. Someone will snap you up when they see you. Trust me. You just need to believe in yourself sweetheart. Make the move and see what happens.' Lillian knew her mother was eager for her to go with her notion to change things – she had chickened out too many times. She knew there was an opening waiting for her to take by the horns, figuratively speaking. That meant she had to get shifting things if she wanted it that bad.

She began to cry, her mother's words released the torture a little, one way of stopping her heart from drowning. Rose comforted her and everything emptied in front of them like a shaken can of fizz, apologising between convulses.

'Don't apologise love, we know,' Rose answered, rubbing her back and squeezing her hand tighter.

'You know?' Lillian blew her nose in a red serviette, anxiously tearing it apart. Martin was paused in motion, his eyes darting from Lillian to Rose.

'I know you're not happy where you are, in work.'

Lillian glanced at her mother then back into her lap. 'I'm not sure how I feel about that, I just know I have to make a move. The managers are whispering.'

'Yes, whispering about their bonuses!' Martin interrupted. Rose continued while she ate.

'I know you're not happy in that house, either,' silence fell for what seemed like an age.

'I love that house, my Olly lives there with me. Things are ok, Mum.' Rose put her cutlery down again, this time a little harder.

'You haven't had your ring on for a while. Anything to tell us?' Lillian felt a rush of nervous heat and regurgitated some of her dinner.

'No. Course not. I've lost weight, it's too big for me now, that's all,' hoping that would be the end of the questions. 'It's not that bad mum. I just need a new job.'

Martin shook his empty glass in the air at Rose. 'I need another one of these please, love. It always tastes better from your fair hands.' She gave him a damning look for interrupting the flow, one that held a little humour. Willingly getting her husband another fix.

He linked his hands together and sat back, exhaling, looking at his daughter with a pained expression.

'Give people their excuses bluebell–you won't change him. But he's a hard worker and good at his job, however,' Martin changed position, 'don't put up with more than you have to. Your room is still available.'

Lillian secretly wished that her father would come round to the house and punch Jeffrey in the face.

Rose came back with another glass of scotch, on ice, placing the glass in front of him.

'How about some trifle? That solves most things,' Rose suggested, with Lillian agreeing. She knew it would be the one with Sherry in the sponge, but anything sweet would do.

'Are you feeling better now?' Rose asked as she finished her plate, setting the knife and fork straight.

'Yes, much better thanks, I couldn't be anything else when I'm with you guys,' licking the smears from the spoon.

Martin raised his glass, 'I'll drink to that!' and took a large gulp, with Rose giving him a judgemental glance.

'That's two you've had!' she pointed out. He put the glass down heavily and breathed out.

'Aaahhhh! Family, sunshine, good food and The Carpenters - what more do we need? Eh? Let every other bugger get on with it. It's not my problem.' Rose adjusted herself in the seat and shielded her eyes as the sun began to slip below the protective line of the parasol.

'Why don't you have a shower while you're here?' Lillian looked at her father as he finished the drops in the bottom of his glass, 'cheers, bluebell!' he said in his jovial manner. Lillian smiled sheepishly 'cheers, dad.' Martin let out a sigh of contentment, waiting for Rose to return to the kitchen, before leaning on the table.

'Your mother smells a rat,' he whispered, and winked. That wink. The, 'I got you' wink; a fleeting gesture, one which cradled and wrapped her in an iron fortress–giving silent protection and an unbreakable bond. She would tell him, she had to, soon, when she gets a new job, when things were better with Jeffrey.

It was getting late and time to for her to leave before Jeffrey got back. She hated arriving when he was already there, it made her feel inadequate. Women should be at home, bare-footed and pregnant, away from the night's predators. Martin and Rose stood at the front door to wave her off, Rose carrying Benny and waving his paw. Lillian gave a quick beep of the horn as a goodbye signal. She didn't want the whole thing going off that time of night.

'I'm going to that house Martin. I need to find out what's going on. She's losing weight!' Rose said, still waving.

'No, I'll go. Better if a man faces him,' Martin insisted. They both turned and went back inside. 'Dinner was delicious love, as always.' Martin kissed her hair, and they retreated.

Six

Oliver was on the patio illuminated by the security light, waiting for the kamikaze moths to drop at his feet.

'Hello, fluff ball! Have you been a good boy?' he meowed and rubbed against her legs as she opened the back door.

'You must sort this cat flap thing out, it's embarrassing. You just push it, with your bloody face, for heaven's sake!' Jeffrey wasn't in, he always called into see his mother on the way home from work. She fed Oliver and put the kettle on for some chamomile tea, placing the box back in the wrong place without thinking. Dashing around the house she put lights on, so it looked as though she'd been home a while. Lillian drank her tea at the kitchen table, gearing herself up for her dementor's arrival.

This wasn't home, this wasn't a comfort anymore; just a place, a place she hated and couldn't leave. A place where she sat in limbo, desperately waiting for something to prise her out of it. After twenty minutes of silent reflection, listening to Vivaldi again, Jeffrey's car thundered down the drive. A 1990 Volvo estate in bottle green. It looked like a tank and sounded like a tractor, but Jeffrey loved its robust practicality. She prayed for strength before he came in, watching him pass the kitchen window and setting off the security light, then charging through the door, startling her.

'All right? How were yer parents?' he asked.

'Yeah, fine thanks. Did you call in and see your mum?' she replied.

'What did they have to say for themselves?' he asked, putting the kettle on.

'Oh, you know, just the usual. We had Sunday dinner, on the patio, like we always do.'

Lillian made it sound like it was an ordinary thing to do, because she felt guilty about him not having that nourishment. His mother lived alone after her husband's accidental death, and her children had flown the nest. She never cooked, not even for herself.

Jeffrey was too busy with his tea to notice what she was saying.

'What yer listenin' to that music again for? Ay? Tryin' to make yerself intelligent, is it?' There was an 'F' bomb on the end of Lillian's tongue. It had been hanging around in her heart for some time, but had made its way up, impatient for its release. He noticed there was a box of tea slightly out of place, putting it back perfectly aligned with the others, before getting his.

'You tired?' he asked.

'Uh, yes, very, why?' she replied, rubbing the back of her neck, worrying where the question was leading. Hoping it wasn't anything to do with 'having an early night' - although there hadn't been any of those for quite some time, relieved to be free from the responsibility she felt so dutiful to.

'Just askin,' Jeffrey said, with an indication that it *was* leading somewhere. Lillian looked to the floor and realised she didn't quite get around to all the vacuuming.

'I did most of the chores, it's been a hot day,' she said, and laughed a little.

'A hot day?! I've been bluddy welding for the last nine hours! You don't know what yer talkin' about!!' Jeffrey shouted, pointing to himself again.

Lillian drank the last of her tea and took it over to the sink.

'Shall I put the shower on for you?' Lillian digressed, trying to douse the immanent eruption. Jeffrey looked at Lillian, and she wasn't looking her best lately.

'Looks like you need one before me! Look at the state of ya! You always wear those bluddy clothes. Haven't you got any dresses?!' Jeffrey's sooted face accentuated his dead brown eyes, and he smelt like hot engines.

'Well, I've been busy. You'd better go first though, I'm not as dirty as you.'

Jeffrey gulped his tea and gave his mug to Lillian.

''Ere, make yerself useful – and you'll always be dirty – in there!' he said, prodding her head. He grinned in her face then left, 'and turn that crap off!' Lillian took the insult on the chin, like always. But she felt as though she was about to lose her internal organs.

His harsh words penetrated her skin and remained there like a toxic substance her system couldn't expel, stinging and burning, reminding her of her place. She stifled her cries in case they never stopped. Oliver jumped up and wanted to help, his presence releasing a solitary tear from her. He meowed and purred offering his therapy. She finished up in the kitchen, making sure there were no traces of water on the sink, hanging up the tea towel with no folds or creases and kissed her cat goodnight. 'I love you' she whispered.

There would be no sneaking around tonight, she was frightened. It felt like a breakup when she left Oliver. Lillian needed him, needed him to help her sleep. Before turning off the light she affectionately glanced at the canvas print of the woods, which hung on the bedroom wall; frequently acknowledging it before leaving the house or going to bed. It was her only connection she had left with her close friend, all other means of communication had ceased. Lisa was a keen photographer, the parting gift portraying Lillian's potential. She felt the bittersweet loss in its capture. It was taken when the bluebells were out - lining the dirt path she felt under her feet, as she ran her finger along it. The longer she stared, the more she could see movement. It was time for another visit. If only she could transport herself, that would be something else to perfect.

Seven

Monday: the day to start her iridescent ball rolling. The day when quite possibly, curiosity could kill the cat.

'Where are my keys?' she asked Oliver. Jeffrey was always out by 6.30am. She rifled through her bag, retraced her steps, went out, came back in again–and there they were, on the worktop.

'Oh, for heaven's sake! I'm losing my marbles! Bye Olly!' she left a lipstick kiss on his forehead, closing and locking the door behind her. Oliver sat up straight on the kitchen table with a terse look on his face. He didn't like it when she left, and she shouldn't be going today. Lillian huffed at the heat then went through the window opening routine. Quickly looking through her CD collection, she chose Def Leppard; a bit of 80s soft metal for her rebellion and despondency. It was on full blast as she reversed out, sticking two hypothetical fingers up to discountenance. She felt scared, but the thrill of the risk challenged the monotony, adding an unfamiliar perspective to an otherwise ordinary day. Feeling childlike breaking the rules, there was an invisible calling that she could feel and taste.

The journey felt a little different as Lillian played the drums on the steering wheel, waiting at the traffic lights, ignoring the cat calls from men in vans. It was the usual start to her day being surrounded by untamed testosterone and innuendoes. She just looked straight ahead and left them in a cloud of thick, silvery smoke - like a skunk warding off its predator. The head gasket was on its way out again, her signature arrival and departure.

Arriving a little earlier than usual, Lillian's enthusiasm was waning in her job. The industrial estate with its corrugated roofs were looking tired. Pulse's sign was weather-beaten and the name of the company had changed so many times, they just stuck the next sign over that last. The office staff were already in and all the electric fans were on because the windows only opened so far. They were sat in silence going through their paperwork, when they heard Lillian's Honda booming its way into the car park. 'Lilly's here' one of them said, without lifting their head. The others craned their necks to look out the window and smiled at the comical entrance. They admired her, she was one on her own and always brought light to any situation.

She felt good today, saluting to the factory workers stood outside the entrance, relishing their early morning puff and quick snatch of natural light.

'Hey Lilly! What's the word today?' asked the shop floor supervisor, Dave; a tall, attractive, wannabe rock star, with a permanent five o'clock shadow and long, wavy black hair, which he annoyingly swished from one side to another – the envy of all the women. Sleazy tattoos adorned hidden parts of his body, privy to those he bedded. He chewed on cocktail sticks when he wasn't smoking. His team of staff hung around him like wasps around a jam pot - but it was Lillian he was after, his ultimate trophy. She just humoured his advances knowing there was something shady laying beneath the inked facade. Lillian had a random word for each day. Neither of them could remember how it started – but it was Dave's perfect excuse to interact with her. She knew exactly what it would be on the out-of-the-ordinary Monday, she'd seen something on the way into the estate.

'Heli blimp,' she said and carried on walking. Dave laughed, shaking his hair over his shoulders, 'I like it!' raising his chin to blow out smoke.

'Catch ya later Dave.' Lillian walked off to her domain, the sunlight shining through her skirt, briefly revealing her figure. He watched her until she disappeared, the probability of never having her enticed him, toying with the idea was pleasurable, like a cat with a petrified mouse. He heard the music she was playing when she arrived. Her outward image didn't reflect it, but her inner struggle and magnetism, did.

She quite liked being on front desk, it was a prominent position but a lonely one - Lillian preferred to work amongst her peers. Positioning her head set so it wouldn't ruin her hair style, she pressed the dedicated line to dial out, holding the piece of paper with the agency's number on it. She shook when she heard the dialling tone, it was too much–it scared her. Lillian cursed herself, she just couldn't do it. She hung up, promising herself to do it later.

Two men walked into reception, looking official, clutching black briefcases. One man had quite a presence, mature, experienced- he hadn't taken his eyes off Lillian since walking in.

'Welcome to Pulse. How can I help you?' The visitors warmed to her pleasant nature and sweet voice. They had come to see her boss, Simon D'or, who never arrived before nine thirty. It was always an apologetic and embarrassing wait for his visitors.

'Phil Hathaway,' the mature man introduced himself, the other one was quiet.

She stood and returned the handshake 'Lillian Tate,' feeling awkward. He was charming but reserved. A domineering woman-hater, and that was just from a handshake.

Breaking the moment, she asked them to sign the visitors' book and to take a seat in the shabby reception area, while she made excuses for her boss. They sat fanning through old car magazines and the company's promotional leaflets, which desperately needed an update. Some had faded and fell apart when you picked them up; a paper reflection of the company. The Hathaway man stood with his hands in his pockets, looking out to the carpark, eagerly awaiting Simon D'Or's arrival. He was getting impatient. They were on a tight schedule and just wanted to get his appointment over with.

At nine forty, the man himself pulled up in his white Porsche, with its personalised number plate; SDOR 1, revving it to let everyone know he had arrived. The first space, right in front of the entrance, was exclusively his - complete with initials painted in gold. Lillian grimaced at them every day. The top was down, and he looked like a cartel boss dressed in chinos and a Hawaiian shirt. He walked in chewing gum, his Ray Bans on his head, beautifully tanned from his frequent and expensive holidays. Regarding his guests contemptuously.

'Good morning, Lilly! Beautiful day, beautiful lady - what more can a man ask for? You're looking gorgeous as ever and can I smell a new perfume?' he leaned on the counter reeking of Paco Rabanne, the gum moving around his back teeth while undressing her with his eyes. Lillian just smiled, her defence and protection. He looked her up and down and winked before turning to his guests. But it wasn't a wink like her father's, it was more of an 'I own you' wink. His invading glances had made Lillian adjust herself and cross her legs, leaving her feeling conscience of her bare arms and low-ish neckline.

The guests weren't greeted in his usual cringe-worthy manner, just leading the way to the stairs. 'Can you bring coffee and biscuits up love?' he asked. She nodded and waited for them to disappear, shivering with disgust when they left.

The Hathaway man had also left an expensive scent behind, although she preferred Simon's. Lillian transferred the calls upstairs to the sales office, they weren't as busy as finance. She left work bored and fed up lately, rather than stressed and exhausted.

Waving to the factory staff through the glassed walkway, she made her way to the brewing station and staff room. She quite enjoyed making the coffee, the silence of reception was apparent beyond the door, down to earth people resided in that section, not like the stiff white-collars upstairs. Dave could see her from the production line and made his excuses to join her.

'Heli-blimp!' he said, 'are you being the hostess with the most-est again?' he asked as he walked in. Lillian smiled to herself at his predictable entrance. The superficial, underhanded attention he gave her was the only thing that kept her alive sometimes.

'Yes, I am. It gives me a break from that screaming switchboard.' He watched her position the cups on the saucers, turning them so that the handles were all facing outwards and became mesmerised as she put the biscuits on a plate in circular patterns. His cologne of Avon and cigarettes, difficult to endure. 'Who's that for then?' he asked, intrigued.

'Some visitors for Simon, not sure who they are, but just trying to make a good impression,' she answered as she placed the last biscuit in the centre of the symmetrical spiral.

She took the tray, it was a little heavy. 'Excuse me, please,' she asked politely.

'Oh sure, sure, sorry. Catch you later Lil,' he said and stood to one side, discretely sniffing in her scent as she passed.

'See ya, Heli blimp,' she called back. Lillian precariously carried the tray upstairs and then continued along a short corridor to Simon's office, her arms aching. She pushed the door open with her back. The crockery rattled as she made her way in, everyone turning as they watched her place it on the mahogany sideboard. Simon's executive man cave, with bare brick walls, chesterfield sofas and golfing trophies. Lillian always felt awkward in there, especially after the incident in the stationery cupboard. The subject and cupboard were avoided after that. She never did anything or told anyone about it. She was scared to– such things were all part of the entitlement. It was a difficult scenario when he was the CEO.

'Thank you, gorgeous,' he said and winked. 'Can you do the usual for me please?' he handed her another sealed envelope, full of cash. She still didn't understand why she was doing it and not the cashier in finance. He told her not to mention it to anyone, so she dutifully did as she was told. The visitors gave her an empathetic smile, but coffee and biscuits would not sweeten the purpose of the visit.

Eight

She stared at the mannequins in the window. They stared back, lifeless, with rigour mortice and badly positioned wigs. Half expecting them to make a face at her. Lillian could see people milling around the perfume and makeup counters, that's where she used to wait for Jeffrey to pick her up, before her shift ended. It was a Saturday job, not much money. She hated it with every bone in her body, but Rose said it was good experience. Yes, good experience of ill-mannered people she was a magnet for!

The reminiscing brought on a sudden panic. She couldn't go through with it - she was betraying him, going against his orders. Lillian closed her eyes as she tried to deal with the rush of shameful emotion. Recoiling, looking at her watch. There was enough time to get a prawn sandwich and just head back to Pulse, and stop being so ridiculous. Her reflection in the window looked disappointed; the Lillian looking back, needed her help.

A member of staff entered the window to redress one of the mannequins. She changed the dummy out of the t-shirt and shorts - into a revealing black evening dress. Lillian looked on in awe, with one raised eyebrow. The woman pulled and altered it, to fit the disproportionate figure. The dress suddenly became a showstopper, people were gathering. A sale price ticket was pinned on, and Lillian's shoulders slumped, it was out of her league and out of her pocket.

'Skiving off, Lillian?' came a voice from behind her. She turned around, and Jeffrey's mother was standing there, clutching her handbag in a stand-offish pose. Her hair just blow dried.

'Oh! Uh...hello Celia. Um, I'm just, uh, getting a sandwich. I needed some air. You?' Celia looked at her suspiciously.

'I just came for a browse, 'ave me 'air done. Have you got your eye on that dress?' Lillian just smiled and glanced nervously at her watch, there was still time to change her life, or slip back into the Cunningham's grip.

'Well. Don't let me keep you. I can see you're not in the mood for conversation. Tell Jeffrey I said hello, I haven't seen him in a while.' Celia smiled bitterly, disappearing into the swarm of excited on lookers.

'Ok, I will! Bye!' Lillian called out. Battling with her nerves, she made her way through the lunchtime crowds, picking up some of their vibes. That's why she never went out much, there's only enough room for one soul. The bank was next to the recruitment agency. She looked at the door – their name etched in gold on the glass made her mouth dry. Who was she kidding? Closing her eyes and exhaling, she made a dash for it -pulling hard on the door. The echo of her steps up the long stairs, sounded official. Her stomach churning.

As she got to the top, out of breath and dishevelled - the hustle and bustle of the town was shut out. Three women were sat behind desks, all facing her.

'Can I help you?' one of them said as Lillian tried to control her breathing.

'Um, yes,' she panted, 'I...I'm Lillian. Lillian Tate,' she said, with everyone looking on. 'I'd like to register with you if I could. I mean, if it isn't too much trouble.'

A woman at the back stood up, 'yes, of course, please, take a seat,' she offered the chair in front of her desk. 'I'm Brenda by the way,' they shook hands. Lillian winced at the wet handshake, immediately distrusting her decision, and Brenda.

'Sorry, I just ran up those stairs!' Lillian said with her hand on her chest.

'It's ok, take your time, I get out of breath just walking up them!' Brenda, a little plump from her chocolate cravings, handed Lillian a small glass of water and a registration form.

'Thank you. Um, I've brought my CV.' Lillian placed the plastic wallet down. It had a deep fold down the centre after being in her bag for seven months.

'What sort of profession are you looking at?' Lillian was beginning to perspire.

'Uh, well, I'm a receptionist, currently. Looking for something similar or a change of departments. I cover other tasks in my current role. They are all listed, in here,' she tapped the pen on the wallet, reminding Brenda of it.

'Who are you working for at the moment?' Brenda asked, fanning through the pages.

'Pulse. They called it something else when I first started. Trident Solutions.'

'Forgive me but, what made you come into this agency?' Lillian's stomach squelched - she took that as a 'what the hell is someone like you doing here?'

'Well, err, I'm hoping for something in Sales administration. I'm not just a receptionist, as you can see. I help with other departments. I want to progress, and this looked like the perfect place to start.'

'Yes, I can see you've gained a lot of experience in your current role. But you have limited software knowledge. It's in great demand now. However,' she stood, 'we just might have the right one for you. You came at the right time.' Brenda opened the steel cabinet, she'd been trying to get rid of a vacancy for a while. No one wanted it.

'Here we are,' Brenda held a manila pocket file 'it's a vacancy right here in town. Working for the rental offices. Says here…' she read through the key information 'previous experience of handling customer enquiries, blah, blah. Good telephone manner, ability to work under pressure, deal with public, and so forth,' she sat back, her cheeks rosy as she smiled 'how does that sound? Want me to put you forward?'

Lillian just said yes to be polite, but she envisaged the job in her head - steel filing cabinets and worn wooden desks, with all the atmosphere sucked out of it. She got an instant knot in her chest, it wasn't quite what she meant.

'Okay, that's fabulous. I'll get everything faxed over and hopefully we'll hear something soon. I think they'll be very interested in you. Why are you looking to leave your current role, Lilly? Can I call you that?'

'Sure. I want to find my dream job,' she answered. Brenda nodded, amused, like she hadn't heard that before. 'I see. Well, nothing wrong with chasing your dreams. I will call you as soon as we get a response. Is there anything else you would like to add?' Lillian had lost the will to live and was ready to leave.

'I don't think so, I've covered all my duties on my CV.'

'Well, if you think of anything, it'll be a bonus.' Brenda handed her a business card. 'I can be reached on that number,' they both stood up and shook hands.

'Thanks. I look forward to hearing from you.' Lillian added. Rushing out she said goodbye to the others, with them all watching her leave. When she was out of sight, Brenda sat back down and looked at her peers.

'Well, that was weird! I'm sure she was here last week! Did you recognise her?' Brenda trawled through the appointment book, breaking chunks off of her chocolate bar.

'She's that girl. The one...you know? Does the sandwiches,' her colleague answered.

'How can she be? She works at a place called, Trident something. Must have been her doppelganger then. I hope they take her for that position. I'll be glad to see the back of it!'

Lillian left cautiously, looking both ways to see if Celia was still hanging around. She half ran back to the car park, just making it back to Pulse. Realising she had no lunch. Had she done the right thing? She would have to go through with it now, not exactly in a position to look a gift horse in the mouth. Annoyed with herself again, for going along with it, just to be 'nice'. It was a disappointment, she had a better feeling about it prior to going. She hurried to her position and exhaled; pleased with herself that she had made the first step, feeling tired as the nerves dispersed.

'Hey Lil,' Dave said, breezing into reception.

'Hey, Heli Blimp,' she put on her headset, feeling like her job wasn't so bad after all.

'Did you have a nice lunch?'

'Well, actually, I didn't get any. Big queue at the bank. Is there anything left in the vending machine?' the brewing stations vending machine was the last resort if you hadn't bought your own lunch. The other option was the Greasy Spoon burger van in the lay-by, with mechanically reclaimed lips and arseholes on offer, distastefully bundled into stale buns.

'There might be something edible in there. I'll go check it out for you babe.' Doing any favour for Lillian was a step closer to her loins.

'Thanks Dave. Anything will do. Cheers,' she handed him some money. He took it - checking how much she had given him. There would be enough change to get that chocolate he had his eyes on all day, she wouldn't notice. He'd observed that she was leaving on time every night, off in a rush somewhere. Dave didn't like it, gearing himself up for the next move.

Nine

Throwing the car keys on the worktop, she went to the check the post, which was lying by the front door. Bills, advertising, and a plucked dead crow that Oliver had left for her. How he got that and himself through the cat flap, beggared belief.

She picked it up by its curled foot, holding out in front of her, grimacing as she took it outside. They had a special ceremony for the bird under one of the roses, with Oliver watching – pleased with his clever disposal. After the mass clean-up of black feathers, she called her mother, telling her about the epiphany and timely presence of Celia Cunningham. It was a start, but it wasn't the 'one'.

Sitting outside with her glass of Mateus and a bowl of nachos, because the two went together beautifully, she ran her eye over the neighbours' gardens; the tops of matured shrubs and Maples in contrasting colours, complementing the view as they took your appreciation off in different directions.

Barbeque smoke rose from the family at the very end. Lillian tutted with envy, they were always having one! No one invited them round anymore, Jeffrey had upset quite a few people, always having to leave early before finishing their food.

She reclined the chair slightly, enjoying her time alone, drinking it in as she studied the Honda at the end of the garden, solemnly facing the cemetery. She felt sorry for it, often putting souls into inanimate objects, making it difficult to let things go or throw them out. It can't be easy not having a shine or something about you to admire. No fancy gadgets, just a wonky headlight that Lillian affectionately called its lazy eye.

The drive went all the way to the bottom of the garden in case you wanted a garage included in the package. A raised foundation that wasn't aesthetically pleasing - portraying the workmanship of cheap labour. Closing her eyes, she faced the sun, its fading zenith gently warming her face and chest as she drifted off into a catnap, one that was dream-filled as her brain emptied its unwanted, nonsensical contents. The Hathaway man made a fleeting appearance, then the visit to the agency - thumping in like a drunk elephant.

Jeffrey's unexpected arrival woke her abruptly. His Volvo came hurtling down the drive, just missing the Honda. Sitting up quickly, going a little dizzy as her vision flashed blue - she grabbed the glass to look normal; heaven forbid if he thought she was sleeping. He slammed his car door, muttering as he made his way round to the patio. Lillian used her hand like the peak of a cap over her eyes, trying to make sense of his bulldozed entrance.

'What's happened?' she asked.

'Happened? What makes you say that? What do you know?!' Jeffrey answered, uptight with adrenaline.

'You're home early, that's all.' Jeffrey sat down in the seat next to her.

'Oh, right. I finished me jobs, thas awl.'

Lillian nodded, waiting for the next instalment, 'just got a bit of damage on me car. Nothing serious. I'll take it to Adrian, he'll patch it up for me.' Adrian was Jeffrey's mate who fixed cars and did resprays as a side-line. She didn't know what his day job was.

'Is there much damage?' Lillian asked,

'Bumper.'

Lillian was waiting for more, but that was it.

'Well, since we're discussing Adrian, can he give me a quote for the Honda please?' Jeffrey stood up, 'quote? For what?!' he pulled off his jacket and threw it down.

'A re-spray. Blue, metallic. Please.' He frowned at her request.

'You're talking four fifty at least!'

Lillian took a sip of Mateus. 'Oh, that much? Um, your mother says hello. I saw her in town lunchtime.' Jeffrey tutted and scowled.

'What she want? And how did you see her lunchtime?' Lillian was quickly back peddling.

'Uh, I fancied a sandwich, from that new place. We just happened to bump into each other.' Jeffrey huffed.

'Ha! You should make yer own bluddy sandwiches! I'm havin' a shower and get me a tea when I come down,' he called out.

She gave the 'V' sign, then the middle finger, then she ran out of fingers. When he was out of sight, arguing with herself about not making him tea, she went to have a sneaky look at the Volvo, so she could revel in the misfortune - squeezing between it and the house to get around the back of it. Running her hand along the dent, she got a good feel of the damage. There were streaks of black paint. The other car must have been worse off from the Volvo's steel girders. Picking up mixed messages, which made her doubt Jeffrey's story.

She squeezed back though, to make his tea. Jeffrey made dinner and brought the food outside, much to Lillian's surprise.

'Oh, are we eating out then?' Jeffrey just nodded stiffly, pushing up the parasol. She looked at him and wondered what the sudden change of personality was all about.

'How did the dent happen then?' she asked, strengthened by her covert information.

'Down by the roundabout, by that big place,' he answered. Lillian frowned, Jeffrey was at the wrong end of the motorway if he was where he said he was. 'The big place' was a central roundabout to all other routes and link roads, with a large office building next to it, owned by a local entrepreneur.

'What were you doing there?' she asked.

'What's it to you? I just was, that's all!'

Lillian picked at her food. 'What are we going to do about the Honda? I'm fed up with driving a car that's two colours.'

Jeffrey scoffed at her. 'Do what yer like? I ain't buying ya a new car! You'll wreck it.' She touched his arm and transferred her vibe, because somehow it worked. Jeffrey flinched and pushed her hand away. Lillian got the hint and amused herself with her favourite view-but yearned for light, intelligent conversation, it would be such a pleasant change.

They both retreated to their personal spaces. She glanced up at Jeffrey now and then, but he avoided eye contact - he was hanging onto something, which was on a need-to-know basis.

Ten

Seventeen days had passed, and no word from Brenda. All with the longest twenty-four hours she cared to endure. She was relieved, if a little deflated. It meant the job was for someone else, someone with cat-eye glasses on a beaded chain.

There was a funny atmosphere hanging around Pulse, everyone seemed to be in a suspicious mood; each day was torture. If it wasn't for Dave, she was sure she'd disappear into the dusty carpet, never to be seen again. The little words of the day and banter were all she looked forward to, and the barbarian long hair. Lillian had been to the woods nearly every night after work, a ritual that was becoming addictive. It was getting close, but not everything was revealed. Dave's insistence on a 'no strings' drink after work was wearing her down, the woods came first.

This night, he'd had enough of the rejection, so he waited for her to leave the carpark and followed her out. Pulling up alongside the Honda in his red Ford Capri, the cigarette drooping from his mouth - he grimaced at the surroundings, it wasn't a good place for a rock star to be seen. Leaving the door ajar, he tiptoed in his pointed, black ankle boots. Stood at the stile, blowing out smoke-rings, he peered into the labyrinth of trees, examining the path that lay ahead of him and asking himself what the hell he was doing there. Mind you, a romp in the woods was something he hadn't done before, apart from the mile high club, but that was 'highly' unlikely.

He flicked the cigarette to the floor crushing it with his boot, replacing it with a cocktail stick before straddling the stile with ease. Looking good in drain-pipe jeans and an Iron Maiden T-shirt, his jacket hooked on his forefinger. A hostile environment confronted Dave and he wasn't sure where to start - the pathway seemed the obvious choice, but maybe it was too obvious. He walked in, his head slightly ducked, wary something would drop into his hair. He tried to look for her footprints–he saw something that resembled a shoe, but they stopped by a tree. He checked either side, she must have veered off the path.

Sighing and huffing as he continued, he occasionally stopped to gaze. He was a little awed by the sight, but his shallow soul could only take so much, incapable of anything deeper than acknowledgement. He'd been walking for a while, it seemed like a while, thinking about his life and needing another cigarette, his mind emptied and quiet, no banging and crashing of drums and symbols. The terrain off the beaten track was difficult underfoot, making it an effort to tread. Although the sound of his feet crushing the undergrowth was hypnotic, comforting. He stopped to get a sense of direction - he was going nowhere fast, it all looked the same! Noises had been leading him off in different directions. Coughing from the tar that lay thick on his lungs, he bent over to catch his breath, supporting himself on his knees.

More snapping twigs could be heard off to the left. He tutted, swearing under his breath. An animal was probably taking the piss. He straightened and wiped his nose on his sleeve, heading in the movement's direction, sniffing and spitting out phlegm. Trawling through the bracken, stray protruding branches pulled at his hair, if his female fans could see him now, he would lose his credibility for sure. He put his arm over his face and pushed forward, clenching his teeth and grunting. His foot suddenly gave way to a different surface, letting out a shriek.

'Finally! Christ!' he said aloud, standing on a pathway. He brushed himself off and redressed his hair, pulling out an elastic band from his jacket pocket to tie it in a ponytail. A narrow, dirt path wove through long grass, leading to an old railway tunnel. Dave looked warily at the opening as he approached; trails of ivy hung over the foreboding mouth like green waterfalls, curtaining the pitch-black abyss that lay beyond. He was hesitant, the sight of it unearthed childhood fears - the flap of unseen wings overhead, pushing him forward.

Parting the ivy cautiously, he felt sure he'd gone the wrong way - it was dark and dank, the ground uneven. He placed his right foot forward, testing the gravel under his weight, wishing he had something to hold on to; it was so dark in there! The tunnel's residue was sombre. Dave felt heavy-hearted as he stepped over potholes, trying not to get his boots dirty, they had cost him nearly two weeks' wages. He felt odd, like his body wasn't attached, something was in there with him, lurking in the alcoves. Dave squinted at the other end, the escape eluding him. He picked up speed, feeling desperate to get out, his ankles twisting over in the crater-filled floor, clumsy efforts echoing around the lime-soaked stone.

To his relief, a dog walker appeared, casually standing by the exit.

'Uh! 'Skuse me! - You seen someone come through 'ere mate?! Girl, uh, woman?' the man didn't acknowledge him, he was too busy watching his animal sniff the perimeter. Dave tutted and proceeded, mumbling obscenities, stepping in large puddles, cursing loudly as the water splashed up the leg of his jeans escalating his short temper. But the thought of the reward kept him motivated. He looked up and the dog walker had gone. 'Shit' he uttered. The darkness was interfering with his faculties as he looked at both ends. He stood still, trying to remember if he'd seen the walker move on, or even come in.

Then he heard the release of a mournful moan, 'who's there?!' followed by the tinkling of a dog collar, which made him relax. He whistled 'here boy! Where's your owner mutt?' he said, searching blindly.

'Here!' came a sharp whisper from behind him. He gasped and turned.

'Jesus! You scared me!' he snapped.

'Are you lost, David?' came another whisper - deep and masculine. Was it his father? He frantically turned his head from side to side as he tried to locate the voice, it was away from him but in his ear at the same time, blinking with confusion as his eyes played tricks on him. He saw movement, but it was hard to focus on, a large, black figure, indecipherable - moving quickly, darting from one place to the next. Disappearing into the walls, reappearing and sliding up them, hanging above him. A shard of light caught the apparition, Dave held his breath, certain his heart would stop at the flash of silver eyes that stabbed the dark, speaking to him in woeful mumblings, chilling his core.

All that was sinister within, was drawn out, joining in with the emptying of mercy. In a split second he was scratched in the face with three sharp nails. He cried out, it burned and throbbed. Rooted to the spot, he was trying to work out which way he was facing, the tunnel seemed to spin. He held out his arms in front to balance himself, not wanting to touch the slippery surface, his breath visible as he panted with anxiety. Dave was cold, his skin goose bumped.

The dog walker suddenly reappeared, silhouetted at the other end as he stood and watched him, with the small, strange looking dog at his feet.

'Ok, that was hilarious!' Dave shouted, but there was a pressing silence, 'which way out?!' The shadowed figure pointed behind him.

'Cheers! Arsehole!' Dave hastily headed out, unsteady on his feet, tripping, falling to his knees as he made it into the light. Shielding his eyes, whimpering, filled with fear and frustration. The sun's warm welcome and solitary call of a cuckoo offered temporary solace. He wiped traces of tears from his eyes, unsure if it was his imagination running away with him, or what he saw in there was as real and as terrifying as it felt.

'Jesus. Jesus!' he said hopelessly, out of breath, trying to pull himself together by rubbing his face. He looked at the trees, then at the small bug that was struggling over the uneven surface, the brambles and dropped crisps packets, trying to absorb a bit of reality. But the outside was as real as the tunnel. Dave the rave wasn't feeling so good; he felt sick and vulnerable, like the time his brother made him keep his eyes open on the Ghost Train. He got up and looked down at his clothes and boots, they were covered in grey clay.

If he did eventually find Lillian, he didn't want her seeing him like this. He checked his mouth, the cocktail stick must have fallen out, but he wasn't about to go back in and get it, cigarettes were in the car. Limping slightly along the path, he broke into a hobbled sprint, eventually leading him back to the car park. He tried to get the key in the ignition as his hands shook–stopping to breathe and regain composure. Looking back into the woods, he saw the dog walker stood halfway in, 'what... the... fuh...?!'

Dave narrowed his eyes, mesmerised at first. The dark figure stood tall, motionless and menacing. Then he realised, the warning stance was for him. He turned the ignition, almost snapping the key, then rammed the car into reverse gear, forgetting his seat belt and pushing it into first, leaving the car park in a cloud of red dust and blind panic.

Eleven

The sky was changing as she put the key in the door. There was a wind from nowhere. She could feel a storm brewing. Everyone, especially the gardens, would welcome it. Lillian prepared dinner as she listened to Sting in her pyjamas - soothing the jagged edges with his silky-smooth lullabies. Following the list Jeffrey had put together for her, sticking to them religiously.

It was hard to do something from someone else's instructions, she liked to be creative. Chopping onions, the phone rang. Wiping her hands down her front as she trotted to answer it.

'Hello?'

'*Hey, Lilly? Guess who?*' it was Lisa. Two years and no word.

'Lisa? Wow, how are you?'

'*Fine, fine. Look, I know this a bolt out of the blue – but I hear Pulse isn't doing so good and I have a proposition for you.*'

'Uh, you have?'

'Yes. Anyway, I have a position that would suit you. Working with moi!'

'Are you still working for the same people?'

'No. Somewhere much better. You know the big place, on the roundabout? It's them.' Lillian studied the stained-glass roses on the front door, stuck in the middle of somewhere as she listened.

'Take down this number and fax over your CV when you get a chance. I'll do the rest. It's in International Sales. Really good company Lil. So, what d'ya say?' Lillian spluttered, the impersonal contact was a shock.

'Well, I'm with an agency at the moment, I'm not sure...'

'Forget the agency Lil, cut out the middleman. It's what you've been waiting for, trust me.' She got a piece of paper out of the little draw and a broken pencil.

'Okay. I'm all ears.'

She returned to the kitchen, perplexed. It was a garbled call, Lisa had to rush off and it came with a whispering decree from the woods – that's why the visit tonight felt different. The light dimmed quickly as dark grey rain clouds consumed the blue sky, accompanied by low rumbles and subtle flashes.

Lillian stood by the back door, breathing in the fresh aroma of ozone. The wind dropped suddenly, everything fell silent and waited. First it was slow, splatting on the patio, and then it came down like stair rods, sweeping the area. Hitting the roofs and washing off the lichen. Lillian stood outside with her arms outstretched and tongue out to catch the drops. She was getting drenched quickly, but it was warm and refreshing, a relief from the long drought. The scent of the parched earth being quenched gave her a sense of fulfilment, as the garden drank and bathed. There was a sudden clap of thunder which made her scream and take cover, screeching with excitement. Another clap of thunder came, shaking the house, scaring her. Then another rumble, but this time, it was the Volvo.

Jeffrey got out complaining, running inside and holding his sandwich box over his head. 'Bluddy 'ell! Where did that come from?!' he shook himself off and wiped his boots on the mat. 'Why are you wet?'

'I was standing in it.' Lillian casually answered. He flumped down at the kitchen table and sighed, like always.

'What a bluddy day I've had. You can cook. I'm too bluddy knackered. Is there Tea?' Lillian made him tea, while she listened to him going on about his day. How everyone didn't have a clue what they were doing and how he could run the place single handily.

'Right. I'm havin' a wash. Make something nice and don't make a mess.' Lillian confidently cooked her favourite pasta. She could hear him coming downstairs and placed the largest bowl on his side, feeling as uptight as an apprentice waiting to be judged by a Michelin star chef - although her pastas were complimented often, but not by Jeffrey.

He sat down and smelt his food then straightened the condiments before starting to eat. Lillian pretended to do something else in the kitchen while she waited for the demeaning criticism.

'What were you doin' with yerself today?' Jeffrey asked, between mouthfuls.

'Well, working,' Lillian answered and sat down with her small portion of pasta.

'I know you was workin. What have you been doin' in work?' Jeffrey asked again, not looking up.

'Nothing special. Pulse didn't set the world on fire if that's what you mean.' Jeffrey hummed suspiciously.

'Did you have another drive to the woods?' he asked. She ignored it.

'How about your day?' Jeffrey scoffed his pasta, tilting his bowl to get every morsel. He dropped the bowl and threw the spoon in it, making a racket.

'I've been workin 'ard, that's what–and all you could muster up from that fuzzy 'ed of yours, was a poxy bowl of pasta!' Lillian pushed her chair back a little, preparing for flight.

'It's all I could think of under the circumstances.'

'What circumstances? You're always makin' bluddy excuses! Why don't you get yerself down the library and borrow some recipe books? Teach yerself summat.' She got up from the table and walked off to sit in the lounge, her legs just about getting her there, she'd lost the bones in them when Jeffrey shouted and ridiculed. She switched the TV on and watched through it, concentrating on keeping her herself together with tears in her eyes and fire in her belly. Jeffrey tutted at her childishness, and followed her.

'You could've put some bluddy meat with it or something, where's your imagination?!' he stood in the doorway, filling it.

'There was no time to put meat in it because that needs two hours.'

Jeffrey raised his eyebrows. 'Since when do y'know how to bluddy cook?! I'll do it meself next time, bluddy useless you are!' Lillian focussed hard on the news, feeling dizzy, 'you listening to me?!' Jeffrey yelled, making her jump, she nodded, wanting to punch him in the face until it bled; dislocating his jaw... clenching her fists as the murderous vision took hold. The TV lost the channel and hissed its white noise through a different frequency. She could hear them, trying to get through, their syllables in bursts.

'What's up with the bluddy telly now?' he went over to it, slamming his hand down on the top. Lillian looked out to the garden, and the news flicked back on.

'Ah, there, must be the aerial. I'll have to get on the roof and 'ave a look on the weekend. Right. Well. I'm going to see mum, 'ave some proper food. See ya lata,' and he left the house, like a tornado leaves town; devastated with irreparable damage.

Oliver jumped on Lillian's lap and she stroked him along his back and to the tip of his tail, repeating it as he purred. She should have gone for that drink with sleazy Dave, she thought - switching off the TV from where she was sat, it was interfering with the noise in her head. They both watched the rain from the patio doors, getting hypnotised by it. Lillian's tears fell like the drops racing down the window. Her soul had lost something, perhaps it was a bit of her sunshine or good nature. Whatever it was, wouldn't be returning.

Jeffrey was deep in thought as he drove to his mothers, thinking about what he would do with Lillian – she was getting dangerously itchy feet. The Volvo effortlessly climbed the steep lane that led to the farmhouse, rocking and bouncing over the potholes. He held on tight to the steering wheel, his face close to the windscreen as he tried to see through the downpour, the wipers on super speed. He hadn't seen rain like it for months, neither had anyone else come to that matter. As he reached the brow of the hill, hedgerows squealed on the door panels as the lane narrowed; it was his sign you were near the house. Then the dirty-white building loomed out in front of him. Cracked render and faded window frames made it look derelict in the rain- reminding him of an animated screaming face.

It had become dilapidated since his father's passing. The younger brother did the odd job under duress, but the old place needed an expensive overhaul, or pulling down. His childhood home was fading fast. The old tractor was still there, tucked down the side of the house, where he once played with his two brothers, pretending with sticks and getting grazed knees. Birds used it for nesting now, and buddleia grew through the engine. Two acres of land behind the house was an idyllic setting for children to grow up in. Celia recently rented it out to a neighbouring farmer, for some extra income.

Jeffrey felt alone without his father, no one to banter with or discuss the ins and outs of welding and steel fabrication, he needed his advice. They knew his father's job would eventually take him away - it was a freak accident they said, couldn't be avoided they said. Corners were cut from being used to working in elevated risk conditions, so he became complacent with the dangers. The sudden death meant Jeffrey had to support his grieving mother and help bring up his two younger siblings, stealing his childhood and family unit that made all his bones fit together. Now, they just felt like they were floating around in his body.

He could see the lights were on in the kitchen, pulling up alongside his mother's Citroen BX. Sighing heavily, he felt bereft, knowing darn well there wouldn't be any food, not better than Lillian's anyway. Running to the front door with his face screwed up- he noticed the old tractor tyres were used as planters outside the front porch, full of caked soil and dehydrated weeds. Jeffrey regarded them with a turned down mouth. Knocking the stable door loudly, he walked in and called out, leading him straight into the kitchen, the smell of fousty milk hit him first. Terracotta tiles were cracked in places, some missing. Jeffrey's favourite item in the kitchen was the big green Aga - warm and welcoming, with a freshly boiled kettle. Where they all sat round in the winter, warming the hearts and feet.

There was just one mug out, so Jeffrey took another from the shelf above, running his finger along it, astonished at the amount of dust that was piled up on his finger. He rinsed his cup out, feeling slightly panicked from the dirt, giving it an extra wash to be on the safe side. God only knows what was breeding in the tea stains.

'Mum!?' he called out again, putting two tea bags in the large brown teapot.

'Jeffrey? That you?' she called back, coming down the stairs in her pyjamas and gown, clutching the lapels.

'You been sleepin'?' she shook her head, 'just got out the bath. Where have you been anyway? You sure you could spare the time to see me?' she said, looking hurt.

'This place is in a bluddy state mum! Why don't you sell up and move somewhere smaller? There must be rats in 'ere!' he sat down at the pine table in the middle of the kitchen.

'Yer father is here. It's all I got left of him.'

'He ain't 'ere! There ain't nuthin left! Don't know what yer 'anging on for!'

'What you here for, anyway?' she answered, pouring two teas.

'Just come to see ya, that's all. Want you to do me a favuh.'

'A favour? That's what you come to see me for, is it?' she placed the mugs of tea down and sat with him. Both slurping loudly.

'I think it's time you came back home. You got no intention of marrying that girl, have ya?' Jeffrey was eyeing up the table, noticing the mouldy crumbs and smears of food that had crusted over; making him feel nauseous.

'You just want me back 'ere to clean up after ya! Look at the bluddy table!' Celia ignored him, doing up her top button.

'You've just got problems, Jeffrey.'

'I ain't the one with bluddy...' he paused, throwing his hands about, '... last week's food stuck to the table. Oh, and enough dust up there...' he pointed above the Aga, '... To make bluddy mole hills!' Celia felt slightly ashamed but was unwilling to do anything about it. She was happy to sit amongst the dirt and die. No one would notice. Her other sons rarely came.

'I ain't marryin' no one. Told ya that. But things have taken a turn...' he paused, picking grease from his nails, 'I might 'ave to go to Birmingham,' he said solemnly. Celia felt sick. All she wanted was her son back. He was right about one thing, he would keep the place looking nice and clean. But she wasn't sure if she could put up with all that again, it was an overbearing pressure. She regretted being so self-absorbed with her grief, letting her children slip through her fingers, needing to be needed again, to be depended upon, completely. It was the only thing that would replace the void that she carried around with her every day.

'Have you got yerself in some sort of trouble?' Jeffrey toyed with the mug handle.

'Not exactly. I can't say anything right now. Just sit tight. Why don't ya come with us?'

'What's this favour you want done?'

Twelve

A recurring dream had been waking Lillian at 3am every night, one that was becoming increasingly lucid. Rushing through people in the same place as they spun her around, while she tried to keep her eyes on a dark figure who was catching all her attention. Feeling overwhelmed and fretful when the alarm went off, she hit it aggressively and the realisation of Groundhog Day made her groan.

Getting ready in a daze, she wished she was in bed, sleeping, telling herself that the day would go quickly, and she'd soon be back in it. She wore black trousers and a long sleeve flowery blouse, in violets and reds. Wearing proper shoes was quite a nice change, adding a little security to her feet. With tea in hand, she opened the back door - the sun blinding her as it reflected off the wet patio. The storm's devastation was clear from the rose petals all over the lawn and borders, almost pulling them from their sockets. It had ruined the luminescent blooms of the Geraniums too, all soaked and drooping.

The wind hung around, drying the saturation. Oliver sat on the doorstep, wincing from his fur being ruffled by that invisible hand, unwilling to step out.

'There'll be work to do on the weekend, Olly.' She said to him. He enjoyed helping her in the garden, even though he just sat there, it was still important, nonetheless.

Lillian drove to work in silence, needing to listen to what the voices were saying, what her gut was feeling. But it was just a mishmash of squirming business, excited whisperings made it hard to listen.

She was later than her usual time and rushed to her post before Simon noticed. Approaching her station she heard a commotion behind the factory doors; pressing her ear against it, closing her eyes to help decipher what was going on.

'Lilly!' Simon called down the stairs, making her jump out of her skin, she shrieked and turn around. 'You need to be a part of that. Don't worry about the calls. Just go in.' She nodded and entered a hubbub of activity. The staff were waiting for an announcement. Dave was standing with his fans and just looked at Lillian. She waved and made a face, but his response was a dip of the head, looking vacant, with bloodied scratches on his face.

Pulse's Finance Director stood on an upturned crate. His shirt collar undone, tie loosened with vigour - sitting slightly skew whiff. He held a piece of paper and cleared his throat before starting, Lillian could see it quivering as he tightened his grip on it. He started thanking everyone for their support, then moved swiftly onto the purpose of his disruption. Cuts, financial cuts, assuring them there was no cause for alarm, but the company would look for a buyer or move production overseas. Competition was tough and Pulse had not found a niche and their products would be obsolete if they didn't keep up. There was an eruption of conversation and it was growing louder. Lillian thought Radar could be one of the competitors, but she still wasn't sure what they did and access to such information was very limited. Perhaps this announcement was because of the Hathaway guy.

The factory staff talked amongst themselves, as his words echoed through the warehouse.

'Uh! Quite please! We will continue to improve our marketing strategies and expand our client base and products we offer! Your line manager will inform you of any further change. Thank you.' He got off his mock podium, sweating. Lillian watched him leave the warehouse with Simon D'or, both of them with their heads lowered as they went, talking to each other from the sides of their mouths.

She thought the speech was more of a deviance from the inevitable, than a courteous procedure. They had lost a few big customers, barely surviving on the ones they had left. Warehouse and production staff were ushered back into action, but everyone was discussing the hot topic, which gave them an excuse to meander. Lillian returned to reception, feeling Pulse's sombre mood - it felt like the end of a party, time to turn the lights on, sweep up and call a taxi. She didn't see any management for the rest of the day, most of them went out for a very long lunch to puff on their cigars and scratch each other's backs.

Dave plucked up the courage and paid a visit to reception, see what else he could pick up on - his next guitar was riding on it.

'Hey Lil,' he said, reflecting the whole mood of the factory. 'What do you make of that speech?' he asked her.

'I think it was a cover-up and you need some antiseptic on those scratches,' she answered, as she did her filing. He just nodded at her answer and touched his face, remembering, flicking his hair over his left shoulder, which was a little dulled that day.

'Oh... uh... yeah, sure. I was just fooling around with some mates. So, uh,' he cleared his throat, 'what's the word today then, Lil?' he asked. Lillian looked at him and smiled, her aura had altered, and he mistrusted her.

'Integrity,' she responded and held her glance. Dave swallowed nervously and stepped back, getting the same vibe off of her as the tunnel.

'Oh, right. That's a new one. Cheers. Ok, uh, catch you later. I'd, uh, better be getting back,' he tapped a little tune on the top of the counter and left. Lillian watched him leave, then carried on filing without a second thought, dealing with calls, mostly for finance.

He left reception not feeling like he usually did when he spoke to Lillian; fired up and living off his ego, looking to the floor as he continued to his post, processing her 'word', feeling paranoid. Taking a detour to the brew station, he needed another caffeine fix, joined by one of the shop-floor workers on their break.

'Watch ya Dave. S'up?'

Dave acknowledged him with a nod, 'hey Stu.' The co-worker chose his coffee from the vending machine and sipped it loudly, needing it.

'Are we looking for another job then boss? And what did you do to your face, man?'

'I dunno mate. Just a load of bullshit if you ask me. Uh, Stu, have you got a dog? Small one? Was that you, pranking me?' he asked, laughing falsely.

'Dog? Me? No. I don't follow, sorry,' Stu replied.

'Never mind, just. Uh, anyway. Umm, listen, could you do me a big favour?'

The switchboard had gone quiet, and Lillian was staring out the window again, daydreaming, fantasising and expecting – wondering what this Radar was all about. It was solid when it crossed her mind, physical. Stu came into reception and interrupted her.

'Um, hi Lilly. Have you got a dictionary at all? Just to borrow, please?' Lillian smirked, retrieving it from her drawer, marking the page he needed with a post it note.

'Sure, here. Tell Dave I need it back before he goes, please.' The production worker flushed red and agreed. He handed it to Dave, who was waiting impatiently.

'Here. She said she wants it back before you go.' Dave took it and saw the yellow note hanging out of it.

'Dude! I told you not to say it was for me!'

Stu stepped back with his hands raised.

'I said nothing! Straight up. She already knew! Are you two an item or something?' Dave slapped the dictionary in his palm and exhaled despondently.

'Uh, no, we're not. Bit out of my league,' he answered, playing with his hair, and finally admitting.

'Yeah well, she's out of everybody's league mate. Not even slimy Simon can get a look in. We got no chance!' Stu jeered. Dave pretended to laugh along with the comment, but deep down he knew it was cheap, too cheap for Lillian.

'Ok, must get back to it. Cheers Stu, I owe you one.' Dave went to the men's toilets to look up the word of the day, shutting himself in a cubicle, sitting on the toilet lid. Lillian had placed the top of the post it note directly under the word for him – he held his finger on 'Integrity' and read the meaning aloud. Nothing made sense, closing the intimidating reminder that he was less than educated in that department. Looking at the floor between his feet, he mulled over what he read, thinking of his one-bedroom flat above the kebab shop, he used for his salacious arrangements and pointless display of electric guitars; he couldn't even play them. He touched the scratches on his face, ashamed of his intentions. He should have gone with the sole purpose Simon gave him, but he couldn't help it. What was a rejected, skint man to do? Anyway, all that nature and tree stuff wasn't his bag.

He opened the cubicle door and caught sight of himself in the mirrors. Dave the rave looked outdated, like the place he worked in. He needed to be more boy band than rock band; denim and BO was so last decade. He didn't venture Lillian's way for the rest of the afternoon, feeling rumbled, wounded and truth be known, still recovering from his experience in the tunnel. The nightmares he had since were the worst, and that took some beating. Dreams of his father's abuse were getting frequent, waking up at 3am every night in sweats, fearing the noises and presence from within the room. It hadn't left him in the tunnel at all – it had followed him home, keeping tabs on his movements.

Thirteen

Pulse had hit rock bottom - the radio wasn't playing in the warehouse, everyone had resided themselves to being out of a job and Dave never came for the 'word', he was simmering. Lillian could feel the bolts loosening on the bridge she was trying to burn, biding her time until the week was up - waiting for Lisa's call.

Having a reflective drive home, she was too hungry to wait for Jeffrey, so she started to cook herself. People would often say how lucky she was to have someone cook for her all the time, but it wasn't out of devotion, it was about not meeting standards. It was more of a nervous hunger than anything - arguing with herself whether to tell him about Pulse, almost hyperventilating as the scenario built up in her head, overthinking it. He also wouldn't be that happy that she cooked without his instruction, either.

Jeffrey burst through the door, smelling of solder.

'What yer standing there for?' he asked and took off his boots.

'Dinner is ready.'

Jeffrey scanned the kitchen like a Meerkat, 'you *made* dinner?!' he said in disbelieve, checking every section he could lay his eyes on.

'Yes, you've been missing out on my stews,' Lillian answered, fussing with napkins and cutlery.

'What's come over ya?!' he answered, angry at this new disobedience of hers.

'Just be grateful you've got another night off, Jeffrey.'

'Right, well, keep some by, me Mum's coming ova lata cuz she ain't been eatin' properly.' Jeffrey instructed as he walked off to have his shower. Lillian's heart sank and she had a sudden loss of appetite, throwing the tea towel down in defiance. She stood by the sink and looked out to the garden. His mother wasn't welcome – another ruined evening. They ganged up on her when they were together. Celia resented her, she had been wanting her son back since he left, making her feel inadequate – criticising and bragging about how she was better at things.

Jeffrey returned to the kitchen and sat at the table in exactly fifteen minutes, smelling slightly sweeter than before. It was Lillian's favourite smell, which pulled at the lost affection, making her stop and push away those feelings - they weren't welcome, they just muddled up everything. She was on track to leave and wanted nothing sentimental impeding it.

'This better be good, I've had 'ard day.'

She wanted to throw it over him, not feed it to him. Jeffrey looked at her, frowning.

'Well, what ya waitin' for!? What ya gawpin' at?'

'Nothing.' She served him his stew, her heart pumping.

'What's up with ya? Ay?!' Jeffrey asked, puzzled at Lillian's behaviour. He tore the fresh loaf of bread in half and dipped it in the bowl, doing his best not to get any on his fingers.

'Am I eatin' with me hands now then?' he asked. Lillian got a spoon from the drawer, tutting as he snatched it off of her. She stood with her back to the sink and stared at him with a heart so vengeful, it could have set the place on fire. He started to splutter and spit his food out, choking, leaning over whilst having a coughing fit. Lillian stood and watched, hoping for a bigger development, but her conscience and good nature sobered her up. She rushed over to him and patted his back, hard.

'Christ! You tryin' to bluddy kill me?!' he said through a constricted throat.

'You need to chew your food more!' Lillian answered, still hitting his back.

'Okay. Okay! That's enough! I'm all right!' he said pushing her away. He wiped his mouth and looked at her suspiciously with his lifeless eyes.

'Do you want a drink of water?'

'Yes.... cold.' Jeffrey was feeling slightly shaken.

'What did y'put in this? Arsenic?!' he asked between coughs.

'Vegetables and things,' Lillian responded.

Jeffrey had another go at it. 'Yer put too much bluddy pepper in it! Yer bluddy choking me!' She joined him with her small bowl of stew and side salad, a little disappointed he was still breathing - watching him eat the rest his food like an animal; psyching herself up to tell him about Pulse.

'So, how was your day?'

'Like bluddy usual and stop bluddy askin' me that every day! It's the same as yesterday was and the day before that! I don't work in a circus, like you!' Lillian chased a cherry tomato around the plate thinking about Lisa's call, dealing with Jeffrey inwardly, betting with herself that it wouldn't come to anything. She stabbed the tomato with her fork and took a sharp intake of breath as she watched it explode and make its way across the table, landing on Jeffrey's arm.

'Oops! Sorry! They're just little red bombs, really. Getting their own back on the world,' he was unimpressed and sucked the pips off his arm. Lillian waited for a bit of a smile, but there was nothing, not a thing.

'What's up Jeffers?' she asked. He looked up from his trough, wiping his mouth with the back of his hand.

'Tomatoes ain't funny, and its Jeffrey to you!' he rested his elbows on the table and looked at her. 'There's summat different about you. Chancing yer luck, is it?' Lillian swallowed and her appetite had passed again.

'What do you mean?'

Jeffrey cut the bread and ladled on butter. 'You're up to summat, bluddy shifting stuff. I told ya to leave things alone! Y'see that dent out there?' he said, pointing his knife towards the drive, 'well, whatever y'been up to, you'd better put a bluddy end to it!'

'You won't tell me about the dent!' she said.

'It ain't none o'ya business, that's why! 'Ave you been in them woods again?' He noticed something in her hair. Lillian followed his eyes and took the pine needle out, looking at it before leaving it on the table.

'Y'see? You 'ave been there! I bluddy knew it!'

'I didn't say I hadn't, and I don't know what you're getting so excited about!' he glared at her, chewing on one side of his mouth, breathing heavily through his nose.

'I think Pulse is going into receivership,' she said and waited. Jeffrey acknowledged her briefly, helping himself to more bread. There was no way she was mentioning Lisa, they never quite hit it off and there was an exchange of expletives before Lisa disappeared. Jeffrey pushed his bowl away from him.

'Oh yeah? I knew you were 'iding summat.' Lillian swallowed nervously.

'I wasn't hiding anything. That's it really.'

Jeffrey hummed. 'I'll 'ave to get yer a job now then?'

'Why are you getting me a job? I can get my own!'

He stood up, laughing.

'You couldn't get anything on ya own without messin' it up! The receptionist is leaving our place, good timing. I'll get you in there. Then I can keep an eye on ya!' The phone rang and Jeffrey threw down the tea towel 'I'll get it.' Returning from the brief call, with a face like thunder. 'Who was it?' she asked.

'Me muther. She ain't coming. Changed her mind. Lucky for you, eh?' he retreated to his armchair and newspaper.

After the dishes, Lillian tendered to her peace roses; September would bring the last blooms. Oliver sat with her, absorbing the vibe of the garden and Lillian - his ears tuned in to the songs of his feathered victims, keeping an eye out for any crows. She looked up and saw the muted girl, two doors down, staring at her from an upstairs window. Lillian waved to her, the girl reciprocated by raising one hand, then turned away. She got a twisting sensation in her gut, hearing the phone ringing again.

'Some woman on the phone for ya!' Jeffrey called out. Lillian took off her gardening gloves and her mind raced as she made her way to the phone.

'Hello?'

'Lil? It's me! I know I've called at a really bad time! But just listen and answer yes or no. Okay?' it was Lisa, whispering.

'Yes.'

'I got some bloody good news! Radar want to interview you!' Lillian checked the lounge door; a rush of adrenaline hitting her stomach.

'But I didn't fax...Yes?'

'Monday at ten. You need to ask for Hannah Bresworth.'

'Oh err, that's short notice...'

'Lil! Yes or no! You'll be fine. Are you okay to go?'

'Yes.'

'Fabulous! So excited for you! Speak soon. Au revoir!' Lisa sang her last words and hung up. 'Who was that?' Jeffrey called out.

'Oh, just some survey thing.'

'Huh! Bluddy nuisance they are! Is the kettle on?'

Fourteen

Lillian was on pins for most of the weekend, rehearsing her interview while she sorted through her wardrobe. She found clothes she'd had for years; some had gone out of fashion, some had come back in. Trying to remember the last time she bought herself something, because the bills he expected her to pay took everything she earned.

Jeffrey wouldn't let Lillian go to her parents for dinner because he was in a bad mood about his mother. There was shouting and crying, but he won. He got himself ready for his journey to Birmingham, storming around with clenched fists, muttering things about the stupid women in his life. Lillian was eager for him to go, she loved it when he went away and so did Oliver. She broke out of her hypothetical straight jacket when he did, and it meant she could watch The X-Files in peace.

He packed his bag in military fashion, doing a last-minute check in the bedroom.

'Right, I'm off. I'll call ya when I get chance.'

Lillian took out a blouse and held it up, 'what do you think about this one? Shall I keep it?' she asked him.

He looked at her up and down. 'You won't be needin' anything posh where you're gowin. You'll be full o'grease an'dirt!' he yelled 'See ya!' and he left, slamming the bedroom door so hard that her picture of the woods fell off the wall.

The back door finally closed and the whole house heaved a sigh of relief. Lillian sat on the bed and slid off it, crying into her hands. She was going for the interview and that was that. Was she? Should she? Oliver came in and pushed her with his head, 'hello you.' She took immense comfort from his thick fur and vibrating body.

'Get my mirror for me Olly, I can't get up, my legs are heavy,' he sat and blinked his blink at her. He could do most things, but not having thumbs had its limitations. She sniffed repeatedly, using the blouse to soak up her tears and running nose, needing her father and her magic. She made her way to the music centre in the dining room and searched for something to match her mood – 80s Prince fitted the bill just nicely, trippy and purple. Her hate for Jeffrey had jumped up several notches, a bit of head banging and air-guitar would be her celebration of his absence; crying and connecting when Purple Rain played.

Emotionally exhausted from her day of nothing, she lay on her side watching Oliver going through his own nighttime ablutions. Preening every inch of himself, hoping it would soon be over. He shook the bed and made nauseating gobbing noises for those hard to reach places. She leaned over and switched off the lamp, darkness fell with a 'click'. Her mind woke her periodically throughout the night because it had something else to say or think about, which meant she tossed and turned and spoke loudly in her sleep. She was having the same vivid dream- it gripped her tightly, greeting people in a long line, all smiling, with fresh faces. There was one person in particular that she couldn't quite see, they remained in a shadow, waiting for her with purpose.

The alarm sounded and made Lillian sit bolt upright, feeling she'd had about 2 hours sleep. 'Oh God,' she moaned, holding onto her chest; full of butterflies and buzzing wires. Looking through her clothes to find a suitable interview outfit was a trauma, doing breathing exercises to loosen her lungs. She decided on her lilac skirt suit with a cream tie neck blouse. The skirt was just above the knee and she would carry the jacket because she didn't want to arrive sweaty. Then there was the shoe dilemma. Lillian dressed casually at Pulse so didn't exactly have an 'office' wardrobe. After throwing everything over her shoulder, she pulled out a pair of beige suede sling backs that were misshapen from being forgotten.

'You can do this Lillian Tate. It's now or never,' brushing herself straight in the mirror. Oliver was watching her on the bed, she turned to him 'wish me luck!' and kissed him on the head. He stretched out his legs and laid on the bed in complete bliss, trying his best to reach both ends - forbidden fruit was always the sweetest.

Lillian drove to Radar Networks without song. As she got closer, her mouth began to dry and her heart felt like it was beating in her throat, her panic blurring the road signs. She arrived in the visitors' car park at precisely 09.50 am, covertly parking the Honda between two other cars. If anyone caught sight of it, it would surely be their topic of conversation for the rest of the day. The building was huge compared to Pulses'. The blue and white signage illustrated success; concentric rings struck through the word 'Radar'. The building was 3 floors high in brick and tinted glass, surrounded by Spruce trees and manicured lawns. Boulders strategically placed as barriers - holding some historic connotation.

She could still hear Jeffrey's ridicule as she walked to the reception down a sandstone pathway - straightening herself and breathing in. Black columns held up an extended entrance to the glass double doors. As she pulled on them, she was being watched by the receptionist and Security Guard, feeling sure she would faint. The reception desk looked like Simon's chesterfield sofas. Tendered, real plants adorned the area on flag stone flooring, carpeted stairs led up to another floor, boasting a plush landing surrounded by glass panels. Every door and wood trim were in a dark oak and there was a smell of freshly printed paper and the subtle ringing tone of an up-to-the-minute switchboard. The security guard smiled at her as she passed him, tilting his jobs-worth hat. The receptionist wore a blue suit, her headset far more advanced that Lillian's, feeling sure she'd just stepped into the future.

'Good morning, how can I help you?' the receptionist said with a smile, her name badge matching her suit, edged in gold.

'Uh, good morning. I'm here for an interview with Hannah Bresworth? I'm Lillian Tate.' Lillian's hands were clammy, her blood was pushing its way to the surface, making her skin blotchy. The receptionist checked her appointment book and then tapped on her keyboard.

'Ah yes, welcome to Radar Networks, Lillian. If you could just sign-in for me please and take a seat over there, she'll be with you in a moment.' With that, she handed Lillian a visitor badge to clip on a lapel. She signed herself into the visitors' book, having to concentrate on writing her own name.

The bespoke seating area in black fabric, with a smoked-glass table in the centre, displayed Radar's promotional leaflets. She picked one up and looked through it, but still didn't understand their position in the industry. None of Pulse's products were referenced - just shiny, expensive ones provocatively photographed.

Lillian's nerves were almost out of control as she waited and took in the surroundings, feeling she had bitten off too much. She looked towards the stairs and saw a woman descending them wearing a red suit, with neatly tied up blonde hair and a perfectly made-up face. She walked over to Lillian with her hand held out.

'Hello Lillian, I'm Hannah, pleased to meet you.'

Lillian stood and reciprocated the greeting, in her best telephone voice. Hannah Bresworth led her up the stairs to an office on the landing. A maturing man stood up and greeted her, with that expensive scent she recognised.

'Hi Lillian, good to see you again.' It was him, the Hathaway man, boasting a good physique, greying wavy hair and noticeable green eyes. His brow line protruded, resembling a gargoyle. They shook hands and lingered for an awkward moment.

'Please, take a seat,' he suggested. They all sat down at a round table which relaxed her, she hated sitting on the other side of a desk. You could see the visitors' carpark from the window and the Honda's nose protruding between the other cars. Lillian got a hot flush of embarrassment - maybe everyone else was looking at it.

The interview began with small talk, then onto the questions. Asking about her previous role, her attitude and reaction to given scenarios, how she would deal with difficult customers, was she a team player, can she work under pressure – all the usual textbook stuff and spiel. Lillian was confident in her answers, she felt quite at home and her nerves were subsiding. Phil Hathaway was listening and watching intently, taking notes.

'Can I call you Lilly?' he asked and couldn't help but stare at her, not really taking any notes, but rather brainstorming about other things.

'What are your weaknesses, Lilly?' looking directly into her eyes. It froze her to the spot as he held his glance without blinking, as if he knew what her answer would be. Lillian was unprepared for that question, we have weaknesses by default and she had quite a few: dominating men, inability to say no, people pleaser. Would she have to go through them all? Feeling pressured to answer appropriately and professionally, the first thing that came into her head, came out instead.

'Mateus on the patio,' she answered. There was instant laughter and Phil sat back in his seat, smiling with amusement and adoration, moving on quickly. Lillian felt like her inappropriate answer might just have cost her the job, but at least it broke the ice.

'Why are you looking to move careers, Lilly?' Phil Hathaway asked. She was careful about this one, he must be an associate of Simon's.

'I want to progress and utilise my skills, there's no room for me to do that where I am.' Would he be telling Simon she was here? She was feeling set up. He smiled again but wrote nothing down this time.

'Ok, thank you Lilly. I guess that's everything from our side. Do you have any questions?'

'Yes. Could you explain what it is you do, exactly?' Hannah Bresworth sat back and handed this one over to Phil.

'You're the only candidate who has asked that.' Lillian felt a little redeemed about her weakness answer. Phil continued.

'Radar are a major provider in the telecoms industry. Developing routers, switches and other network elements, to help facilitate our clients' requirements.' Lillian stared blankly.

'We are a leader in the global market. With offices in Europe, the Middle East, Canada and the US. What languages do you speak, Lilly?' she swallowed hard and the colour drained from her face. Suddenly the chunk she'd bitten off was choking her.

'I don't. Sorry. Well, a little German,' she wanted to kick herself. The contact with Munich on the telefax was the only other language she spoke, and that was just 'Guten taag'. Phil sat back and linked his fingers.

'It's ok, don't look so worried, it's not a requirement. We can put you through some courses if we have to. You'll be dealing with a diverse range of clients and colleagues, and they all speak English at the end of the day.' He finished with a smile that teachers give a struggling pupil. Lillian's hopes faded fast as she felt like the bottom rung of an enormous ladder - wishing she had done more with her education, but she couldn't wait to get out of the school environment.

'Well, I think we've covered everything. Hannah? Do you have anything to add?' Bresworth flicked over the pages of her notebook, Lillian eyeing up her perfect red nails.

'What's your availability, Lillian?'

She answered without even thinking, 'I'm available immediately.' Hannah nodded and jotted down her answer. The interview was over and she just wanted to get out of there. She was feeling traumatised by the different environment, needing to hide somewhere, desperately craving the woods and her parents.

They all exchanged their farewells in turn.

'We will be in touch with by the end of the day. It was great to meet you, Lilly.'

'Thank you. You too,' Lillian responded, feeling deficient. Hannah escorted Lillian down the stairs, with Phil Hathaway watching them leave. She knew deep down that she'd be walking those stairs again, not wanting to believe or trust it because the disappointment would be crushing.

'If you could just sign yourself out, please, and return your badge. We will speak soon. Thank you, Lilly. Have a safe journey back.'

Lillian left the building dazed and confused. There were positive comments, but the languages thing ate her alive as she walked back to the car. She took one last look before she drove back to Pulse. It was good experience - she told herself, trying to make a joke of the huge goofy moment that rendered her defenceless.

Fifteen

Walking into Pulse, she hit a thick mist – a sales colleague was manning the desk, with Dave hovering, beckoning her to quicken her step.

'Lilly! Oh my God, where have you been?!'

'Dentist. Why? What's going on?!'

'These guys came in with clipboards and black uniforms! They're upstairs! In his office!' she said, oozing schadenfreude. She looked at Dave, who seemed falsely surprised.

'Bailiffs?' Lillian answered, putting her bag down and taking over the headset.

'I think so!' her colleague said. It was the best thing that happened at Pulse for a long time. They heard deep voices at the top of the stairs and heavy feet descended, which made them scuttle out of the way. The bailiffs began noting the equipment in reception - discussing values amongst themselves. They weren't hopeful of getting back what the client was owed, it was all well passed its sell by date and the value would be minimal. Lillian looked on and reflected at the many times she wished this would happen, so it could set her free - never wanting to make the break herself. There was an uneasy feeling in the air, one of change, a shift pushing her out of her uncomfortable comfort zone. She watched them from the other side of the desk.

'Right ladies,' he thrust his ID badge at them, 'we are removing the equipment and we'd appreciate it if you would just step aside,' with a gruff voice and a few city miles on the clock. He wasn't to be messed with, bursting out of his black shirt and stance of a bulldog. The girls stood together on the other side of the desk, Lillian still with the headset on, the cord stretched to its limit - while Dave stood back and watched in silence.

Suddenly the fire door flung open, and the Finance Director made an appearance, trying to buy time and make other settlements. But the bailiffs weren't hanging about or listening to any excuses - the High Court writ was impenetrable. Their attention was shifted when a large tow truck began to position itself, ready to take Simon's Porsche. Lillian cringed inwardly, looking away – even though Simon was, who he was, she didn't like seeing them humiliated. The large men ripped plugs out of their sockets, taking the fax machine, electric typewriters, and telefax – Lillian was sad to see it go.

'Goodbye Munich,' she said, as the Bailiffs struggled with it out of the building. It would probably end up on the scrap heap, after the equipment she'd seen at Radar. The phone was going crazy, the lines flashing all at once. Lillian leaned over and selected line seven...

'Good morning, Pulse, which extension please?'

'Hi, Lilly? It's Lisa!'

'Oh, hi Lisa, sorry I didn't call, it's manic here! Um, well, I think it went ok, some drops of gold I thought of when I left, you know how it is, but hopefully I came across ok.' She didn't mention the faux pas, hoping they wouldn't either.

'Great, well, I think you did more than ok – Phil Hathaway wants you to join our team!' There was a long pause as Lillian waited for the 'just kidding!'

'Are you serious?! Really!? That quick? Oh My God! Even with my non-existent language skills?' Lillian tried to take in what she'd just been told as she watched the reception area being emptied of its contents.

'Never mind about that. Congratulations Lil. Now, we need to talk about your availability, do you have to give a months' notice?' Lillian watched her notice period and the collapse of Pulse, unfold before her eyes.

'No, I think it will be less than that somehow. Can't talk now. Can you call me later?'

'Ok, no problem. I'll wait for your update. They want you to start as soon as possible. So pleased for you, Lilly. Can't wait to see you! It'll be just like old times! I'll leave you to sort things out there. At least you can enjoy the rest of the day off! Ciao Bella!'

Lillian closed the call and felt light-headed as she watched the switchboard lights retreat.

'So, I guess that's that then – I hated here anyway, it's the kick up the arse I needed.' Lillian's colleague said, gathering up her lined pad and pen, not sure what she was going to do with them.

'I mean, what happens to all the paper and stuff when everyone leaves a sinking ship? In chronological order, painstakingly co-ordinated, like a life?'

Lillian shrugged, 'they burn it, like a life. Where's Dave?' she asked.

'Get his stuff from the locker.'

He was on his way upstairs to Simon's office. 'Ok boss?' he said, breezing in.

'What you got for me?' Simon asked, chewing gum 'and what have you done to your face?!' Dave sat down on the chesterfield, his arms stretched out along the back, feeling cock-sure of himself. 'She spoke to a Lisa. Sounds like they've offered her a job.' Simon nodded.

'Oh, and she goes to the woods, by herself.' Dave added.

'Yes, but who does she meet?'

Dave shrugged, 'No one. Well, I don't think she does. No other cars there. I got lost, so I can't really say.'

'You got lost?!' Simon laughed as he opened his top drawer, 'I gave you one job...' he put two white, unmarked envelopes on the desk.

'I'm wondering whether I should give you this.'

'They ain't just woods. Okay? It was, something else. Nearly took me. Killed me!'

'Killed you? There was someone with her then?'

Dave sat forward, 'it wasn't - 'a someone'.'

Simon gave him a cynical look, 'have you been smoking something?'

Dave stood up in defence. 'No! I ain't done that shit for years! It wasn't human and that's the truth, man! Believe what you like! I haven't slept for days because of it! Don't pay me then. I'm done!' he was feeling nauseous and uneasy again, like it knew it was being talked about. Simon held up his hand.

'Calm down, calm down. I believe you. Here. Take it and go ask Lilly to come up please.' Dave took the bulging envelope and left, feeling guilty, but affluently fulfilled. He strutted back to reception confronted by raised voices from factory and office staff, packed into the small space, pushing hard on the door and squeezing through the gap.

Lillian was behind the reception desk, holding her plant. Dave waded through the angry bodies to get to her, they acknowledged each other with a look of astonishment. The Financial Director stood halfway up the stairs waving his arms about to stop the tension and possibly, a difficult situation arising. He raised his hand to get everyone's attention.

'Uh! Listen up everyone, PLEASE!' he shouted. Dave whistled with his fingers, piercing Lillian's ears - silencing everyone immediately.

'Thank you, Dave. Listen up. Leave the building. Just take your stuff and go home, we will contact you in due course.' Everyone erupted again, all asking him questions that he tried to bat back with his hands, hoping they would all go away. Lillian grabbed her handbag, it was all her fault and she had to get out. Holding her plant in the air, making her way through the squirming mass, Dave pulled her back. 'Lil! Wait! Simon wants to see you before you go.'

'Now? Ok, take this,' she gave him her plant and hesitantly went upstairs.

Simon was sat on the chesterfield, looking slightly broken; the Paco Rabanne having minty undertones.

'Close the door love, and come sit next to me,' he said, patting the space beside him. Lillian stood with her back to the door, holding the handle behind her.

'It's ok. I'll stand.'

'I have a proposition for you,' he said and stood.

'They've taken your car,' she pointed out.

'Yes. Let them have it. They'll be another one, what do you think about red?' He laughed. 'This has all happened faster than I expected. However, I am starting up another venture and I would like you to be my secretary.'

Lillian released the handle, 'I don't understand.'

'What's there to understand? This is business, Lilly. You fall, you pick yourself back up.'

'I've been offered another job. Thank you.' Simon walked over to the window, watching everyone pour out of reception like panicked ants.

'How much are they paying you? I'll double it.'

'I haven't had that confirmed as yet, but I'm keen to work for them, sorry, but I appreciate your offer, thank you.' Lillian nervously observed his body language, portraying a determination she'd seen before, it made her throat close - the stationery cupboard still resonated between them. He picked up a photo frame, thinking of the next persuasion.

'Dave's accepted my offer, it would be nice if you two stayed together. I think you make a nice couple. I'll make it worth your while, Lilly.'

'Oh, I see. Well, like I said, I appreciate it, but I really want to work for this company.' Her legs began to shake. She returned her hand to the door handle, gradually turning it, wincing when the mechanism made a noise. Simon sat in his leather office chair and made a tune on the desk with his nails.

'Who's the lucky guy?' he asked.

'I don't want to say too much yet, sorry,' Lillian responded, thinking Phil Hathaway must be involved in this conversation.

'Ah come on, what's the difference now? You can tell me.' But she shook her head insistently. 'I see' he said and held his glance. She was too close to the door, he was hoping she would sit down, give those sexy little knees a squeeze.

'Well, that's a great shame.' Simon pushed the second envelope towards her.

'Can you do me one last favour then, please?' Lillian regarded the envelope, it was a lot thicker than the usual ones. 'Account details are inside. Different bank. You'll see which one.' He poured himself a scotch from the wooden bureau - which Lillian thought was for files and stuff. Raising his glass to her, with a feeble smile.

'I wish you luck, Lilly. You'll be an asset. Thank you for your loyalty and honesty. Here, take my card. Call me if you change your mind. Now, you'd better leave before you're thrown out. How about one last hug before you go?'

Lillian overstretched and took the envelope. She nodded a goodbye to him then left the office. 'Remember!' he called out, making her stop and come back, 'big doesn't always guarantee longevity,' she left, checking behind her as she took to the stairs, relieved to be leaving him behind. Dave was holding her plant by the entrance. She stuffed the envelope in her bag and took it off him, 'thanks Dave,' smiling sympathetically at him.

The warehouse and production staff congregated outside, smoking and laughing at the turn of events - watching the bailiffs loading up the white vans; like watching a good bonfire. A large electronics firm were employing production staff by the hundreds, so they enjoyed the last moments of their poorly paid, poorly lit jobs. Office peers felt less fortunate as they stood and discussed the situation by their cars, some of them with families to support. Lillian felt it was inappropriate to mention her dream job. They all decided to mull over the shocking turn of events in the pub, to straighten their heads and prop one another up. Lillian opted out and said her farewells.

'Uh, Lilly, did you speak to Simon?' Dave asked.

'Yes, I did. But I didn't accept. Sorry.' Lillian held out her hand. Dave looked down at it but gave her a hug instead.

'You take care Lil. It's been a blast, hasn't it?' he closed his eyes and lapped up the brief contact he had with her.

'Yeah, it sure has Dave. Won't be the same without you. But I have a feeling I'll be seeing you again. Simon will look after you. What's the position?' she asked.

'Oh, sort of similar thing really. I'm looking forward to it. Here, why don't you call me if you change your mind? You should really think about it Lil,' he said and handed her a piece of torn off paper with his number on it. Lillian smiled at him and wanted to pinch his cheek, not the one with the deep scratches on it though.

'Thanks. I'll keep it in mind. Today's word is... 'Goodbye.'

'Don't be so hasty, Lil.'

'I hope it all works out for you Dave, and don't forget the other word I said. It will save your life,' she turned and left, waving to everyone, but not without glancing up to Simon's office - who was standing in the window, raising his glass to her.

Dave watched her leave in bereavement. What did she mean about seeing him again? He failed miserably.

Lillian put the plant on the passenger seat and buckled it in. As she watched the others milling around wondering what had just happened, she couldn't help but feel responsible for it all - because once Lillian shifted things, everything shifted.

She looked at the business card Simon had given her, 'Phoenix Solutions' printed in gold on a black, glossy background. She snorted a laugh, turning it over to check the back. Driving out of her parking space for the last time, she stopped at the entrance. Pulse was a shell of its former self, its day-to-day life and soul it once held, just residue. Waiting for someone else to take over and put it all back. She grinned at the hand of fate and the precipice she was tittering on – then headed off, into her hypothetical sunset.

Sixteen

Lillian needed time to reflect, she felt exhausted from the release. Sitting in her usual place with a glass of Mateus, Oliver relaxed with her on the garden table reminding the birds of his indomitable presence. She called into see her parents on the way home to tell them the news. A pleasant surprise for them both, Rose even got the special biscuit tin out.

Staring at the bubbles in the fluted glass, ascending in straight lines, their transient formation represented the way forward and happiness had returned, softening the snagged fibres in her body. Her clairvoyance gave her courage, renewing the third eye. Lillian felt as though she'd received another awakening, her soul emerging from the trauma as a different being; disassociating itself from the once ordinary world around her. Even the same view looked different.

She was looking forward to seeing Lisa again, having a good chat over the phone. The reunion made everything fall into place. She never had a five-figure salary before, fourteen thousand was more than double. Not having Jeffrey around meant not having to prepare dinner. Rose gave her something to take home to reheat - could the day get any better?

The phone interrupted her peace, making her jump. She dropped the glass, smashing it on the floor. Oliver scarpered off the table while she ran into the hall to answer it, maybe it was Lisa - perhaps she forgot something.

'Hello!? Oh, hello,' she said with deep disappointment, it was Jeffrey. Lillian sat down on the phone table, there was a convenient little seat incorporated.

'What's 'appenin' there then?' he asked.

'Pulse went bust today… we're all out of a job,' she held onto her new shiny thing and wasn't about to divulge it, she'd lie her way through it.

'You had summat to do with that, I bet!'

Lillian screwed up her face. 'What's that supposed to mean?!'

Jeffrey wiped his brow in anxiety. *'Nuthin. Anyways. You're workin wi'me. So, enjoy your week off. Cuz you'll be doin sum propa work soon!'*

'Right well, I've got the dinner on,' Lillian said, trying to leave, poking her tongue out down the phone.

'Oh yeah? What yer cookin'? Pot bluddy Noodle?!'

Lillian tutted, 'No! Something Mum gave me.'

'Ha, well, I knew it wouldn't be summat you did. Just behave yerself and don't go buying anything stupid. You need to hang

onto yer money. There's bills to pay. Speak to ya lata,' and he hung up. Lillian grunted in frustration, slamming down the receiver.

She swept up the glass, taking pleasure in the sound it made. It was a pleasant change not having Jeffrey tutting and huffing about it. Oliver was already back on the table, not wanting to give up his look-out and if it wasn't for him, she would have left the glass there a little longer, just for the hell of it. Dusk was falling and a bit of stargazing would be heaven on her own when she'd finished washing up. A different stress had materialised, and she needed help from her guides. How was she going to wriggle out of this one? Maybe she should just leave - maybe now was the time. She put her face in her soapy hands and screamed at the top of her voice, annoyed at herself and him. As her blood pumped from the exertion - Celia popped in her head, hearing a noise coming from the hallway.

She listened with her eyes, it sounded like the front door, strange - no one used that anymore.

'Hello?!' she called out walking to the hallway cautiously. Her heart sank to the bottom of her flip-flops when she saw Celia taking off her shoes.

'I came in through the front 'cos I wasn't sure what was gowin on in the kitchen,' she said, holding an overnight bag.

'Oh, I was, erm, just washing up,' Lillian answered, pointing over her shoulder. 'Jeffrey isn't here, he's in Birmingham,' hoping his mother would leave.

'I know. Jeffrey thought y'needed a bit o'company.'

Lillian's stomach regurgitated some of its juices, and she felt slightly incontinent.

'I'm fine. I don't need any company. Thanks.'

Celia gave her a look of contempt. If ever there was a stereotypical image of a mother-in-law, she was it; bitter, jealous and self-opinionated. She didn't just bring a small, overnight bag with her but a whole load of other baggage, ready to dump on Lillian. It was her coping mechanism- tearing everyone and everything apart because she was angry with God. Her face portrayed her resentment - she had a permanent scowl, her hair rollered in tight curls that she never brushed out, they just remained there like copper pipes, some a little flattened. Lillian's rage rose from her stomach and up to her neck. Her week of self-care, dabbling and slouching had ended abruptly replaced with a female version of Jeffrey. She wanted her confidence back - it was there just a minute ago and it felt good. Celia placed down her bag and walked off into the kitchen.

'Is the kettle on? You've got soap on yer face an awl.'

Lillian followed her, the red mist descending fast. 'Jeffrey tells me they've made you redundant?' she leaned on the worktop.

'Yes, well, not redundant, the company went bust. At least I think it did.' Celia had a habit of looking at Lillian like she was trashy, starting from her feet upwards.

'I bet it's easy getting a receptionist's job. You don't need any qualifications.' Lillian blew into her mug to cool down the hot liquid.

'I'm not looking for a receptionist job. I need something that will stretch my imagination.' Celia turned down her mouth.

'Jeffrey will sort you out. There's a job gowin apparently, at his place. Be ideal that. You'll only need one car then. Or you could always become a housewife.' Lillian just listened, doing her best to keep the anger under control and her choice of weapons. Oliver had finished eating, looking at Celia with a turned-up nose, sitting on Lillian's feet.

'Isn't he a bit overweight?' Celia said, looking at Oliver in disgust.

'He's a Persian. They are bigger than your usual cat. They also have a lot more fur.' She wanted to eat that answer.

'Huh! I bet it gets everywhere. I don't know how my Jeffrey puts up with it. All those germs from the bins!'

Lillian finished her drink and wanted to get away from her.

'He doesn't go in bins! Not even ours.'

'You're lucky you have Jeffrey, he's a big softy letting you keep it,' Celia responded sharply. Lillian raised her eyebrows while she had her back turned, she couldn't imagine Jeffrey getting soft over anything. She really didn't know her son very well, a rod she had constructed all by herself. She could have him back if she wished hard enough. They could live together in that dirty farmhouse, out of everyone's way and kill each other in peace. She had the same harshness in her voice as her son, but the accent wasn't as strong. They all moved to Wales when Jeffrey was young for his father's job relocation. But their estrangement made him feel like an only child.

'I'll get meself changed then.' Celia went to make herself at home. Perhaps this was a good opportunity to sort out that kitchen drawer, Lillian thought. She tugged on the handle, trying to free whatever was jammed, nearly breaking it in annoyance. There were odd pieces belonging to whole pieces, broken pens, sofa casters, hairbrush and different lengths of string. She spotted something, moving everything aside to get to it.

'Ha! Well, I never.' An old photo of her in the garden with her dog, just before she died. Remembering the wholesome life, full of yellows and greens - like it was yesterday. The photo deserved a better place, she left it out then continued the rummage. Another find, the world's smallest recipe book. It was from a Christmas cracker, an exclusive edition Rose bought one year. The little book brought on a nostalgia that was long lost. She strained to read the small print, just making out the ingredients for quiche Lorraine. The happy memories made her tearful, she wanted them all back to fill her emptiness, fill up the holes in her bones and love her inner child again.

Lillian put her hands back in the hot water, her body shuddering, squeezing her eyes shut trying to suppress her hate. It overflowed, drowning her goodness, the most powerful emotion for her telepathic contact. Staring at her reflection in the window, resisting the alluring pull of the hidden doorway to dark temptation; everything she held in was the energiser for its calling. It came to her, expanding the space - solid, heavy and electrical. She begged the dark presence to rid her of her stresses. The contact made her blood warm, running through her like strong liquor, pulling her further. Revenge's bittersweet smell wafted under her nose - if she could just kill them both once, that was all, it wasn't too much to ask.

She broke off the connection, being good was better – no one could pass judgement, her image intact. It was important what people thought of her, at any price and the reason why she was always so eager to please. She dried her hands, succumbing to it all was easier than fighting. Oliver came in and jumped on the kitchen windowsill to have a more sheltered peruse of the garden; preferring to stay inside close to Lillian. She stroked him while he preened, feeling tearful and missing home. Where was that now? The cat suddenly stopped - his tongue protruding, paused in action. Something caught his attention outside. He stared motionless out the window, his tail swaying from side to side. Lillian felt the static fill the kitchen and run up her arms. Her left side tightened, squeezing her scalp and making her eyes water. He rose to his feet in jerked movements, arching his back - making high-pitched warbles, forming recognisable syllables, '*no, no, no.*'

His pupils large, bowing his head in submission and backing away from the window. She didn't want to look, the window had lost its reflection – blacker than night. Hitting the security light switch she shut the back door, locking it. Oliver changed instantly when the garden was floodlit but was still breathing heavy - leaving mist on the window as he snorted like a bull, snapping his head round at everything that moved, scanning the outside and vigorously flicking his tail. She stroked him, but the cat jolted and spat at her, he didn't want anyone touching him yet, his fur still on end.

'What's wrong with that cat?! It needs castrating!' Celia said as she scuffed into the kitchen, dressed in a silk navy robe, which desperately needed a wash.

'He saw another cat outside,' Lillian answered, feeling a little hurt at Oliver's reaction.

'Open the door and shoo it away then!' Celia opened the back door. 'What's it locked for?' Lillian didn't try stopping her. Celia brazenly went out. A warm wind rustled the trees and played with the wind chimes, setting off a distorted tune. She wrapped the robe around tighter as the garden looked back unassumingly. There was something fleeting in the cemetery that caught her eye. She made her way down the garden path, regarding Lillian's roses as she went. They made her stop and look longer, putting something back in her heart. She delicately touched them, bending to smell the centres – the scent making her crave something sweet. There was a slight change in wind direction, slamming the back door shut.

Celia decided not to pursue what was out there and made her way back in, using the light from the house to guide her.

Lillian could see the handle being tried, stepping forward to help.

'What's wrong with the door?!' Celia called out.

'Just a sec!' Lillian pulled and tried the handle repeatedly.

'It needs oiling! I'll go round the front. Let me in there, will you!' Celia heard something coming up the garden path; narrowing her eyes, trying to make out what was approaching.

'You push your side and I'll pull at the same time!' Lillian was pulling hard, using all her weight. Celia must have gone, she couldn't see her through the frosted glass anymore. Tutting, she when to the front door to wait for her to appear around the corner. She was taking her time - perhaps smelling the roses again. 'Celia?' there was no response. She walked down the drive, setting off the light as she got to the patio. Celia was sat on the floor still holding the handle, staring out and looking pale, her chin quivering.

'Oh my God! Celia!' Lillian rushed to her pulling the robe around her exposed, frail body.

'What happened?!'

'I want my Jeffrey! I want my Jeffrey!' she sobbed.

'Come on, let's get you inside.' Lillian helped her up and released her grip from the handle. She tried it, the door opened with ease. It was an effort to get her in, setting her down at the table Celia seemed to have aged twenty years.

'Can you hear me?' she looked into her lost eyes hoping for life.

'Yes, I can hear you! I'm not deaf!'

'Can I get you anything?'

'Tea. Sweet, please.'

Celia cradled the mug in silence, staring at the table - she'd been like that for fifteen minutes. Lillian touched her forearm, she flinched.

'What happened? Did you fall? Are you hurt?'

'You know what 'appened,' she nodded her head towards Oliver in the window. 'He saw it, before I came down.'

'A cat?'

Celia straightened herself, glaring at Lillian. 'It wasn't a bluddy cat, and you know it!' she put her mug down and pointed her finger. 'You knew what it was. That's why you had that look on yer face. Knew it was summat you shouldn't 'ave known about. You're a witch! That's what!'

Celia felt nauseous, vulnerable; she needed the strength and physique of her son. 'I wanna go 'ome.'

'Maybe that's not a good idea on your own, in the dark. Why don't you stay here until the morning?'

Celia grunted, 'spose you're right. I'd be safer there than 'ere though!'

'What did you see?' Lillian asked. Celia adjusted herself and began to cry, trying to stifle it. 'Bad news,' she wiped her nose and eyes with the back of her shaking hand. 'That's what it felt like - when yer body empties, all at once. Y'know?' Lillian didn't know what to say, relating to Celia's analogy of it. 'It was whispering something,' she grimaced, 'it all happened so quickly. Then you came and it went in them trees, back there.

Can it get back in?' Lillian shook her head. 'Have you got anything, t'make me sleep?'

'Sure. It's upstairs.'

Celia grabbed her arm 'don't leave me!'

'Come on. We'll go together.' Lillian locked the front and back door, not that she needed to. After some essential oil therapy, Celia settled in the spare room.

'I'm sorry,' she said, pulling the cotton sheet over her, 'that's all,' she turned her back, rigid with fear under the cover.

'Ok. Just call me if you need anything. Night.' Lillian wanted to tuck her in. Poor woman with her disorders. She turned off the light and went to her room feeling guilty about letting her anger get the better of her again. But it had alleviated many things, renewing a part of her. Every piece put back, was building another Lillian.

Seventeen

Rose tooted the horn on the little red mini. Martin's XJS was too much of a guzzler for town. She was buying her daughter some new clothes. Lillian put her bag on the back seat and got in the front, kissing Rose on the cheek - feeling the tension.

'You look nice, Mum.'

'What the hell is she doing here?! Lilly! Get out of there! What a bloody nerve! Use this week to pack up and get the hell out, please, for me, for your old mum. You have my permission.' Lillian buckled up while Rose did a U-turn in the crescent, blaring the horn at the children. The relief from her mother's blessing almost broke her. She expected it to happen differently, but this bus wasn't stopping, there were no perfect moments. They left the close in the little red bean tin.

'Why must you settle for so little Lilly? I don't get it, I don't.' Lillian looked out the window, thinking about Celia.

'Well, I have a roof over my head and...'

Rose laughed mockingly. 'Ha! Don't give me that 'be grateful' crap - you're not homeless! Oh, and F.Y.I, I know what goes on in that house. You needn't have panicked when I came early.' All Lillian could do was listen, trapped. Mothers had a habit of doing that - losing their shit in the car. 'What happened to that Dave?' Lillian daydreamed about him before she answered. She wanted him back, sordidly - he paid attention to her, and that's all she wanted.

'He accepted the offer from Simon. His main goal was to get me in bed – and I could have, just like that,' she said clicking her fingers in front of her, 'but I didn't, I turned him down. He was snooping for information. Shame, really.'

Rose recoiled a little, 'it would have done you a bit of good if I'm honest! Opened your eyes a little. Was he a looker?' Lillian grimaced at the very thought of it. But that hair, was mesmerising.

'Mum! I dread to think what lurked behind those zips.'

'Zips? Oh, I see, put it about a bit, did he?'

Lillian adjusted the seatbelt, enjoying being in the passenger seat. She could have a good look at the Victorian houses she liked, lining the roads into town. Picking up their vibe as she studied each one, some housing good feeling, most, not – especially the ones with dark exteriors. If only people knew how much they contributed to the attraction of unwanted guests.

'Yes, something like that. He wasn't sure about himself, that's all. Another one with mother problems.' There was an awkward silence while they stopped at a crossing, watching an elderly couple cross hand in hand, supporting each other. Rose felt humility as she watched them, smiling at the sweetness of everlasting. The very sight of them prompted self-pity in Lillian, she had to look the other way. Feeling bitter that a dragon had high jacked her fairy tale.

'Bless them,' Rose said, 'you, see? That's what you need to be striving for, a life-long partner. A best friend. Not someone who saps the very soul out of you! That's not love. He doesn't even share your interests! Why do you feel the need to stay with him? Do you love him?'

'I don't know mum.'

Rose tutted loudly, grinding the mini into first gear. 'Is there something you're not telling me?'

Lillian's heart thumped, 'like what?'

Rose screeched off the zebra crossing, 'oh, I don't know, must be something keeping you there! You're not pregnant, are you?!'

'No, I'm not!' Lillian didn't want to continue; she kept her guard up and blocked her mother's prying.

'Well, that's a relief!'

They entered the underground car park, searching for the 'right' space, which irritated Lillian. After passing umpteen vacant spots, Rose found a space, with four others either side of it.

'I don't want to park next to other cars - they forget I'm there.' Lillian rolled her eyes and reached in the back to get her bag. 'You can't stay with someone you feel sorry for sweetheart. He needs a check-up, from the neck-up, if you want my honest opinion,' her last comment echoed around the car park, along with their slamming doors.

'Not today, Mum, please. I've missed you,' she hugged Rose and closed her eyes, containing the melt down.

'How's dad?'

'He needs to get himself a hobby, he's driving me mad! And drinking too much Scotch! Right then, what's the plan? My treat, whatever we're doing.'

They linked arms and walked to the elevators. Although Lillian preferred the stairs, she hated the awkward silences and pungent smell of stale urine. The carriage pinged and juddered to a halt, the doors squeaked loudly as it slowly revealed the eagerly awaiting shoppers. Everyone nodded and smiled as they passed each other. A new mini mall was the latest addition to the little town. They entered under cover, it was white and cool. The smell of new clothes and coffee was always in this area. Their shoes echoed on the glossy floor, her mum's cork sandals making that noise again, like little farts. Lillian wore her brown, flat sandals and long, white cotton skirt, with black t-shirt. All the other girls were wearing denim with pink Bubble skirts, but she didn't want to follow the crowd, even though it got her bullied at school. Lillian was grateful to be different.

'What do you think I should wear mum?' Lillian asked, it was a long time since she'd bought anything for herself.

'What was everyone else wearing? That should give you an idea. Or just wear what you feel comfortable in. I think you should go office smart on your first day. Are you going to change that old rust bucket, now you've got a bit of extra cash?' Rose answered, stopping at a shop window, 'you won't know yourself, I think it will be a wonderful experience for you.' Lillian was trying to see what her mother was so fixated on.

'Jeffrey won't be letting the Honda go in a hurry, I think I'll give it a re-spray.'

'Give it a re-spray?! My God, it needs crushing! You make sure you get yourself something decent, that car makes me nervous. I'm waiting for it to fall apart like something off wacky races!' They both laughed and moved on, chatting constantly as they made their way around different shops.

'There was one dress I had in mind, actually.' Lillian said as she pulled Rose in the department store's direction. Disappointingly, it wasn't in the window. They frantically searched through the rails inside. A shop assistant, carrying around returns, asked if she needed help.

'I'm looking for a dress you had in the window, two weeks ago. It was a black party dress,' Lillian replied.

'Oh, I know the one. We only had a few in, sorry. They've all sold out.' It was crushing, Lillian swore she saw herself wearing it.

'Is there anything else you had your eye on?' Lillian just picked out a plain purple dress. Not as ego boosting as the black one, but it was new, albeit a poor substitute.

'Changing rooms are just over there madam,' she knew where they were, it was the department she used to work in. The smell of old carpet and disinfectant hadn't changed. The dress flowed like a silk flag behind her as she made her way to the cubicles, with faded brown curtains for privacy. She chose the first one, tugging at the flimsy screen. It wasn't Lillian's favourite pass time, clothes shopping, especially when things didn't fit. But this dress was far from it, looking at herself in the mirror and admiring herself from different angles. She sighed with content, happy with her new thing and new life approaching. But she still had that stinging sensation in her gut. The move was long awaited but felt uncomfortable. Rose poked her head around the curtain.

'Hmmm... a bit plain. But it's a good colour on you. It would pass for office.'

Lillian ran her hands down the front of it 'I love it.'

Rose held out her hand, offering to buy it. 'Meet me at the till.'

It was time for a well-earned cappuccino and the department store's café was in stumbling distance.

'Thanks mum.' Lillian said and gave Rose a kiss.

'My pleasure sweetheart. Shall we have lunch here? I could eat a scabby cat.'

'Yes. I fancy a Caesar salad, please.'

Rose chose a table where you watched the clientele browse the store.

'Why didn't you have pie and chips? You could do with filling out that dress!'

As they ate, Rose could see the colour starting to come back in her daughter's cheeks, although there was a dark cloud still hanging over, and under her eyes; ones she wished she could take away and carry herself. 'So, tell me about your boss.'

'My boss? Well, he's not a Simon. Mature. Seems nice enough. He smelt amazing. But he has something about him, something, edgy.'

'Is he single?'

'Wow. That wasn't predictable at all, mum.'

'How does Jeffrey feel about the news?' Lillian swallowed hard, almost choking on a Crouton.

'Oh. He. I didn't tell him. I'll wait until he comes back, break the news then.'

Rose looked up from her lunch, 'you won't tell him though, will you?' Lillian took a large gulp of her sparkling water.

'Yes, of course I will. Face to face,' and laughed it off.

'I know I say this a lot, but you are worth much more. I think you need to meet someone else, who will fight for you and watch Jeffrey run off in the other direction.' That aroused Lillian, how delicious that would be.

'He can't help the way he is, it's his mother's fault.'

'Why do you always defend him?! He's a bloody adult now, he should deal with that stuff and move on. If he can't move on, he should at least get some help for it. He's just a petulant child thinking the world owes him something. I think I should move in with you, that'll loosen a few bolts!'

Lillian was still picking at her food, long after Rose had finished hers.

'I hung on because I didn't want to upset anyone. You and Dad spent a lot of money on the engagement party. I wish him dead, every day. He'll be gone then, won't he?' Rose smiled sympathetically, reaching over and squeezing her hand.

'It hurts me to hear you talking like that. Why didn't you speak to me about it? It doesn't matter about the damn party! Your father and I thought you were happy, and we wanted to celebrate that with you.' Rose held back her tears, feeling a little helpless and severely let down. 'Sometimes, the only thing holding you back is your perception of it. You've got a fresh start next week, but tame that tiger you've got in there.'

Lillian sneered, along with another tsunami of letting go.

'Do you remember that time we came in here when you were little? You picked up a crystal vase and dropped it?' Rose asked.

'No! I don't! Oh my God Mum. What did you do?'

'I didn't know what to do. I checked the price tag before you got your hands on it and saw my purse flash before eyes! The manager was very courteous, more concerned whether you were hurt. I wanted to wring your bloody neck! Your tiny hands were just too small to hold it, but you still wanted to try. That's my Lilly, determined and headstrong – that's the Lilly I need back.'

Lillian poked the salad, 'she got lost mum, stitched up tight under someone else's weight. Let her come out on her own. All this pushing and shoving will just make her hide further into dark. You're not trusting her,' tears appeared in both their eyes.

'I got all the time in the world, but she'd better get a move on, or she'll miss the boat!' Rose got overwhelmed by the moment. Since her daughter moved out, she pined for her daily, especially knowing her unhappiness. 'Have you finished dissecting your lunch? Come on, deep breaths and let's go buy some scented candles. They always make everything better.'

Rose pulled up outside the house, with the little red mini full of bags.

'Thanks mum, I love everything.'

Rose leaned over and kissed Lillian on the cheek, 'the pleasure is all mine. Come on, I'll help you in with your bags and I promise, no trouble.'

'Ok. We'll have a cuppa then.'

They emptied the car and poured through the back door, dumping the bags on the kitchen table. Lillian flicked the kettle switch and sighed with contentment.

'Where's Celia?' Rose whispered.

'Well, her car is still here. Probably having one of her attention-seeking-lie-downs.'

'Oh, hello, I didn't hear you come in,' Celia walked into the kitchen, yawning and scratching her head, 'I was having a lie down,' Lillian and Rose looked at each other, sucking in their grins. 'What with my condition.'

'Condition?' Rose questioned. Lillian rattled the mugs to divert what was inevitably coming.

'Yes, well, you know, me legs and my fatigue and my heart isn't what it was, and I hurt meself the other night, did she tell yer?' Rose had an answer but bit her tongue – she had been biting it for a long time, it's a wonder she hadn't bitten through it.

'Right. Well, I'll take these upstairs for you Lil.'

'No, it's fine, just leave them, I'll take them up later Mum, thanks, have a rest.'

Rose just took them before she said something, secretly wanting to have a nose around. They hadn't been there for several months because it wasn't somewhere they enjoyed going. Putting the bags on the bed amongst the clothes and Oliver, 'hello you'. Rose tickled him under the chin, he had missed her. She looked around the prettily decorated room, she could tell Jeffrey was away, the mirror was out - picking it up and feeling sentimental, studying it, turning it in her hand. Lillian had looked after it and God only knows how many years it had been in the family. It seemed to be in good working order, apart from the blemishes. She put it back, adjusting its position so it would look untouched. Looking to the ceiling and down the walls, picking up everything on the dressing table – like she was at a boot sale. Jeffrey bought the bedroom furniture from a house clearance, you could still smell the previous owner's dry rot and moth balls.

She lifted the cloth that covered up the dressing table mirror and peered beneath it. There was a large crack that ran across its width.

Turning the black rococo key on the wardrobe, stiff at its first turn, she pulled on the handle and winced when it creaked. There were a few bottles of perfume in the pocket hole shelving, half used, but she still had the one Rose was hoping for. She took it out and unscrewed the black, ridged cap. Holding it up, shaking the liquid to gage the content. It had almost gone and Rose had only gave it to her a month ago. Placing the bottles on the windowsill she took out an identical one from her trouser pocket, pouring her oil into it, filling it almost to the brim. The sour scent rushed at her and jolted her head back, it was a stronger mix than the previous one with a few added extras. She put it back in the same place and closed the door. Rose noticed a ring mark of oil left on the windowsill, smearing it left to right with her forefinger as far as it would go, reciting with the movement, putting a barrier between the inside and out.

'Mum?! You ok up there? Tea's ready!' Lillian called up the stairs.

'Kay! Coming!' she had once last look, making any presence known that she was watching, before going downstairs.

'Tea? Celia?' there was a feint nod from her.

'So, are you all spent out now? Poor Jeffrey will have to do some extra hours.' Lillian handed her the mug and sugar bowl.

'I haven't spent a thing, my mum did. I desperately needed some clothes for....um....' Rose returned 'what's all the mess upstairs?'

'She was trying to make a quick getaway this morning, until I interrupted her,' Celia answered as she sipped her tea.

Rose looked happy, but surprised Lillian had kept it from her.

'Oh, that,' Lillian dismissed with the flap of her hand. 'I was just sorting out my wardrobe. I was too tired to do anything about it. I'll sort it out later.'

'And the mirror?' Rose asked, making Lillian freeze.

'Mirror?'

'Yes, dressing table mirror, it's cracked.'

'It's nothing. I've just been a little clumsy,' she answered.

'She probably cracked it doing that stuff she does,' Celia commented in her tea.

'I don't know what you're talking about, Celia – is my tea ready?' Rose answered and sat next to her at the table. 'So, how long do you plan on staying?'

'Gowin home after me tea. Did she tell yer?'

'Tell me what?' Lillian was hyperventilating while she washed up the dishes.

'I just thought she could do with some company while he was away, keep any eye out, y'know?'

Rose gave an aggravated nod. 'She's a big girl now. Needs her space. It's good of you to come though, Celia.'

'So, what's all this buying for then? What's the occasion?'

'I thought Lillian could do with a wardrobe boost, seems there wasn't much in there for a young girl. She has no money to herself. She'll be looking for another job soon, so I wanted her to look smart for interviews and such. How's the house coming along?' Celia looked away, studying the cobweb in the window frame.

'Bluddy place is fallin' down, and I haven't got the means to fix it,' she responded solemnly. 'No one comes anymore. Not even my boys. They know how to do things. I can't manage it on me own.'

'I think it's about time Jeffrey moved in and helped you out. Have you thought about getting into residential accommodation?' Celia pushed the chair back with her legs, the scrape loud and teeth shattering.

'I'm off. Me cat'll need feedin. He ain't mine exactly, but he's made himself at home wi'me. He's all I got. Anyway, you never know what she's up to while you're sleeping. I'll be back on Friday to check the house, don't want my Jeffrey coming home to a mess,' and she left to pack her bag. Lillian felt pained for the poor woman, stuck in that house living in just one or two rooms, with mice and ghosts and a cat, apparently. She had a worried brow when she looked at Rose.

'You promised, Mum!' Lillian whispered sharply.

'I couldn't help it, sorry. Were you getting ready to leave?' Rose whispered back.

'I was looking forward to spending time on my own. I got mad!'

'This is the last time though Lilly, it'll be the death of me. Sort it out, quick!' secretly, she was happy Rose had come. Celia walked back in with a morose look, carrying her baggage.

'Right then. I'll see you Fridee,' Lillian felt awful for her, regardless.

'Ok, thanks for coming Celia. See you Friday. Just call if you need anything.'

'I won't be needing anything from you. Bye Rose. I'll see meself out,' she left, slamming the front door.

'Well, you can see where Jeffrey gets it from. And why does she use the front door?!' Rose asked.

'I feel awful now that she's gone and you've put your guns away...' Lillian played with the condiments in the centre of the table, she felt Celia's loneliness – something she had created all by herself.

'Some people are their own worst enemies. Her heart must be like pumice. I've been in touch with Myriam, by the way.'

'Oh Mum! Why?'

'Because I'm worried about you, that's why! Far too much of that bottle had been emptied for my liking. I've had to ask her for some more! And you've covered the mirror! You need to kerb your anger, Lilly.'

'You'll be sending me there to be exorcised, next!' Rose didn't comment.

'Look, Lilly, whatever is going on, I trust you, but don't get complacent. You're blocking me and it's very concerning.' Rose felt the shift in her daughter, she had missed it, but she wasn't there to keep it under control.

'I've topped up the tincture by the way, it was nearly all gone!' Lillian just thanked her, there was no elaboration on it.

'Don't abuse what you've got. I don't want to keep saying it. Be careful. Our gift is to be respected, remember that. You're messing with things that, well, you know what. There's something hanging around and I hope it's nothing to do with you.'

Eighteen

She sat bolt upright, grasping her chest. The bed clothes damp from her sweat, her recurring dreams were getting lucid.

After a quick shower, she lumbered down the stairs in her fleecy pyjamas, needing the fluffy comfort. Although she enjoyed being alone, she was feeling a bit vulnerable of late, the change made her feel unattached. But Oliver's protection was all she needed, to guard the doors and windows. The post lay on the straw mat at the front door – there was a large white envelope face down, it was heavy. Turning it over, Radar's navy-blue logo was inscribed on the left-hand side, she gasped, opening it in haste. She pulled out the sheets of bespoke paper; they had spared no expense on the GSM.

She skipped the welcome letter and turned to the contract, skimming it as she walked to the kitchen, reading the salary several times so it was real. The back door was open, and it felt a little too breezy for patio musing. The sparrows were tweeting bringing beautiful light to the day with Oliver sitting on the doormat just checking and watching, purring and dozing, happy with his life – it was just him and his favourite person. Lillian read and ate trying to take in the conditions and agreements without dropping marmalade on them. There was a separate page for Confidentiality – not remembering anything like this for Pulse. It was serious stuff. She read on…Phil Hathaway was her manager under Lisa's supervision, and it will feel a little strange having her best friend as a supervisor. Were they still best friends? Lillian was looking forward to being in her company again and she would sign everything when her hands weren't so sticky.

The peaceful week was spent decluttering cupboards, keeping the garden maintained and cleaning – without paying too much attention to it. Just enough to create a comfortable environment. Her soul was light being free from the toxic behaviours of Jeffrey, the same feeling you get when the bully has a day off. Radar made her nervous, she just wanted to get the first day over with, feeling anxious from the anticipation of meeting new people – but not as much as Jeffrey's return. Celia never came Friday either. She called to say she wouldn't be coming to the house anymore, and Lillian wouldn't be losing sleep over it.

The depression set in as the evening drew close on Sunday. But there was the positive side – her shiny new thingy she kept in her pocket for Monday morning. Relived Jeffrey left at 6am every day, at least which was one less headache. Getting back a little earlier than usual from her parents', Rose was grilling her again. Martin just sat back and listened, and Lillian had noticed something different in him, he was distant and preoccupied with his thoughts. Rose made trifle but without the sherry this time.

Lillian's week of eating when she wanted made her feel much healthier, and she looked radiant, determined to continue with it. She rushed around the house lighting the new scented candles and closing all the doors upstairs, so Oliver couldn't get in them. Grabbing a handful of clothes to put in the washing machine, she liked having the sound of it on in the background, it was comforting and it made her sound domesticated and busy when Jeffrey came home. Lillian mournfully wiped around the kitchen sink, looking out to the garden with a confronting glare.

Brutus's back end was suddenly lit up as the Volvo came down the drive, highlighting its imperfections and that number plate she loved - RLC 277W. He flung open the back door.

'What's wrong with the bluddy light again?' he said as he threw his bag down.

'How was your week then?' she asked. Jeffrey had a face like a wet weekend, and she was waiting for the tearing down to commence.

'It wasn't bad. Is there tea? That journey gets bluddy worse!' he flumped down in the kitchen chair, wiping his hand over his face.

'So, what you been doin' with yerself?' he asked and took a big slurp.

'Why didn't you call? Then you would have known.' Lillian was wondering why he hadn't mentioned Celia first.

'I been too busy to phone,' he answered. His stocky physique was looking a little weak tonight. 'Got summat to tell me then, 'ave ya?' Lillian sat down with him.

'Yes. Your mother came but left. She was worrying about her cat.' Jeffrey just looked at her, perplexed. He undid the laces on his boots and prised them off, throwing them at the back door. *Bam*!

'I got some news for ya. I been offered a job – in Birmingham,' she sat there, watching the most beautiful opening and way out present itself like a magician's assistant glamorising a cheap trick. 'And you're coming with me,' Jeffrey added.

Lillian looked at him finish off his tea.

'I don't want to go to Birmingham!'

He huffed and took his mug to the sink.

'Tough! You ain't got no say in the matter. I'm taking it. Makes life easier for me anyways. Think about what I said, if you know what's good for ya. Don't bother getting a job, you can get one there.' He dried his hands, took his bag and left to go upstairs 'and what's that funny bluddy smell?!'

'Candles,' Lillian murmured.

Nineteen

Her heart was beating so hard, it was pulsating in her vision. She didn't know where to stash the car until she got there – the contract made it clear that she was no longer at liberty to park in the visitors' area. The drive there was clumsy, her nerves affecting her co-ordination. Their security barrier was down, which meant she had to sit there with the Honda in all its glory, squirming, wishing she could morph into something else.

The staff stared at her, some sniggered while others didn't take much notice, the barrier lifted after an agonising wait and she made sure she parked the Honda right down the bottom, out of sight. There weren't many other old cars, and she stuck out like a sore thumb.

'You'll be all right here. It's in the shade and it would be so nice if you just changed into a black beamer, or something.' Lillian breathed out before opening the door, pulling at her clothes to get some air between them. Wobbling in her heels, walking alongside the building, the noise and the size of the air-conditioning fans indicated the vastness behind them. She kept her head down as she passed the huge, tinted windows, feeling all eyes on her. There was newbie in town, and it felt like the first day at school in her stomach.

Reporting in, she waited for her colleague to come down to meet her, clutching her bag. People from all walks of life regarded her as they entered. It was all very exciting, but Lillian felt alone - she would have to make friends all over again, not that she ever had any trouble with that. But she missed walking into Pulse and acknowledging her peers and giving Dave the 'word' of the day. Lillian was part of the elite Radar party now, but she felt like the poor relation, who was the first to arrive. She stood awkwardly, glancing at her watch then up towards those infamous stairs- Lillian stopped breathing, fixed to the spot, watching her estranged best friend coming down them, not knowing whether to run to her or just wait for the prompt on how to react.

'Lillian Tate,' her friend said, coming towards her with open arms. They hugged, then released their hold and looked at one another with huge smiles on their faces, searching one another's eyes for answers. Lisa hadn't changed much; she still had her hair in a strawberry blonde bob. Her clothes neat and straight, with a whiff of branded perfume and femme fatalities.

'So, how have you been Lisa?' she asked.

'I'm good thanks Lil. You look gorgeous. Come on, let me introduce you to the rest of your proxy family,' they climbed the stairs, linking arms.

'I've missed you,' Lillian whispered.

'Me too, Lil.' Lisa took out her security card to open the door.

'Wow, that's very Star Trekky,' Lillian said, as the door clicked to let them in.

'That's nothing, wait until you see the rest of it,' Lisa let Lillian go first. Beyond the oak fire door was a hubbub of activity. Departments sectioned off by blue partitions, managerial offices off to the left and right, the latest photocopiers and hum of air conditioning. Groups of people stood chatting and laughing in the kitchen area, with their morning fix. She didn't know where to look first – it was like an amusement resort. The tannoy announcements jolting her and adding to the ambience. Lisa led the way as they turned left into International Sales. Light flooded in through large windows, which ran the length of the building, overlooking the motorway; your very own view of the rat race, as you swivelled on your bespoke chair. Everyone had their own desks, surrounded by lower, blue partitions with name plaques on each one. Before Lisa introduced everyone, Phil Hathaway came out of his office, which faced the entrance to the department.

'Ah, you're here. Welcome to International Sales Lillian,' he said in a gentle and confident tone. 'I will let Lisa take care of you today and we'll catch up later. It's good to have you on board,' he dipped his head then retreated, closing the door on his office.

'Right then, can I get you anything before we start Lilly?' Lisa asked. An awkward moment had descended, and Lillian suddenly had hot flushes, feeling everyone looking at her. She was shy and embarrassed, but at least her clothes were new.

'I could do with a tea please,' she answered.

'Ok. Sure. Let me introduce you to the team and we'll sort that out.' The team were all male, each with a part to play in their exaggerated titles.

'Everyone, this is Lilly, our new recruit,' Lisa announced. They all greeted her as Lisa said their names desk by desk. There was one man, who was the oldest, that made a point of standing up and shaking Lillian's hand.

'Hi Lilly, Tim Smith. Pleased to meet you. Welcome to the team.' A stocky man in his late fifties with a cockney accent and beer belly, wearing strong aftershave; everyone's favourite wealthy uncle. He was old wood, but they kept him on because he had a knack of getting new customers on board, flashing the cash at dinner. He'd made his way around all the departments, but International Sales earned him the most, with offshore bank accounts and shares. 'I cover most of Italy. Well, it ain't that 'ard with my stature!' and he laughed at himself, Lillian laughing with him.

'You never know, you could be on the next trip to Rome with me, but we'll let you feel your feet first though, ay?' Lillian raised her eyebrows and needed pinching.

'You makin' tea? That's the most important job here.' He returned to his desk and started a conversation with a quiet guy, who chose the corner desk, about his latest finds on the index. The kitchen area was near the exit door to the stairs, with a sink, coffee maker and everything else you needed for your caffeine. Lillian watched Lisa retrieve logoed mugs from the cupboard, with taped notices about keeping the area as you found it.

'That could be open to interpretation,' Lillian commented.

'That's what we say. There have been comments written on it to that effect, but they get renewed. We don't know who sticks it there. Some busy body. We had bets, once.'

'What do you give visitors when they come?'

'Oh, that's all done from the landing. There's a separate area for that. I'll show you later. Although the canteen staff usually do most of the big meetings.' Another member of staff joined them. A slender woman in a navy skirt suit, precisely manicured with permed blonde hair.

'Morning. Who's the newbie?' she asked curtly.

'Hi Sian, this is Lilly, she's joining our team.' The woman regarded Lillian with an air of self-importance.

'Welcome to the madhouse.' Lillian smiled passively, the woman reminded her of an old bully from school - the one that threw rolled up tin foil at her during assembly.

'Where did you work before?' The woman asked.

'A component company.' wishing she'd made something up.

The woman frowned and would be taking a look at her file.

'Great. Well, back to the grindstone, see you around no doubt,' and the woman left with her black coffee.

'She's from HR,' Lisa whispered.

'Oh right. With Hannah Bresworth?'

'Yeah, that's them. Double standards league. All precise and perfect. Bloody irritates me. So, how are things with you?' Lillian hated that question, she had to think on her feet, think which answer to give – so there was no need to justify herself.

'I'm still with Jeffrey, if that's what you mean,' she played with grains of sugar on the worktop.

'Have things improved then?' Lisa pressed while stirring.

'Not exactly – he doesn't know I'm here. Look Lisa, I'm...' Lisa held up her hand to stop Lillian mid-flow.

'Lil, it was my fault. I shouldn't have made you choose. I just got tired of seeing you being treated like that. I was hoping you'd leave so I wouldn't have to watch you being controlled by that nutcase! And here you are, here we are, back where we started.'

Lillian held Lisa's arm, 'and thank goodness for that. It's not the same. Would I have come here two years ago?'

Lisa shook her head, 'no, I guess not. So, what's changed?'

Lillian patted her heart and smiled. 'Me, the stars, and the woods. Let's not forget them.' Lisa handed Lillian her mug of tea, 'here you go, mystic Meg, get that down your neck -we've got a lot of walking to do.'

They returned to the department, everyone greeting Lillian as they passed, swelling her heart. 'That's yours, right opposite mine,' Lisa pointed out Lillian's desk.

'Oh wow! I get the one with the view!' Lillian touched her name plaque and got a sense of pride from her fortune. Pulse seemed like a distant memory, and it was like going from pot noodle to surf and turf with a side salad. She put her bag on the back of her chair and sat down – looking out to the cars that were in perpetual motion. The stationery was neatly arranged in a special holder, along with stapler and hole-punch. Lillian just regarded the computer; a small Apple Mac with a mono screen.

'That won't be there for long. We're having upgrades! I can't wait. Monitors will be bigger, with a separate hard drive under your desk.' Lisa said.

'Oh, okay.' Lillian wasn't sure what that meant, she didn't use computers at Pulse, just an electric typewriter that she wished she'd brought along. Sitting back, she absorbed her beautiful dream. It was strange, one minute she was there, now she was here. Having the same feeling you get when you had all you asked for on your birthday, wrapped in expensive paper. Lillian studied her friend - modestly dressed in a light blouse and tweed skirt, with subtle makeup. A little jealous of her stable life.

The size of the building amazed her. It didn't seem that big from the outside and was a far cry from being in a dusty, 1980s one as a receptionist. Radar's staff were the beautiful people. Their positive energies enthralled her; free rein and appreciation had straightened their backs.

'When you've come back to earth Lilly Lil. Get yourself over here and I'll take you through the telephone quickly.' Lillian's awe humbled Lisa, she deserved it more than anyone in the building.

Lisa went through the technicalities of the telephone, but Lillian was getting distracted by passers-by. She didn't really need that amount of training for a telephone, anyway.

'I'll give you the grand tour now, then we need to get our heads down with the heavier stuff.' Lillian took her new notebook and pen just in case, peering over the partitions as she followed Lisa along the walkway. She was buzzing from the charged atmosphere.

'That's marketing, but we have nothing to do with them, but just so you know who they are.' Lisa continued with Lillian lagging behind, watching marketing draw on whiteboards and rehearse with props.

'Lil! Come on!'

Lillian trotted after her. 'Sorry, I got distracted!'

'Well, they're a permanent source of entertainment if you look long enough.' She opened a door that led to a flight of stairs.

'Now, down here are the departments you will deal with. It keeps you fit.' Although it was a different section, the layout was exactly the same as upstairs. She met her international contacts in the ordering department. Some down to earth, others took their job seriously, some not so – with their favourite characters adorning the top of computer screens, stuck on with BlueTak. Lillian's head was spinning as she picked up everyone's vibes, and she could feel the stuffing begin to leave her, needing to move on. It was something she hadn't quite mastered, her mother had learned to block out their silent screams, but Lillian was so open to everything, she was like a sponge.

They briefly visited the technical department in the basement. It seemed to be the bones of Radar where engineers worked in artificial light on network cabinets. The ambience cooler and quieter than the Mardi gras above, full of tech geeks and nerds. Lillian was glad to get out of there and away from her impostor syndrome.

'Are you ready to go on?' Lisa asked.

'Ready.' More stairs, down and down, then through a door which led them into a fair-sized warehouse.

'This is your very own stationery cupboard. Only, it's a very large one,' Lisa said with pride. 'You can pick whatever you want as long as you list what you've taken on the piece of paper, by the door.'

Lillian regarded the shelves stacked with boxes of pens, rulers, paper and everything else you really didn't need. The word 'stationery cupboard' still gave her a wash of dread.

'I can just take, anything?'

'Yup.'

'Do I hear ladies?' came a voice from the back.

'Hey, Fitz.' A young black guy emerged from a messy desk, with a bright and confident personality, strutting his way over, almost dancing.

'What's this? A new face?' Fitz immediately made Lillian blush.

'This is Lilly. Just joined us.'

'Cool. Good to meet you, Lilly. What do you think of my candy store?'

'I, uh, like it.' She looked around again, spotting new items on offer.

'If you can't find it, just ask Fitz,' he patted his chest, smiling. She knew this would be her place to escape to if she needed. Putting the world to rights with Fitz the stationery man - there were no negative vibes, only vibrant and liberating ones. Maybe they would have a 'word of the day', she could start that off with anyone she pleased, if they were game.

'Ok then, that's us, more to see. Thanks Fitz.'

'My pleasure. Here, a little souvenir,' he gave Lillian a Radar logoed pen.

'Thanks!' She already had about four in the holder, but this one was a little bit special. They left, Lillian feeling uplifted.

'He's such a great guy,' she said.

'Yeah, Fitz is one of my favourites. But he's leaving.'

'Oh, that is a shame. I was looking forward to getting my pink highlighters from him and get away from you. I only had green ones, by the way. You know I like the pink ones. Where next?'

The noise of copiers and franking machines greeted them and a suffocating heat with trolleys lined up ready for mail distribution.

'Hi Pam! Sorry to interrupt! This is Lilly!' Lisa shouted over the din. The post-room controller peered over her glasses on a beaded chain. Pam, a maturing woman-widowed, enjoying life with her best friend and family.

'Well, pleased to meet you Lilly, welcome to the pleasure dome. I'm mad Pam, but you can just call me Pam,' she said and cackled, her bracelets rattling on her wrist. She smelt of cheap cologne, but it made Lillian feel welcome. There were a few holiday souvenirs on her desk and pictures of her grandchildren, you could tell she was the stepmother of the company. The little whimsical gifts were probably from colleagues.

'You're churning them out up there, aren't you? So, where did they find you then?'

'She was hiding, amongst the dust,' Lisa answered.

'I came from a company called Pulse.'

'Pulse? In the industrial estate?' Pam took off her glasses, gawping.

'Yes. They've gone into receivership,' she felt she could tell Pam anything. She had that openness about her. Probably went home tired after listening to everyone's problems, telling her best friend about them.

'I don't believe it! I used to work there! On reception! I'm going back a few years now, mind you.'

'Really?! I was on reception too! I did some work for Sales.'

Pam sat back in her chair.

'Well, well, well – what a small world we live in. Looks like this is the place for the poached!' Pam chuckled to herself, shaking her head. 'I can't believe they've gone through the hoop! I was glad to get out of there in all honesty. How is Simon? Still up to his old tricks?'

Lillian nodded, hoping Pam would get what the nod meant, she still needed to talk to someone about that.

'Do you two know each other then? Sisters?'

Lisa and Lillian looked at one another. 'Yes, we were, we are best friends' Lisa answered.

'Hmm, I thought so, you seem very connected. Well, I shan't keep you, I'm sure you've got a lot to cover. I dare say you'll be dizzy by the end of the day. Last post is 4.30pm sharp – but I'll overlook that if you've got one of those last-minute deadlines. Don't tell everyone I said that,' she cackled again, like an old witch, a nice one.

'I'm looking forward to seeing you again, Lilly. This one's a bit frosty,' she said from behind her hand.

'Thanks Pam, none taken. We'll catch you soon.' Lisa closed the door.

'How about that then? I mean, Pam working at Pulse!' Lisa pulled on the fire door to the canteen. 'No one mentioned her, not once, there's something about Pam though, isn't there?'

'Yes, she's bloody nosey and only tell her what you want repeated.'

'Oh, ok. Noted. Where are we going now?'

'Canteen. You still manage to soften the hardest of hearts, I missed that the most – you need to take off the rose-tinted glasses though.' Lillian smirked at Lisa's comments.

'Still pissing on bonfires, I see.'

'You can keep them on for this week.' Lisa stopped and turned to her, 'look, Lilly, you're in a corporate environment now. This isn't cosy Pulse. Don't get me wrong, it's great working here, but just keep your wits about you and your eye on the ball, ok?' Lillian caught a whiff of lunch cooking, and it made her stomach rumble.

'My dad said that,' Lisa reminisced about the laughs they had with Martin, which brought a smile to her face.

'How is your dad? I miss him.'

'He's still dad. What did Pam mean about churning people out?' Lisa held the large oak door open for Lillian.

'She has something to say about everything, take no notice.' They built the canteen like a conservatory; full of organised tables and plush blue chairs, two vending machines and the stations where you chose your hot food, which were lit up and steaming, ready for the lunchtime rush.

'Well, here we are, this is where you kiss your waistline goodbye. I only come here when it's raining, or I've had enough of everyone's shit. They have custard, Lil, custard,' Lisa said as she introduced the area like a guide in a museum.

'Mmmm! I can't remember the last time I had custard, except in mum's trifle. Jeffrey...' she stopped.

'Jeffrey what? Doesn't allow it? Because you like it, and it makes the pots messy? Freak!' Lillian looked to the floor - the grand tour around Willy Wonka's had masked the reality outside, and she was reluctant to let it in. 'Watch the chef, he's as greasy as the deep-fat fryer.' Lisa said from the side of her mouth. With that, he came out in his stained whites, quite a large man and a victim of his own success.

'Good morning, ladies! You're early, what can I get you?' Lisa shielded Lillian with her arm and pushed her back a little.

'Is that another new face? I'm losing track!'

'Yes, this is Lilly, she's working with me.'

The greasy chef held out his hand. 'It's a pleasure to meet you, Lilly. If you have any favourites, let me know, and old Colin will make it especially for you. I like to keep my ladies happy,' he said, tapping his nose and winking.

'Oh great, thank,' Lillian prised her hand away from his, wiping it on the back of her skirt.

'Custard, she likes custard,' Lisa answered for her.

'Well, you've come to the right place then. We have that here every day, pretty much.'

'I don't think I'll be here every day, you'll have to roll me out of here!' Lillian said and laughed nervously.

'Yes, look at me!' he said, rubbing his large stomach, 'all paid for though. Ah well, I must get on, pleasure meeting you Lilly and seeing your lovely face, Lisa. There are fresh sandwiches in the machine. See you later ladies,' and he retreated into his den of boiling cauldrons and flustered staff.

'Well, there you have it - there's always a cheese roll from the vending machine, if the thought of him touching your plate puts you off. But things get a little limp in there after one thirty.' They left the canteen and headed for the stairs.

'Are you still with Ken?' Lillian asked.

'No. But that's for lunchtime, I'm taking you out.'

'Oh, sorry to hear that. Anyone else?'

'Married.'

'Wow! Lisa! Still not doing things by halves then?'

'I'm happy, I will reveal it all later. We're off to see UK Sales now, then it's time for more tea.' Lisa opened the door with her badge. Lillian was resentful that everyone else had their happily ever-after. But Radar was like a sweet shop when it came to eligible knights in shining armour.

She sat down heavily at her desk and took her shoes off.

'My feet are killing me! Can we do sitting down training for the rest the day, please?' Lillian's lack of stamina amused Lisa.

'You can tell you've been a receptionist, lightweight – you'll be walking that stretch daily. Better get the custard in, you're already wasting away!' Lillian looked down at herself and felt her face.

'Custard it is then,' they both laughed but Lisa kerbed her joviality when Phil came out of his office, doing her coughing thing.

'Did you enjoy your tour, Lilly?' Lillian gasped and almost stood to attention. It was those piercing green eyes. He had an accent of the area, but he'd worked hard to educate it.

'Uh, yes! Thank you, it was um, a broad experience,' Phil acknowledged with a nod.

'I have a conference call in...' he flicked his wrist to look at his Rolex, 'fifteen minutes. I'll see you after lunch. Bring your notebook and pen,' and he left. All that lingered was the smell of his fabric softener and air of authority.

Lillian looked at Lisa in horror, 'oh my GOD! Of all the people to catch me with my shoes off!'

Lisa sniggered. 'Well, you'll get away with it today, I'm not so sure about tomorrow.' She beckoned Lillian with a tilt of her head, 'come on, broad experience - wheel yourself over here, time for some hard stuff.'

Twenty

Just about everyone she had seen on her tour, were there. It was your typical franchised establishment; dark oak, tiffany lamps and velour seating with loud carpet. The Royal Oak pub, Radar's staff haunt, with their own tab.

'I am starving!' Lillian said, the smell of freshly griddled steak knocking her flat. Lisa found them a seat, after weaving their way through everyone, standing with their half a pint of something and lemonade.

'Right, I'll order. What are you having?' Lillian didn't need a menu, the aroma had decided.

'Steak. Medium rare and chips, you know, those big ones. Please,' her mouth was watering at the very thought of it.

'I need you awake for the rest of the day, steak is out, sorry. I'll get you something lighter.' Lillian's disappointment showed all over her face, she needed rare meat.

After watching the intellectually vibrant, she looked out the window while playing with a beer mat, sighing with gratitude at her shiny new thing. The pub was situated on a busy main road, leading to the town and link roads. Lillian hated any sort of city life, it was nice to visit, but the call of trees and greenery was preferable. Concrete and streetlights messed up her aura.

'Hi, Lillian? Isn't it?' her daydreaming was disturbed by one of the tech staff.

'Yes, Hi. Sorry, I've forgotten your name. I've seen so many people today. You're the guy, in the glass box?' the handsome fair-haired guy shook her hand.

'Uh, no, I'm Darren, from IT. Darren Marshall. It's ok, I still don't remember everyone's name, and I've been working for Radar for five years!' he pulled up a stool and sat down.

'Oh. Do you always come here for lunch?' Lillian asked, not knowing what IT was and vaguely remembering Lisa showing her that department. She noticed his band of gold, while he noticed she didn't have one.

'I'm not always lucky enough to have lunch, sometimes I forget to eat because we're so busy. So, where did you work before?' Lillian had enough of that question, why did it matter? She was trying to move on from Pulse, shake it off her back, secretly missing it.

'A computer component company, but they went into receivership,' Darren was nodding, pretending to look interested.

'Right, right. Yeah, shame. This is a fast market now. You need to be ahead of the competition nowadays. You, erm, with someone?'

'Yes! ME!' Lisa scolded, standing there with two lemonades.

'Oh, right, sorry, I was just, uh, keeping Lillian company. I'll see you around Lilly. Enjoy your lunch,' and he left, with Lisa glaring at him.

'Creep! He didn't hang about!' Lisa said under her breath, as she placed the drinks down.

'Lilly, you will be like jam to the wasps and shit to the flies here – Just remember what I said. That was Darren, the bike.'

'Darren the bike? He's an Eco warrior?'

'Christ, Lilly. Here, drink your lemonade, Rapunzel.'

'We were just having a chat. I thought it was nice of him. He had a ring on anyway.' Lisa laughed a little too loud while she zipped up her handbag and put it under the table.

'That doesn't mean jack! Trust me, not with everyone. You worry me Lilly, you're too naïve. Just stay away from men like Darren, with bikes!'

Lillian frowned at Lisa's damning report on the opposite sex, she didn't quite understand all of it. Some new jargon people had made up in corporate environments. She could detect that Lisa had an unhealed scar that still wept and itched.

'What did you order?' Lillian asked.

'Tuna baguettes.'

'Ugghh! We could have had that from the canteen!'

'Too many nosey ears in the canteen,' Lisa checked the small screen of her Nokia.

'Ok. So, tell me, about your Brian.'

'Well, after you and I, you know, fell out – I left Ken and my job and went looking. A bit like yourself, only you've got to muster up the balls to do the other bit.'

Lillian picked at her fingernails, the pressure of the 'other bit', was a bit too great right now.

'You've got more courage than I have Lisa. I have no guts left.'

Lisa leaned on the table and into Lillian, 'it takes more guts to stay with Jeffrey. It takes a little bit of insanity. You're here, aren't you? I'm sure the rest will fall into place Lil.' They both held hands across the table and united in silence. Lisa pulled away first, afraid to let the emotions run away with her.

'Anyway. I got a job here, met my Brian and we've been married for two years. He's a good man, looks after me. He's an executive at Radar. Brian Finlay. He's away a lot in the Milan offices. I can't wait for you to meet him, he's heard a lot about you.' Lisa detected Lillian's envy, as she looked down into her drink.

'You need to go somewhere with a passport Lil, broaden your mind, and I need to go somewhere I hate, so I'll miss this shithole. It's just fear holding you back. It ain't easy, I'll admit. You've been through enough and you owe nobody nuthin. You're a good person. Jeffrey has some serious issues, and you need to be free of him, pronto. Muscle and aggravation, that's all he is.' She repeated the same old lines. Lillian was half listening as she watched their order making its way to their table, devouring her baguette, not caring if anyone was watching.

'My God! When *was* the last time you ate?' Lisa watched her taking huge bites out of her food.

'Months,' she answered, her voice muffled by white bread.

'Oh Lil – he's not still doing that thing with the food again, is he?' Lillian shook her head as she shoved crisps in her mouth.

'Not exactly. I just haven't felt like eating. I was waiting to come here – it took all my heart and soul.'

Lisa nibbled on what she left on the plate, she had lost her appetite, watching Lillian speak and spit out food at the same time. Lillian picked up on that and wiped over her mouth with the scratchy white serviette.

'How did you know that Pulse wasn't doing well?'

Lisa brushed crumbs off her lap, 'it was hot news in the industry. Anyhow, have you still got the canvas?'

'Of course. It's what kept the connection alive – I've been talking it to it for the past two years! Didn't you hear?'

Lisa straightened herself and finished her lemonade. 'I needed some Gin in that. Yes, I did hear. I went to the woods once, but I wasn't welcome - it still protects you.'

They caught up on the rest of the news they had missed over the last two years, and Lisa gave her the lowdown on all the departments and people to watch within them. As glittery as it was on the surface, office politics was rife beneath it.

Phil Hathaway was waiting for them when they got back, in his black suit trousers and striped shirt, with an air of Daniel Craig about him.

'Could you bring two coffees with you, I have mine black, no sugar.' Lillian put down her bag and forgot the rest of the world around her, as she scurried to the kitchen to follow orders. While she waited for the percolator, she looked at the notice board. There were internal vacancies by the dozen, and most of them looked made up. Team building and motivational props were a new thing in the nineties – Radar spent thousands on it, making them a magnet for young professionals. Lillian walked back to Phil's office, being careful not to spill any coffee. He left the door slightly ajar so she could enter, pushing it open with her shoulder. Relieved he wasn't there, she placed the mug down on a glass, logoed coaster.

The office was sparse. Not a scrap of paper in sight. His chair was high-backed in black leather and the smell of his clean clothes filled the space. No trophies, photographs or egotistical displays, just one large framed picture on the wall, which halted her abruptly. It was the woods. The path she walked. Not the same angle as her print, but similar.

'Isn't it great?' Phil said as he walked in, startling her.

'Uh, yes. I have one the same. Not this big, but the same. Is it one of Lisa's?' she answered, with a buzz of providence.

'It is. Have you been there lately?' he asked, stood next to her. This could be him; the same interest alone was immense for her.

'I have. They've been felling quite a large area. Have you seen it? There's nothing wrong with the trees!'

'No, I haven't. Right,' he cleared his throat. 'Did you bring your notepad?'

Lillian was so preoccupied with making sure the coffee was perfect, she forgot the first instruction. She grabbed what she needed from her desk and trotted back into his office, with her pen poised over the ring-bound paper. She studied his chiselled features, reminding her of someone. There was no ring on his manicured hands either- giving her a little sting in her belly and another tick on the list. Phil linked his fingers and rested on the desk.

'If you have a habit of forgetting my instruction, may I suggest that you write them down? That way, it saves me repeating myself,' he said, and held his glance with those eyes. Sending Lillian weak and afraid, attracted by his efficiency.

'Yes, of course, sorry, it won't happen again. I'm bamboozled, with all the information I've had to learn today,' she laughed nervously. Her stomach gurgling loudly, echoing in the office.

'Well, now that's that out of the way. I want to go through what's expected of you. You'd, uh, better write this down,' he waggled his finger at her notepad. Lillian was nodding while she wrote his name and circled it several times. She felt a little light-headed in his presence, imagining all his shirts were ironed by Geisha girls - bringing him sushi and tiny cups of Jasmine tea, stooping and fussing. As he spoke about himself and his needs, she stared passed him out of the window, daydreaming – having a virtual walk around his house. He noticed she had lost focus, feeling slightly irritated, coughing loudly.

'I have my coffee black! One at 9.30am, then I will let you know when I need the others. Unless I'm in a meeting.'

Lillian began writing, a little in disbelief, slimy Simon had his faults, but he rarely asked her to make his coffee. Just made her think she was responsible for satisfying his whims and entitlement to twang her bra straps.

'You'll take minutes in some meetings and make sure there is plenty of coffee for our visitors. Organise refreshments with the canteen staff, in advance. Lisa will advise you on that one.' Lillian was writing in shorthand, something she learnt when she left school. Although it was fast becoming extinct. Phil leaned back and swivelled to face the window.

'We have large tenders, and you will be responsible for putting them together, after all the sections are completed by those involved. Again, this is something Lisa will hand over to you. I will give you the odd letter and memo to type, I expect little or no mistakes. So, make sure you check everything before you give it back to me.'

She finished her notes then looked up.

'Okay. No problem. Is that everything?' she asked, swallowing nervously.

'For now, yes. There is one last thing.' he said, swivelling back to face her, 'your clothes.' Lillian looked down at her black suit and chiffon blouse, 'my clothes?'

Phil placed the tips of his fingers together.

'Yes. They're a little, managerial,' he tilted his head to the side, 'there's no need for you to wear a suit, relax. Wear something comfortable. Some flat shoes, perhaps? Must be hell trying to walk in those heels all day,' he said and raised a wistful smile. Lillian stood, holding her notes, desperately needing the toilet.

'Right. I will. Thanks,' she turned to leave. She let out a puff of air when she shut herself in the cubicle. There were persuasive voices in that toilet, too. She noticed the places that were secluded, oozed a 'watching'.

'So? How did it go?' Lisa asked. Lillian turned to her when she returned.

'He's got one of your prints.'

Lisa fiddled with her pearl necklace. Red patches started to appear on her neck and chest.

'Um, yes, he has. What else did he say?' Lillian put her head in her hands, feeling mentally exhausted and secretly needing Jeffrey's protection. She came running to Radar to hide from him, now she just wanted to run back.

'You've got to show me the tenders.'

Lisa adjusted her collar. 'Ok. I'll do that tomorrow. I think you've had enough for one day. You can sit with me and just watch. Ask questions.'

Lillian rubbed her eyes with her forefingers, they were itchy and dry from the air-conditioning; forgetting she had mascara on.

'Oh no! Do I have black eyes now?!'

Lisa laughed at her new gothic look. 'Yes, you look a panda! Here, I have a wet wipe.' They belly-laughed for the rest of the afternoon at stupid things and memories of nights out and foibles. Neither of them had done that in a while, it was welcome therapy for them both. Lillian didn't want to leave or go home. The reunion and new environment filled all the gaps. They walked to the car park arm in arm, Lillian feeling relieved that Lisa's car was parked well before hers. Even though Lisa had seen the Honda before she didn't want her seeing it again, just so she could look at it with a turned-up nose.

'I'm exhausted, not sure I want to go home. Do you think they'll put me up for the night?' Lillian yawned loudly, breaking away from Lisa's hold.

'You'd have to sleep with one eye open, if you did. Why don't I come with you? Please Lil, I'm worried about you. Or just come with me now, I got some clothes that'll fit you.' It all sounded so easy, so tempting, but the very thought of it made Lillian sweat.

'No, I'll be fine, really. But thank you for the offer, I appreciate it. I just need my bed. I will take up your offer soon, I promise.'

Lisa shook her head, perplexed. 'I don't get it Lilly, I don't. What's holding you? You're a free woman. If you had kids,

I'd completely understand, but you have a cat, Lil. It's a no brainer.' Lillian was itching to get to the Honda, the pressure to justify herself building.

'Look, here, let me give you my number. Just call me, in the middle of the night, anytime, I don't care.' Lisa wrote her number down on a page of her diary and tore it off.

'There's my mobile number on there too. I'll pay for the bill if you call it.'

Lillian took it and read it just to register the numbers, 'thanks. It's been an amazing day. I've missed you so much,' they hugged again.

'Ditto. Don't have nightmares and stay strong, you know you can do it Lillian Tate. I'm sorry I left you, but I'm here now,' Lisa clutched her keys. They blew kisses in the air at one another, and parted. 'Love you, Lilly Lil!' Lisa called out, raising her hand, making her way to the white Audi Quattro -that looked like it had just rolled out of the showroom. Lillian waved back and walked to her Honda, which was a complete eye-sore.

'Well, I see you didn't morph into that beamer I asked you to!' getting in quick, waiting for Lisa to drive out first. Once the white Audi had proudly left the car park, Lillian started up the Honda.

'I think it's time we thought about getting rid of you! I can't face another day driving in here!' she said, hitting the steering wheel. Lillian hoped that no one would see her, which was a bit of an impossibility, considering everyone was leaving in their droves. She put on some music and left the car park, looking straight ahead, ignoring the eyes on her. Fabricating in her head what she would say to Jeffrey.

Arriving home first, feeling everything drop when she parked and switched off the engine - she rested her head on the seat. The silence and moment alone was ringing in her ears, mentally going through the entire day. She was overwhelmed... needing a long sleep. Jeffrey disturbed her, pulling up behind her. Lillian's stomach hit the floor when she saw a purposeful look on his face in the rear-view mirror.

She got out of the car, whispering prayers of support.

'Where the bluddy 'ell 'ave you been today then?!' he yelled, almost letting out steam through his nose.

'The agency,' she answered and walked passed him.

'What for? I'm getting you a job! I've been bluddy ringing ya and you weren't 'ere!' Lillian opened the back door and winced at her lie.

'I went to see mum, and then we went to town. Why didn't you call there?' Jeffrey took off his boots and followed Lillian like a storm cloud.

'I don't believe ya! What you wearin' that bluddy suit for?! Ay?!' he grabbed her arm. Lillian nearly lost control of her bladder as she felt the charge from his aggression.

'Get off me! Believe what you like! I wanted to look smart!' Jeffrey flicked the kettle switch on. The neighbours rolling their eyes when they heard the shouting.

'Listen! if I find out y'been bluddy lyin' to me, you'll be going to stay with yer bluddy muther!'

'Fine! And that's not a threat, Jeffrey! I don't want food either.' Lillian's honesty elf was dancing about in her mouth, threatening to fall out and trip her up.

'You're doing dinner! So, get yerself back 'ere and do some bluddy work!' he shouted, pointing to the cooker. Lillian wanted to retaliate and keep the rumble going, but the beast needed taming, and she wanted to avoid any confrontation, her greatest fear.

'Ok, just let me get changed. I'll be there in a sec,' she answered calmly. Jeffrey wiped over his head and sighed heavily as the red mist subsided. His anger and anxiety had been eating away at him all day and it needed to vomit. The new life in Birmingham was calling even louder.

Lillian took off her suit and hung it up on the back of the bedroom door, her limbs quivering from low blood sugar and the threat of safety. She wanted Jeffrey's protection earlier, now she needed someone else's, something else – a fill of power. Changing into her grey tracksuit, she held on tight to the fact that she would return to Radar tomorrow. Although that felt like a sinful pursuit and the hole she was digging was getting bigger. Lillian nervously placed the food in front of Jeffrey and joined him. She watched him eat, in disgust, as he shovelled the food into his mouth, holding the fork like a caveman.

'What yer lookin' at me like that for?!'

Lillian shook her head and shrugged her shoulders. 'Nothing. How was your day?' Jeffrey finished his food in record time and belched loudly, without a pardon.

'What did I say about askin' me that? It was the bluddy same. Birmingham is still on the cards, and you'd better start thinkin, cuz you're coming with me. I ain't going up there without ya!'

Lillian stopped chewing. Was that a bit of love, squeezing through Jeffrey's barrier?

'I'm not coming, sorry. I can't leave mum and dad.' Jeffrey wiped over his mouth, then slammed it down his hand on the table, making Lillian jump out of her skin.

'Gotcha! Bluddy fly been drivin' me mad.'

She moved her legs from underneath the table, so she could make a quick dash for the door. 'Get yer bags packed. We're leaving in 2 weeks. If you know what's good for ya.'

Lillian relaxed and released her hold on the table. 'That omelette was nice, for a change. You want tea?' Jeffrey asked as he took the plates. She sat, wary of the sudden mood change, all her senses were on red alert, and she could not move.

'I know Birmingham ain't all that good, but I think it will be one day. Lots to do and see up there. The house won't be as big as this one, cos they're more expensive. Company's offered us a two-bed terraced. I ain't seen it yet, but we could have a look this weekend, if yer like. No garden though, just a back yard sort of thing they said.'

Lillian hated the sound of it already. Imagining moss covered concrete and dripping drainpipes. She listened as Jeffrey washed up, trying to polish a turd - becoming suspicious of his insistence. Although the change of heart had left her a little confused, just when she was ready to up and leave, his bit of charm made her think it was all going to be okay again, making her relax and feel drowsy, nestling back into the compromise.

'We could take mum and dad with us,' she replied and turned in the chair to face Jeffrey at the sink.

'They don't need to come. Anyways, it might upset them,' turning his back.

Lillian frowned and recoiled.

'You go then. I trust your judgement. Just let me know what it's like.' Jeffrey placed their tea on the table and sat down heavily.

'I'm just lookin' out for ya, that's all,' he slurped loudly. 'You ain't bringing that animal though. Anyway, he might get lost or try to make his way back 'ere and get run ova or summat.'

Lillian had an exasperated expression on her face. 'I'll think about it, that's all I can offer at the moment. If I had other sisters or a brother, then maybe I wouldn't be so hesitant,' she said, not meaning any of it.

Jeffrey gulped his last drop. 'Don't get too attached to yer parents, does ya no good. If you listen to them, you won't do anything. Just go with yer gut, it'll be yer best mate all ya life.' He left the table and retired to the living room, to heckle at the news. Lillian looked out of the small side window; all she could see was next doors bricks, following the lines of the mortar, it was a good distraction and mind dump. She could feel the stress leaving her shoulders, he must love her, in a strange, Jeffrey kind of way. But the detachment he had to all that she was, kept her feet firmly on the ground. She was right to wait, Lillian knew it would be there at some point, it would just be nice if everyone just trusted her intuition.

As the week went on, the lie she was trying to uphold wore her down. She was running out of excuses when Jeffrey pressed her for information, trying to trip her up. Phil Hathaway was a stickler for punctuality and wasn't very lenient with missed deadlines, or laughter, come to that matter. He rarely came out of his office, but when he did, he stood and talked with his hands in his pockets, looking a little socially retarded. Lillian had taken on board what he said about her clothes, wearing dresses or trousers instead. They were better to explain away to Jeffrey, than suits. All the departments played a part in preparing the tenders. It was up to Lillian to nip at their heels to meet the deadlines. She was over the moon with the role - the entire world had opened up to her, even though she had to blag most of it. She left on time every night and arrived earlier in the morning, to avoid any confrontation from either end. It was like being in a pin-ball machine, with spikes! Radar was seeping into her veins; the opiate she needed daily. But Friday would be the day, which changed everything.

Twenty-One

The new arrival walked through reception, feeling a little anxious. It wasn't what he was hoping for, after leaving a prestigious establishment. The building looked successful enough, but the area felt strange, outdated, crowded and a little backward. The company car would do for now, the hefty pay rise and perks made up for that. He parked in the elite spaces, feeling anxious about stepping into a new environment, and country.

Lillian received a call from reception to collect the guest. She brushed the croissant crumbs off her lap; a regular Friday treat from Tim Smith.

'What do I say?' she asked Lisa.

'Just talk about the weather or their journey and that will take you to the top of the stairs. They're out of your hands then.'

When she got to the top of the landing, she breathed in and rehearsed what she would say as she casually descended the stairs, trying not to stumble - stopping halfway when she saw him, waiting in his sharp navy suit, clutching his briefcase. She hesitated, not sure if she had the confidence to step off the last stair. He watched her, a little captivated by the flowing material of the dress, walking towards her with his arm outstretched.

'Hi. Sorry I'm late. M25 was a nightmare! Robert Courtney.' He announced confidently, in a southern accent, London or the suburbs. They shook hands, a handshake that felt different. He had a Mediterranean look about him; black, wavy hair, soft brown eyes and subtle cologne made her blush. Something he noticed above all else.

'Lillian Tate. Welcome to Radar,' she could feel her smile quivering. He smiled back, revealing a set of perfectly straight teeth.

'Pleased to meet you, Lillian. Any chance I could grab a coffee, please? I'm flaming garsping!'

'Sure, this way please.' Lillian led him up the stairs, 'how was your journey?' she asked.

'Oh, it's hellish – I think I need to stay in Wales while this tender is on. I don't fancy traipsing back and forth!' they arrived at the top of the stairs, just like Lisa said, revelling in opening the door with the card, already feeling part of the elite.

'Phil Hathaway wants to see you first. I'll bring your coffee in.'

'Great. Thank you. Uh, which one?'

'Third on the right. The name plaque gives it away.'

'I will open the right one. Milky with two sugars please,' he replied with a beautiful smile. Lillian took great pleasure in making his coffee, it was the same as she took it. She placed the mugs on the desk and left, nodding and bowing like a wench, returning to her desk with a red face. Two sharply dressed men, smelling clean, with that male presence that demanded respect - gave her hot flushes. Male will always feel like that to her.

'Was that the visitor?' Lisa asked.

'Uh, yeah. Robert Courtney,' Lisa frowned and looked through her diary, licking her index finger to turn the page.

'Robert Courtney? Are you sure?'

'Yes. Why?' Lisa was still looking through her notes, front to back, running down the pages with her pen.

'I had a different name down, John Smythe. Strange. Was he dishy?'

She stared blankly at Lisa, 'uh...he, uh.'

'Spit it out! Do I need to buy a new hat, or what?'

'A hat? No! He, um,'

Lisa screwed up her face and shook her head, huffing a laugh.

'I think you got the hots for him. Are you going to be writing- Lillian Courtney on your notepad, for the rest of the day?' she said mockingly.

'No! And cut that out!' Lillian smelt her hand behind her partition and got butterflies from his scent. Robert Courtney's arrival had violently shaken her tree and heightened her senses.

She went back to typing up her training notes. Sadistically wishing she was still at Pulse, praying for something to happen; missing the dark, delicious hunger longing gave her. Now she was being force fed with everything on her bucket list, unsure if she was actually ready for it.

Phil's office door clicked shut, and she froze when Robert Courtney walked in.

'So, this will be my new home for a while? You must be Lisa,' he said, walking over and shaking her hand.

'The very same. Welcome to the department. I have set up a desk for you.'

'Thanks. I'll get settled in and then I need to go through the Apex file with you Lilly.' Her stomach squelched as he made direct eye contact, leaning on her low partition. 'Looks like you and me are working on this,' he said and grinned like the Cheshire cat. She just agreed silently, the dopamine causing her neck to throb.

'How long have you worked here, Lilly? Sorry, Lillian,' Robert asked.

'It's okay, you can call my Lilly, everyone else does. I've been here a week, seems longer.'

'About the same then?'

'What part of London are you from Robert?' Lisa asked.

'Oh, I'm not from London. I live in Surrey. Guildford. London is just the nearest office. Mind you, it was quicker to get here from Surrey, driving into the smoke is a bloody hassle!' That's what they called it, The Smoke, a term used by the older residents of London, but one that stuck amongst salesmen and the likes. Lillian was breathing through her mouth so she wouldn't smell his cologne, the marked presence was filling her personal space and having a walk around her boundaries. 'Right well, I must get on, we'll chat later Lilly,' he tapped the top of her partition and winked at her; that wink, like her father. It made her gasp, he'd overstepped the line, loosening her iron guard. She exhaled, her hands shaking... feeling Lisa's eyes boring holes in her.

'You've gone bright red, Lillian Tate!' she said with an intrigued and flirtatious look. Lillian wasn't sure what was going on, and these feelings weren't familiar to her; intense and filling her with shocks.

She speed walked to the car park at the end of the day. She was frightened, it was here. The chemical compound was explosive, undeniable. It was him, definitely him. Lillian caught herself gawping when Robert Courtney held conversations with her peers, taking comfort in his soft, south-eastern twangs - giving her a warm feeling, like sitting with her family. His aura was dark in colour, indigo perhaps - not one that held any malice, but strength and a steadfastness that held her captive.

Pulling the door shut on the Honda, she felt protected. She cried, in frustration, in a clumsy mess. What was she supposed to do now? Turning the ignition in a hurry, trying to shake herself out of it - the car wouldn't start. Its shell was hanging off the bones, but it rarely let her down engine-wise.

'What?! Are you serious?! No, no, no! Come on, come on!' Lillian put the throttle to the floor and willed it to start; pulling the choke out to various positions, but it was no use. She rested her head on the steering wheel.

'I hate you, I just hate you,' she stayed there for a moment, hoping Brutus would change his mind. 'Look, I'm sorry about what I said, the changing into a beamer thing. Okay? I like you the way you are. Please start!' she tried again. It was fruitless. She looked in the rear-view mirror, nearly peeing when she clocked Robert Courtney walking towards her. Lillian tried to wind the window back up before he got to her – but her elbow just wasn't moving fast enough.

'Is everything all right, Lilly?' he asked. If there was a time she wanted to ground to swallow her up, that would be now.

'Oh, erm, yes, it's fine. I'll try again in a minute.' She answered nervously, hoping he would just go away. Brutus seemed to worsen in appearance since he arrived.

'A Honda Civic?!' He said excitedly.

'Yeah. It's just something I use now and then. I wouldn't want to ruin the other one. It gets me here and back home, just about. It runs on good luck, mostly.' Lillian felt like a low-class citizen, and she was ashamed of it, and herself.

'Well, I never. 1980s, isn't it? Shall I have a go for you? I used to tinker a while back.'

'Oh no, it's fine, really. I'll just let it settle,' she replied, wringing her hands with anguish.

'Look, it's no trouble, please, it's worth a try at least.' Robert worked hard on the handle to open it. There was an awkward moment when they tried to move around each other without touching. He studied the interior as he got in, feeling the fake leather seats in toffee, smiling evocatively to himself. The carpet matched the seats, worn away on the drivers' side. It had manual windows and a push up sunroof, basic dials and a really long gear stick. Lillian had a sweet-smelling air freshener hanging up on the rear-view mirror, to mask its musty aroma.

Robert tried to get it started. The starter motor was turning over, but his will wasn't working. It disappointed him, his ego needed it to start. Lillian just watched, squirming. Robert Courtney, from the London office was sitting in her rust bucket, in a suit!

'It's not the battery, lights are working. Could be the starter motor. I can pop the bonnet up, have a look. Listen, tell you what, why don't you borrow mine for now, at least to get you home. Leave the keys with me and I'll see what's up with it.'

Lillian froze, 'oh no. Really, I couldn't, I...'

'Please Lilly, it's fine. You can sort it out tomorrow.'

'I couldn't possibly, it'll be okay....'

'Just take it, please. I mean, it's not really mine, is it? I'm staying at his Lordship's hotel for the weekend anyway, so I can walk.' The owner of Radar ran a prestigious hotel, hosting international sporting events and conferences, which was a five-minute walk away. Another perk for his pampered staff. He held out the keys between his fingers. She just looked at them, portraying a small step closer to something bigger, dangling like a gold carrot. Lillian took them and looked around the car park.

'Don't worry what anyone will say, you're allowed to drive it.'

'Thank you, I really appreciate it. Uh, which car is it?'

'My pleasure. Lock up, I'll take you to it, show you how she works.' Lillian manually locked the Honda and followed Robert to his car.

'Bleep it then,' he said, looking round at her.

'Bleep it?'

'Yeah, bleep it – open it, with the top button, on the key,' he said and pointed to the fob in her hand. Lillian looked at the key like your dad looks at his mobile phone – when she figured out how to do it, she got a hot rush when the 'bleep' made the indicator lights flash on a black BMW; 520i M - opening it with a sophisticated 'clunk'.

'Watch your speed in her though, she does a tonne with her eyes shut!!' he said and smiled. 'You all right, Lilly? You look like you've seen a ghost.' Lillian was watching Robert as he spoke; those teeth and chocolate eyes were talking to her all on their own. 'Come on - get in.' Lillian got in the driver's seat. She buckled up and nearly lost her senses as Robert leaned in to show her how everything worked. It looked like a cockpit with dials lit up in orange and symbols she didn't even understand. He was showing her how to operate the CD player, but Lillian didn't really take it all in, she was holding her breath and putting up her barriers, pressing herself further back into the seat - the static she got off him almost made a noise. When he finished his tutorial, he crouched down to her level.

'Are you sure you're okay, Lilly? Don't be scared of it, you're the one in control, not the other way around.'

Lillian started it up and it instantly intimidated her; it was a pristine piece of German engineering which demanded the utmost respect. She'd only seen one like it in Pulse's car magazines, and high-end forecourts.

'Enjoy it, but don't prang it!' Lillian laughed nervously. Robert closed the door and hand gestured for her to wind down the window, it took her a moment to find the button. As the window descended in a futuristic whir, Robert admired her in the seat, it suited her. He knew she wasn't used to such luxuries, which made her even more attractive.

'Right then. Just enjoy it and, ooo! Have you got a mobile? While I think of it, in case you need anything,' he said, patting all his pockets. Lillian just shook her head - her thoughts preoccupied with what story she would make up when she got home with a strangers car.

'Ah, shame, ok, never mind. Well, if you need anything, it's tough,' he joked. 'Just call security on reception and they can contact me, okay?'

'Yes. I will, thank you. Thank you.'

'Look, you know it makes sense, don't worry about it. Why shouldn't you share some free fruit, ay?'

Lillian was conscious that she was looking like a nodding dog. 'I will look after it, thanks again.'

He banged on the roof as a signal for her to leave and she pulled away carefully, watching him in the wing mirror waving her off like a big brother. He didn't quite know what he was doing, he had no transport for the weekend. But he didn't want to let her go, offering the car was the only way to keep a hold.

Lillian drove home with the biggest grin on her face, drunk on torque – a gluttony of fancy lights and expensive nonsense had fed her rebellious soul, doused when she pulled up behind Jeffrey's Volvo. He came out when he saw the car.

'Look what I got!' She looked different; a large hole temporarily filled with heady endorphins.

'What the bluddy 'ell is that doin' 'ere!?' Jeffrey yelled, losing the colour in his face.

'Honda wouldn't start. I borrowed it, from a friend. Uh, Dad's friend. He lent it to me, it's an animal! Have a sit in it!' Lillian left the door open for Jeffrey, but he didn't get in.

'Which friend? What's his name? What's he let you have it for? You can't bluddy drive properly!' Jeffrey asked with a worried brow.

'So, I could get home. Honda wouldn't start as I was about to leave, would you believe it?' Jeffrey just stuck his head in and studied at the interior. 'Shall we go out for a spin in it?!' Lillian suggested excitedly.

'No. I've already made dinner,' Jeffrey answered curtly and went back inside. Lillian looked up to the heavens and crossed her fingers... bleeping the beamer. Oliver greeted her with an impatient meow, Jeffrey never fed him. She picked him up and rubbed her face in his fur.

'Why didn't you call me? I would've picked you up.' Jeffrey asked.

'Well, it all happened at once I guess,' Lillian replied.

'Yeah well, it's all happening at once if yer ask me,' Jeffrey said as he laid the kitchen table.

'What's that supposed to mean? I didn't want to hang around waiting for you and how was I going to get back to, uh, town? He just lent me the car, so I could get home, that's all.' Her lie wasn't even a credible one. That car had spurred on the need to go to Birmingham, and if it was feasible, they would go tonight.

Her heart beating hard, she carried Oliver over to the kitchen window to look at the beamer, the evening sun reflecting in its black armour. Her eyes ran over the flawless contours, it was alive. The feelings from the day came flooding back and the car took on the form of promise - and presence of Robert Courtney.

Twenty-Two

The beamer looked positively provocative with its chrome trims against the black paintwork. Lillian took another look inside, reluctant to give it back. Pulling a guilty face opening the glove box, stuffed with the tangible life of Robert Courtney.

She picked out items and smelt them, receiving quick glimpses of his existence. He had the same compilation albums as her; Depeche Mode, Crowded House and Cypress Hill - obviously for those bad days at the office. She put them back, not exactly how they were which meant it wouldn't close properly, pushing it hard in a panic. What did Robert do all weekend? It was tempting to drive to the hotel, and then what? Picking at an opening she didn't have the guts to continue with. She had been grinding her teeth in her sleep from holding onto such a terrible lie, too. Her dreams tormented her, Robert came to the house while Jeffrey was there, eating his stew at the table. Even the lie in the dream was bad. It was one of those dreams that refused to let her wake until she turned herself inside out, needing to pray when you woke and be thankful you did.

All eyes were on her as she drove into Radar; something she didn't mind that day. The security barrier ironically lifted quicker than usual. She parked it closer to the door so Robert wouldn't have to see the Honda again. Walking up to her department with a spring in her step and a million butterflies in her stomach.

Lisa was in before anybody else and stressed out as usual.

'Morning!' Lillian called out.

Lisa was peering at her over the top of her glasses. 'Morning. You look different. Anything to tell me?' Lisa asked in a coercive tone. Lillian explained everything while she settled in. Lisa typed, non-responsive and held reservation on the sickly–sweet gesture.

'I'm making tea then,' Lillian said.

'Please, strong one, got a shed load on,' Lisa requested, pushing her mug forward. Phil came out and made his way around his staff, making light conversation and asking how everyone was getting on with their deadlines. He stopped at Lillian's desk, before heading back into his office.

'Don't forget coffee at nine thirty and we need an extra one for Robert,' her mouth went dry when she heard that name. 'I noticed you were early again this morning. Keep it up.'

Daydreaming at the notice board, she was waiting for the coffee and thinking about Robert, playing footsie with her shoe, not noticing him tapping on the glass panel. She pressed the release button.

'Sorry! Haven't they given you a temporary badge yet?' she asked. Robert was crisp and fresh again, in the same mood as Friday.

'Two weeks they said, no temporaries left. Shall I help you with those Lilly?'

'Oh, yes, ok, Thanks.'

'How was your weekend? Did you get on okay with the car?' he asked, making his own coffee.

'I didn't use it, really. I'll leave the keys on your desk. I really appreciate it.'

'No worries. Anytime. Hope it starts later. I can't give you the car if not, change of plan. I have to be back in London tonight. Sorry.' Lillian felt bereft, a feeling she didn't like. She couldn't concentrate, having second thoughts about pursuing him. It was better not missing anyone.

'I'm sure I've done something to it, it'll probably start. I'll try it lunchtime.' Robert took the mugs, 'I'll take these. Give me a shout if you get stuck.' He showed his pearly whites and went to Phil's office, relieved it was Monday so he could see her again. The weekend was tedious, luckily, he found someone else from the Maidenhead office at the hotel, someone to talk to and pass the time with - otherwise he would have lost the will to live.

Lillian was heavy on his mind the whole time, wondering what she'd been doing and with who; tempted several times to try and contact her at home. He wanted to look back at her but fought against it, feeling her eyes burning his back. She wasn't like all the other girls in their black stilettos and alter egos, this woman held his attention with something, squishing him like putty, her blue eyes giving him a sense of familiarity.

Lillian sighed heavily when she looked at the pile of papers on her desk.

'What do I do with these?' she asked Lisa.

'Filing. Just put them in alphabetical order and hand them back to Phil. He does the rest.' She got lost in the clerics, organising the piles of correspondence, still having to sing the alphabet song in her head. She didn't shift the Universe to do filing! Wondering why Lisa had all the good stuff to do. The department was quieter than usual, although the frivolities in marketing kept the dream alive. Lillian peered over the partition to watch the staff toying with one another; they did this motivational 'whoop' every morning. They were all high on group hugs and monetary goals. The married couple that headed up the department was like the head boy and girl of the company; popular and fully aware of it. Lillian saw a baby arriving soon as she studied the woman.

She took the finished piles of paper into Phil and put them on his table, heaving a sigh of relief when he wasn't there; maybe he did go to the toilet, after all. But Robert was, quickly closing a file when she came in. It was time for her to sprinkle some fairy dust. She needed Robert closer, work out what needed airing between them to release the trapped imp from the jar.

'Okay Robert, ready when you are.'

'Uh, what for?'

'Phil said we have to look through the Apex file.'

'Got it. Right. Just let me, um, sort some things and I'll be there.'

Her heart was racing as she waited for him to return. Breathing in slowly, connecting, opening, letting it in as it knocked loudly and burst through. She was resisting but it was like running downhill.

'Here you go, I hope that's how you like it,' he gave her a sweet cup of tea and sat beside her, their souls dancing above them.

'It looks perfect, thank you,' she took the file out of her drawer and didn't have a clue what to talk about. As she looked through it, Robert's name was appearing on nearly everything, something she hadn't noticed before.

'Oh, it's your name,' she said, reading through the letters.

'Yup. I used to work for Apex,' Robert answered and sipped his tea. 'I was poached. Dropped in hot water and left to cook,' he chuckled to himself. Lillian continued looking through the file.

'Look, this may be a stupid question but what am I supposed to be looking for in here, apart from realising that you used to work for them?' Robert took the file from her and rifled through the pages.

'Here, I think this is what Phil wanted you to see,' he handed her a sheet of paper full of codes and numbers, with descriptions of products and prices.

'This tells you what the competition is supplying and for how much. This isn't from Radar, see, it's from a company called Sisco,' he pointed out the name across the top of the page, in a deep red font. 'One of our biggest competitors. American-based and highly efficient.'

'Ok. So, how did Phil get hold of these?' she asked.

'That's not important right now. I believe a gentleman called Steve Turner is your man for that. Pre-Sales, in saint Helier. He will compete with the pricing, then the techy stuff comes back to me. Make sense?'

'Yes, it does now, thanks, but isn't this cheating?' Robert gulped down air with his tea, almost choking- no other girl had ever questioned it before, they just blindly went with it.

'Well, uh, that's the just the, uh, name of the game. It's all about the winning,' he winked that wink and drank.

'Where is saint Helier?' Lillian asked, with a straight face, Lisa listening in.

'You don't know where that is? Uh, it's in Jersey. Look, just send it over to Steve as soon as and chase his tail, I'll need it back this week.' He got up and went to the spare desk, feeling rumbled. That was it, he thought – she was a woman of integrity and that just may have lost him the opportunity.

'Shall we go out for lunch, Lilly? My treat,' Lisa interrupted.

'Yeah, fine. Not if we're having tuna baguettes though, you can go by yourself otherwise,' Lillian replied. Lunching became quite a habit, and the novelty was wearing off.

'Ok, deal.' Lisa needed a chat with her, she was getting anxious from Lillian's movements.

They went to the usual Radar haunt for lunch. Lillian just ordered a prawn salad and a soda and lime, she was in no mood for chips and a Spritzer, her appetite was being suppressed by her crush and a big, fat lie. Although she felt a bit confused about that now. They chatted about work, Lillian pressed Lisa about Apex, but she brushed it off - then Robert Courtney came up in the conversation.

'Lilly, I know you're looking for a way out, but don't use a man as leverage, you could come out of one hell and into another. Robert seems like a nice guy but he's pushing your exposed buttons right now. You know nothing about him. Just because he's got a job here doesn't mean he's had an integrity check.'

Lillian rolled her eyes and just played with her food. 'It's him.'

Lisa stopped eating and raised her eyebrows. 'You've known him for five minutes! It's just a coincidence, it's not him. He's not the one.' Lisa answered, devouring her breaded scampi.

'Since when has it been up to you? I don't get you! One minute you're trying to get me out of Jeffrey's grip and when I meet someone that might be what I've been looking for, you're putting me off them! Oh, and there's no such thing as coincidence. Didn't I teach you anything?'

'Well, you know what I mean. Don't just fall at the feet of the first man that smiles at you, Lil. You need something more concrete than that, he's probably just sniffing around. Men are clever at reeling you in once they see a vulnerability they can chip away at. Just let Robert Courtney work for it and don't let him see you're impressed all the time. They need to feel a little threatened to keep them grounded, stops them getting too big for their boots.' Lillian listened attentively.

'I'm not very good at hiding my feelings. I fall easy, you know that.' There was a silence between them while they both reflected.

'They are not very good at our body language, or take hints very well. If you laugh at their jokes, they think you fancy them. Jeffrey doesn't realise or even think you hate him. You have to tell him.' Lisa held Lillian's hand and made eye contact with her, she looked woeful, and Lillian didn't like what was screaming from her eyes.

'What? What is it?'

Lisa let go, finishing her Gin and tonic. 'I love you, that's what. I don't want to see you get hurt any more, Lil. Just rein in it in a little. Anyway, Courtney might be married.' Those last words made Lillian feel sick.

'He's not! No ring. I looked!'

'Maybe he takes it off and puts it back on when he gets home.'

'What?! Why would he do that?! There would be a line. There was no line, or mark. There has never been a ring. That's just a nasty assumption.'

'What makes you so sure? Don't be fooled by the no ring thing, Lilly. I don't think he's single.'

'I know it. Don't ruin this for me, please Lisa. I'm not falling out with you over this as well.'

'There's nothing to ruin. You're not going to pursue it. Let it go, save yourself the heartache.' Lillian didn't want to listen. Lisa kept her head down and ate the last of her lunch with her fingers.

'Look, just wait and see who else is out there, ok? I don't trust Courtney, he's too... happy-chappie-full-of-shit, kind of guy. If he is single, he's probably gay or a serial killer.' Lillian grimaced and just didn't get Lisa's analogy, and it hurt. She watched her suck on the lemon from her drink, with thoughts of ending the friendship.

'We'd better be getting back. Come on.'

After an awkward atmosphere in the car and walk to back to their posts, Phil was perched on Lillian's desk again. It was starting to intimidate her.

'Did you enjoy your break, ladies?' he asked, Lillian checked her watch, they were five minutes early. She'd had enough of watch checking with Jeffrey.

'Yes, thanks,' they replied in tandem. He stood up and ran his eyes over the rest of the team who all had their heads down, afraid to look up.

'Can you come to my office please,' expecting her to follow. She grabbed her pad and pen, straightening herself before she entered.

'Close the door,' he asked. Lillian was a little nervous about what he wanted. His face was stern, but he gave her a sympathetic smile. 'Sit down,' Phil said and sat in his seat, chewing his pen. Lillian got a déjà vu moment, and her heart beat faster. She braced herself for questions about her and Robert's discussions in the car park, unknowingly tapping her pen on the notepad. He took the pen out of his mouth and sat forward, resting his elbows on the desk. 'What did you bring your notepad for?' he asked and pointed to it.

'You told me to. I write your requests down and tick them off as I go. It's better than trying to keep them in my head. The rest of the day has a habit of erasing them,' Lillian answered with confidence. There were two elephants in the room, head-to-head, pushing against one another. Phil leant back and clasped his hands on his head.

'How is everything, Lilly?'

'Everything is fine, thank you,' she replied, her hands in her lap.

'You've settled in very well and I'm pleased with your work. I made the right choice, but don't do anything to jeopardise that.'

Lillian's stomach dropped. He paused and studied her with a smouldering look; he was a beautiful man in his own right, but his presence resembled shards of ice, impaling on impact.

'How is the car now?'

'I must check it later if I can please. It should start,' Lillian was smiling, waiting for a bombshell, she could feel it approaching, their bodies tensing.

'How is everything at home?' and there it was. She checked his hand for a ring again, the conversation with Lisa made her question it. There was always someone's husband or partner, chancing their luck. Her dancing soul, child-like mannerisms and mirrored attributes aroused their inhibitions. She was what they had been 'looking for all their lives', but none of them had any honourable intentions. Being spoken for was their safety net, curiosity eventually burning them.

'Uh, fine, thanks. Why do you ask?' she replied.

'Just wondering. As long as you're happy. I don't want your work being affected. That's all.' That wasn't all. Lillian got a sudden headache from the pictures and words that came pouring in – like her dreams, the office felt like her dreams.

'I'd like you to arrange a function, for the department, invite the other regions too.' She wrote it down, wincing at the sharp pain in her temple. 'Entertainment would be good. I'm thinking of a suite. We'll need a decent sized one.'

'At the hotel?' she asked.

'Yes. Book it as soon as possible. Get back to me with availability. I'd also like to extend a private invitation, to you.' She stopped writing.

'Call it, an ice breaker, if you like. I'm inviting you for dinner at my house. Lisa and Robert are coming. Tomorrow night.

Seven o'clock, sharp. I'll have a taxi pick you up at your address. I hope you'll accept. It's a bit of a surprise, so keep it from the others. I'll call them in individually.' The air was escaping from the office. Lillian held her head as it began to spin, steading herself on his desk, hoping it would pass and he wouldn't notice.

'Are you all right?' he asked. She made her way to the door, leaning against it and twisting the handle, opening it enough to get some air. Phil looked on with a lack of empathy and a chilling grin.

'Shall I take that as a yes?' Lillian managed to nod, intensifying the pain and pressure. Lisa was walking back to her desk with coffee, taking Lillian by the arm.

'Sit, sit. I'll get you some water.' Lisa got her a cup of cold mineral water from the up-side-down gurgling bottle. 'Here, drink this. Jesus! What happened to you? Bad prawns? You're as white as a sheet!' Lillian held her head up and waited for the dizziness to subside.

'I'm ok, just give me a minute,' she said, waving her hand to show she didn't need the fuss.

'What did he do to you?!' Lisa whispered, agitatedly. Lillian just put her finger on her lips to silence her.

'What's happened? You ok Lilly?' Robert asked, breezing through, like he always did. What was he so happy about all the time?

'It's nothing, just a dodgy lunch. I got this. You can go,' Lisa answered curtly. He went to his desk and opened his laptop, feeling a little bruised from Lisa's rudeness. He could see that she guarded Lillian like a barbed wire fence, making him more determined to cut through it.

'Lilly, Lilly, say something,' Lisa pressed, tapping the back of her hand.

'I'll be fine, really, thanks. Stop fussing!'

'Drink your coffee then, maybe you didn't eat enough, shall I get you a sandwich or something?' Lillian refused and took a sip of her coffee.

'No, it's fine.'

'Okay. Umm... maybe you should sit with me and go through anything you're unsure of, shift your focus a little.' Lisa looked over to Robert, who had been watching her closely. After Lillian got over her incident, all the dazzling lights and whiz bangs had ceased - her rose-tinted glasses, a little cracked. There was a pressing force in that office, she picked up on every sordid detail.

'I'm just going to see if the car starts, I won't be a moment,' she said sullenly. Feeling woozy from her experience.

'Ok, no problem Lil, you'd better pop your head into Phil's, let him know what you're doing,' Lisa replied.

'I'm doing no such thing. Send out a search party if I'm not back in half an hour.' Lillian walked off, regretting saying yes to dinner but it was the only way in.

As she left reception, feeling shaken, Robert called after her.

'Lilly! Wait up! How are you feeling now?'

'I'm fine thanks. Low blood sugar and Phil Hathaway.'

Robert snorted a brief laugh, 'yeah, I know that one.'

'Oh? You two know each other then?'

'You could say that. Anyway, listen. Let's see if we can get this car started, ay?' Phil watched them from his office window as they made their way down to the Honda.

'I can tell you're embarrassed about your car, don't be. I used to have one,' Robert's confession comforted her, injecting a warm, fuzzy feeling.

'Really? Same model?' Lillian responded, her embarrassment subsiding.

'Yes, it was my pride and joy. My father bought it for me.' Lillian delighted in his openness; it was like talking to a member of the family on her father's side. The man behind the Saville Row suit was surprisingly unpretentious. She opened the car, put the key in the ignition and sounded the horn, playing a brief version of General Lee. Robert put his hands over his ears and laughed loudly, checking to see if anyone was around.

'Did it have one of these in it?' she jested. 'It's my signature tune. It's annoying, but I didn't want to change it.' Robert's ears were still ringing, trying to clear them by waggling his finger in them.

'I think the whole building heard that!' his heart leapt and beat a little faster from Lillian's humorous side, which added to the adoration. He was grinning as he studied the Honda's bodywork.

'It came with it. I just never took it out. I didn't know it was there until I nearly gave our neighbour a heart attack.' Lillian looked at the car then back at him, Robert was making his way around the Honda, running his hand over the chinked panels and dull surface.

'Don't do it, don't make me fall in love with you, because it's working,' she said in her head.

'Where did you say you got it from?' he asked.

'Uh, I didn't. It came from Bristol, I believe,' Lillian's hair began to stand on end and her right side was burning, her indication of a clairvoyant arrival.

'Look. Don't freak out or anything,' Robert said, holding his hands out in front of him.

'This car, well basically, this is my old car. It's mine, the blue bits... and the horn,' he said and waited for the ripple to settle. Lillian's eyes watered as a rush of stinging magic ran through her. 'That's my personalised number plate. But I didn't want you thinking I was crazy or anything, or making it up, or trying it on...' he explained, hands still in front.

Lillian was silent as she stood there gawping, looking at the plate several times.

'I don't know how you got it Lilly, it's all a bit weird!' She got in the driver's seat in a daze, and put the key in the ignition... pausing, stopping at every stage as she turned it. On the final one, it started.

Twenty-Three

She revved the engine, making more silver smoke billow from the exhaust. Robert leaned on the door frame, wafting his hand in front of his face, still shaking his head in disbelief.

'It's like it didn't start on purpose, ain't it?' They looked at each other and the invisible force buzzed excitedly around them, rejoicing at fate's impervious timing.

'See that dent?' he said, pointing to the centre of the bonnet. Lillian looked at it like she'd never seen it before, yet it was her annoyance every time she drove it.

'Cricket ball. Smack!' he clapped his hands together 'the kids were playing in the street, and it was always a target.' Lillian began to sweat, her gut was churning, and she had a different feeling about Robert.

'Have you been listening to me?' she asked suspiciously.

'Listening? To you? Well, now you come to mention it, yes, I can't stop listening to you Lilly,' he replied, his face softened and those eyes caressed her. She looked away quick and tried to swallow her saliva that was gathering in her mouth.

'Was it something I said? I swear, Lilly, this is all hocus pocus, but I swear to you.' Lillian looked out the windscreen and suddenly felt uncomfortable. Droplets of rain began to fall, dampening the moment.

'Ok. I think I need to be getting back now, Phil will be on my case otherwise.' Robert moved aside as she got out, 'thanks for helping me, I really appreciate it.' She locked up and started to walk back, feeling stupid again and hearing Lisa in her head telling her a 'told you so', the rain falling heavier. Robert panicked, trotting after her, grimacing at the sudden downpour, pulling up his shirt collar.

'Lilly, look, I'm telling the truth! I know what you must think...' the rain was loud as it hit the tarmac - soaking him, his hair dripping styling gel into his mouth.

'You're just telling me that to trick me into something!' Lillian answered, tearful, walking faster, swaying her arms.

'What? No! I'm not trying to trick you Lilly, why would I?!'

'You find it easy to cheat!'

'No, that's just, well that's just how it is. Look, you of all people should know I'm telling the truth!'

Lillian stopped dead. 'What do you mean by that? You know nothing about me!'

Robert ran his fingers through his hair, flicking the rain off his hands. 'Now I'm just digging myself a bloody big hole. I know you're special Lilly, I can feel it. Okay. What can I say to make you believe me?'

'What's your middle name?'

'Don't laugh, okay? It's Lance. Robert Lance Courtney. The numbers are random.'

'How many clicks for the choke?' Lillian having to raise her voice.

'One. It's always one, two in the frost,' he answered. Lillian couldn't help but raise a smirk. 'That was just a lucky guess.'

'Ah come on Lil! Give the guy a break! I'm dying here! I'm drenched and squirming!'

'It's Lilly,' she corrected.

'Lilly, sorry.' Robert reacted timidly.

'Okay then. Where's the leak?' reaching the shelter of reception.

'Back door, near side. Leaks through, God knows where, but there's always a puddle in the back when it rains. They'll be one there after this lot! Which means you're opening all the windows through summer. Get rid of the smell more than anything. Although I like your pomander thing you've got hanging up,' he said, spitting out rain. She began to giggle and looked down to hide it.

'I'm right, aren't I? Go on, say it. I'm right and telling you the truth! Who could make that stuff up?!' he wiped the excess water off his face. She could see his skin and nipples through his saturated shirt and looked away shyly, jiggling her head at his right answer.

'You see?! Hey, how come you're not wet?' he asked, puzzled that Lillian just had a few drops of rain on her. She affectionately wiped rain from his face with her thumb. He gulped at the mammoth tingle that ran through him, twisting his gut. 'I'll have to go the hotel, get another shirt, well everything really. Rain has reached the parts where rain hasn't reached before.' He pulled on the reception door for her.

'We can't leave it like this – you know that,' he took a logoed umbrella from the holder by the entrance.

She watched him run up the hill to the hotel. Bright and colourful popping things danced around in her head, looking forward to seeing him at Phil's dinner.

***

'Is this a social visit, Jeffrey?' Rose asked, as she handed him tea.

'I came to sort out the Honda and see Martin,' he said, after turning up unexpectedly at their house.

'The Honda? Oh! The Honda! Yes. Martin's taken it for a run. So, he's, uh, just taken it out for a run, yes, to um, keep it running. Did you leave work especially? Bit of a long run.' Jeffrey slurped his hot tea, wincing as it burned his tongue and feeling awkward in her company.

'I hear you and me muther had a bit of a fallin' out.'

'Uh... well, we don't exactly see eye to eye, but I mean no malice. It must be tough for her, living up there all by herself,' Rose answered, plumping the cushions nervously.

'I know you ain't happy with me, but there's reason things are the way they are,' Rose sat down and was ready to listen. Jeffrey looked at his mug and toyed with the pattern. Startled by Martin when he came in, holding milk and a loaf of bread.

'It's pouring out there! Oh, hello Jeffrey, what do we owe the pleasure?'

'Martin! You're back early. How was the Honda?' Rose said quickly.

'The Honda?' Martin questioned, Rose glaring at him, hoping for the penny to drop.

'Can I get you anything Jeffrey?' Martin deterred.

'No. Thanks. I just came to see if I could get the Honda started.'

'Right. Well, it's ok now. No need. Was there something else?' Martin asked.

'Yes. Err, but in private,' Martin thought a drive would be best, and this was his opportunity to have a word about his behaviour.

'Sure. I'll take you out.' Rose was reluctant to let Martin go; she didn't want him getting angry while he was driving.

'It's ok, I'll take Benny out for a little walk. You two stay here,' the men agreed. It was a long-awaited moment for them both.

Rose felt like she'd let go of a heavyweight as she walked to the park with Benny leading the way in his little red raincoat, hoping Martin would finally sort it out. With a bit of luck, it would push things forward.

'So, Jeffrey. More tea?'

'No. Thanks. Why didn't y'stop her?'

'There's no stopping Lilly once she gets a bee in her bonnet, and it was too precious to see her happy again,' Martin answered from the kitchen. 'You haven't exactly fulfilled my wishes, Jeffrey. If anything, you pushed her to it!'

'I can't 'andle her! She's been doing that stuff again. I had a threatening nudge the other week! I can't go back to that Radar place. Christ, what are we dealing with 'ere?'

'I don't know why you had to go. It was foolish! You've probably made things worse! Have you got anything secured?'

'Yeah. We 'ave to leave soon, but there are some things that need tying up. She ain't exactly keen to go!'

Martin closed his eyes as the bereavement stung him, hard. He didn't want his daughter to hate him and was waning from the idea.

'Right. Well, we might already be too late.'

'You wanna back out?' Jeffrey could see Martin was weakening, he also looked physically incapable of dealing with any stress.

'Just promise me one thing, be gentle with her. If she really doesn't want to go, leave it. We must think of something else.

You have contacts in the force. We might have to go down that route.'

'Police? What are they gonna do?'

'I'm not sure. So, how is work?' they got onto small talk before Rose returned with Benny; his little coat soaking wet and so was she.

'Goodness! This rain! We had nothing for months, then it comes all at once! Sorry, it was too wet for a walk.' She shook the rain off by the front door, aware of the silence in the house. Martin and Jeffrey were just sat, chatting.

'Well, I best be going then, if the Honda started.'

'Oh, don't go on my account,' Rose insisted. 'I have to get back to work. Thanks for the tea,' and he got up to let himself out.

'Ok. You're welcome anytime, Jeffrey. We're here most days to lend an ear,' Rose offered.

'Yeah. Maybe. Cheers. See ya Martin.'

Yes, see you, Jeffrey. Thanks for stopping by.' Rose watched him out of the window, leaving in a bit of a hurry.

'What was all that about?' she asked.

'He came to see the Honda.'

'Did you have a word?'

'I did,' his gut was churning. Rose affectionately patted his hand as he rested it on her shoulder.

'Since when did you care about him? I had to think on my feet! Lilly hasn't told him she works at Radar, and that BMW she brought here on the weekend, well. I don't know what she was thinking! You can't keep a lie going like that, it trips you up eventually.' Martin listened, looking over her shoulder as they peered through the net curtains, watching Jeffrey leave.

'He will realise you were also lying when he didn't see the Honda outside. He won't be coming back for tea and sympathy, anytime soon I don't think.'

Jeffrey's stress levels were increasing. He took the drive a little too fast and nearly ended up in the cemetery, slamming on the breaks and swearing. He stayed there, the Volvo ticking over, composing himself. He could see Oliver through the fence just sitting, looking at him – sheltering under the oaks.

'Stupid bluddy cat. I'll be sortin' you out soon, an awl!' getting out, huffing in despair. Opening the back door, he stopped to sniff before he went inside. He could smell something. He checked the bottoms of his shoes, then where he was standing.

'What's that bluddy smell?' sure it was Oliver. Pushing the back door open, he stopped, immediately putting a bent wrist up to his nose. The kitchen stank of sewage. He went over to the sink, grimacing in panic at the black, sticky substance that was bubbling and popping out of the plug hole, getting splashes of it on his t-shirt, taking it off and throwing it on the floor. He heaved while running the hot tap and squeezing bleach down there, but it repelled the liquids.

'What the bluddy 'ell is that?!' he said aloud. Watching it latch onto the sides with what looked like small, clawed hands, expanding, the pipes gurgling loudly. He looked out the window for an idea. Oliver was still in the same place, waiting, watching amongst the long grass, giving Jeffrey a shiver. He ran upstairs, turning on the shower, dodging the first cold blast – it was all he could think of, logic was in there somewhere. More black goo spat and spurted from the plughole, filling the surface, holding onto to rim of the sink and pulling itself out, resembling something giving birth; something that was already dead.

'Arrgghh!' he looked for anything to add to it – he grabbed a shampoo bottle, emptying all of it, hitting the expanding mutant with the empty bottle. Opening the window and turning the taps on full. Bubbles and foam were increasing, spilling over the edge and taking the substance with it. Jeffrey shut the door afraid it was going to sprout legs and run, or attack. He felt dizzy, scared and the house was different and unnerving. He suddenly thought of the plumber three doors up – he would know. Jeffrey ran up the hill topless, in slippers, knocking the door and ringing the bell several times. The door swung open.

'Uh, yeah, can I help?' he wasn't that happy to see Jeffrey.

'Sorry to bother ya, but can you come an' 'ave a look at me drains? Got some stuff coming out of them. Black stuff!' he panted.

'Black stuff? Is it blocked?'

Jeffrey shook his head, leaning over out of breath. 'Don't think so. It's in all of em!' The guy was reluctant to help, he'd just got home.

'Well, ok, just give me a minute,' he closed the door, leaving Jeffrey looking back at the house.

The neighbour was regretting his good will. They entered through the back door, Jeffrey pushed past him. Stumbling when he was confronted with the contents of what looked like the streets' bins, strewn all over the worktops and floor.

'What the bluddy 'ell?! I bet this is to do with them bluddy kids o'yours!'

'I'm sorry?!' the plumber was aghast.

'Yeah. Winding me up as per bluddy usual!'

'Look, I don't know what you're insinuating, but this is nothing to do with my children and I don't like your tone! Do you want my help, or not?' He showed the plumber the sink, but there was nothing there.

'I put bleach down this one, must 'ave done the trick. Come and 'ave a look upstairs.' The bathroom still had shampoo bubbles everywhere, but no smell, or black goo.

'It was comin' out 'ere!' Jeffrey pointed to both plug holes. The plumber sniffed in the sink, running the taps.

'Looks like it's all going through fine. Was there a smell?'

'Yeah – awful, like sewers! It was thick, sticky stuff. Black! Looked like summat off one o'them horror films!' Jeffrey laughed embarrassingly as his statement. The plumber shrugged, feeling a little uncomfortable in Jeffrey's company. Blaming the mess on his children, just to cover it up.

'Well, whatever it was, has righted itself now. The water wouldn't go down if there was a blockage. Maybe you had some air in the pipes.'

'It wasn't bluddy air! There was bluddy black stuff coming out of them! It was alive! I ain't bluddy joking!' There was an edgy pause. A loud noise was heard on the landing, alarming them both.

'What the 'ell now?!' Jeffrey pushed passed the neighbour.

'Who's there? You'll be sorry!' Then all the upstairs doors slammed shut a once, causing a vacuum and shifting their hair. The plumber ran downstairs, two at a time.

'It's just the bluddy wind!' Jeffrey ran after him. 'I'm sorry I bothered ya. Must 'ave been the bleach. I swear by it. Kills anything. Do you use it?' the plumber smiled nervously and began leaving, visibly shaken, nearly tripping over Oliver as he backed out of the house.

Twenty-Four

She waited for the taxi by the front door, checking every set of headlights that came down the hill; dressed in black slacks and a red, collared blouse. It had been difficult keeping it secret from Lisa and Robert. Jeffrey was working late so she left a note, overthinking about that too. An unmarked car arrived at exactly seven.

She got in the back; it was brand new, clean and untouched. The driver didn't speak, just made sure she was safely in, and drove off– it felt like it was gliding. Lillian looked around noticing the stitching in the seats and polished walnut panels. It didn't look or feel like a taxi, no one had been in this one before. The Mercedes headed back down the motorway and out towards the woods. Not knowing Phil's address unnerved her - observing every street she passed so she remembered where she was if she had to run back home. The houses were getting bigger, detached and boasting wide driveways and immaculate frontages.

They stopped outside Phil's, his car on a blocked paved driveway; a freshly painted white house with cosy table lamps lit in the front room. Lisa wasn't there yet, making her heart thump, she wasn't happy about being alone with him. Relieved to get out the taxi - it had been an awkward, silent drive. She rang the doorbell. A short *brrriinnng* brought Phil to the door, seeing him through the frosted glass.

'Ah, good evening, Lilly. Please, come in.'

His house was as sparse as the office, but tasteful, and there was a distinctive scent of floor wax and fabric conditioner. After taking off her shoes, he led her into a large lounge, her feet thumping on the hollow floor. A grand room with a marble fireplace, a carriage clock ticking softly. Original parquet flooring covered the downstairs, complimented with Persian rugs and brocade curtains with golden tassel tie backs. The furniture was dark antique, housing artefacts and abstract souvenirs.

'Lisa won't be long, although Robert is putting in some overtime. Drink?' Lillian nodded, feeling blocked and squeezed by the house.

'Mateus, isn't it?' he shrewdly suggested. 'Annie!' he called, and in came a lady in her mid-forties from the Philippines. Not quite a Geisha girl.

'Yes, Mitter 'athaway?'

'A Mateus, for Lilly!' raising his voice. She grinned at Lillian, jiggling her head.

'Nice to meet you, Miss Lilly,' and she scuttled off.

'That's Annie, my maid. She's a diamond. But her English is a little comical. We're having Beef Wellington with seasonal vegetables. Does that suit?'

'Oh, uh, yes, thank you, sounds lovely,' she checked the time again, stood there looking awkward. Phil opened a mahogany drinks' cabinet, displaying crystal decanters, pouring himself a scotch.

'Do you have to be somewhere?' he asked.

'I have to be back, on time.'

Phil took a large gulp of his poison. He made her tremble, his demeanour and features were daunting, coupled with an overbearing confidence. Swirling the golden liquid, he raised a condescending smile.

'Why do you let him control you?'

Lillian gulped, stuttering to answer. 'Uh, who?'

He sat in an Oxblood wing-backed chair, positioned in the bay window, overlooking the bespoke garden; it was his favourite seat. 'Jeffrey,' he answered, after a big swallow. Annie came in with her drink on a silver tray, offering it to her.

'Thank you, Annie.'

'S'ok Miss. You like der menu? Is very nice.'

'Yes. It sounds wonderful, thank you.'

'Annie, enough talking and can you bring Lillian some slippers.' Phil demanded.

'Yes, mitter 'athaway,' she left the room, bowing and shuffling backwards. Phil stood from his resting place. 'Would you like to see the rest of downstairs? At least until Lisa arrives.' Lillian took a large mouthful of Mateus, holding it in her cheeks.

'Yes, of course. Thank you.' The pink fizz burned her belly, calming her nerves that were making her quake. She needed something stronger to block out what was residing in the walls. As they entered the hallway, something flashed passed her, shooting up through the staircase - a blue and white blur. She said nothing. He gave her the history of the cornices, but she didn't hear what he said, she was concentrating on keeping herself together. Phil had finished his historical tour of the hall and led her to the large kitchen, with a utility room full of wine bottles, then into the dining room. She hovered at the doorway, not wanting to go any further. It was a psychic's lair; a room with floor to ceiling bookshelves filled with highly sought after collections.

The walls were decorated in a damask flock paper in dark green, and a mahogany dining table, all set for his guests, with a matching green billiard light overhead.

'Can Annie take your bag for you?'

'Oh, uh, no, it's ok – I'll hold on to it. Thanks.'

'You seem uptight. Here, take a seat,' he pulled out a chair for her. The room made her nervous. She looked around discreetly, spotting a basket of onyx runes – swallowing her

Mateus down too hard. Where was Lisa? And the absence of Robert left her feeling vulnerable.

'You'll be home in time, you have my word. But we need to rid you of this oppression.' She just drank, unable to react. Was he offering to kill Jeffrey? Suddenly losing all morality since stepping into the room. The alluring psyche coaxed the darkest part of her ego, feeding her desires. Phil finished his Scotch, drawing the last drops through his teeth.

'I want to help you, Lilly. I'm sure you've realised that you and I have quite a lot in common. I'd like to show you how to perfect the gift we share.' Lillian couldn't absorb what he was saying, what she wanted someone to say, for so long. This man wasn't what she envisaged. He was single, seemed generous and thoughtful enough and psychic, far more powerful than her. But the negative presence that filled the room was quietly strangling her.

'How long have you had your ability, Lilly?'

'Oh, um, since I was young,' she nodded, not wanting this conversation to go any further, she was burning, her facial muscles contorting. 'You?'

'The same. You know…' he studied her, she was trying so hard to stop him entering.   'The mirror intrigues me. I'd like to take a closer look at it sometime. However, your projection is not reaching far enough. I could hear you, but it was faint.'

'You… you *heard* me?'

Phil hummed his confirmation. 'I know you're desperate to get out. What's stopping you?' he left the table and took a book from one shelf; leather bound. 'You'll be surprised what's on the other side of fear, Lillian. That's the only thing holding you back, wouldn't you say?' He handed her the book.

'What if you could see *beyond* your fear?' he said with an element of sensation. She regarded the book with caution; an embossed pentagram on the front, the sight of it going against her morals. Now it all made sense. Phil's foresight had entered a place where Lillian vowed never to tread, thankful she had been warned against the borrowed powers of the unseen, knowing the book also had its limitations.

'Take it home with you. A bit of bedtime reading.' It was as tempting as the keys were to Robert's beamer. What did it matter now? Might as well keep the ball rolling.

'I'm impressed with your gift, Lilly. But you're not using it to its full potential. I imagine it would be deadly,' he sneered, feeling slightly aroused.

'It's none of my business, but you can do better than Robert Courtney.'

Lillian drank every drop in her glass, 'you deserve better treatment. Someone like you needs guidance and nourishment. You shouldn't have to explain your soul to anyone.' Phil was speaking from her heart, not his. Lillian was trying hard to suppress a loud burb –any bodily functions would seem inappropriate in front of him. He was a sophisticated kind of evil.

'It's safe to assume there'll be no more secrets between us. Which leads me to say, I know you have something of mine.'

'Have, something?'

'Yes. You've been unwilling to let it go since you arrived,' she nearly threw up. Did he mean *that* something? Planning how she would get out. Annie would help, she was probably desperate to leave, too. They would hit him over the head with one of the large crystals he had adorning a small, round table. All shapes, sizes and purposes. Lillian held on tight to her shoulder bag.

'Why have you still got it?'

'The onyx?' she answered, trying to knock him off the scent.

He blurted a laugh. 'That is mine, granted. But I don't want it back. You found it so I could find you,' he rested his elbows on the table. 'I'm talking about, the money,' those eyes had changed, his face had changed. Pinning her in the seat, numbing her. He held out his hand.

'Just hand it over and we'll say no more about it. You're not in any trouble.' She shook her head in protest. 'Why didn't you bank it?' he asked.

Lillian wanted rid of it, starting a war with herself since Simon gave it to her. 'I'd rather not say.'

'Oh, come on now, what did I say about secrets?' he leant back in his seat. She could see something around him making her chest tighten, wanting to stare longer; giving her the feeling of being thrown over a vertical drop. Infatuated and terrified in the same breath. A shadow dipped in and out of Phil, unsure of its place, trying to gain a comfortable position. We were hollow to them, making themselves as small as mosquitoes to 'fit' inside.

'Simon owed me that money. I know you are a loyal individual, Lilly – lucky for me,' he grinned. 'The money is mine. He won't miss it or pursue it. You can tell me. It's all right.' She manipulated the zip of her bag, having another fight with her conscience.

'I didn't bank it because... he owed me too,' she looked down at the detail of the tablecloth, her plans for it dashed. Releasing the trauma he caused, wiping away a tear before Phil noticed.

'No man has the right, Lilly. No man. Would you like to meet one of them?' he asked. Lillian looked up from the table, 'one of who?' she stiffened, watching his shirt ripple from within – like something was trying to get out of it. Pushing herself back in the chair.

'Don't be afraid,' he said soothingly, his left arm going into spasm. She watched closely as the table blurred from the apparition that left him. It turned disturbingly cold, something pushing down on her shoulders. The ghostly figure moved in a melancholic manner, reaching the chair next to her, its alien features a distinctive portrayal of discontent. She'd seen them before; condemned to this realm from threats of harm and murder to fulfil black magic practices. Lurking in derelict places away from human intrusion.

'This is Bal, he's a Jinn. You've heard that name before, haven't you?' Phil said. The jinn was trying to imitate something, shapeshift, changing in sporadic movements, tired from its despotic keeper.

'Come on, we have a guest – show Lilly what you can do.' Lillian's stomach filled with a sickening heaviness, she stood, trying to catch her breath - watching Bal's transparent limbs abnormally stretch, feeling pained for its reluctant effort under Phil's pressure.

'Stop, please! Leave it alone!' Phil nodded at Bal, his signal for it to leave. The being shot upwards and disappeared through the ceiling, shaking the billiard light.

'Why feel sorry for it? It has no other purpose other than to serve us. He can get you anything you want. Be anything you want. Just imagine?' He held out his hand again with a persuasive, threatening look. 'The money.'

Lillian reached into her bag, her face flushed red, tipping the bag out onto the table; makeup, pencils, change, tissues, onyx and crumbs, dirtying the crisp, white cotton tablecloth. It wasn't there, but she still separated everything just to be sure.

'It's gone! I had it, I swear!' The doorbell rang – startling them both.

'Just make sure you find it!' he said before answering the door.

Phil kept his word, ordering an early taxi for Lillian, keen for her to find the cash. Dinner was delicious but awkward, although she couldn't eat, she kept thinking about Bal. Lisa and Phil had a lot to say, with Lillian just listening, feeling like a spare part. The house was the most oppressive atmosphere she'd ever been in. Every time she went to the toilet, she had to run back down the stairs; afraid of being grabbed by the ankle or pushed from behind. Lisa stayed behind, too drunk to drive back. Poor Annie went home, exhausted from her duties.

Lillian's gut wrenched when she saw the Volvo on the drive. She thanked the driver, the same one she had, who just looked straight ahead. Walking down the drive, she was thinking about the excuse and where she could've dropped the envelope of cash. She opened the back door with her eyes closed, feeling bruised from Phil and dinner. Although he was respectful of her, which seemed odd. Looking at the note she'd left still pinned on the cork board, wincing at it – what a rubbish lie! She tip toed through the house. The atmosphere was a blessing.

'Hello?' she called out. No answer and no Oliver. The house was in upheaval; bulging black sacks were everywhere. It felt sad in there now, like Pulse - the chapter was smouldering, preparing for the next. Jeffrey sat in the lounge, with a face like thunder.

'Hi, I'm back,' she said coyly, walking in, tucking her hair behind her ears. There was no answer. 'Where's Oliver?' still no response. She took herself off to the bedroom, hoping she'd got away with it. Lillian shoved the book under the bed and began looking for the envelope, searching in places where she knew darn well it wouldn't be. Regretting carrying it around with her, maybe it was lost, for good; someone had an early birthday.

'Lookin' for summat?' Jeffrey asked by the door. She didn't hear him coming up the stairs.

'Oh, uh, I've lost a letter. You haven't seen it, have you?'

'You mean this?' he held the envelope of cash in his hand, waggling it. She thought she would pee herself. 'What the bluddy 'ell 'ave you been up to? Ay?!'

'Look, I can explain. It's not mine and I need to give it back. Where did you find it?'

'I got it outta yer bag! Looking for a clue!'

'A clue?'

'Yeah. A Radar clue! Think I'm bluddy stupid, is it? BMW man give you this, did he?!'

'What? No! The money belongs to Pulse!'

'You stole it?'

'No! What do you take me for?!'

'Well, yer must 'ave – why else would you have six grand in yer bluddy bag?!'

'How do you know it's that much?'

'Cos I bluddy counted it!'

'You had no right going in my bag! I'm not touching it, you've opened it. Your fingerprints are all over it now!' Jeffrey's face changed, throwing the hot potato on the bed.

'Go on, I'm waiting for it,' crossing his arms.

'Simon gave it to me to bank. I always did his banking. He gave it to me on the last day and well, I just kept hold of this one. Can't explain why exactly, I had no intentions of touching it. That's it really. But I'm going to bank it.'

'And when were ya gowin to tell me about Radar?'

'I wasn't. But now you've found out, well, what else is there to say?'

'So, where yer been then? And not at yer muthers, cos I rang her. So, you'd better think, quick!' Lillian wasn't as scared as she thought she would be, Phil's sinister support gave her strength.

'They invited me to dinner. My boss, Phil Hathaway and, some colleagues. That's how they welcome new staff. Break the ice. I hid the whole thing from you because of your over dramatic reactions. It's well paid and I love it.' Jeffrey's eyes glazed and reddened. In a split second he grabbed Lillian by the hair, dragging her out of the room and downstairs into the kitchen.

'Think yer bluddy clever, is it?! Yer getting us into serious trouble! That money ain't clean!' He shook her head violently, emphasising every word through clenched teeth. Lillian closed her eyes as the pain of his grip shot through her scalp, fearing that something would tear.

'Okay! I'm sorry! Let go! Please! You're hurting me! I'm sorry!' she screamed, trying to release his hold. He threw her aside, breathing heavily.

'You stink of bluddy booze an' all!' Lillian cowered down, holding her head and covering her face, hoping he wouldn't notice she'd wet herself.

'I bet Lisa was there! You're a bluddy idiot! I ain't listenin' to anything yer say, you're coming with me to Birmingham and that's it! Everything has a consequence. We're gowin, SOON!' he shouted in her face and left, unsure if he was happy with what he'd done, feeling sick and regretful as the red mist dispersed.

Oliver scratched his leg from under the table as he passed, hissing. Jeffrey grabbed him by the scruff of the neck and lifted him up. 'I'll bluddy kill ya!' the cat writhed, trying to free itself from the grip.

'Jeffrey! No! Please! Leave him!' Lillian screamed, shaking from the charge, covering her eyes. He dropped Oliver and walked off, fists clenched. Lillian waited, with her hands still over her eyes, her head throbbing. She got up slowly when she heard the lounge door slam, and unravelled the roll of kitchen paper, trying not to make a noise in case he came back. Tears filled her eyes, making it difficult to see; her stifled cries coming out in patchy whimpers. Oliver came creeping over to her, sniffing her and the floor. She held him and sobbed silently, massaging the back of his neck – amazed how he still managed to purr.

Everything bright had left, replaced by a nauseating atmosphere. She was fragile and empty, desperate for someone. Searching her buzzing head for a solution, needing her father and Robert - needing Phil's sordid offer that would beautifully fulfil her desire for Jeffrey's death. The house was like her kryptonite; powerful and confident outside of it, weak and bullied within it. Where could she put the pee-soaked paper? Jeffrey would be mad if he found it in the kitchen bin. She took it with her, carefully taking off her wet shoes and leaving them outside the back door.

Tip toeing upstairs to the bathroom, locking the bathroom door behind her, she slid down it and wept in her hands – screaming from her heart, feeling it would burst from its calling, feeling ashamed of everything. She cried herself to sleep where she was, numbed and wretched. Jeffrey woke her, knocking on the door.

'Lilly? Lilly? You in there? You done anything stupid?! Lilly? Look, I'm sorry. Lilly?' she got up, steading herself.

'Yes, I'm here. I need to shower. Just leave me alone, please.'

'I don't know what came over me. I just got angry with ya. I couldn't 'elp it. I'm sorry Lilly, please open the door!' She closed her eyes tight, fighting the feeling of pity for him.

'Please Jeffrey... just leave me. I need a shower.' Jeffrey laid his hand on the door trying to connect, wanting her comfort he sorely missed, feeling confused. Having no control over what he had done, knowing there was no way she was coming with him willingly. He'd blown it and there would have to be another plan.

'I'm sorry,' he whispered, his eyes glistening with emotion, leaving Oliver sat outside. Lillian took the soiled clothes in the shower with, rinsing them through. She crouched like a foetus, drifting off from the hypnotic tap of warm droplets falling on her back, cleansing the outside, but not the in. Washing herself in disgust, every movement hurt - whatever resided at Phil's had followed her home and wreaked its instructed havoc. Or was it that book? Afraid to leave the bathroom, she opened the door about two inches, checking the landing - holding her ear to the gap, hearing the TV and Jeffrey making nervous noises in his throat. She ran to the bedroom, clutching the towel tightly, Oliver following. Sobbing anxiously, she shook like a leaf, dressing in something fleecy, needing the cushion comfort on her goose bumped skin. Her head ached- she kept feeling it to see if her hair was still there, checking her hands for blood. Holding Oliver close, her tears fell into his fur, the light soul offering comfort and clarity. But she needed something else, something more.

Crawling on her hands and knees, she pulled the book out from under the bed - she would only look at the first page and then close it, that was all. The leather hardback smelt musty like the Honda. The cat settled next to her as she read the first page, skipping it then onto to next, looking further in to find something particular to her needs.

'Here you are,' she muttered. Holding up the mirror, she followed the instruction, opening the lines of communication, the colours brighter than she'd ever seen them. Her breaths became shorter, lighter intakes, her whole body entranced as she was pulled through its reflection.

Twenty-Five

Robert slumped in the greenbelt semi, the lounge furnished with bare essentials: a fashionable grey sofa, a little table for stuff, standard lamp in the corner and a sepia canvas print of New York City on the wall. He was tired, staring at the TV, coffee in one hand and remote in the other, surfing the cable channels. He'd spent the rest of the day working from home after the long journey back. A drive into the London Office tomorrow meant it was a stupid o'clock start. He could barely lift his arm to use the remote - closing his eyes, willing himself to go to bed. Drifting off into a twitchy sleep, Lillian's strange perfume woke him, forcing him to sit bolt upright in a daze. It was strong and danced around him, drawing him to the hallway.

'Lilly?' looking into his mug and tipping it down the sink of the cloakroom, 'that's enough of that,' he needed a hot soak to wash away the pressure.

Satisfied with the depth and temperature of the water, he got in, holding his breath as the hot water hit the sensitive parts, immersing himself up to his chin. He wiped his face and breathed out, thinking about his father as he rested on the bath pillow, closing his eyes and letting his mind bring forth its images and memories, reminiscing about her comments and wit - getting a flutter and squeeze in his stomach when he relived their conversations and the Honda moment. He wasn't like Lillian, just trusted his intuition, noticed it – few people do, theirs were off for whatever reason.

Robert held his nose and immersed himself for a few seconds, moving his head from side to side; his hair resembling seaweed. Coming up for air, releasing his breath like a blow whale, he laid back and played with the plug chain, wrapping it around his big toe and studying the engineered layout of it. Lillian came through again and he sat up, half getting out, listening with his eyes - sure he'd seen something flash by in his peripheral vision.

'You're going bloody mad Courtney!' he told himself, grabbing a towel off the rail – creeping to the bedroom, and looking around the generous space. Robert waited, he felt uneasy, there was something hanging around.

'Hello?' he whispered, questioning his own sanity. He quickly dried and put on a pair of boxers; checking out his physique in the mirror. His lavish lifestyle had been piling on the pounds, not looking as stealth as he was. He stood sideways, holding in his stomach, then letting it out again.

'Before, after. Before, after. Before...' stopping mid-flow, sure he caught sight of Lillian out the corner of his eye.

'Aaarrggh! What?!' he yelled, stumbling backwards. He could smell her again, sniffing around the room like a bloodhound.

'Lilly?!' he called out, walking cautiously towards the mirror and staring into it, was it moving? 'I think you've lost the plot, Courtney,' checking out his eyes as he pulled down the skin underneath them. He felt someone behind him, twisting – nearly cricking his neck, 'who's there?!' Holding onto the dresser, waiting for the intruder to come out of a hiding place.

'I have a gun! This is your final warning!' he said, gripping a can of deodorant. She came again, the smell burning his nostrils – he felt she needed him and could feel her urgency, but where was she? The top stair creaked, he ran to the landing and leaned over the banister.

'Hello?! Hellooooo?! Helen? It ain't funny now! You're freaking me out, you win!' He returned to the bedroom confused, sitting down heavily on the bed, guessing she was in trouble. Taking out his mobile from the trouser pocket he called Radar's reception, looking toward the mirror, he was sure he saw her, blinking, trying to clear his vision as the reflection darkened. An apparition of hands appeared on the inside, pressing against it - they were her hands; she still had that old watch on. Robert creeped over to it with his arm outstretched, looking away and squirming as he touched the cold surface. Then the rush came, hot, he looked round, just hands, but hands that were connecting, calling. Lillian could be felt like she was actually there. Robert grinned as her playful vibes came through, but there was an urgency there, too. He was mesmerised and struck with fear; his hair stood on end all over, sniggering at the sensations. Putting both hands on hers she washed over him, stinging his senses – she was in him, moving around in his head. He closed his eyes and swooned from her contact, taking him off somewhere else -somewhere we all long to go, away from the prison of our own minds. The mood changed quickly to desperation; tears appeared in his eyes from empathy. Robert grappled at the surface trying to get her out, trying to hold her. Why was this so familiar? He felt this before, searching his mind for the answer. 'Lilly? I don't know what to do!' An acute drowsiness began to take over and the hands retreated – the mirror resuming to its other purpose. He heard ringing, the mobile! The line was picked up, hearing the faint voice of the security guard. Robert hung up, soothed and drugged - yawning and rubbing his eyes. His body fell sideways, and he slept; having the worse and best dreams fused together, with a silly grin on his face.

**

Robert had woken a bit earlier than usual, he was restless and had to send Lillian an email after the night before, hoping she would answer him. Deciding to give the caffeine a miss today and work from home. Going into London was too much of an effort this morning. Lillian was in every fibre, his day was different and disturbed because she wouldn't let him forget her.

He rinsed yesterday's dishes while periodically looking up at the garden. The grass was getting long and dying but he didn't want to go in the shed, not if that big spider was still lurking above the door; threatening him with sudden movement - it gave him the eebie jeebies. It would be another slog on the laptop outside this time, where he could get some natural light, wires and extensions trailing everywhere - the squeaking of the modem could be heard a few houses down.

Most of the garden was on a slope, leaving the back quite shaded, ideal for computer work. Betty, the elderly neighbour, was hanging out her smalls and striped flannelette pillowcases, when she caught sight of Robert.

'Morning!' she called out and waved.

'Oh, great,' he muttered under his breath. 'Morning Betty. How are we on this fine day?'

'Ah you know, my bones ain't what they were, but can't complain. You on that thingy again? You'll have square eyes!' she chuckled.

'It pays the bills. Gotta be done. Helen might be popping into town later. Do you need anything?'

'Oh, now, let me think. Pegs. No, Fairy liquid. That's it. Fairy liquid, but only if it's no trouble.'

'No trouble. Fairy liquid. You got it,' Robert responded, not looking up while checking his emails for Lillian's response.

'How is Helen? Haven't seen her lately.'

'She's fine, thanks.'

'You know me, I use my front room as my look out, waiting for my Vera. I must have missed her. Well, this won't get the baby washed, must get on.'

'Ok Betty. I'll drop your fairy round later.'

'Thanks love. Such a good boy. Tell Helen to come and see me, I got those biscuits she likes.'

'Okay, I'll tell her. See you later.'

'My Vera is taking me out later. Bye Richard.' Robert raised his hand then rolled his eyes once she'd gone. Two hours into his work, he needed a break and went inside to make himself a coffee – he couldn't help it, the pressures of his new role and Phil needed the accompaniment of a stimulant; a liquid cigarette. He watched the percolating coffee drip and make ripples as it filled the glass jug, not feeling so good today. There was a funny atmosphere hanging around. He was desperate to call her, he could feel the pull of it, or maybe he just imagined the whole thing last night - too many late nights and screen work. There was a soft knock on the back door, shifting his thoughts; his five-year-old nephew, Michael, bursting through it.

'Uncle Robert!' running to him and wrapping his arms around his legs.

'Hey there little buddy! What's cooking?' ruffling the gangly child's blonde hair. His sister Helen, followed.

'Morning. Is that fresh coffee?' she asked. A slender woman with the same features as Robert; dark, shoulder length hair and very attractive.

'Well, ain't that funny – smelt it, did you?'

'Is there breakfast to go with it? We're starving!' she said and kissed him on the cheek.

'There's hard cheese and hard lines – be my guest. Batty Betty was asking after you.'

'I just waved to her in the window. She still waiting for invisible Vera?' he poured two mugs of coffee.

'Yeah. Poor old dear. Must be nice being batty though, I could live with that.'

Helen opened cupboards, searching for anything that passed as edible.

'Have you got any potatoes?' she asked, looking in the fridge.

'I think my potatoes have grown potatoes.'

She slammed the door and huffed.

'Robert, you need to sort your food situation out! What do you live on?' she said, hands on hips.

'Coffee, mostly.' Michael was being an aeroplane around the kitchen, with the other two having to dodge him.

'Right. Come on, we're going shopping for Uncle Robert,' putting her bag back over her shoulder.

'Yaayyy! Can we get a milkshake please?' asked the boy.

'Get me a Fairy liquid please sis. For batty Betty.'

'Shall we pop into the castle on the way back? Have some lunch in The Keep?' Helen suggested. Guildford boasted a Castle with Saxon roots, surrounded by beautiful grounds and a place to rest after your historic excursions.

'Bring lunch back here, I haven't exactly got time for gallivanting today. I'll cook.'

When Helen returned with bags laden with cupboard essentials, Robert took Betty's Fairy liquid round. She was sitting in the window, waiting for her Vera. Robert waved it in the air at her. At the door, she seemed a little bewildered.

'Well, this is a nice surprise, Richard.'

'It's Robert. One Fairy liquid for the finest lady in the street.'

'Oh, thank you. I've just run out. How did you know? Let me get you something.'

'No, no – its fine, my treat,' he insisted.

'I've got some biscuits for er...' She tapped her head with two fingers, hoping they would jog her memory. 'I got them especially. Oh dear, my old brain, it'll come to me, next week!' she laughed at herself.

'Come in, won't you. I just need to remember where I put them!' she called out as she disappeared into the back of the house. Robert walked in gingerly; her house was decorated the same way it was fifty years ago, smelling of churches and boiled washing. The loud, slow tick of the grandfather clock in the hallway caught his attention, he studied the clock face and pendulum, taking comfort in the silence of the rest of the house. He heard a noise in the front room, someone shifting, putting things away – he began backing out of the house to wait for the biscuits.

'Here they are,' Betty said as she came out with a packet of chocolate digestives.

'Thank you, Betty, that's kind. I didn't realise you had a guest. Sorry.'

'Guest? Oh, it's only my Vera. Bye Richard,' and she shut the door on him, leaving Robert bemused and slightly spooked. He looked back at the house as he made his way home, Betty was watching him out of the front window with an odd-looking woman stood behind her.

'Oh, for god's sake!' Helen scolded, retching as she emptied the fridge.

'Don't be such a baby –it's just a bit of mould,' Robert just heard her as he came in through the back door.

'What's mould?' asked Michael.

'It's green stuff that lives here with Uncle Robert on a regular basis!' the boy screwed up his face and wanted to see. 'Do I have to come here every week and do this?!' she shouted, pulling a face as she put perished food into bags with Michael curiously studying the tins and containers with a sheen of decay.

'You know you like it. Right. While you're doing that, I'll put some lunch on. What time have you got to get back?'

'Not for another hour or so. Michael's got a playdate.' Helen lived alone but the boy's father looked after them financially. It wasn't ideal, however it was better than trying to survive off the Government; not a good status to have in such an affluent town.

'A playdate? I see. Got a girlfriend, have you?' he asked Michael, nudging him.

'Don't dirty him please, Robert,' Helen protested, while she wiped her hands.

'Dirty him? Helen, you need to chill out. I had a girlfriend when I was four, I think. Everyone needs to love, Hel.' Helen just dismissed him and got her son's hands washed for lunch.

They all sat down to steak and a side salad, with a baguette; it was a regular thing on a Saturday.

'You okay? You seem... different, today,' Helen said.

'Do I?' Robert replied, buttering his half of the bread. 'I have a lot to get done, I'm preoccupied I suppose, and I had some really weird dreams last night. I felt like I haven't slept!'

'You got something to tell me?'

'Like what?'

'I dunno...something. Some'one' maybe?'

'Leave it. What's the steak like?'

'Ah! So, I'm right? Come on, spill the beans.'

'You just bought some.'

'Robert! Tell me!'

'Okay! Okay!...Lillian.'

Helen paused 'Lillian what?'

'Tate. That's all you're getting.'

'I knew it! What's she like?'

'Like no one I've ever met.'

'What's a Lilliantate?' asked Michael. Helen stopped eating and looked at her brother, he was serious for once, and he'd changed.

'Oh? In what way?'

'Do you remember my old Honda? She has it. I don't know how, but she has.'

Helen frowned.

'But how? That's...'

'Impossible? Not with Lilly it's not. I'm beginning to find out, anyway. I couldn't believe it when I saw the number plate! The same one! I thought I was seeing things!'

'That's weird on many levels. So, is it serious?'

'That's all you're getting.'

'Okay, fine! But you know I'll get it out of you later. We have to talk by the way.'

'No, Helen, we are not, no,' he shook his head in defiance, taking more salad out of the wooden bowl with his fingers.

'We have to.'

'Helen, please, I got a load on, don't say it.'

'We have to see mum.'

'Strike a light, she said it!' Robert threw down his cutlery.

'She needs us, please, think about it. Soon, Okay?'

'It's times like these I wish I drank and smoked!'

'Don't be such a sour puss! She must be lonely.'

'She lives about, twenty-seven minutes away, for Christ's sake! Sorry Michael. Why can't she come here? I got a spare room. What's the problem? There's these things called trains you know – they're very useful.' There was an awkward silence as they finished their lunch.

'I want to see Grandma! Can we go?' Michael asked as he bounced in his chair.

'Look. I got a big job on at the moment, and I haven't got any head space for mum. Why don't you go?' Robert said, vigorously chewing on steak.

'She won't be happy, you know that. Has to see her Robbie.'

Robert sighed and winced, 'can't believe she still calls me that. Haven't you had a word with her about it?!' Helen just looked up at him, waiting for an answer.

'Who's Robbie?' asked Michael, picking out the green leaves from his plate and leaving them on the table.

'Okay. Okay. Once this job is tied up and I get what I'm owed, we'll go. Promise.'

Robert cleaned up after them, daydreaming while he washed up, listening to the compilation album. Phil said he was needed in the London office, he still hadn't got a sensible answer as to why. The coming week would be the longest one to date – working and killing time until he was back in Wales. He played the drums on the worktop singing at the top of his voice, feeling euphoric as the tracks fed his feelings about her and reminded him of the fortune he was about to ensue; ignoring the angel prodding at his conscience.

When the ballads came on, Robert sat outside with another coffee, he was falling in love with her as the music sang their lyrics. Lillian made him feel like a child again… that petite figure and heart-shaped face – how did someone so small contain such an immense personality? Everything pushed its way through their boundaries and got serious in the blink of any eye. They fell quickly because they were each other; temporarily separated by life's lessons. He tried to work out what the hell that was all about last night, forcing him to perceive life a little differently today. Reminiscing about the Honda, the memories of his father came flooding back – everything had come full circle. Letting go of the Honda when he did was like throwing a boomerang; coming back and hitting him on the back of the head, bringing him Lillian and much more than he bargained for.

Twenty-Six

Lillian watched the kettle boiling in a melancholic mood, imagining screaming in Celia's face about her son and what a discredit he was. Then punching Jeffrey square in the jaw and the beautiful commotion that went with it. Leaving the house with bags packed, while Celia nursed and fussed over her son - a delicious and dark gratification. Her scalp was still hurting, wincing as she touched it, trying to feel what the damage was. The quick visit to Robert kept her heart pumping, she hadn't gone that far before in a while and couldn't wait to try and stay longer next time. That book was good.

She carried the coffee down the walkway and entered Phil's office, he pushed the coaster to the edge of the desk, like he always did.

'Are you okay today?' he asked. There was a little humility there, but not much. Lillian just nodded, handing him the envelope of cash. She held her head again, certain movements pulled on it. 'You have the power to stop whatever is holding you back, Lilly. Don't be afraid to use it.' He raised a smile, looking inside the envelope; fifty pound notes batched in one thousand.

'This has been opened,' he stated.

Lillian tucked her hair behind her ears. 'Uh, yeah. Sorry. Not me. It was taken, from my bag.'

'Don't go just yet, take a seat,' he took one batch, counting out five hundred pounds. 'Here. Go get the car done and buy some new shoes. Red.'

'Oh, no! I couldn't, thank you anyway.'

He gave that persuasive look again. Lillian took it gladly. 'Thank you. I...'

Phil held up his hand to pause her, 'no thank you needed. Have you read the book?' Lillian blushed.

'Um, yes, just quickly though. I haven't read it properly yet.'

'Is the suite booked?'

'Just waiting confirmation. I'm expecting a call later today.'

'Excellent.' He opened his top drawer and took out a flat, flimsy present; wrapped in black paper. 'This is for you,' sliding it across the table to her. Lillian regarding it suspiciously. Carefully tearing the paper and frowning as it revealed a black material. All the paper was off, she unravelled it, gasping – it was a black dress, *the* black dress from the window. Glory expanded Phil's face at Lillian's astonishment.

'Well, do you like it? It's your size. I want you to wear it to the function, with the red shoes.'

She held it up, feeling special. 'But how did you...?'

'Really Lilly? You're going to ask me that question? No strings, just wear it,' he returned to his laptop, which was her que to leave. Lillian went back to her desk with the dress screwed up in her hand, quickly stuffing it into her bag, shaking. She opened up her emails and immediately saw Robert's, marked urgent. Hot tears filled her eyes, she felt alone since last night because she couldn't tell her parents. But Phil just made her feel whole again. She waited for the crying to stop, not knowing what to write or where to start and not wanting to sound selfish or needy.

"Hey you. Wow! I think I got your FedEx thing last night! Although, I could be hallucinating from all the coffee! It scared me, to say the least, you'll have to warn me next time. I hope you're okay though. Just call me. RLC x"

She read it several times, getting a new feeling every time she did. It was the initials.

International Sales had been quiet this morning, she didn't like what she was picking up from Lisa either. It looked like she didn't get a taxi home and she couldn't bring herself to speak to her.

'You avoiding me, Lilly Lil?' Lisa called over. 'What are you doing on the weekend?'

'Nothing much. You?'

'Brian's away again. Shall we do something?' Lisa asked. Lillian wasn't sure, not wanting to be in her company; Lisa was affecting her nervous system.

'Okay. Fine.'

'Would the real Lillian Tate please step forward? You're actually leaving the house?!'

'I leave the house every day, and last night. What's your point?'

'You're coming to mine, no questions. Saturday. Eleven. Seems like something has finally given you some balls!' Lillian's stare was filled with malice, she held it, emanating instruction for Lisa to turn to her – she did, jolting at the colour of her eyes and the empty glare.

She was up early Saturday; fretting if Jeffrey would leave before Lisa arrived. She booked the Honda in for that respray, so Lisa had to pick her up, telling Jeffrey the money was from her parents. But he was onto her now, lying for fear of his reaction need not have been a concern.

'You still not talkin' to me then?' Jeffrey asked. Lillian shook her head.

'Right. I'm off, get this car done. I hope you're bluddy grateful.'

'Why wouldn't I be?'

'Yeah, well, I'm just sayin' – it ain't a beamer, that's all. You'll have to ask what's-his-face for one.'

Which 'what's his face' was Jeffrey referring to? She thought. Taking the keys off the hook, he murmured a 'see ya lata' as he left. She thought heavily about Robert while stirring her first cup of tea, smiling to herself, repeating everything he said in her head. She savoured the moment, daydreaming out the of kitchen window while observing the cemetery visitors laying their flowers, silent in their prayer and grief - a constant reminder, blatantly on view.

Oliver pushed his way through the small gap in the back door relieved he didn't have to go through that flap thing, which caught his tail every time. He sat, looking up at her, meowing persistently.

'Hey! Where have you been? What's up?' he jumped on the worktop and meowed again. 'I know, I know,' but she didn't, she never did – especially when all his needs were met. She tickled him under the chin, his favourite spot. They put their heads together, connecting – his illuminous soul bathing hers; a moment she didn't want to break.

'Phil bought me the black dress,' she told him. Their peace was disturbed by something hitting the window. 'Arrgghh! What was that?!'

A crow hung on the kitchen windowsill, looking in. They both watched and waited. It tapped the window again with its beak, seeming curious at first. Then again – harder, chipping the pane aggressively.

'Hey! Stop that!' She pulled the back door open, shrieking as she was confronted by it, perched on the railings. 'Good morning, Sir. Didn't I bury you already?' It gave her a *kaarr*! She stepped out, hoping it would fly away. It moved a fraction, raising its wings to balance itself, the sunlight catching the teal and copper sheens in its dense, black feathers.

The bold, black bird's presence was imposing and out of place. She studied the matt black beak and the way it looked at her with intelligence; the bird of death, the trickster.

'What do you want?! Shoo!' waving off the bird with a free hand, holding her cup in the other. It hopped to the left, giving her another *kaarr*! Its beady eye looking her up and down. Oliver was in the doorstep, arched and hissing. Lillian got a wash of dread, which dragged down to her feet. She knew this bird was a warning; a vivid and unmistakeable representative of one.

'Ok. I heard you. Thank you for breaking the window. Now, SHOO!' she shouted louder, getting closer to it. It took flight, but only to the end of the wall. 'Unbelievable!' They regarded each other for a moment. Remembering she was thinking about Robert before it came.

'No God, please, not him.' She grabbed the hosepipe, turning the tap on until it nearly popped off the fixture, spraying the bird 'Go!' It took flight, swooping over her head, making her duck and scream as the force of the take-off moved her hair. Landing on the roof, it pecked off the moss clumps in disgruntlement, throwing them down at her.

'Bugger off! I heard you, ok?!' Did she though? Her gift was powerful, but she only took notice when it suited her. It pushed its head forward and flapped, calling once again, *Kaarr*! *Kaarr*! *Kaarr*! - Happy with the deliverance, before flying off. Oliver crouched by the doorstep, keeping his distance, chattering to the bird as he watched it disappear over the rooftops. Lillian watched it leave, her heartrate accelerated. She sat on the end of the patio, deflated; her happies thwarted. The visit wasn't clear, but if she took it for what it was, she had to take heed. A precaution perhaps. Oliver joined her, rubbing his scent on her back before settling by her side. A blanket of grey cloud covered the sun and instantly cooled the air - she could feel the change approaching. The Oaks' leaves blew in hushed rustles, comforting her, giving insight. She gazed in awe at the enormous branches supplicating to the heavens. The Crow was a mere blot in comparison, but had a similar impact.

There was a 'toot-toot' out front, at exactly eleven. She quick stepped around the house to the white Audi.

'You look nice. Is Jeffers here?' she got in a buckled up.

'Thanks, no, he's taken Brutus for a makeover.'

'Is he paying?'

Lillian felt pressured to answer, 'it's paid for,' was her response.

'Christ! What happened to him? Find out about Robert, did he?'

'No. Well, not yet anyway. He knows I'm at Radar, I was clumsy with my lie, you know I'm no good at it. He's flipped his lid, thinks I'm packing up to go to Birmingham with him.' Lisa drove out of the crescent with most eyes on her, there weren't many cars around like that.

'Well, he's in for a shock. But then it's all his own doing.'

Lillian took pleasure in the drive to Lisa's. The countryside views on the way there made her feel proud of where she lived, the car smelling of money and a sensible life, one without worries.

'So, you and Robert keeping touch over the weekend? Or have you come to your senses?'

'I don't have a mobile, do I? He suggested calling the house, but I didn't think that was a good idea.'

'Well, it would have shifted things a bit quicker! He'll just have to buy you one then, won't he?' The gravel drive affirmed the prosperity as they arrived at the exquisite white, thatched cottage. No roses or wisteria over the door though; Lisa had modernised it somewhat. A solid oak door with a diamond-shaped window in the centre, big enough to put your face in. Two perfectly clipped box balls in terracotta pots either side, with tendered borders underneath the windows. Tucked away off a narrow lane you could just see the hint of other houses, concealed by their clipped shrubbery.

'Oh! It's beautiful Lisa! It's a far cry from the flat you were living in,' she shamefully felt envious.

'Not bad, is it? Come on, let's get you in.' Lisa opened the door; a thin black cat ran out and meowed impatiently.

'Hello! What's your name?' Lillian asked, trying to coax it back in.

'That's my Jet. Come on, come and see aunty Lilly!' The slinky cat followed them back in, mewing for attention.

'I've only been five minutes, you're such a baby!' Lillian followed her, while having a good look around. The smell of new carpet hit you first. With stairs to the left, an antique cabinet faced you, hosting a cream-coloured telephone and some gold framed pictures. The carpet was beige and thick under your feet. The furniture Oak tastefully decorated.

'Come through to the kitchen!' Lisa called out. The kitchen was also in Oak and large, with an island in the middle.

'Oh, Lisa, you have landed on your feet.'

'You think so? Thanks. Mia casa su casa. Now, Mateus, is it?'

'Yes please, not a big glass though.'

'Nonsense, I'm driving you back. Let your hair down a little. We're having steak.' Lisa opened the large American-style fridge. 'I think I owe you one of these, for being such an arse.'

'You're not an arse, well, maybe just a little one.'

Lisa poured the Mateus in what looked like a wine bowl.

'Whoa! Are you trying to kill me, or what? That's plenty!'

'Oh, don't be such a matron – here, just sip it. The steak will soak it up.' They chinked glasses. 'It looks like you're finally getting rid of that arsehole – what luck!' Lillian looked into her glass. It was an obvious step to take, but still a difficult one.

'Yeah, about that,' she hoicked herself up on a bar stool, positioned by the island.

'He's running from something since he found out about Radar. I don't know, there's something going on. He doesn't seem too keen on Robert's beamer either – what's that all about?' Lisa was heating the frying pan, her face getting hot from it and Lillian's question.

'He's just jealous. Saw something he couldn't give you, and didn't want anyone else making him look inadequate – the fact that he is, is besides the point. It's all about phallic competition at the end of the day.' Lillian felt sorry for him, hearing bad words spoken, even though she wanted to kill him frequently.

'Jeffrey won't change Lil – and what do you think he has to offer you in Birmingham? You're not thinking of going, are you?' Lillian took a sip of the Rose, secretly looking around the kitchen taking in the workmanship that must have cost the earth. The drink tasted much better than the one she buys, too.

'No, I'm not, but I made him think I was. I'll duck out at the last minute. But I need to disappear, he'll just come and cause a ruckus at Mum's.'

The steak sizzled loudly, and it was making Lillian feel ravenous.

'You can hide here. He'll never know where this place is. Think about it.' Lillian's sipping was increasing, making her feel woozy, racing into her bloodstream and numbing her frontal lobe. She held the glass up, studying the drink, suspicious of its potency.

'You sure this is Mateus?' Lisa placed a white bowl of peanuts on the counter.

'Steady on there, vicar – have some of these. Wait 'til you've eaten, that Mateus is going straight to your head!' Lisa felt slightly anxious, laughing nervously.

'What about Jet and Olly?' Lillian said, as she slid off the stool.

'You and that bloody cat! He's a weight around your neck!'

'Hey! Don't speak about My Olly like that. He's a part of me so comes with.'

'Well, one of them will establish a pecking order. They'll have to fight over Brian's chair.' They sat at a large kitchen table which overlooked the landscaped garden through large patio doors.

'This is great. It's so beautiful here, Lisa. I never socialised after we parted.'

'Me neither. I can't wait for you to meet Brian. He's such a lovely man. I'm grateful every day. Anyway...' she held up her glass 'here's to new beginnings Lil. Be careful when you go home. I worry about that man, he's unhinged.' They chinked glasses again, taking sips while their eyes were on each other. Lillian looked down at her plate; the food beautifully presented. She immediately started on the meat.

'I don't think he's jealous. He's stupid if he thinks I won't find out. He should know better than that.' Lillian devoured the meal. Lisa swallowed a bit too hard and nearly choked.

'Finish up and I'll show you the grounds.'

'Aren't you going to say anything about it? Don't you think it's odd?'

'What do you want me to say?' They ate in an awkward silence, Lillian longed to have a conversation with someone on her wavelength. She was tired of being the 'freak', because she wasn't that at all. She just got called it because people didn't understand, or want to understand. Generations and tribes had influenced their incapacity to accept, perceiving Lillian as someone to fear and avoid. Not willing to see past what they already knew that she was a gift. It was refreshing talking to Phil.

With satisfied bellies, Lisa took the plates and left them on the side of the sink, she would put them in the dishwasher later.

'There's pudding. Now or in a bit?' Lillian looked at her watch.

'Never mind about the time, well?'

'Now please. What is it?' Lisa went to the fridge and took out a large plate of strawberry gateaux.

'Oh! This is getting better by the minute! Did you make it?' Lisa gave her a look of distaste. 'Do I look like I faff about baking? Cream?' They ate the cake in bliss while talking about Radar- cream and sponge always breaks the ice.

'How are you finding Phil?' Lisa asked.

'He's not the same man. I've got used to him. He's been quite helpful, with things. But he still makes me feel nervous and I just do what he says, oddly enough. I have that problem, don't I?' Lisa didn't answer.

Something didn't feel right, it hadn't since she arrived at Radar, either. Lisa made patterns in the cream with her fork. 'He overhears, Lil – without even being there,' her voice was low, defeated. Lillian's stomach churned. Shame, she was enjoying that gateau.

'The garden looks amazing. How do you find time to do it?' Lillian quickly changed the subject, for fear of being heard.

'I'll take you around, if you like?' They took their glasses, casually strolling. The cottage garden portrayed everyone's idea of a blissful life. Lillian loved the informal design, one that would give Jeffrey a nervous tick. Posing goddesses leaned provocatively amongst the dense herbaceous borders. All that was missing, was Vivaldi. Lillian wanted to fall amongst the Delphiniums and never wake again. The beauty and heavenly scents withered the dark, forcing Lillian to rethink her rebellion, feeling guilty and ashamed that she chose it over what really bloomed within. Thinking perhaps that's why she was hurt, a subtle punishment and reminder. Lisa pulled a leaf from the red Acer they passed, tearing it apart and throwing the bits over her shoulder; she fiddled when she was anxious. Lillian winced at the disregard.

'I would be quite happy dying here. Must take up all your time.'

'We have a gardener.' Lisa responded. There was a silent moment at the society gap.

'Oh, nice. Is he dishy?' Lisa tutted and snorted.

'He's seventy years old! But he's very fit for his age. Like your dad. I suppose you could look pass the numbers. Be ideal for you Lil.'

'Ewww! – Nearly fifty years between us? It would be like dating my dad! But then again, I suppose I wouldn't mind that. At least he'd be happy with a sloppy sandwich for lunch.' Lisa held onto her arm and led her to the summerhouse. A white, wooden construction with Wisteria trailing over the front. Two wicker chairs with Laura Ashley cushions, and a matching, circular table, positioned for the best view. The sun was getting weak and a relief for everyone, including the plants, making sitting in it less suffocating.

'Summer didn't last long.' Lisa commented.

'This is such a wonderful life you have Lisa. What's the catch?' Lisa sighed and looked out to the view.

'I'm a lucky girl, aren't I? I got what I wanted. Funding all this has its downsides though. I'm alone most days and weekends. You know me, I'm reckless when I get bored. I let my hair down once in a while, then come scuttling back here when I get scared. It's nice being married to an older man, like you say, I'm looked after and appreciated. But sometimes, the age gap can be a bore. But I'm happy, I'm safe, well, when Brian is here, anyway.' Lillian admired the straight edges and carefully placed annuals, which sat away from the grass in consistent measurements. Alternate pinks and whites, with some purples and yellows; all doing their utmost to please.

'Does he know Phil comes here?'

'How did you know that? Oh, stupid question. No.' Lisa looked away. The high life that surrounded her had a nasty blemish. Lisa drank all the glass, nearly losing her breath as she gulped it down.

'He's my distraction from my lonely life. He comes here when he wants to assert his power, and I let him. Phil makes me feel something that, well, I've never felt before. It's addictive, and so sexy - it's what I crave. He frightens me, too.'

Lillian grimaced. 'Oh my God, Lisa – what are you doing?! I'm guessing you stayed the other night. I felt like a gooseberry at the table and what is it with that house?' she could see clearly what went on; something that she couldn't always avoid. Her gift had a tactless approach, like that of a child.

'I don't know what I'm doing!' Lisa cried desperately. 'I can't stop it, I can't! He's so hard to resist! There's something about him!' Lisa thought, sniffing, wiping tears from her face. She looked up, 'a Vampire! That's it, he's just like that!' she stated.

'Has he taken anything of yours?'

Lisa's eyes moved back and forth as she tried to digest Lillian's question. 'Uh, like what? What do you mean?'

'Something from you - hair, nails, clothing, photo? Have you noticed anything missing?' Lisa raised her eyebrows 'what the hell would he want with those?!'

Lillian looked pensive, quickly sobering. 'Oh, don't play the innocent with me, Lisa. God only knows how many times you've been to that house. Even a non-believer would feel uncomfortable in there.'

'I swear Lil, what do you mean?'

'Spells,' she said calmly, looking back at the chocolate box house.

'Spells... spells?!' Lisa's body was taut and upright. 'Oh God,' she held her chest and tried to swallow the bile that reached her throat.

'He goes upstairs to use the toilet; he prefers that one to the one downstairs. Oh shit, you don't mean...?'

Lillian saw the spell in Lisa's face. A fleeting image, rippling like a mirage - unwilling to give itself away. Another face appeared over Lisa's; scared and confrontational. Not human, but something trying to copy one, copy her. Lillian's innards stung when she saw it, her hair standing on end. There was a sudden change in atmosphere, it became heavy, charged. She looked at the flowers trying to grapple at something divine.

'Have you been feeling off-colour lately? I noticed you're picking at your food.'

'Well, no or sleeping very well. I wake up suddenly, thinking someone is there, not when Brian's here though. Oh my God, I feel sick. How do I get rid of it?'

'You can't. He either has to die or you need to break all ties, or burn what he has of yours. You're unprotected. I'm worried about you,' Lillian replied, quite matter of fact.

'Christ! Is this real? I mean,' her eyes darted again 'can someone do that?' Lillian felt the teasing of the spell pressing at her darkness, aroused by its presence. It tried to convince her to let it stay, if she did, then it would serve her too, having an abundance of specialities that would enhance her life. If she didn't, there would be a consequence. The presence of spells was something she picked up on, they had a special feeling, threatening and with an awareness of dread. But something else whispered to her, the one that was always looking out for her.

'Yes. It's real and easy to do, once you know how to 'see'.' Lillian finger quoted the word, unintentionally grinning provocatively.

'Why are you looking like that? You're scaring me, Lil. Please, do something, I know you can, please!' Lisa pleaded, dropping to her knees. The thud of Lisa's bones on the wooden floor snapped Lillian out of the seduction.

'I need my water, to help you.' She suddenly felt tired, her energies were being used.

'But you, you've got a gift! It can't touch you!'

'I'm like an open vessel because of my bloody gift!'

'I wish I had what you had Lil, don't knock it. Must be amazing seeing the unseen and knowing everything that goes on,' Lisa knelt by Lillian's feet.

'Don't wish that on yourself, Lisa. Believe me, it has its perks but also its downfalls. Right, we need to get you some of Mum's water. But it's at home. Come then make a quick dash for it.' Lisa agreed.

They arrived at Coed-y-Ffrind Close; it looked a little dowdy in comparison. Lisa's conscience was playing havoc with her, making her feel worse, feeling ill. He was listening, always, listening. Both of them burst through the back door, panting.

'Do you think Jeffrey's here?' Lisa whispered. Huddled together, they walked cautiously into the kitchen.

'Wait here, it's upstairs.' She left Lisa looking around their small kitchen - all plastic and white, she hated new houses. Oliver came through the back door swaying his tail. He jumped when he realised Lisa was standing there, arching his back and hissing at her.

'What is it, Olly? It's me, Aunty Lisa,' she bent down, clicking her fingers at him. He hissed again and hid under the table. She tutted 'what's up with you?' She opened some drawers to pass the time, having a good look through the junk drawer.

Lillian returned, unscrewing a bottle and shaking the droplets out into her palm. Lisa stood by her side her hands cupped, waiting for the cure like a disciple at the feet of Jesus. Lisa looked on, watching her every move. She wiped over her head with both hands, barely touching her hair, the back of the neck then round to the chest, doing the same to Lisa.

'Thank you. What do you say?'

'Something to seal the protection. You'll be ok for a while, but you must repeat it. I'm not sure how long it will last. Close it. Time for *you* to grow some balls. Here, take it with you, but I need it back tomorrow.' Lillian's eyes seemed to sparkle, her complexion rosy. Lisa often imagined her sat on top of an Amanita contemplating the stars.

'I love you, Lil. That was lucky you came today.'

Lillian was a little sceptical. 'Nothing to do with luck. You'd better go before Jeffers gets here. If he sees you, I'm not sure I'll survive the night.'

'Don't say that Lil!'

Lillian smiled affectionately at her. 'Go on, you'll be all right. When's Brian back home?' Lisa had lost all recollection of anything that happened before today.

'I'm not sure, Friday night, I think.'

Lillian led her out, 'go home, have a bath and get some rest. You'll probably be feeling hungry later, too,' they walked to the Audi, Lisa fumbling with her keys.

'What do I do if he comes back?'

'That's up to you. Now, be off with you and thank you for a lovely lunch.'

'Thanks Lil. I hope the Honda is all you expected. You need a new model, really. Oh, and don't get your hopes built on Robert. Just a feeling,' the window went up, and she drove off. Lillian waved until she left, glad to be rid of her; the performance deserved an Oscar.

Twenty-Seven

'Was 'appened to the bluddy winda? Them bluddy kids throwing stones, I bet! Little blighters. They 'ad summat to do with them drains an awl!' he swept Lillian's crumbs off the worktop into his hands, brushing them off in the sink. 'You excited today then?' Jeffrey asked. Lillian shrugged her shoulders.

'Still mad with me, are ya?' she ignored him and sat outside. Oliver was fussing around her and insisted on jumping up.

'You just had to ruin it, didn't ya?' Jeffrey said as he made his own drink. Lillian just drank, burning the view with her anger-filled stare. Humiliated, worthless, scared, stuck, self-blaming, wrong and guilty – all flying around in circles, hitting her as they passed. She wasn't sure how she felt, the mental abuse was something she had got used to, expecting nothing physical, even though the threat of it lay dormant.

'Aide will be here soon, drop off yer car. Be about an hour. You'd better change yer mood – you got a face like a smacked arse!' Lillian closed her eyes as tears rolled down her face; it had given her another golden ticket, one she wasn't bypassing this time. The phone rang and she didn't want to answer it – if it was Rose that would set her off crying.

'I'm not here!' she called out. Jeffrey came out to the patio.

'They hung up. Why ain't you speaking to anyone?' Lillian flicked debris off the garden table, turning her attention to Oliver.

Adrian arrived an hour late. He drove the Honda down the drive where Jeffrey had left a space for it. Lillian stood there, with more tears as she looked at her and Robert's car, gleaming a beautiful, metallic blue. It stood proud this time, overlooking its view. She was sure Brutus was smiling.

'Oh, my goodness! That is just perfect! Thank you!' afraid to touch it in case it was still wet.

'Not too bad, is it? You can touch her, she's dry.'

'It's a He,' Lillian corrected.

'Fair enough. I think the white would have been better with the interior, but blue is as good.' He opened the doors to show Lillian he had sprayed all the sills and inside the doors.

'This is a fantastic job, Adrian. I love it. Thank you,' she walked around, running her hand along the glass-like paint work, all the dents and flaws had gone; missing them. But the old Brutus was still underneath.

Jeffrey stood with his arms folded, 'don't get bluddy scratchin' it!' they ignored him. Adrian watched Lillian appreciating his work, an unlikely reaction from a female. He found it attractive, it meant there was tom boy in there somewhere.

'Right. I'm glad you like it, Lilly. You taking me back then, mate?' he asked Jeffrey.

'Yeah. Just give me a mo. I'll change me shoes.'

'This has cheered me up no end. I can't believe my eyes. I suppose I had another vision of it.'

'She took the paint well considering the state of her. He, sorry. So, what have you got planned for the rest of the day?'

'My parents for Sunday lunch. How about you?'

'I've got other jobs to do then I'll have to take the dogs out.'

'Where do you take them?' she asked.

'Oh, just over the fields at the back of us. Twice a day usually.'

'They keep you fit then.'

'Yeah. Must be hard being out of work. You, uh, found anything yet?'

'Didn't Jeffrey say? I've got a new job.'

'Oh, right. Good. Where?'

'You'll have to join us for lunch one Sunday Adrian, as a thank you. It'll be the best lunch you've ever had, I'm sure.'

'Thanks. I'll hold you to that.'

'Hold ya to what?' Jeffrey asked as he came out.

'Lilly just invited me for lunch,' Adrian answered smugly.

'That's more than I get. C'mon. Stuff to do. See ya lata and don't scratch it, got it?' Lillian just nodded, with a stern expression. Jeffrey had become the most hated person in her life, and the thought of killing him, was becoming a daily thought. How she would do it, and would she be clever enough to get away with it. It was available to her if she wanted.

The men left, Adrian taking one last look at Lillian, who was looking back at him. When they were out of sight, Lillian kissed the Honda.

'You wait til Robert sees you!'

Dinner wasn't what it usually was, bright and beautiful. It was a little strained. The Honda seemed the only topic of conversation, not telling them about the money or Robert. Lillian didn't mention the incident either, unsure if she could cope with their reaction. She already felt degraded, any other blame would have been detrimental. The book was calling, and the mirror. She was restless, wanting to get back. Leaving Martin and Rose, feeling bereft at the loss of her cocoon, she knew it was time to walk through a bit of hell on her own, she'd been avoiding it for long enough. Her nervous system wasn't quite ready for it, but it was so close, she could feel it in her mouth. Repeating Phil's words in her head, gave her encouragement. Jeffrey was home when she got back, but she no longer dreaded going in and there was an imminent change hanging around. She walked in through the back door, throwing her keys on the worktop instead of hanging them up.

'So, do you like your newish car then?'

'Yes,' she answered, looking for Oliver.

'That all yer got to say?'

'Yes.' Lillian went to the bedroom, getting the book out from under the bed while Jeffrey ate supper alone. She held up the mirror, the reflection was dulling. The little bit left was still enough to make contact, and receive her messages. She was angry, hurt – making the connection a good one. There was something attached to her negative feelings, overbearing and in control. Her third eye seeing nothing but black and red. She entered into the gap between the mirror and the next reflection, setting off panic. It hadn't happened before. Her ability had changed – it seemed she could choose which exit she made. She saw Robert in his hotel room, her parents' house and Michael's bathroom and another place. Dark. Feeling delighted and horrified. Pondering over her choice. When she eventually came downstairs, she needed something sweet to replenish her energy. It was late. Jeffrey entered in the kitchen, scuffing his feet.

'Look. We need to talk.' She hated it when he said that, when *anyone* said that.

'About what?' her back turned, putting four sugars in her tea while eating chocolate biscuits.

'Birmingham.'

'What about it?' she answered.

'We're going, soon.'

'*We* are not going. You are!'

'I thought you said you were packing up yer stuff?'

'That was before you dragged me in here by my hair!' she inhaled, holding back her tears.

'I said I was sorry, it's forgotten now, let's move on from that, you made me angry!'

The security light came on and he shifted his glance from her. 'You brought it on yerself. We're leaving, soon!' The light came on again and the distraction was starting to annoy him - it was Oliver setting it off, tip toeing at the foot of the garden.

'Anyways. We gotta new life to look forward to and…' the light went on again. Pushing Lillian aside to look out the window.

'What the bluddy 'ell?!' Jeffrey shouted, making Lillian drop her cup, smashing as it hit the floor. He stood still for a moment with a look of terror on his face. He scrabbled at the door handle. Lillian looked out into the garden and saw Jeffrey running down to the trees, searching between them. She watched him pace back and forth, stretching to look over the wire fence into the cemetery.

'What is it?'

'Did you see it?!' Jeffrey was coming back up the garden.

'See what?' Lillian looked out to the trees; she had goose bumps and rubbed her arms to stable them.

'It was black and big. Like that…' Jeffrey tried to represent its size by stretching out his arms. 'Bluddy thing stopped by the kitchen window then went across there, and disappeared!' Jeffrey pointed towards the trees.

'Black? What, like a cat?' Lillian said, humouring him.

'No! Not like a bluddy cat! It was bigger than that!' Jeffrey snubbed.

'A bird then, Crow.'

'A Crow? In the dark? Don't be so stupid! It was just black, thick! - I'm going round the neighbours, see if they saw anything.' Lillian watched Jeffrey as he searched his practical mind. She took intense pleasure watching a sceptic squirm in front of unquestionable evidence. 'I bet it's them bluddy kids! Clean up the tea and I'll be back inna minnit.'

With that Jeffrey left, leaving Lillian stood on the patio looking back out to the trees. They swayed in the dark, their leaves whispering to her - she waited, moving her eyes from left to right; shifting her gaze to look at the stars adoringly - they were still there if needed. She went back inside to mop up, checking the garden from the window. Jeffrey came back, out of breath.

'Nobody saw anythin. They think I'm mad, don't they? If it's them bluddy kids, I'll 'ave their guts for garters! You 'ear me!?' he called out into the night. He was disappointed and Lillian could see he was uneasy.

'I think you've just seen your own demon,' she said calmly.

'My what?! Rubbish, I know what I saw, there must be some....'

'What? Rational explanation?' she had regained a new position in their relationship; one that had taken back power.

'Do y'know what? I think that had something to do with you out there.' Lillian frowned and handed him his tea.

'I don't know what you're talking about,' Jeffrey's hands were shaking as he cradled the mug.

'Yes, you bluddy do! You been upstairs too long!'

'I've been upstairs, to get away from you!'

'Why? What 'ave I done? I got yer bluddy car resprayed. Ungrateful little bi...' he stopped, her look was contaminated, the colour of it. Jeffrey closed his eyes as the thought of the vision in the garden made him shiver. He put his mug down and looked at Lillian with his arms folded. She was silent, sipping...expressionless. He blamed himself for the change in her; she'd hardened since the other night. What had he done? There was probably no recovering from it, the moment he feared. He went back out not willing to be defeated or made a fool of – walking back down to the fence. There was movement in the grass behind it. He was looking for human figures because that's all his practical, closed mind knew. Stomping back up the path, the light went out, waving his arms around to set it off again, but the sensor wasn't picking him up. Lillian stood on the patio, shrouded by the kitchen light. Then, she saw it, behind him,

'*Jeffrey*!' it whispered sharply, making him turn around.

'Who's that? That you bluddy kids?! Ay? Think yer funny do ya?! I'll wring ya bluddy necks when I get 'old of ya!' the security light clicked back on, illuminating the garden and illuminating, Bal; towering above him – the fear of death in its face and empty, silver eyes, stopping Jeffrey's heart and blocking out life in a split second as it sucked in everything around it. He tripped as he turned and ran to the house on all fours, briefly seeing his breath in front of him.

'Get in! Get in!' he shouted, but Lillian didn't move; her stare focussed, concentrating. He got to her, and side tackled her into the house, they fell in the door in a heap. Jeffrey scrabbled and shut the back door, locking it, sitting with his back against it 'stay down!' Lillian propped herself up; her hip feeling numb from the fall and Jeffrey's weight.

'Jesus!' he said breathlessly, his heart straining to keep up - Lillian could see his t-shirt moving from its effort.

'Did you see it? Did you bluddy see it?! What in God's name was it? Summat to do with you?! Ay!?'

'Why would it have anything to do with me? And since when do you speak of God?' she asked calmly, her tone unsympathetic.

'What d'ya mean?' he answered, still panting and shaking with fear. 'I don't know what yer sayin. I'm sorry! Okay?! I'm really sorry! It wasn't your fault! It was mine! I just don't know how to 'andle things!' Jeffrey stifled a cry, running his hands back and forth over his head; eyes wide, almost popping out of their sockets.

'You been doing it again? Haven't ya! Ay?! You just can't leave things alone! Always bluddy meddlin!' Jeffrey started rocking back and forth, hugging his bent legs.

'I'm just trying to protect ya!' he began to sob, Lillian looking on as she watched him shrink.

'Protect me from what? It's you I need protecting from!'

'I ain't sayin no more. You got no choice, you're coming with me. You, you 'ave to! Y'see?!' He was a snivelling wreck, and it was starting to upset her.

'You really need to calm down Jeffrey!' He reached above him to get his tea and winced as he drank it, it was stone cold - welling up again.

'I'm sorry. I never meant to hurt ya. I hate meself for what I've done,' he grabbed the edge of the worktop and pulled himself up; his legs weak, he was shaken to his core. Washing his face in the sink, he slowly slipped back into Jeffrey. Lillian felt pained and regretful as well as feeling foolish for wanting to comfort him. He searched the fridge for her Mateus, then the cupboards for any brain-numbing medication.

'You got anything? Calm me nerves? Is that why you drink, cos you can see em?'

'One sec,' she went upstairs and got her bottle of mixed oils. Jeffrey's colour had completely drained from him; Bal repeating its appearance in his mind's eye. Lillian returned with her bottle of women's therapy, the scent alone would help.

'What are they? Jesus! Is it that old man, I upset in number thirty? He was a miserable old bugger.'

'Give me your hands,' she asked him, he obliged. Lillian tipped some oil into his palms, 'rub them together and spread it over your head and back of your neck,' he did what he was told, closing his eyes as the pungent scent comforted him. She watched, he was just a lost human being that needed the love of a mother and a purpose.

'How does that feel?'

'Yeah, better. What is that stuff?'

'Just some plants, all crushed together to release their magic, that's all.'

'It ain't coming back, is it?' he asked, feeling fulfilled from her affection.

'You should sleep well now,' his lifeless eyes opened up, revealing a broken man.

'I don't deserve ya. I'm sorry. That's all I can say. But you just gotta listen to me!' He insisted, yawning, his body slumping.

'You'd better go to bed before you end up sleeping here.' Jeffrey agreed and trudged upstairs. The oil worked quickly, he was tired, but his body was still reeling, his mind racing – having visions of never sleeping again.

The house fell silent; all that was pent up had been released and dispersed. Lillian's chest felt light with new strength, new blood. Pressures had subsided, her heart pumped with ease. She tidied up in the kitchen, no folding or wiping this time. Oliver came back in and sat in the window, just checking - the extreme tip of his tail moving lazily. The opening had arrived, its door wide, with a treacherous space that lie beyond.

Twenty-Eight

Robert rushed to the beamer with a piece of toast in his mouth, throwing his briefcase on the passenger seat. His car phone was ringing as he buckled up, adding to the stress.

'Robert Courtney!' he announced, looking both ways before leaving the drive, leaning forward so he could see past the parked cars.

'I've been calling for the past hour!' Came Phil's stern voice over the speakers.

'I got up late, I've been up most of the night, working for you!'

'Good. Is it done?'

'Patience. I'm on my way to you. Couple of hours or so, hopefully.'

'Come straight to me before you talk to anyone else.'

'Affirmative,' and he hung up. He did have plans to go to the London Office, but making the journey to Wales was his priority this morning; seeing Lillian was all he was thinking about.

She typed requests via email to Italy and France, trying to keep to the broken English she used to type to Munich; her stomach full of butterflies.

'You're quiet Lilly. How was your weekend?' Lisa asked.

Lillian looked up 'eventful.'

'Oh. Don't tell me, Jeffrey wasn't happy about you going out with me.'

'Something like that. It's all escalated quicker than I thought. I got the Honda sprayed though.'

'Great. Still going to Birmingham, is he?'

'So it would seem. Did Brian get back ok?'

'He did, tired and exhausted like usual. Poor love. I think it's all getting a bit too much for him. Do you fancy lunching today?'

Lillian wanted lunch with Robert. 'Uh... nah, not today, thanks. I'm going out with Robert.'

'Oh, I see. Dumping me for another is it?' Lisa said and winked, 'well, if that doesn't happen, let me know and we can go somewhere different. I'm worried about you today.'

'Thanks. No need to worry. It's all good. How are you feeling now?'

'Amazing. That stuff you gave me really worked! I slept like a log!' Lisa could feel her friend was a little frosty. She tugged at her pearl necklace; her worry beads.

'Did you remember to bring it back?' Lillian asked but knew she hadn't.

'Oh damn! I forgot. You know what my head is like.' Lisa pulled herself along by her feet on her wheeled chair to Lillian's desk. 'You need to sort out your current situ before you jump into another,' she whispered, making Lillian bristle. Lisa had slipped back into that old record again; like Saturday never happened.

'I want to show Robert the car.'

'I don't think he'll be that interested, no offence.'

'You're wrong. My Honda, used to belong to him.' Lillian answered as she typed.

'That's bullshit Lil, and you know it! He's full of shit, I told you that.'

'Actually, he's not.'

'Believe him, or want to believe him? Jesus Lil, haven't you been listening?' Lillian stopped typing and looked Lisa in the eye.

'Shouldn't you be telling yourself all of this?' Lisa sat up straight, her neck and chest flushed with red patches, her expression as blank as a porcelain doll.

'What's that supposed to mean?'

'Just because I don't react the way you do, doesn't make me defective. I know what I'm doing and the least you can do is give me some credit.'

Lisa was gobsmacked, losing her control. 'What the hell happened to you?!'

'I found Lilly,' she stood, taking a pile of papers off the desk, 'and I gave you tap water.'

Robert arrived at Radar, after an agonising journey along the M25. Driving to the end of the car park, the stress of the drive was lifted when he saw the Honda. He parked a couple of spaces away, walking over and admiring the flawless work, nodding with appreciation with moist eyes - transported back to his late teens. He couldn't wait to see Lillian now, if a little nervous. Bleeping the beamer, he walked up to reception, taking a few more glances back at the Honda.

'Good morning, sir,' the security guard said and tilted his hat.

'Morning. Haven't been called that in a while. It's always a good feeling to come here.'

'That's cos you're in Wales, sir,' the guard responded.

'I'm beginning to believe that.'

'You had a tough journey? – Londoner, by the sounds?'

'Not quite, Surrey. I'm still a southerner here I guess, whichever way you look at it.' Robert signed himself in with a stressful scribble, taking his temporary badge from the receptionist.

'Cheers. Any ideas when I get one of these for real?' he asked, holding up the badge.

'You're still classed as a visitor at the moment Mr. Courtney. There seems to be a restriction on your access.'

Robert frowned. 'Oh? I'm officially employed here, can you get it checked out please?'

'Of course. I will get onto our facilities department straight away for you,' the receptionist answered, with an 'attention to detail' promise.

'That's great. Thanks, I appreciate it. I'd like to spend more time here.'

'It'll be the making of you! All this fresh air!' the guard called after him.

'You're not wrong!' Robert replied as he made his way up the stairs, his stomach squirming.

He panicked when he got passed the oak door, deflated when he couldn't see Lillian. But at least he could prepare himself instead of saying something goofy, going straight to Phil's office with two coffees. Lillian was distributing orders downstairs when she felt Robert arrive; her mood immediately changing, wanting to run and cry to him. Hearing those internal voices again 'you don't need a man to complete you' she did, and that was that. Why were they called 'other halves' otherwise? She called in to see Pam before going upstairs, she'd been going there regularly. Pam was her Rose substitute, the one she could tell everything to.

'Hey Lilly. What's going up on in the lap of the Gods?'

'Oh, you know, everyone is getting cranky to meet deadlines.'

'Do you know what I do with deadlines? I watch them fly over my head and land in that basket,' she chuckled, Lillian too. 'I need a nice young man to help me with the post. Don't know of any, do you?' Lillian immediately thought of Dave. Although he would need a personality transplant first.

She quite bravely knocked on the glass panel to Phil's office, forming her hand into a cup, gesturing a drink to them both. Robert grinned with delight, she was radiant in his presence, and he nearly giggled from the love rush. His whole body relaxed from the affirmation he needed.

Making the coffee, going against her own wishes, she just wanted to make one for Robert, feeling the tension when she entered the office - she avoided eye contact with Phil. He said nothing, but his thoughts were radiating, looking at the other two as the sparks flew and ricocheted off each other. Robert discretely held his breath so he couldn't smell her perfume, it would be the trigger to his inhibitions and long await to see her. The purple dress she had on complemented her skin and portrayed her catharsis. Phil was stood with his hands in his pockets; her scent was his way in, a brief visit, one he was getting addicted to. Her gift colourful and child-like.

'We can't afford any distractions!' he sat down, tasting his drink.

'What?' Robert answered, with a look of innocence.

'Just keep your eye on the ball!'

'I can multitask and it's none of your business.'

'It is my business when our necks are on the line!' Phil said, banging the table with his fist.

'O ye of little faith,' Robert answered, 'what's spooked you?'

'Nothing,' Phil adjusted himself and looked out the window.

'I'm in by the way, it wasn't easy, but I'm in.' Phil grinned and looked to the ceiling in gratitude, praising himself.

'I'm sorry I doubted you, Robert Courtney. I congratulate you.'

'Apology accepted,' he slurped. 'Lay off Lilly.'

'Oh, serious, is it?' Phil answered.

'What does it matter? You need her on your side, wouldn't you say? Treating her the way you do doesn't gain trust and I don't like it. What's with the coffee regime?' Phil was amused by Robert's protection over her.

'You're losing focus, Courtney.' He was hard to 'read', his beliefs weren't strong enough to pick up on anything.

'I've finalised the quote with the info I had, so we're good to go.' The atmosphere changed as the two men regarded one another with mistrust. Phil lowered his malicious gaze, deadpan in his response.

'Show me what you've got.'

Twenty-Nine

Lillian checked her watch every twenty minutes, waiting for lunch. The affection void was getting bigger, and she needed it filled. She tidied up her desk drawers and pen holder, unable to focus on the serious stuff. The Apex tender was almost ready.

Robert was busy, totally focussed on his screen, eating an apple, his facial muscles having a workout. She was covertly watching him bite down on the fruit with her hand up to her mouth, manipulating her bottom lip. He took a break to flex his fingers and arch his back, about to fill up on more caffeine – when he looked up, Lillian was looking at him, holding a provocative glance over the partition. It made him jolt in surprise, a little scared. He affectionately raised his head to acknowledge her, but she didn't move. He hadn't noticed her shaped eyebrows and long eyelashes before; the universe in her eyes, like an enhanced close-up.

The centre of his soul was being pulled towards her- shutting everyone and everything else out, it was just the two of them. His breathing becoming heavy as the rush of endorphins pressed on his lungs, unable to move from an invisible hold. He was silently panicking, but surrendering to the erotic trance. Thoughts entered his head, raising his temperature. It was like a trip from a rare and expensive drug; full of deep reds and magenta with images that held his attention.

Tim Smith was watching him with interest while he chewed on his ham sandwich. He leaned over his desk to see what he was fixated on, but everyone was busy, heads down, even Lillian.

'Earth calling Robert, come in Robert,' Tim said into cupped hands. Lillian broke off the connection with a smug look on her face as she casually made a call to St. Helier. Her gift had resurfaced, tenfold - all it needed was love, encouragement and a little bit of darkness to flourish.

'Huh? What?' Robert said, as he felt himself being thrown back into his chair, looking round at Tim.

'You were proper gone then, mucker. Was it sunny there?'

Robert undone his top button and loosened his tie, 'uh, yeah. One ten in the shade.' He laughed nervously.

'You wanna slow down a bit. It ain't worth it. Cut the coffee out before you give yerself a bloody 'art attack!' Tim laughed, his belly jerking up and down.

'Good advice, thanks.' Robert tried to focus on the keyboard, concentrating on acting normal, whatever that was. A cup of water was placed on his desk by Lillian.

'You look like you need one,' she said, with a glowing presence.

'Thank you,' he drank it in one.

'You look positively gorgeous today, Lilly,' Tim Smith commented.

'Why thank you Tim. You're off to Rome soon, I hear?' Robert was looking up at her, the secret between them was exquisite, stripping off a layer. His primitive instinct ignited the fierce need to protect her.

'Right then. We fit to go?' he asked, needing to leave so he could at least brush passed her skin, and that would suffice.

'Watch him,' Tim said, 'have to keep yer eye on these young lads,' he added.

Lillian giggled. 'I will. Thanks Tim.' He ogled Lillian's behind as they left, amusing himself.

It was an awkward, charged walk to the door, until they got to the landing.

'Was that real?!' he whispered, exasperated. 'I saw things!'

'I needed to open you up a little.'

'Open me up?! For what?'

'I'm taking you out, in the Honda,' Lillian discouraged.

'I've seen it already. Bloody good paint job. Who did it?'

'Oh, spoil sport! I wanted to surprise you. Still, it sticks out for other reasons now I suppose. Yeah, I'm really pleased with it.'

Robert was finding it almost impossible to control his feelings as they walked together, the overwhelming need to hold her was making his arms twitch.

Brutus stank of new paint and body-filler. Robert had a good look around.

'At least it doesn't smell like wet socks anymore. They've even done inside the doors. Impressive job, Lil. Who did it?' he asked again. Lillian started it up and she was taking them to the woods.

'I missed you the other night - I nearly got sucked into another dimension at Phil's!' Robert swung round to face her. 'You were at *Phil's*?'

'Yeah, you know, for dinner. Why didn't you come?' he closed his eyes despairingly, curling his fingers into angry fists.

'I didn't know there was one! Sneaky bastard!' They brooded, looking in different directions. 'So, where you taking me?' At first, he was trying so hard to be civil, being trapped in a small space with her was all he could stand. But the reveal of Phil's intentions, doused it all.

'You'll have to wait and see.' This would be the test, to see if he was a tree person or not.

'Look, Lilly. What happened on the weekend was...the FedEx thing.'

'A great alternative to FedEx, don't you think? You're very receptive.'

'You scared the hell outta me! How do you do that?'

'Sorry, it wasn't meant to scare you. I just had to reach out to you, I needed the connection. It was selfish of me.'

'Lilly, I'm just an ordinary guy. This stuff is way over my head. I'm not sure what it is you do, but curiosity is gonna kill this cat that's for sure.'

'I mean you no harm Robert. I'm sorry, I was impatient. Forgive me.' Their blood was thickening as their hearts pumped furiously from giddy attraction.

'And that, in the office just now? My God. I have no words,' he waved his hands in a dismissive manner. Lillian grinned wickedly; her halo was a little crooked today. She read how to do it from the book.

'You've brought my gift back. That was nothing.'

'Were you hurt, Lilly?' Robert asked with a serious tone. Those words flicked the cap off the volcano and Lillian couldn't hold onto her emotion any longer. She burst into tears, because all she wanted was for him to rescue her out of it.

'Hey, hey – you would cry when I haven't got a tissue,' he said gently, handing her the shammy leather he found in the glove box. 'This is all I got, don't judge me.'

She took it and laughed through her convulsions.

'Take your time, okay? You'd better pull over,' she shook her head, determined to get to the woods.

'Is it your husband?'

She stopped crying instantly. 'He's not my husband! Why does everyone think he's my husband?!'

'Well, that's a relief! Makes things less complicated!' he was immensely relived, much more than he realised.

'Are you trying to get information out of me, Robert Courtney?' Lillian sniffed, taking in little breaths.

'Is it that obvious? I must be losing my touch.'

'Please don't ask me right now, that's why I contacted you.'

'You should have hung around a little longer.' The static in the car was building, but Lillian was determined to hold onto her dignity, for the time being. She had to see his reaction when he saw the trees as well as what they had to say about him.

The tyres crunched the gravel when they arrived. Lillian was looking at his reaction from the corner of her eye; he craned his neck to look up.

'Whoa! You wouldn't think this was tucked away here, would you?' he got out and admired where he was 'this is beautiful, I'll give you that.' Lillian was already swooning from 'whoa'.

'Come on,' she waited for him to follow her.

'I'm taking it we have to climb over that contraption?' he asked, pointing at the stile. Lillian did the thing with her dress, so she cleared the obstacle without any embarrassing mishaps. She waited for him at the entrance, watching him take the stile very well in his office attire. Walking on, she turned around and walked backwards, still observing his reaction. Beckoning him down the dirt path, deeper into the trees. The noise of life began to fade, and the silence enveloped him. Robert could feel the earth's heart beat as well as his own, vividly aware of breathing, giving him a sense of awakening. The smell of a dry floor and heated pines grounded him - he never felt this way about woods before. He followed Lillian who periodically skipped in front of him, looking round now and then to make sure he was still there. 'Mind the bugs!' she called out. Robert stopped where he was, searching the floor.

'Huh? Bugs?' turning up the soles of his shoes.

'Don't squish them! If you do, say sorry!' her voice echoed around the invisible walls.

'Okaaayyy...' he answered, his voice drifting off. He was a little bemused, and carried on walking, checking the ground as he did. There were plenty of little mushrooms, and not many bugs.

'Sorry. Sorry. Sorry,' he whispered a little mockingly. He was drawn to touching the barks and looking up. 'Amazing. I bet these have seen some life.'

'They sure have! Hug one, they'll tell you.'

'What?'

'Hug one! Go on! Your kudos is safe with me. Hug it and look up, let it take you.' Robert picked his tree, did as she said and she was right, he felt as though he was being pulled gently from his centre. The tree's majestic silence resonated through him; calming his elevated senses with the smell of its maturity.

'It feels warm.'

'Yes, they soak up the sun.'

'Ok. I'm hugging and looking up. What next?'

'Just be patient,' Lillian tingled all over as the connection opened.

'I think something's happening,' he said nervously, feeling the pull, making him feel insignificantly small. Lillian looked on adoringly at him, hugging a tree in a shirt and tie. She walked over and held both his hands from the other side, praying for them both as the pulling picked up speed. Robert was transfixed by the feeling he had once felt before, but couldn't recall when. Lillian closed her eyes, he began to struggle and tried to release her grip… the contact was too intense.

'Just relax, trust me,' her voice low and soothing. The pulling was full of static, their heads felt light. Robert was feeling uncomfortable, it was pulling on his buried emotions; reluctant to release them. She heard a whimper from him, then he began to cry. His crying turned into sobbing, and he fell to his knees, Lillian going with him.

'God, what is it?' she tried to prise his head from his hands. Robert continued to sob. It was a heart breaking but beautiful moment, if a little awkward. She stroked his face and hair to comfort him.

'My father, it was my father!' Lillian held his head and closed her eyes as she felt his grief, absorbing it, taking it for him.

'You weren't supposed to cry. What happened? Tell me,' she spoke softly.

'He died before I got to him. I didn't have a chance to shake his hand or say goodbye. I was too late, too caught up in my bloody job!' he said through tears, his voice distorted. Holding onto her arms, the sobs kept coming.

'I felt him Lilly, I felt him - he was here... as clear as anything!' he broke free from her embrace and sat back, leaning against the tree, frantically wiping his eyes.

'You would cry when I haven't got a tissue. You'll get your posh trousers dirty. If that's not character building, I don't know what is.' Robert let out a laugh through his sniffles, resting his arms on raised knees and slowly composing himself.

'I just wanted one last chance to speak to him. It was my fault, too busy to drop everything, it broke me. I thought he'd pull through, he always did - but he left, he quitted, without me...' Robert's tears flowed again and he squeezed his eyes as the pain of the emotion stung them '.... we did everything together. I should have been there, hold his hand, talk about old times. But I took it for granted that he would fight back.' Lillian studied his pained face and quivering lips; completely changing his features.

He looked at Lillian 'I said that I was sorry, as I looked up, it sort of pulled it out of me. I felt...forgiven,' Lillian smiled with empathy.

'When did he pass away?' the man of her dreams before her all muddy and dishevelled, making him real with his armour a little chinked.

'Five years ago,' Robert started to feel better but extremely overwhelmed and exhausted.

'You've been holding onto that, for five years?! Was he a proud man?' Lillian rearranged his soft, black wavy hair.

'Yes, I suppose he was,' he grabbed her hand and kissed her palm.

'Well maybe he didn't want you to be there if he was. You were late for a reason.'

'You think? Y'know, you could be right.'

'I think you've had a bit of a revelation. It's ok now, you know that you can let that go. Come on, I have one more place to show you.' Lillian pulled him up by his arms. Robert dusted himself down, exhaling, feeling baptised. His emotional breakdown left him feeling completely open to everything around him, taking in the source.

He looked ahead to check Lillian was still in his sights, she'd ran ahead of him again. Purple flowers started to appear, everywhere, making him wary, feeling sure they weren't there before.

'What are all these flowers?' he called out.

'Bluebells!' Lillian called back.

'Bluebells? In July?' he said to himself. More carpeted the way as they continued. He laughed with delight, 'isn't it a bit late for bluebells?' hurrying his steps as more popped up wherever he looked.

'It's never too late for bluebells!' Lillian shouted, slowing down as they reached the centre. She arrived at her den and stood beside it while he caught up. When he entered the clearing, he halted, scuffing the dirt beneath him. There was a scattered ring of bluebells around where she stood. Lillian looked like a child, her face alive with innocence, eyes enlarged in excitable anticipation; resurfacing a memory.

'What is it?' she asked, titling her head. He swallowed, afraid of what he was entering into. Something wasn't normal about all this. But then he laughed to himself, ready to dive in - he'd had enough of 'normal'.

'Uh. Nothing, nothing.' He walked on, looking up to the trees that seemed to be the governors' board of the woods; the way they stood, seeming older than others they'd passed. She excitedly beckoned him into the den. Robert cautiously sat down on the log, not sure what he was doing, fearing it was some kind of initiation ceremony. Well, it was.

'If my sister could see me now, I would never live it down.'

'Helen?' he was surprised she knew, then not.

'Yes. Helen. I briefly told her about you. Wait til she meets you.'

'I'm meeting her?'

'Yeah, why not. Are we pretending then?' Lillian picked up some pinecones to deter him, placing them amongst the ashes.

'We have to cook, for the woodman.'

'What? That's not what I meant, Lilly.' Robert's words were serious, it made her heartbeat loud and slow; the child retreating as her female desires resurfaced. The woods fell silent, she listened, waiting for a warning but none materialised.

'This is where I came to contemplate, and wish for you,' she looked into his soft, dark eyes, and the urgency returned. They caressed hands over the cinders and charred beer cans; he smelt so good today, his skin fresh and clean.

'Ah, it was you then, making me restless and pulling my hair. Well, I'm here now. Tree Wife.' Robert looked sincere and defenceless, she could see the little scars on his face she hadn't noticed before. Maybe from pox, or just being a boy. A reservation through his touch resonated through her, there was something holding him back. He pulled her towards him, she hesitated, fighting with her conscience and the wood's gentle whispers. The agonising scream of longing saw its opportunity, she touched his face – getting electric shocks in her stomach.

He took her hand 'No more hurt, it stops here. Okay? I won't allow it. I got you,' she took her hand away.

'Don't put that kind of pressure on yourself. Or make promises you can't keep.'

Robert held his gaze, full of sincerity. 'It's no promise. It's how it is. No need to put something empty on it.' The rush returned in her torso. They both salivated as their souls urged for touch, feeling the fall approaching. She lunged at him, wrapping her arms around his neck - kissing his full lips with the same fire she'd released from the volcano. They fell backwards, collapsing the den, oblivious of the sticks piercing and scratching their skin. Entwined in a clumsy mess, they consumed one another, euphoric and dizzy from the anticipated contact. Their souls connected and they became the half of each other. Mutually resisting deeper intimacy; it wasn't the time, or the place, yet. Laying on the forest floor, giggling, covered in ash and pine needles, their sighs muted and absorbed into the barks.

'I guess you won't be contemplating or wishing in there anymore.'

Lillian rested her head on his stomach, while he looked up to the blue sky feeling rescued and complete.

'You're gurgling,' she said as her head was rising and falling from his exaggerated breathing.

'I've never noticed the trees like this. They're almost speaking. This is you, isn't it?' He caressed her hair, pleasantly surprised that there was no hairspray holding it all together. She flinched, sitting up, placing her hand where it still hurt.

'What's up? Pine needle?' Robert said provocatively.

'Um, no. It's....' she stopped, lying on her side, propping herself up on her elbow - looking down upon him.

'Do you believe in God, Robert?' he turned, her eyes waiting for the answer. It made him swallow nervously, feeling under pressure. Was it a trick question? Could this be the game changer?

'Uh...' he sat up, 'there must be something. I guess?'

'If everything is random, an accident – then there wouldn't be a purpose. Don't you think?' she responded, going back to admiring her surroundings.

'Am I supposed to say yes?' She lay back, her hands clasped behind her head.

'Once you realise there's no such thing as coincidence, the rest should fall into place.' He looked to the floor, thinking, studying what was there with a deeper interest.

'Your turn to tell me now,' she coaxed, softly.

'Don't spoil it, and we should be getting back. You know what's happening.' Robert got to his feet, although he wanted to spend the rest of the day rolling around in the bracken with her.

'Brush yourself off first though, and your hair, you should see your hair!' he said giggling. She tousled it, shaking her head.

'There, is that better?' Robert was a bit love struck from her action, flushed cheeks and enlarged pupils. Her eyes had changed colour too, he noticed, dismissing it.

'Yeah. But I think you need to get up quick, we could be here all day.' She held her hand out for him to take, he pulled her in, and they petted again. Becoming fiercely aroused, she could feel his pressing against her, a little threatened by it. Hair was being grabbed and pulled, buttons were being undone, they were rushing downstream about to hit the immense waterfall – but Robert pushed her back gently and broke off the embrace, his chest heaving.

'Let's go. Okay. Let's just go, this could get us into trouble. Not here, ok? Not here.' Expressing the point with his hands.

'Why not here? I can't think of anywhere more perfect than here,' Lillian answered.

'I know, but I don't want to be looking at my watch when I'm with you.' He pulled on his shirt to create air, suddenly feeling overheated.

'My chest is burning?'

She had a coy look on her face 'yes, sorry. I don't know why that happens.'

'*You* did it?!' she nodded. 'But, how?!'

'I just don't know.'

'Oh my God, I'm a dead man.' They corrected themselves, holding hands as they made their way back.

'I knew this would happen when I saw you in that dress on my first day. I was speechless when you came down those stairs. I felt like I'd been hit by a train. My life changed, in that moment,' they swung their clasped hands.

'Well, I knew it was you when I saw you. I just wanted to give you a big cwtch.'

'What the bloody hell is that?'

'A cuddle, hug. It's Welsh.'

'Oh, right. Cooch. I like it.'

'No, it's C'tch,' she said, forming the phonetics with her mouth, 'not Cooch! Although I think we'll have that as our word, especially with that accent.'

'Cheek. Can I drive the Honda back?' Robert asked. She handed him the keys and he studied them in detail. 'These here, have a lot to say. Don't you think?' he clutched them tight in his fist, then let go of her hand.

'Marry me. Marry me right now, here, under this tree!' he stood, perfectly serious, under the largest pine in the woods; one that you couldn't get your arms around.

Lillian frowned, unsure if he was joking or not. 'Don't be silly,' she giggled.

'I ain't joking. Marry me, here. No paper, no people. Just us, in this place, with strange bluebells and bugs, and those little mushroom things. Then I'll feel better about taking advantage of you.' His sense of humour was intensively attractive to her, after being engaged to none.

'I do,' she said, walking over to him. They sealed their already unbreakable bond, hugging, crying, and laughing. Both feeling saved and blessed.

'They say you don't need someone to fulfil you ... because they haven't found that someone,' she said into his shirt.

'You're beautiful. Come on...miss bluebell.' Lillian gasped.

'You said Bluebell!'

'Uh...yeah, is that bad?'

She beamed, shaking her head. 'No. But only my father calls me that.'

Robert struggled with the gear stick, getting accustomed, laughing at himself and feeling a little bit embarrassed. But he soon got used to it and grinned, the drive back to work a nostalgic one. They touched each other's hands, knees and thighs along the way. It was the first time Lillian had sat in the passenger seat and a long time since she could be affectionate.

'I was twenty-one the last time I sat here. I parted with it because I became a highflyer, or so I thought, and it was cramping my style – it was hard to let go of. But here I am, back in it; humbled, in love and bedazzled by a wisdom far more complex than I dare comprehend.' He looked at Lillian and she gave him a smile that would light up the dark.

'You've brought back something Lil, with extras.' His eyes were full of devotion; looking like expensive chocolate.

'What's that I feel when I kiss you Lil? I can call you that now, can I?' s

She nodded an eager yes. 'It's me. That's all,'

They held hands. 'I don't want you to go back home, Lilly. You still haven't told me what's going on.'

'You know what's going on,' she answered.

'Ooh! Ouch. Touché! Seriously though. I'll kill him if he hurts you!'

'Not if I get there first.'

'Listen. Do what you gotta do, in your own time, okay? Well not kill him obviously. Would you do me the honour and spend some time with me this week? Not on a work level, but I'd love to take you out, spoil you, please? What day could you make it?'

'Any day.' Lillian responded.

'It's settled then, we'll go straight after work one evening. Let me know, on a post it note. So, did I pass your initiation?' Robert asked. Lillian tried to hide her smile, unbuckling as they reached Radar's car park.

'We'll see.' He loved that answer, it wasn't the one he wanted, but her strength was his other pursuit, even though she didn't believe she had any.

'What about the hotel dinner? Are you coming to that?' she asked, as they walked together.

'Are you going?'

'I have to. I'm part of the celebration.'

'Ok. But that's not our night out. We're going somewhere on our own.'

'Oh my God! Have you seen what time it is?!' Lillian looked at her watch in horror.

'What? We were only an hour.' Robert said looking at his, 'shit! How did that happen?' realising they had been two. 'Don't worry, I'll sort it.'

They trotted up to reception and swiftly sat at their desks. Robert suggested he was going to see Phil, which made Lillian nervous. Suddenly the moments of fantasia had come to an abrupt halt; busying herself with nonsense. Phil frowned when Robert walked in with dirty trousers and an untucked shirt.

'Looks like you've been busy. Anything to tell me?' Robert sorted himself out and sat down, trying to brush the ash off his trouser leg.

'She's not stupid, Phil. I tried to coax something out of her but, there's more to Lilly than meets the eye. I don't feel so good about this anymore.' Robert looked down at his hands, getting a stinging rush from his memory of the woods.

'What do you mean?'

'You wouldn't understand. She's precious.'

Phil drummed his fingers on the desk with a sanctimonious look on his face.

'Let's get back to the job in hand. Could you ask her to bring two coffees in, we need to finalise this tender.'

'No. I'll make the coffee. I meant what I said.' Robert got up from his seat. 'Oh, and make her a coffee in the morning,' he left the office, feeling like he'd taken back power.

'Idiot!' Phil blurted, swinging his chair around to face the car park, with his hands on his head.

Thirty

She had an insatiable appetite - having a sneaky peek into Robert's hotel room was probably not a good idea. Toying with him. Studying the way he did things, talking to himself while he prepared his clothes for the next day. She quickly backed out before he noticed. The significant use of energy always made her hungry.

Jeffrey left her dinner on the worktop, cold and congealed. She turned her nose up at it and made a sandwich instead, the biggest one she'd ever made in a while. Rare stake would have been a good filling but there was only cheese; revelling in the feel of her stomach being filled.

Jeffrey scuffed in.

'Oh, decided to show yer face then? What you been doing up there?'

'I'm hungry. Packing is hard work.' she mumbled sarcastically.

'You wouldn't know what hard work was even if yer bluddy fell ova it!' Lillian wasn't affected by his words anymore. She ignored him and knew, she was enough. Robert's beautiful persona made him look like a bargain basement.

'Where's the Mateus?' she asked, seeing that the bottle had gone from the fridge.

'I tipped it down the bluddy sink!' she just nodded and poured herself some juice. 'What d'ya see in him? Ay?' he asked.

'What do I see in who?' Her emotions were leaping about as she was put on the spot, feeling instantly guilty, it was as if the whole kitchen was judging her.

'You know damn bluddy well who! Robert Courtney!' Lillian froze. She felt her face burn. It was like the dream, hearing him mention his name. Robert metaphorically looking around the kitchen door.

'How do you know his name?' she asked, sitting at the table.

'I called ya today, lunchtime. They said you were out, been gone a while. Said you were with him!'

'Who said? He's a colleague. Working with me on the Apex tender. He's gay, anyway,' she answered calmly, finishing her sandwich.

'Spect me to believe that, do ya?! We shoudda left soona!'

'Ok. You got me. We got married under a tree, sorry, I really am, but that's how it is. I'm a tree wife now.'

Jeffrey turned and leaned on the sink, looking out into the garden.

'You don't have to be bluddy funny about it. At least have a thought for me feelings. Have you slept with him?!' he asked and didn't look round.

Lillian stood up, 'No I haven't! We just went for a walk! What were you calling me for anyway?' Jeffrey was relieved and hung his head down.

'What's the attraction? Ay? His car? His job? What?'

Lillian folded her arms 'neither of those.'

Jeffrey swung round to face her. 'So, what then?! Or don't I want to know?!'

She moved forward to confront him.

'If you must know, there's compassion, sensitivity, acceptance, uh, devotion, kindness and respect!' Jeffrey stood motionless, watching her list Robert Courtney's attributes on her fingers.

'How is there? How can ya pick up on that in such a short space of time?! How is respect there when he steps on my bluddy patch?!' Jeffrey shouted and pointed downwards.

'*Your* patch? You don't own me Jeffrey, no one does. It didn't take much, even if all those things were that of an atom's weight, he would have still won me over, just have a little think about that!' Jeffrey was hurt and felt hollow, but deep down, he knew this was coming. He picked up her handbag up and threw it outside.

'Go on then! Bugga off! If I'm not good enough for ya!' he pushed her out and slammed the back door. Lillian was left looking at the contents of her bag strewn all over the patio, the onyx skidding across the floor. She picked it up and brushed it off, holding it tight. Scanning the gardens, checking for onlookers. In that moment, she realised she'd let go; grown an extra two feet. It was a quiet thing, not bad, not good, but she felt it. Leaving the old Lillian behind, feeling her slip away as the new one took her place – a release of something she couldn't describe, which was both renewing and painful.

Jeffrey opened the door, wiping his eyes. Lillian stood, paused - rubbing the pebble between her fingers.

'You got a nerve, throwing me outside! Oh, how the guilty claim victimisation! You're nothing but a bully!'

'Shut up. Get in! And stop using them stupid words!' Jeffrey beckoned her back.

'Please,' Lillian said, standing firm, her gut buzzing.

'Ay? Just get yer arse in 'ere!'

'I will. When you've said, please,' she shook inwardly, holding her ground, still afraid.

'Please,' he answered sheepishly. Lillian put the rest of her stuff in the bag and walked back in the house.

'Sit down!' he said, but Lillian remained standing. 'Please!' he added, and she sat.

'Name it. Just name it. Whatever you want, I'll get it for ya.' Lillian frowned and shook her head.

'You haven't been listening, have you?' she squinted, trying to make sense of Jeffrey's idea of what love really was.

'I thought the other night would've cured you of your ailments! This isn't about materials, Jeffrey. It's about someone making you feel whole. Someone who wouldn't dare lay a finger on you and stand up to anyone who did. Someone who lets me be me, without ridicule. Someone who doesn't shout when I spill something. Someone who thinks my ability is amazing, not strange! That's how I loved you. Do you understand?' Jeffrey looked blank.

'I dunno,' he felt lonely. There was a truth, he didn't want to look at, and it was sitting on his drive a few days ago. But now he wondered if he was being set up.

'Does he know you, y'know, do that witch stuff?'

Lillian ignored it.

'I'm doing this, not what everyone else wants me to do! Have you got that Jeffrey?'

'I don't care! I'm tellin ya, you 'ave to come with me!'

'You can't force someone to love you, Jeffrey.' Lillian was still shaking her head, leaving the pebble on the table.

'Now you ain't listenin! Use yer bluddy 'ed will ya! You don't have to love me, you just have to come with me! I know that's gone now. I accept that. But your father...' he stopped, wanting to put his hand on his mouth.

'My father what?'

'Nuthin. I don't think your father will mind, if that's what you're worrying about.'

Lillian narrowed her eyes at him, 'oh, he *will* mind, trust me. Running away isn't going to solve anything, why don't you tell me what's going on?'

'You just have to learn the 'ard way, don't ya? What's that?' Jeffrey pointed at the onyx,

'I hope it's not that mumbo jumbo stuff!'

'It's for you. You're going to Birmingham, by yourself.' She took her bag with her and the glass of juice, 'Olly!' she called out. The cat jumped off the lounge chair and eagerly followed her upstairs.

Jeffrey was holding the onyx up to the light, turning it, waiting for it to do something.

'Bluddy load o'rubbish,' pushing it into his pocket.

Thirty-One

Helen Courtney rattled around in the three bed detached - obsessively locking all the doors and windows, closing the curtains, with no gaps. After she'd done all of that she 'smudged' the house, crossing the entrances and doorways - a routine she went through every night. She needed a new method; burning the sage wasn't working.

Michael had gone to bed, but in hers. He refused to go in his own for past few weeks – afraid of the man that came in his room. She put it down to a growing phase, in denial that maybe there was a problem. The school called her yesterday, concerned that he didn't want to play outside anymore. She dismissed it, he was a complex child and needed his own space at times – they were reading too much into it.

She picked up her magazine from the long coffee table, fanning through the pages to savour the time alone. Michael had been getting up at 6am every morning. He usually amused himself with his building blocks or imaginary play, while she slept in.

Envying the models looking perfect in everything they wore, she felt her stomach, pushing the muffin-top into her jeans. She sighed, perhaps the gym was the first step, still not feeling good about herself. Regretting her decision often but she had no choice, battling with her situation every night. She never told Michael about his father. He grew up thinking he just didn't have one. When he asked why, she said God decided it was best, and left it at. She knew that would wear thin as he got older.

Determined to start supporting herself rather than be totally dependent, the contact from him was unwanted. He engulfed her, still owning a considerable proportion of her life, including the house. She had never met anyone so detached from compassion, so obsessed with himself and the dark side of life. When he started getting involved with unscrupulous business deals, that's when she made the tough decision. He was cold about it, but insisted she stay in the house. Perhaps it was time to get back to work, she missed her career in the office. But he disallowed it and she was to remain in the house as a kept woman, have all she wanted, to keep her quiet.

Now, all she had were friends connected to child activities, which was beginning to suffocate her. Sitting around in play centres, talking about sleeping and eating habits of their children, comparing development stages – they had nothing in their heads. Nothing! Licking Apple puree off of their fingers and pretending that's what they've always wanted.

She turned all the lights and switches off as she made her way to bed, leaving the table lamp on in the hall, climbing the stairs, thinking about Robert. She loved her brother dearly, feeling a little jealous about this new woman in his life, she was a lucky lady. Fearing she would be seeing less of him if things got serious, and probably move to Wales. She had her mother but her whims and opinions stifled her. Jean Courtney never took to Michael, either.

Helen thought it would be the replacement gift they all needed after her father passed away. She hated herself for being fooled by a devil, one she thought was the answer to all her prayers. Getting into bed carefully, trying not to disturb Michael, she stroked his face and completely adored him when he slept. His features were fair but his soul was like hers and Robert's. Helen lay on her back, her eyes getting heavy as she watched the passing car lights sweep across the ceiling. She slept, twitching and murmuring - her worries up in pictures that made no sense, but she knew what they were. Michael suddenly sat bolt upright looking at the dressing table mirror, staring at it. He needed the toilet but was too terrified to go alone. He looked at this mother, thrashing her head from side to side. He lay his small hand on her stomach and shook her gently.

'Mummy? Mummy?' she awoke startled, alert.

'What is it Michael?!' she snapped.

'I need a wee. Can you come with me?' Helen tutted and huffed, fed up with having her sleep disturbed.

'Oh, Goooddd Michael! Okay, come on.' She waited outside the door for him, leaning on the frame with her arms folded, her eyes struggling to stay open. Michael screamed and ran out, scaring Helen half to death.

'Bloody hell Michael! What is it?!'

'The man! He's in there! In the mirror!' he pointed with a straight arm, his back against the wall.

'What man? What you talking about?!' Helen went in the bathroom annoyed and frustrated at these dreams. She looked around, humouring him.

'Look, no one,' she said, slapping her hands down on her thighs. Michael shook. Helen crouched down to his level.

'Sweetheart, there's no one there. Okay? If there was, I'd bop them on the nose,' he nodded, frowning with fear.

'But he was! He just went when you came!'

'You see? Mummy's a superhero,' he was still shaking his head.

'But he comes back! I want to stay at Uncle Robert's. I don't like it here anymore. You're not making him go away!' he screeched at the top of his voice, angry he wasn't believed. Helen sighed and held his arms, gripping tightly, wanting to throttle him, throttle her situation, close to losing her marbles. It was breaking her, seeing her son like this, which she couldn't stop or kiss away.

'Have you seen him in a film or something?' Michael shook his head.

'No. Just in the mirror, and I saw him at school, by the gates.' Helen was angry, her mother had been telling her he needed to see a Shrink.

'Okay, I've had enough of this. Let's get you back to bed. Don't think about him anymore Michael, he's not real! We'll do something nice on the weekend.' He ran back to the room while Helen took one last look around the bathroom. She noticed something on the side of the sink. Black, round; an onyx rune. Briefly studying it, another random item to add to Michael's collection. She placed it back on the glass shelf and thought nothing of it.

'Are we going with Uncle Robert?' Michael asked, as he hid under the covers.

'Yes, if that's what you want. We'll get some ice cream in that shop you like.' Helen got between the cold sheets, shivering a little as she settled. Michael curled up, thinking, clutching the cotton cover under his chin; his tummy hurting.

'What's that black stone in the bathroom?' she mumbled.

'I found it, in the park. It's my lucky stone. I keep it in my pocket,' he answered. Michael listened in the dark, his eyes moving around. 'He is real mum. He spoke to me, at school.' Helen's eyes snapped open, the pupils expanding.

'What did he say?'

'He said, he was my daddy.'

Thirty-two

Rose checked her watch; just past 2.30am. She had one more visit to make after this one. Cynthia was her weekly call, a lady in her late eighties, terminally ill and waiting to die in her ground floor council flat. Rose relieved the family of the round the clock care. Plumping pillows, changing the intravenous, talking to her as she carried out her duties. Even though she had her eyes closed for most of the visit – Cynthia knew she had company. Rose was her favourite, she brought something with her, something invisible but noticeable. It calmed her, feeling shrouded while she was there.

The flat was crammed with memoirs and trinkets from boot sales and charity shops. Black and white photos of her wedding day, a few pieces of furniture left from the house clearance. She felt alone surrounded by irrelevant things, our superficial protections we insist on dragging around with us. They didn't matter now, people were needed today; she was feeling scared and expectant. The morphine box at her side clicked and bleeped more than usual today, as she pressed the administration button constantly. The ice cold opium was all that ran through her veins now. Rose took her pulse, it was weak, recording the results.

'Steady with that button now, Cynthia,' she brushed her hair and gave her a quick bed bath. Rose hoped it would never come to this – telling Martin to shoot her if it did. She had a feeling this could be her last visit here and maybe she wouldn't be making the second house call.

After her duties she sat at the bedside, reading a book she got from the mobile library. It was about an artist on the coast of Saint Ives in Cornwall. Something to get lost in, taking her away from where she was. She checked her watch again, it was a watch-checking kind of job, but she did it for another reason today. There was a gentle knock at the front door, one she was eagerly expecting.

It was Myriam; an immigrant from Syria who had become her closest friend and colleague. She missed her culture but had been trying to get into Britain for years to escape her abusive household and loss of her family. This had been her lucky year when the legislation changed; her determination and hard work had paid off, as well as relentless devotion to her faith. She hadn't quite lost her accent, which made it difficult to understand her at times. Her white hijab framed her bright face today. Rose thought it was an art the way it was wrapped and tucked so perfectly and secured with just one, small pin.

Myriam had something special about her too, that's why they connected so well when they first met.

'Asalaamu alaikum Myriam,' they kissed cheeks.

'Walaikum asalaam Rose. How is she?'

Rose shook her head, 'not long now I don't think. Do you have something for me?' Myriam took the amber bottle from her uniform pocket. 'Here. This one not easy.'

Rose clutched the bottle.

'I'm sorry. Thank you, Myriam, I really appreciate it. Hopefully, I won't be needing any more.'

'How is Lilly?' they entered the bedroom, Myriam looking over Cynthia.

'She's doing well, coming out of her shell. Which is why I called.'

'Allah protect you all, Rose.'

'Who done it this time?'

'That is not important. I can't get any more, sorry Rose. This is my last time.'

'It's fine. I won't expect you to. Thank you for all your help.' Rose became tearful. Myriam smiled and put her hand on her heart. 'My pleasure. You accepted and welcomed me, others no. I am happy with you. God loves you Rose, you are good woman. I must go now.' Myriam pulled at her watch in annoyance; the damn thing was her dictator of late, she needed a rest.

'Oh, please stay,' Rose insisted, 'I need you,' she pleaded with a playful expression. The patient's eyes flickered open, she was smiling with contentment, something Rose had never seen.

'Hello Cynthia. Can I get you anything love?' the woman held out her bony, aged hand. Rose took it with affection 'who's here?' the old woman asked in a croaky voice.

'Myriam,' Rose answered.

Cynthia closed her eyes, with a blissful smile. 'Thank you. Thank you,' she whispered.

'No need to thank me my love, you just rest now. I think it's time we sat,' Rose indicated to Myriam with the nod of her head towards the positioned chairs. The two sat on opposite sides of the bed, resting their elbows on the garish pink cover, with embroidered carnations in the centre. Myriam held her hands together with upturned palms, her eyes closed, Rose watched her lips move in recitation. Cynthia lifted her arm, it was an effort for her - the pain had made her weak. Her pale, drawn face began to light up, pointing towards the end of the bed, trying to speak; excited and couldn't quite get her words out.

'She came! Look!' her voice quivering, filled with elation. Rose smiled and stroked her face.

'That's good news. No more pain now Cynthia, you've had enough,' a tear of relief pooled then fell from the corner of the old woman's eye, making a drip as it soaked into the pink pillowcase, her last tear she would ever shed. She was sad to be leaving, so many beautiful memories...difficult ones, too. All that was taken for granted came to her in pictures. The chances she had while on this mortal coil, the laughter and the rain, being human, the little things that made us happy, safe. The songs beside father's piano with small glasses of flat beer. Cynthia wasn't scared anymore, that was taken away somehow when you leave. Maybe she was going to see her Stanley again, at the station, where they met – he must be getting impatient. He always liked to be on time, in his trilby and sharp suit. She strained to look at her mother again, she was waiting for her at the end of the bed. Gentle, benign, but urgent. Wearing her spotted apron, that one she wore for housework. Her brown hair was curled, shiny. Face made up with her favourite red lipstick. It was time to come in, she said, time for bread and jam and listen to the radio. She was ready.

Rose bowed her head, saying the Lord's Prayer, while Myriam continued to recite her passage of mercy from the Quran. The atmosphere changed in the room, it became eerily still - the air left...Rose couldn't hear the grandfather clock ticking anymore. Their moment, and only theirs, had been held. The light took Cynthia away from the bed that had become her prison; swift and graceful like the removal of a silk scarf from around her neck. The bedroom fell silent as Cynthia's hand went limp in Rose's. She stayed, her head lowered, respectful of the passing. The divine visit had been immense on this one, its predominant presence briefly entering this realm; striking fear and worship in them both. They looked at each other with tears in their eyes. Myriam wiped her hands over her face to seal the prayer.

'She's gone.' Rose released her hold of Cynthia's hand.

'It's close Rose. We watch it pass, but it will come. I hope you smile like Cynthia, Insha'Allah.' They stood, overcome with emotion. Rose made her way around the bed to hug Myriam. 'I am happy we cross paths.'

'The feeling is mutual, Myriam.' The women straightened themselves and wiped their eyes.

'The mirror, Rose - you must break it. Not bad luck, bad doorway. You see?' Myriam handed Rose a piece of paper. She unfolded it, verses written in Arabic English.

'Say this, three times, each one, before water.' Rose nodded, trying to decipher the writing.

'You'll have to teach me how to say this correctly, Myriam. I think I'll just be saying anything,' tucking it in her uniform pocket. They held hands for a moment, squeezing each other's fingers.

'No matter how you say. When it comes from heart, it say everything. There is much coming for you, my sister. I pray for you. Hold tight to Allah's rope, he will help.' They hugged again, patting one another on the back.

'Come on, we need to arrange formalities,' Rose said, sniffing. They wouldn't be able to make the next house call, procedures had to be followed. Rose pulled the sheet over Cynthia's face, tapping her forearm - 'Goodbye love. God Bless.'

Thirty-Three

Phil arrived in his silver Audi Estate, parking in the elite spaces. He fizzed and bristled as he walked under the pylon wires, passing through reception without a greeting. An unpopular man, but he didn't care, they were all feeble and lived with their heads in troughs, oblivious of the truth.

The office was quiet. There was no sign of Robert yet. Lillian got on with her work and tried to gage what vibe was hanging around. Lisa was in heavy discussion with Tim. The sun hadn't made an appearance, it was dull and muggy, reflecting the whole mood of the building, even marketing hadn't taken their happy pills.

She silently prayed while typing, asking for her father's recovery. Rose had called her before she left, he had come down with a chest infection and wanted to see her. Lillian's stomach churned as she felt Phil enter the floor. She opened her top drawer and pretended to look for something, blatantly making a noise amongst the rulers and pens, hoping he would just go in his office. He walked straight into the department. Everyone looked up at him, Lillian was pinned to her seat as he stood there looking beautiful, dressed in a black Polo shirt and grey trousers, exuding a confidence that was hypnotic.

'Good morning, Lilly,' he said, walking over to her desk. She pushed her chair back so hard it hit the partition behind, almost knocking it over. He leered at her reaction.

'Morning,' she replied, through held breath. He must have been late due to being professionally groomed before he came in, she thought. Or maybe it was the black against his fair features. She felt oddly attracted to him today, too.

'Could you bring a coffee in, please? It always tastes better from your fair hands,' he asked and smiled, then left, running his eye over the rest of the team. Lillian released all the air she was holding in, her limbs quivering. She hesitated about making the coffee, overthinking it, feeling stupid she was in a quandary about it. He had that way about him, you just did what he asked. She knew the change in him was superficial, but it was the next shift.

'Morning everyone! Sorry I'm late!' Robert came in and brought light. Lillian just wanted to take a running jump at him, glue herself to him.

'You all right, tree wife? What's happened?' Robert asked seriously.

'Uh, Robert, can you come and see me! Lilly? Don't forget the Coffee!' Phil called out.

'Did he just ask you for coffee?'

'Robert, don't. I'll make it. It's fine. Go in, please. It's my job,' she pleaded.

'No, it's not fine! You stay there!' Robert stormed off, with Lillian putting her head in her hands. Robert got three coffees, putting one on Lillian's desk, before going into Phil's office.

Phil regarded him with a disbelieving look, 'have you gone soft in your old age?' he asked.

'I got over myself,' Robert answered, spilling some coffee on the desk as he placed the mug down heavily. He took a large slurp, trying to work out what was different about Phil.

'New hair cut?' he asked.

Phil took a tissue from his draw, wiping away the spill in a methodical manner.

'You start letting a woman think she is equal to you, one might as well start wearing lipstick.' Robert felt nervous in Phil's presence today; something he'd felt before.

'I'm calling Apex. I'd like you to stay and listen in, but don't say anything. I don't want to let the cat out of the bag.' Phil dialled the number and left it on loudspeaker, asking to speak to his counterpart in the company; a director at Apex he knew well.

'*Phil! Good to hear from you. I have some off the record news!*' he announced.

'Good, I hope.'

'*I'm very impressed. If I didn't know any better, I'd say you had some inside information!*' the man chuckled. Robert looked to the floor, feeling sick about himself.

'*The tender meets every spec and you've even added a few new ones. Clever stuff indeed. I think I can safely say, the deal is in the bag. We have to finalise everything, of course, make it official.*' Phil and Robert smiled at each other. Robert wanted to high five, but Phil left him hanging.

'I'm pleased to hear it Frank, good news. When do you think we'll hear officially?'

'*Oh, I would say, no later than end of this week. Excellent work. I'm sure I can trust you with this information, until word is out?*'

'You have my word. Looking forward to hearing from you Friday, Frank.'

'*Likewise. I'll get my secretary to fax over the official acceptance, then follow it up with you. We must have a drink sometime. I want to hear everything about this company.*'

'Sounds good. Have a successful week Frank. Talk soon,' the call was ended, with Robert heaving a sigh of relief.

'I think this calls for a celebration. I commend you,' Phil said.

'Thanks. All in a day's work. Although I think we need to stop there. Let's not get too complacent, that's how we get detected.' Phil was getting amused with Robert's conscience; it must be such a tie having one.

'Oh, I think we can lie low for a while. I've got my eye on breaking Sisco.'

'Sisco?! Are you serious?! No way, no way! Their systems are very tight. Find someone else!'

Phil sat forward and rested on the desk, 'are you backing out, Courtney?'

'You got Apex. Leave it at that. Just give me what I'm owed, and I'm done with it.'

'You'll have that, when we get Sisco,' Phil answered, with a straight face.

Robert stood up. 'That wasn't the agreement! I ain't breaking into Sisco!'

Phil spoke through gritted teeth. 'Sit *down*, Courtney! Stop throwing your toys around and keep your bloody voice down!' he rounded off his shoulders.

'I'll give you treble, plus what we agreed,' he leaned back in his chair. 'Call it, a retainer.' Robert sat down, running his hand through his hair, nodding once to pacify Phil. Phil drank his coffee and smirked, Robert got up to leave.

'Be careful with Lilly. I don't think you know what you're dealing with.'

Robert looked around, 'what do you mean?'

Phil raised a mocking smile as he stirred in the Canderel. 'Lilly is out of your league,' he tapped the spoon on the edge of the mug. 'How is Helen? I haven't heard from her in a while. Is she avoiding me?' Robert's head was plucked out of the sand every time Phil asked about her.

'She's fine, thanks, uh, Michael too,' Robert answered coyly, avoiding eye contact with him.

'I can see you want to protect your sister. I can relate. However, I like to see my son. You can't deny me that.'

Robert didn't want to talk about it anymore and was feeling a little grey. 'I will speak to her about it for you,' he answered and gave him a strained smile. 'Actually, I think I'll go back home tonight. I haven't seen my mother in a while. I'll drive back the following evening.'

'Why don't you go today? Take some leave. Just keep your laptop with you,' Phil said.

'Was that a bit of humility?'

'I'm giving you time off Robert, not a puppy.'

He left and went to see Lillian, pulling up a chair to sit with her.

'Hey,' he said, accompanied with his wink, needing her sweet, consuming affection. She picked upon his unease. They made direct eye contact, wanting to molest each other.

'I'm travelling back home, just for tonight. I need to see my family. Are you going to be ok?'

Lillian nodded, 'yes. Of course. I'll be fine. I need to see mine, too.'

'You can always contact me, you know, by FedEx,' he said, blushing. Lillian gave him a provocative look that would have melted an iceberg. She suddenly looked away when the feeling was replaced by a threatening one. Robert was worried, was it him? Had she changed her mind because he was such a sap? She put her finger on her lips, hard, screwing up her eyes.

'What is it?' Robert pressed. She kept hitting her lips with her forefinger, hoping he would get the message to stop talking. He could see her hand shaking. She looked straight into his eyes trying to convey the message to stay silent, detecting Phil's eavesdropping. She kept her finger there and wrote on a post note, badly.

'Phil...!' Robert didn't understand and shrugged to express it. She used another note, her finger still on her lips, 'listening...with mirror!!' her exclamation marks tore through the paper. He read it twice, eyebrows raised, he shivered and went pale... realisation weighed him down in his seat, his limbs heavy as lead. Everything slotted like flip animation. He put his hands up to his head, breathing heavy, he'd been deceived and didn't even see it. He needed to get out of himself, standing up ... feeling hurt, betrayed, humiliation gripped him.

'Oh no, this ain't good, this ain't good at all,' he murmured. Lillian grabbed his arm, shaking her head, gesturing with her eyes for him to sit back down. Phil broke off the connection, his grin splitting his face. He got off on his undetected intrusions, it was getting easier, and the power increased his arrogance, often feeling he was invincible. He could see Lillian's ability was protected; it was beautiful, pure – scorching him as he tried getting close. It needed to be weakened, to blacken the vibrant colour that surrounded her.

Thirty-Four

They sat in Brutus. It was difficult as they touched, their skin tingling. She put three drops of her oil in his palm.

'Rub it between your hands and over your head.' He did what she said, feeling protected from the scent. It was her scent.

'What is this stuff?' Lillian put some over her and secured it in the pocket of her bag.

'Himaya,' Lillian answered.

'Him-what? Is that French?' she laughed along with the secret, rubbing the last of the oil in her hands and around her wrists.

'It's Arabic. Means protection. My mother gets it for me.'

'Arabic?! Really? Wow!' he looked at his hands, turning them over. 'Wonders will never cease with you, will they?' He smelt the liquid, trying to get a sense from the origin;

imagining how far the wisdom had travelled and over how many generations.

'We've only just started. You'll be fine for a while. Go and sort your family out and get back here. I'm slightly ahead of Phil but only by a short breath.'

'Start him up, follow me to the North Gate, before I go.' He gently pinched her cheek, winking that wink. Giving her a warm shiver.

Robert arrived a few minutes before her, she lost him on the roundabout; the black vehicle was too swift and light on its feet for Brutus. His passenger seat hosted two packs of sandwiches, two bags of crisps and a bar of chocolate and a thermos cup full to the brim with coffee in the holder, which he sipped periodically.

He dialled Helen on loudspeaker, telling her to meet him at their mother's in three hours - scared, in over his head. He'll have to cut his losses and just leave. But not without Lillian. There was no way he was breaking into Sisco's systems, for any amount of money - he was good, but the risk was futile. He may have ignored the warning signs a couple of years back, living a life of close calls. Phil was getting greedy and getting out of the coercive contract, could be costly.

The North Gate was in the opposite direction to the Royal Oak, towards the woods. No one went there, it wasn't trendy enough, outdated and only for the locals. It was a longer ride, close to the resident castle that no longer housed its knightly retainers - but used for film sets and haunted tours. All that historical stone and misery awoke Lillian's psychic responses when she arrived, parking next to Robert. It was liberating not creeping about or lying anymore, but Lillian wanted more than just work time with him; snatching an hour here and there was getting to her already. He was sitting near the fire with a Coke on ice waiting for her. Fleetwood Mac were playing in the background, maybe that would be their new album.

The elderly punters were propping up the bar with their Guinness - the barmaid chatting to them about politics, while drying the glasses with a cotton cloth. Lillian could feel the unseen occupants when she walked in, they rushed through her, hoping to be noticed. She acknowledged them but didn't partake in their woeful whisperings. The pub smelt a little damp, the walls were painted sage green, the curtains and pelmet patterned in Fleur de Lys. It was bright and cosy.

'Mwah!' She kissed him on the cheek and sat down, it was so good to love again. Robert delighted in her child-like attitude.

'Thank you, Miss,' he said as she settled herself and took a sip of her drink.

'Haven't you had enough of fire?' she jeered, her cheeks beginning to glow from the burning logs. Robert beamed at her question.

'It would seem not. Maybe I just wanted to relive that feeling.' They both glared daringly at each other. 'The weather has changed, hasn't it?' Robert turned his glass around on the paper placemat.

'Ah, I see. A bit of small talk to avoid the subject,' Lillian said.

'Lilly,' he took her hand, his expression pensive, 'I will find out one day what I've done to deserve this incredible journey you're taking me on.' Her muscles and sinews flared, releasing the lactic acid that lay trapped there for years. He leant forward and kissed her lips gently, tasting her tears as he did.

'Well, they're salty. I half expected them to taste, strange. Would you be prepared to come to Surrey?' he blurted. Lillian was finding it hard to cope with her wishes coming true all at once; she needed time to process them, one at a time - questioning the normality of his responses after being accustomed to such harshness and one-sided entitlement.

'Are you serious?!'

Robert shrugged 'Yeah, I am,' his eyes held nothing but devotion and a little vulnerability.

'I can't leave my parents, sorry,' she looked down, maybe that would be the tin lid on it. The risk burnt her, panicking, unwilling to let it go.

'I'll just have to come and live here then; this place is growing on me. Are you sure that's all you can't leave?' he was afraid she meant someone else, the fake husband guy, and was just letting him down gently.

'Of course! It's just, difficult.'

'I'm not going to leave you to fend for yourself, Lilly. I'll do whatever it takes, ok? I got you.' Lillian was scared by all she prayed for, bulldozing its way in, the speed of it was loud and confusing. If she could just bring herself to accept that she deserved it, then it wouldn't seem so surreal.

'This gift you have, completely amazes me. I suspect if you used that inappropriately, it would be lethal. Do you read tea leaves? Stuff like that?' Lillian huffed a laugh and ran her finger down the condensation on the glass.

'You can see a face in anything. I see them in my ceiling. It's called pareidolia. Tea leaves create enough images if you swirl the cup long enough.'

'I clearly don't know anything. How did it happen, I mean, how did you start, you know…that?'

'It runs in the family. From an early age I started seeing them. Not really being conscious of what they were. It seemed, natural. They're called the blue ones – preferring children to adults. I think they were attracted to me because I'm an only child. But it intensified after I had meningitis.'

'Meningitis? What is that?'

'Bacterial infection, a nasty one - affects the frontal lobe, the conscience and all the fluid in your joints. I forgot how to function when I left hospital. But I survived it, unscathed, others are not so fortunate. The Consultants were at a loss as to how I managed to live through its advanced stages; they had only just got to grips with the understanding of it. They would come and see me every day, clutching clipboards, staring at me like I was some freak of nature. Ticking boxes and pretending they knew what they were doing. So, here I am, defying logic and textbooks.'

'Wow - that must have been tough.'

'It was, but it wasn't my time obviously. I was meant to come back. During my recovery, I was contained in a room - that's when they came and never left, always after lights out. They talked amongst themselves in there. All I could do was watch and listen, I was too weak to do anything about it. They were hanging around like vultures, attracted to my third eye that had been flung wide open. They present themselves in different forms now, depending on which message they have to give.'

'Do you mean, people spirits?'

'No, not people. Imagine that, coming back here and hanging around toilets and empty places. We would know for sure what happens when we die or who murdered us. But none of them seem to answer that question, do they?'

'I, I guess not. Maybe they're sworn to secrecy?'

'Maybe they are, but what is the secret?' Lillian drank, without taking her eyes off him. She could feel herself changing as she got deeper into discussion. It gets heavier, pressing down on her.

'Many psychics and soothsayers use them, they know all there is to know about everyone and everything passed and future.' She checked her watch.

'How can they know, these, whatever they are? Do they time travel or something?!' he jeered, laughing at his own joke. Lillian held a serious glance, making him shift and cough.

'Oh, right,' he said.

'I use my mirror to connect with you and...' she paused, contemplating to divulge it all, 'well, that's how I connect. How you get the FedEx.' He got an overwhelming sense of familiarity when he looked at Lillian, a dèjá vu.

'But how on earth do you, err, enter the room?'

'It's difficult to explain. I concentrate on you and nothing else - you sort of, project yourself. When I was small it just happened without me thinking. My soul wasn't attached then, y'know? Our connection makes it easy, I can't do it with everyone. Phil has perfected it with something much darker.' Robert processed the information that seemed farfetched and illogical. But Lillian didn't come across as unstable, or suspiciously psychotic – on the contrary. He instinctively believed her when she spoke.

She fished out a half-melted ice cube from the glass to suck on, tipping the drink. Robert stood up with his arms out.

'Whoa! Clumsy!' Lillian recoiled, shrunk, burned from the inside.

'I'm sorry, I'm sorry. I'm really sorry,' she fussed, putting beermats on the spillage.

Robert shook it from his hands, 'don't worry about it, ok? I'll get some tissue.' He returned with something from the bar, mopping it up, wiping the edges.

'I'm so sorry. I just like crunching ice cubes,' he could see she had an instilled anxiety, because it was an irrational and defensive reaction.

'What did he do to you?' he asked, busy with the liquid.

'My spillages are a bit of an issue.' Lillian played with her silver thumb ring, repeatedly turning it, focussing on the action – it was her coping mechanism. Robert noticed.

'Looks like it was more than an issue, Lil,' he picked up the glass and tipped the rest of it on the table. 'Whoops!' There was a beautiful silence, filled with healing and fulfilment as she watched him gather up the heaps of tissue paper. He returned to the table with a brooding expression, looking into the fire, watching the flames lick across the axed wood.

'What's wrong with these men?' he held her hand, finding it inconceivable how she manged to endure such treatment for so long, and how much strength that must have taken. But then, so had he. 'I dread to think what Phil can do with that power,' he looked out to the car park through the bay window, it was a beautiful place with a strong sense of community.

'He's a dangerous man. He uses it for his own gain, it will eat him alive, eventually.' Robert snapped his head round, 'what will?'

'Greed. Sinister addiction, to them. Do you know that his manipulation doesn't stop at humans?' Lillian answered. Her face morphed a little when she connected to them for a brief moment, she was a magnet; they loved her talking about them. Robert stabbed his finger towards her.

'You, changed, then.'

She pressed her lips into a thin, line and raised her eyebrows.

'It's when I connect, sorry. That bit isn't always pretty. My mum says my eye goes funny too, this one...' she pointed to her left eye, 'it goes inwards.'

He smiled, a little unsure. Sometimes she made his blood run cold, it was only now and then, like then. His fear held wonderment, opening up his intuition. He loved this woman in such a short space of time. Her place in his life was enriching, and he would guard that no matter what. He wanted to leave Surrey but didn't feel secure enough, it was a big step. She didn't answer his question with enthusiasm, feeling slightly confused about it.

'I'd better be getting back. Can't have the newbie taking the mick,' startled at Robert just staring at her. 'What? Have you thought of your catch?' she knew there was one coming, at some point, there had to be one, right?

Robert laughed at her determination and shook his head. 'I don't need to think of it. It's there, if you look,' Lillian's blood rushed to her head and back down to her feet.

'It hasn't been a short time for us, it's been longer, much longer. We're just programmed to forget what we see as children.' Robert's eyes widened – unsure how much more he could take, wanting to drop to his knees. They stood, no questions, leaving the North Gate hand in hand.

'Get in, please,' he said with earnest. Lillian opened the Honda's door, letting him sit in the driver's seat. 'Thank you. That's all I got,' he said.

They kissed with open affection this time. Touching each other's faces, caressing and studying their features - something lost, something missed, back in their hands, it was too great, yet so natural. Robert had tears in his eyes from the intensity of Lillian's love, nourishing his core. He touched her lips and was losing himself, her eyes darker than before. Enlarged pupils surrounded by a change of colour; terrifyingly beautiful. He couldn't decide which colour, dark purple perhaps.

'Why do your eyes do that? It sends chills through me!' Lillian sat back, her hand on her heaving chest. She swooned at Robert's form and his essence of man - his arm resting on the Honda's steering wheel, fanning his chest with his shirt again.

'I don't know, it happens when I let my barriers down, or when something breaks them down.' Robert studied her and watched them slowly return to steel blue. Smiling at him with such warmth, his fear subsided.

'Lilly, you are right to feel there's a catch, I can't deny that in front of you. Come to think of it, I can't deny anything with you!' he licked his teeth behind closed lips. 'What are we going to do about your situation, ay?' he tapped the dashboard, trying to come up with a plan.

'You leave it to me, that's what. When are you taking me out?'

'When I get back. I'll be a couple of days, hopefully,' he was worried about leaving her and about the decision he was about to take. The money didn't matter anymore.

'Ok. I want to make sure you get back ok, race you there!' he gave her the beamer keys. She loved getting in his car, it shut out the world somehow and it was Robert in metal form. She turned to him, still watching her from the Honda - turning the engine and reversing without taking her eyes off him; her ego making a rude appearance. He laughed loudly and the race was on. Lillian pulled away and the beamer was on top form, effortlessly taking the lead. She looked in the rear-view mirror and it was weird seeing the Honda being driven by him, slowing down, mesmerised, watching him follow- filling her up with something missing, like a backbone. Flashing the lights, Robert overtook her. She watched the Honda pass, exuding its magic. They pulled up at the roundabout and Lillian caught Robert's eyes in the Honda's rear view mirror, framed and captured, he winked and pulled away, leaving her at the roundabout.

'Damn it!' she shouted.

Driving down to the bottom of the car park, defeated, Robert was waiting with a smug look on his face.

'Okay, okay. It was a case of smart manoeuvre rather than speed, let me tell you. We smashed it until I went all gooey when I saw you two in the mirror.' She said. Robert threw the keys to her, she caught them mid-air.

'Older and wiser beats fast and inexperienced, every time.'

'What did it feel like? Driving him again?' Lillian asked.

'It was special. Right, I'd better be going. You're gonna be ok. Yeah?' Lillian just nodded, her eyes filling with bereavement.

'Hey, no need for that, please, it kills me. Come on. Don't forget, there's always FedEx,' he got in the beamer, a little hesitant to leave her with Phil and Jeffrey. Lillian could feel that nothing was an inconvenience to him. She also noticed that so far, he hadn't failed her. There was one faded, red flag - flapping lazily. But so many things to get used to that was the norm, making Jeffrey look completely abnormal. She waved him off, feeling sick as she walked back to reception. Both of them feeling the pull of separation.

Thirty-Five

Robert pulled up outside his mothers' house in Farnborough, Hampshire. She was waiting in the doorway of her detached bungalow, her heart leapt when she saw her son; dark, handsome and successful.

'Robbie!' she called out and ran to the small gate wedged between two neatly trimmed privet hedges. Jean, a lady in her late sixties, five foot four, slight with short grey hair that was roughly cropped. She wore layers of light clothing, usually in mauves and lilacs, dressed in matching Malas. Her arms were aloft ready to receive him, hugging over the gate.

'Oh, my boy, it's good to see you. You look tired.'

'Argh! Mum, don't squeeze me so tight. How's things?' his mother opened the gate for him.

'Well, I've had better days, but you're here now, that's the main thing. Helen tells me you have some news?' Robert sighed and felt a bit overwhelmed and just wanted to sit down.

'Yes, I have, but all in good time. I really need a coffee.' Robert felt good to step into his mother's home; he missed the smell and feel of it. She had been burning those sticks again from her little corner of worship. A 1950's construction, tastefully decorated with wood and plants. There was a conservatory on the back of a generous kitchen. Robert hung his holdall on the banister as he walked in, something he always did. Helen and Michael followed in behind.

'Come and see my new toy uncle Robert!' his nephew said, tugging at his arm.

'Ok buddy, bring it to me in the kitchen, yeah?' Robert sat down at the kitchen table while his mother made him a coffee.

'Something smells good, mum.'

'There's fruit cake, made it just for you, Robbie.' He cringed at his pet name.

'Good, I'll have a piece with my coffee please,' he looked at his watch, the time meant Lillian was home with Jeffrey. His mother sat down, wincing at her aching bones.

'Mum, you need to see a doctor. Why don't you help yourself?' Robert saw his mother was emotionally tired and started to give up.

'Well, what's the point at my age? Your father's gone, you're flitting off here and there...' Robert looked at Helen, both rolling their eyes.

'You've got us, twenty-seven minutes up the road! Which is more than a lot of people have, and you've got a roof over your head. Yes, dad is gone, but you have to live in the moment mum. I'm here today. Stop feeling sorry for yourself.' Robert's mother listened while she picked at her slice of fruit cake, playing with her beads.

'Here it is Uncle Robert!' Michael came running into the kitchen holding up a toy car. 'It's my favourite one, like you used to have.' Robert looked up at Helen, a little bedazzled.

'He picked it out himself, there were others, but he had to have that one.' Robert held the toy car up and smiled at the miniature Honda Civic, in metallic blue.

'That was a good choice, but how did you know it looked like my old car? Photo?' Michael leaned on the kitchen table and shook his head.

'Nope. I saw it, in my head,' he said, tapping his temple. They all looked at one another.

'He tells us all the time about a lady, a purple lady and a man in the mirror. I think he needs to see a shrink!' Robert's mother said.

'Mum! Don't say that in front of him!' Helen protested and went to the sink, pretending to wash up, hiding her tears.

'What's a shrink?' Michael asked.

'It's what your grandma does to my clothes. Tell me about the purple lady and man in the mirror, buddy.' Robert put his arm around the boy's shoulders.

'The purple lady has that car now,' Michael answered, pointing at the miniature Honda. Robert got goose bumps, overwhelmed from all the amazement - a secret that seemed privy to a chosen few.

'I know the purple lady. Her name is Lilly.'

Michael looked astonished, his mouth and eyes wide open. 'Really?! Can I see her?'

Jean looked at them in disbelief. 'Is this true? Or are you just playing along with it?'

'It's true, mum. And about that, I can shed some light on why he sees things. He's not crazy, he has a gift. An inherited one.'

Helen put her hand over her mouth. 'Oh my God. He's been seeing Phil in the mirror! Aaaand at the school gates!'

Michael stopped playing with the small Honda and hid behind Robert. 'I don't like it!'

'What do you mean by that?' Jean asked.

'I've recently discovered that Phil has a gift.' Helen panicked, busing herself with nonsense in the sink. 'You got some light to shed on that, Hel?'

She gulped, but it was time for a confession now that everything had been pushed to the surface. 'Yes. I didn't want to say anything, he warned me not to. He listens. Please don't make me elaborate. I'm not sure I'll make it out alive. My sage sticks are not working.'

'Sage sticks? What are you using those for?' asked Jean.

'No one makes it out alive. It's time to for me to pull out. Hear that, did you?' Robert comforted Michael. Jean felt uneasy as she picked up cake crumbs up with her index finger. Helen found it hard to deal with the guilt, giving Michael a hug.

'You're a clever boy sweetheart. I'm sorry mummy didn't believe you. I didn't want to believe you,' she kissed him all over his face.

Robert's mother held a sour and bitter expression,

'I still think he needs to see a special doctor. Who is this Lilly? Is that your news?'

'Lilly's my...' Robert played with his watch '...tree wife.' Helen giggled and noticed a change in her brother, a positive one.

'A *tree* wife?! What on earth is one of those?!' his mother asked.

'I'm thinking of moving to Wales too, but it's not confirmed, the brown stuff hasn't hit the fan yet. I married her under a tree, mum.'

Jean was waiting for the joke to emerge, Robert was always winding people up.

'Is this family losing the plot or something?! You married a woman, you hardly know, under a tree? What the hell has got into you?!'

Robert finished off his coffee and was shaking his head as his did. 'Magic. Something. Just, don't worry, mum, it'll be okay, you have to trust me on this one. There are very few people I trust in this world, but I would trust Lilly with my life.'

Jean just huffed, a little jealous. 'Are you sure she's not just after your status?' she asked.

'And what status would that be exactly? A cheat? A spy? Please.' Robert snubbed.

'A single guy, decent job, nice car, big house in an affluent area – bright lights, big city and all that. Isn't that what every woman wants? Isn't that what the others wanted?'

'What others? No one's like Lilly, she has substance and integrity. If anything, she deserves a good status, from anyone. But she's deeper than that and her status is far more superior to mine. I want to give this woman all I have.'

Jean shifted in her seat, feeling envious of this Lilly already.

'If she has integrity, she'll drop you like a hot brick when she finds out about your vocation - have you thought about that?'

Robert picked the melted wax off the candle in the centre of the table. 'Yes, I have. This lifestyle Helen? It has to stop I'm afraid. You'll just have to do without the money, it's my duty to look out for you and this isn't the way anymore. Have you spoken to him recently?'

'No, I haven't heard from him in weeks, five in fact. The money has doubled though.' Robert clenched his fist under the table.

'You need to get yourself a job and move back in with mum, I'm just pre-empting what's ahead.'

Jean raised her eyebrows. 'What?! Since when has this been arranged?!'

'Since a meeting I had today! And don't use that money anymore, transfer it into another account, or better still, block his account. We're going into town. I need to get Lilly something. I'm getting us out of this.' Robert went into the hallway to get his mobile and wallet from his bag. Helen didn't want to move back in with her mother, she had got used to her independence.

Jean began crying at the table. 'Why didn't I have a normal family? If only your father could see all of this. I don't want to believe any of it!'

Robert held her. 'Nothing is normal mum. I don't think anyone actually knows what that means. We got each other. That's near enough normal. Michael, look after your grandma until I get back, okay?'

Michael nodded 'like a superhero?'

'Yes, like a superhero. I'm counting on you.'

'I will bop the bad guys on the nose if they hurt my gran. But what if the Phil-man comes?'

'He won't. Not if your Gran is here. He'll be too scared to,' he winked, that wink.

'What's that supposed to mean? Cheek!' Jean blew her nose in the cotton handkerchief, a little fulfilled by her son's jar of sunshine.

'I'll get you a bar of chocolate, Michael.'

'Yay! One with a wrapper like the lady please.'

'Oh yeah? A purple wrapper? I'm on it.'

Michael and Jean were in the greenhouse, watering and potting up when they returned.

Robert unpacked Lillian's present and wanted to wrap it, 'have you got any girly wrapping paper please Hel?'

Helen wiped her hands on her jeans. 'Yes, I think we have. Pinkie girly or classy girly?' she called, entering the dining room.

'Uh, the latter!' Robert yelled back 'definitely the latter,' he repeated to himself. Helen returned with purple tissue paper and wrapping paper that was deep pink with a black Damask pattern on it, 'will this do?'

Robert took the paper and purple tissue and felt it between his fingers. 'Ha! Well, well, well. How long has this been here I wonder?'

'I don't know, Mum's had it in the drawer for a while.' Helen sat watching Robert make a bad job of the wrapping, 'shall I do it for you?' she asked.

'That bad, eh?' She took over while he tried to learn from the skill that he thought was definitely women's territory. 'You haven't told me about Lilly yet.'

'What is there to say? Ask Michael,' Robert answered.

'That's not funny and you know it! Why does he see her as being purple?'

Robert sighed, 'Bluebells, hundreds of them and her eyes...'

'She has purple eyes?!'

'No, well, yes – sometimes. She smells purple, too. Let's talk about something else, I'm getting butterflies.'

Helen smiled and secretly wished she was feeling like that again.

'What's with the tree business then?' she asked.

'In the woods, her woods. Tall, so tall they were. She took me to see them, somewhere she goes,' he picked at the wax again, 'somewhere, she belongs. I said sorry to Dad there.'

'Are you kidding me?! All these years we've been trying to help you with that, and trees, did it?' Helen stopped what she was doing.

'Yep. I still don't believe it myself. But after that, I started getting a conscience,' he moulded the wax into a heart. 'I miss it there, it calls me – it sort of...' he paused, looking out to the garden at his mother and nephew. 'This may sound stupid, but it feels part of me.'

After homemade veggie lasagne, Robert sat on the sofa with his mother as they watched some late night TV. Helen and Michael had both gone to bed after an exhausting day, but one that had closure. Jean was a sad lady, the loss of her husband meant the loss of half of her, because she not only lost her partner but her best friend, and nothing or no one would ever replace that. She constantly searched for something that would, but it was never quite right or good enough; turning to Hinduism to help heal her open wound. Michael was a very popular man, one that you instantly warmed to when you met him. He would help anyone and sacrifice himself to do so. They never wanted for much, having his own carpentry business and he was a prominent member of the family. He had strong family values, ones that had been passed down through the generations. Robert was the apple of his eye and his daughter, his most treasured possession. His death left them bereft and with a very big hole in their lives. She mourned him every day; her son was her only connection. Robert had the same attributes as his father and she was grateful he'd been such a good role model for him. He'd just lost his way a little when he became consumed by guilt and grief.

'What are you thinking about, Robbie?' she asked as she fussed, picking bits of fluff from his joggers.

'Mum, you know how much I love you, right?'

She changed her position and looked at her son. 'Of course I do, you just never say it enough.' Robert felt guilty because she was right.

'I know, and I'm sorry, I love you mum, but it goes without saying. My point is, what I want to say is, please stop calling me Robbie, I hate it – it sounds like…' he stretched out his arm, reaching for an explanation, '…like that boy band singer! I ain't about to change my image.'

Jean laughed a little through emerging tears. 'But I've called you that since you were a baby, you are my Robbie, and you always will be. It hurts me that you hate it, why haven't you said it before?'

'Don't cry mum, please, I didn't mean it to come out as badly as that. I'm sorry but it makes me cringe! I'm not a baby anymore. Why don't you get yourself a cat? Call that Robbie.'

'Well! If your father could hear you right now!'

'Oh, mum!' he put his head in his hands and was irritated by hearing the same old lines.

'I just miss you. You saturated me with unconditional love and that's what I lived on, every day. Then you left my arms, my hands and I feel silly that I miss you so much. I can't explain it. I call you that because it fills my heart back up. You brought such joy when you were little. Now, well, that's changed. It's the last bit of you I've got left. Do you remember when you had that imaginary friend?'

Robert swivelled round. 'No? Really?'

Jean nodded. 'We had to set the table for it and everything. It got ridiculous in the end. You even rushed home from nursery to see it. Gave me and your father the creeps!'

Robert snorted a small laugh, which quickly turned to a puzzled frown. 'I hope one day I will know what it means to miss a child, mum. I'm sorry.'

She smiled and tidied his hair then held his face. 'I don't think I'll ever get over losing your father, he was one in a million and now with all this is going on, I'm scared of losing you too. But I'm proud of you for wanting to change it.'

'Lilly is a special person, Mum. Just be happy for me.' Jean rubbed his knee, thinking that her son hadn't quite got over his grief and had chosen a woman that fed his imagination. She felt safe in the knowledge that it probably wouldn't last, and it was all just a bit of a novelty, to get over the loss of his father.

'We just need some normality in this family for once, I can't take all this nonsense anymore. I'm tired and had enough of it. I want to run away sometimes.'

'Don't say that, I'm sorry I got us into this but I'm going to get us out of it. All this – will soon be over, then you can sigh at normal and look forward to your beautiful grandchildren filling your void.' Jean looked at the aspidistras and wished her husband was there to apply some sense to this crazy situation.

'If all this brings peace, then I'm happy if you are. Just promise me one thing.' Robert sat up and was relieved that his mother had offered a fraction of her blessing. 'If she accepts you for who you are, do the right thing and let this be the end of it.'

'I will mum. Thank you.' They hugged and Jean felt her grief lift a little, she couldn't help but be a little bit cynical; it kept one's feet on the ground.

Thirty-Six

Robert woke up on the sofa, cold, having just the living room throw over him, which wasn't supposed to be used. He sat up and wondered where the hell he was for a split second. Jean came down and checked the living room.

'What are you doing in here? I thought you'd run away again.'

Robert sighed and rubbed his face, 'morning mum,' he said, exasperated.

'Morning…Robert. Coffee, is it?'

'Yes please, thank you. You're a diamond.'

'You look dreadful. Over thinking last night, were you?'

'Something like that.'

'Well, it's not good to sleep in here with all my plants. They've probably sucked the life out of you!' Robert sniffed and chuckled, getting up to go to the bathroom and kissing his mother on the cheek as he passed. She opened the curtains and the windows to alleviate the heaviness in the room. She never understood how a man managed to generate such a dreadful smell overnight - wafting her hand in front of her nose as she left the room, muttering words of distaste.

He turned the tap on and had a spring in his step, looking forward to seeing his tree wife again - he had mixed feelings about going back to Wales, but the pull was stronger than ever before. Washing his face, he felt like having one of his mother's English breakfasts, the hefty talk with her and small blessing, had given him an appetite. He had stepped into his father's shoes for five years, but had received the permission to move on from that role; liberating him as he let go of the responsibility but daunted by the new one, he had ahead of him.

'Uncle Robert? Is that you in there?' Michael knocked gently on the bathroom door.

'Yes mate, it is. Did you sleep ok?'

'Um, yes, I think so. I'm not sure, I had my eyes shut.'

Robert's laugh echoed. 'Good job. Do you need the toilet buddy?'

'Yes please.'

'Ok, hang on a sec.' Robert unlocked the door and let Michael in. 'Can I smell bacon?' he called out as he walked down the hall.

'Uh, no – was that a hint?' Jean answered, waiting for the coffee to percolate.

'Yes, it was,' Robert clapped his hands and rubbed them together, making her jump.

'Someone's full of the joys of spring. I can hazard a guess why.' Robert kissed his mother in excitement, much to her annoyance. Michael joined them, clutching the little Honda.

'Hey there little fella, are you having some breakfast with your uncle Robert?' Michael nodded proudly, making sure he chose the seat next to his uncle.

'Are you going home today?' he asked.

'Home? He is home,' Jean answered for him. Robert glanced at his mother.

'I'm going back to Wales, but later. So, we'll have some fun together first, okay?'

'Yay! Can I come with you? To Wales?' Robert ruffled Michael's fair hair, ever surprised at his intelligence, feeling uncomfortable at how much he looked like Phil. A gentle, sensitive little soul, with a piercing look.

'Not this time buddy, but you can come and visit any time you want, once I've sorted out a house.' Helen was the last to join them, her hair messy and her eyes smudged with mascara, yawning.

'Morning everyone. Did you sleep ok Robert?'

'Morning squirt. Well, I ended up on the sofa. Mum's triffids were feeding off me all night. I had a plant hangover this morning,' Robert answered, making Helen blurt out a tired laugh. She missed her big brother; he always brought light to any subject. She laughed more when he was home, feeling safe and happy again in his company.

'I'm surprised they're all still alive! The damn smell you left in there!' Jean commented as she started the breakfast. Michael put his hand over his mouth, laughing at something he thought he wasn't supposed to.

'What's your grandma saying about me, ay?'

After a long breakfast and the best family sit down, they'd had in a while, talking about his father, with fondness. It was good therapy for them all. Robert and Michael walked to the park, hand in hand and chatted about boys' stuff and school.

'I'm going to miss you when you go Uncle Robert.'

'I'll miss you too buddy, but you can call me anytime you want. We shouldn't be going to the park, you should be at school.'

'They won't mind. I'm always there usually.' Robert chuckled to himself at Michael's funny comments. The walk was peaceful and meditation for the mind; a bright day with a light breeze that aroused the smell of freshly cut grass and clean air. The street was lined with Maples, full of tweeting sparrows; their roots lifting up the paving, making it a little hazardous. Properties with matured gardens made the place look beautiful - the area knocked spots off Wales, but not as much warmth, he'd noticed lately.

'Is Lilly going to make the bad man go away?'

'Well, maybe, but nobody really goes away.'

'Only if they die.'

'Yes, there is that, but if you love them, they'll always be in your heart.'

'I don't love him. He needs to die, so he will go away.'

Robert was stuck how to answer, silently agreeing. 'Now, you shouldn't say things like that, you shouldn't wish anyone dead.'

'Why?'

'Because.......' Robert thought, taking in the good day, briefly looking up to the sky; which always reminded him of Lillian '.... because God will leave them here on purpose, just to annoy you and make you say sorry, or make peace with them.'

'How do you make peace? In the kitchen?' Michael answered, skipping.

'Ha! No – Peace means not to hate or worry anymore; when your heart feels happy, light. It also means to stop fighting, stop war.'

'Like you felt when you hugged the tree?' Robert stopped dead, looking dumbfounded at Michael.

'How did you know about that?!'

'I saw it, in the mirror.'

Robert blushed, looking horrified. 'Mirror?! You too?'

'And the nice, blue people tell me things.'

'Is that what, they are?'

'Am I in trouble?' Michael's mouth curled. They continued walking.

'How can you be in trouble for being awesome?' Michael radiated at Robert's acceptance of him, and skipped higher.

'Carry me! Carry me!' holding up his arms.

Robert straightened and braced himself. 'Okay. One...two....three...' lifting Michael, grunting, staggering backwards a little, then continued with his extra load.

'I think I need to go to the gym! What have you been eating? Stones?!' Michael wrapped his legs around Robert's waist and held on, closing his eyes as he absorbed his uncle's unassuming energies, ones that nourished him. Laughing aloud.

'I'll carry you to the park big fella then I'll have to put you down, you're breaking my back!' Michael closed his eyes tight and didn't want the ride to stop, he craved male company. They reached the park, much to Robert's relief. Michael ran to the last swing that was left.

'Push me Uncle Robert!' He called out with excitement; jiggling his slight, pale body, trying to get it moving.

'Ok, but are you ready?'

'Yes! I'm ready! Will you push me up to the moon?'

'Five...Four...Three...Two...One! Blast off!' Robert made a noise, hoping it sounded like a launching rocket; he was happy with it anyway. Michael screeched in anticipation and waited for the next push. Robert checked his watch, it wasn't his most favourite thing to do, he found it totally brain numbing. But recently he changed his mind about it, his father always did it, a memory he treasured. Pushing a child on a swing through each stage of their life, moving up to the bigger ones as they develop, until one day they can do it alone. That's when you feel them leave you, leave your hands. He stretched out his legs the higher he got, imagining himself reaching the moon with his feet. Robert went through the motions of pushing, his pressing issue, forefront in his mind. Staring into space going over conversations in his head, whilst managing to keep his face and teeth clear of the swing seat. As he got into a steady momentum, Michael began to scream and kick his legs.

'Get me down! Get me down!'

Robert was snapped out of his daze and automatically grabbed the swing to slow it down, 'sorry buddy, am I going too high?'

'Get me down!' Michael cried.

Robert stopped the swing. 'What is it? What happened? Did I push you too high? Sorry,' he rubbed his nephews back to comfort him.

'Don't let him take me! I don't want to go with him! Please! I'm scared!' Michael was in distress.

'You're not making sense, don't let who take you? What happened while you were on the moon?' Michael slid off the swing. Robert's smile was wiped off his face when he noticed there was a pee patch starting to appear at the front of Michael's trousers, escalating, pooling at his feet, drenching his socks.

'Hey, hey, buddy, why didn't you tell me you needed to go?' Michael convulsed, shaking 'what is it? Tell me!'

'The...bad... man – is over there!' Michael pointed in the direction of the entrance. Robert looked round, scanning everyone to see where Phil was. His mouth going dry.

'I can't see him, he's gone, okay? He's gone. Maybe you imagined it.'

Michael shook his head and pointed again, 'he's there!'

Robert looked, but there was no Phil and no one that resembled him either. 'I can't see him, he's not there. I swear Michael.' Robert got down to his level and held his arms.

'I'm not awesome like you, I can't see him. Is he still there now?' he nervously looked again and nodded slowly.

'Okay, I tell you what we're going to do. Think of us just now, trying to touch the moon.' Michael smiled feebly, sniffing. 'I'll try, but I'm a bit wet.'

Robert wiped Michael's tears with his thumbs and held onto his face. 'It doesn't matter about that. We'll sort it out when we go home. Now, the moon and let's throw some chocolate in there as well.'

Michael was tense but kept his eyes on Robert. 'The moon is made of chocolate?'

'Now you're talking. What's it taste like, apart from chocolate of course?'

Michael squeezed his eyes shut, silently calling for the blue fairies. 'Umm, like the one you bought me, Lilly's one.'

'Ah, the best kind then?'

Michael warily looked round. 'He's gone now. Lilly's chocolate did it.'

'Good, but I think you did it little fella. Come on, let's get you back home and sort you out, I'll carry you.' Robert picked up Michael with newfound strength, wincing as he had to put his hands on the boy's saturated trousers. Checking and looking out for Phil, feeling threatened. They reached the house, Robert opened the front door and called out.

'Some help here please!' Helen came running and saw that they were both wet.

'Oh Michael! You should have gone before you went!'

Robert glared at her shaking his head. 'Not now Hel, just sort him out, it's not his fault. I need to change.'

Jean came out to the hall. 'What's happened now?!'

'It's okay mum, we just had a little accident, put the kettle on please.' Robert got changed, feeling traumatised by the poor child's reaction; his hate increasing. He came down with his soiled clothes in his hands and put them in the washing machine. There was a hot drink waiting for him on the table, 'cheers mum.'

'What happened?' Robert opened the conservatory and sat outside. Every time he thought of Michael, he was choked with emotion. It kept repeating itself in his head, like a stuck record.

'What happened, I said?!' Jean came out frustrated that Robert had ignored her.

'I don't know what to say mum, I really don't.' Robert covered his eyes, faced with an overpowering situation.

'You're scaring me, what?!' Jean asked as she sat next to him and pulled on his arm.

'He saw Phil. He was so petrified, he peed himself.'

She sat back and looked out to the garden. 'Oh my God, that's why.'

'What do you mean? That's why!'

'That's why he wets the bed sometimes, but he won't tell us why, he says he's not supposed to.' Jean put her head in her hands. 'I feel so terrible, the poor boy. What are we going to do?'

Robert sighed and was pained as he thought about the nights that Michael had to deal with his fear alone. 'I don't know right now, but it's too dangerous to do anything about, and who would believe us anyway? Not even his own family do, except me, they'll take him away from us - and forgive me for saying this, but you seriously need to open your mind! There's far too much generational influence in there, Mum! You're too shut off from your own intuition! You do all that, chakra stuff. What are you doing it for, anyway?'

'So, I don't get any nasty visitors. Did you see him?' Jean asked smugly.

'Well, I was waiting for that. No, I didn't. But then I'm not gifted like he is and by the sounds of it, that's how Phil visits him. You need to start believing him before it affects him for the rest of his life. Phil wasn't there physically, I would've seen him. He uses a mirror. Lilly uses....' He stopped, that just wouldn't help the situation.

'A mirror? What do you mean?'

'He uses mirrors to communicate, pass through. Something we laymen can't do.'

Jean shivered, 'poor little mite, what's he been brought into this world for? Life can be so cruel sometimes and all you can do is shake your fists at it.'

'He's here for a damned good reason, just like everyone else is. Life isn't cruel, people are, there's a blessing in everything. Put your hand on your heart, there's a reason. Michael is a special little boy. He just needs a bit of direction.'

Jean rolled her eyes and looked over to the neighbour's garden – envying their normal life. 'Well, that should be fun. Hadn't you better be going soon?'

Robert ignored his mother's comment, 'yes. Trying to get rid of me now? You'll be crying for me later,' he went to see what his sister and nephew were doing. He shouted up the stairs 'are you two okay up there?!' Michael appeared on the landing, changed and looking a bit fresher.

'Yes, all clean now. Mummy had to peel my trousers off, like a banana. She said a bad word, too.'

Robert looked down to hide his smirk; the innocence warming the dire situation.

'Good job. You certainly look a lot better, mummies are clever like that. Come down now, and we'll have a chat,' he held his arms out and waited for Michael to reach him. Helen followed and Robert could see she had been crying, he waited for them both and they all hugged together at the foot of the stairs.

'Just get him, ok, I don't care how, just get rid of him, please,' she said as she held on tight to her brother.

'I'll do my best.' Michael joined his Gran in the garden; having a deep conversation with her as they dug over the weeds.

'I know you don't want to believe me Gran, you're just too scared to,' he saw a bug, stopping what he was doing to study it.

Jean brushed over his hair affectionately. 'I just find you a bit strange, I suppose, but you're still my Grandson, and I do love you.' A new love had washed over her as she watched him, angelic and full of the universe. 'Are you, um, I mean, can you speak to your Grandad? At all?' she asked, looking around to see if she was heard.

'No Gran, it's not like that - it's not like that at all. But he said you have to stop crying and love those who are still here.'

Thirty-Seven

Lillian was going over in her head what she was going to say to Jeffrey about her date with Robert. She would just like to walk through the door and have half an hour before food; being force fed as soon as she got home was beginning to drive her mad. Too busy thinking about what to wear, the For Sale sign outside the house almost went unnoticed. Lillian pulled up looking at it, not sure how she felt. It was the end, finally. Arriving quietly, not how she imagined it at all.

'Hi, sorry I'm late. I got held up. What's the sign up for?' Jeffrey just grunted. 'Were you going to tell me?' Jeffrey put the plates on the table and didn't answer.

'How was your day anyway?' she asked him.

Jeffrey looked at her with that hollow soul of his. 'Birmingham's gettin' closer. You packed yet?'

Lillian gulped. 'There's an event tomorrow night. In the hotel. It's a celebration. I shouldn't be too late.' Lillian waited for the explosion.

'Another one? With whom? BMW man?!'

She held firm. 'Yes, and everyone else.'

Jeffrey tapped the table. 'I don't trust ya. But go and make the most of it. Take it as a leaving do. You drivin'?'

Lillian nodded. 'Good. Well, means you ain't drinkin.'

Lillian's heart pumped, she needed to get ready, but she would have to wait for him to leave first, even though things had moved forward. Jeffrey grabbed her arm as she walked past the table.

'You really thought I was lettin' yer go, didn't ya?' she took her arm away.

'I didn't ask for your permission!' she carried on, but Jeffrey grabbed her again, sending shooting pains up to her shoulder with his vice-like grip, 'let go! What's wrong with you?! Do you want to come as well? I'm sure they wouldn't mind.'

'I ain't losing ya. That's all. I'm not happy you going with them. Cancel it.'

'No. I'm not cancelling it. It's my job. I have to show my face. Now let me go, please!' Jeffrey loosened his grip, leaving white finger marks on her arm.

'While ya dancing with Robert Courtney, think about what you're going to do with that bluddy cat! I'm working late all this week, got a big job on. Make sure yer home when I get back, and start packing!' Lillian ignored him. After he left, she used the front door and fled the house with a tight gut, speeding to the Hilton hotel and feeling nervous.

Robert was already waiting outside reception; dressed in dark chinos and a short sleeve blue shirt and a black, leather jacket. Her stomach squelched when she saw him. He smiled seeing the Honda again and his beautiful tree wife driving it.

She shook all over as she walked to him. Robert was taken aback – she wore a red t-shirt, with a large rose motif in the centre and tight black trousers.

'Wow, you look, wow. You're not going to kiss me with those big red lips, are you?'

'No. Not yet anyway. It was difficult to get out. I nearly didn't make it. If I don't turn up for anything, you know why.'

'I'm sorry, blame me. Uh…what's that on your arm?' Robert stroked the red marks.

'Nothing. So, shall we?'

'Did he do that?' Robert pointed with a creased brow.

'Can we just go, please?' she tearfully asked.

'All right Cinderella. But those ugly sisters are treading on thin ice,' he led her to the beamer and opened the door for her. He could feel what Jeffrey was feeling, it must be painful, and he wouldn't like to be in the same position. But it was no excuse to hurt her. He disliked men who couldn't control their animal.

Lillian huffed out the stress as she got in. 'The house is up for sale,' she sighed.

'That must have been hard for you. I'm sorry. But things don't feel so nice when they're pushed forward. You come out the other side smiling though, you do know that, right? I did say I would kill him if he hurt you, and I'm getting closer to that notion. You have to get out now, no pressure, but pressure is on. Or I'm coming to get you myself!'

'Where you taking me?'

'Do you like Italian?'

'Umm...does it have to be Italian?'

'No, it doesn't. This is Lilly's night. Where would you like to go? Name it.'

'Somewhere restauranty. Where they have steak and custard.'

'Okay. You're the boss. Only you'll have to guide me, I am a foreigner in these parts.' He rummaged in the side pocket of the door for a CD, as he drove out.

'Let's have a bit of, Crowded House, shall we?' he pushed the disc in the slot; Lillian watched it disappear, expensively.

'Haven't you got anything by Prince?'

'Serious? What do you take me for? Can't say I have. I can see why you like him – he's purple. I like the one about the rain, though. Gets me waving in the air, connecting with my inner turmoil. Maybe I should invest. What's the deal with this colour, anyway?'

'You know the answer to that, surely?'

'I guess. It's kind of a ... statement, although I'm not sure what. I have a feeling I'll be finding out sooner rather than later. Anyway, changing the subject. I've never been to Cardiff before. But can I just say that the only big lights worth seeing, are those in London. That'll be our next venture.'

'Why don't we go there now and never come back?'

Robert smiled with fondness, rubbing her knee, 'all in good time, Cooch, all in good time.'

Driving into the city and into a different life; the day had just started over, as the night crawlers lined the streets. The city's castle lights shone on the gargoyles, slumped over the over the walls, each one making different faces at Lillian's excitement overflowing.

'It's better than I thought, here. Good call, Lil.'

'What were you expecting? More sheep and trees?'

Robert laughed coyly, 'well, now you've come to mention it.' He searched for the best multi-storey, still feeling a bit lost. His jacket made a noise with every movement; releasing the smell of new leather combined with his cologne.

'What do you think about this one? It's more central,' he said as he waited for the machine to spit out a ticket.

'You'll pay more here. May have been better to park further out,' Lillian answered.

'The closer the better. No expense spared. Radar are paying,' he took the ticket and stuck it between his teeth. Those teeth: that anything would feel privileged to be clamped in. He parked up confidently and Lillian admired the light reflection in the beamer's bodywork, and it was beginning to feel like their chariot.

'Right then. You'll have to lead the way or maybe we'll just wing it. Follow the scent of beef,' he looked at her and still couldn't believe his luck.

'What?' Lillian asked, feeling a surge from his gaze.

'I am not worthy. That's what. I have something for you,' he reached behind his seat and gave her the present.

'Oh! A present?' she loved the paper, feeling the pattern; signs, were everywhere.

'Why sound so surprised? Don't you have presents?' she looked at the beautifully wrapped box.

'Well, open it then!'

She opened it carefully trying not to tear the paper, catching a glimpse of what it was.

'You didn't?!' she looked again, just seeing the word 'Nokia'. Taking more paper off, her guess was right...a mobile phone.

'You got me a mobile phone?! Oh my God!' she just looked at the box, the smell of the new print and weight of it, adding to the gift. Robert was humbled by her reaction.

'Now there's no excuse. They're easy to use. Contract is already set up. Just use it, in case you get kidnapped, or something.'

Lillian opened the box with a huge smile. 'Thank you so much. I love it,' she took it out of the plastic sleeve; pressing the buttons - it was quite heavy. Now she would have to get a new handbag.

'You're welcome. It needs charging first,' she looked at him adoringly, dying to kiss him.

'Come on, or we'll never get out of here and I don't fancy spending the night in a car park. Put it in the glove box, for now,' he got out and opened her door.

'After you, Miz Lillian,' he said, holding his arm out to the side. 'Let's go live a little.'

Lillian wished for Robert and 'poof' there he was, in the flesh, getting to her through a network of unicorns. They looked alike and seemed like an established couple; she was feeling beautiful and spoilt, as well as a little bit sceptical. Being treated so badly for so long became the expected norm. Walking arm in arm, feeling protected, periodically looking over her shoulder in case Jeffrey decided to have a walk around during his break. The crowds were gathering outside clubs, with women barely covered and men clean shaven. They walked for a few minutes and couldn't see any restaurants that suited; Las Iguanas was a new chain just opened, but it was packed to rafters and noisy.

'Look, Lilly, why don't you want to go to an Italian? They do steak.'

'Jeffrey took me out on our first date to one, and I just don't want history repeating itself.' Robert tutted loudly.

'It ain't gonna happen! Look...' he pointed to a stray black cat, sniffing around the bins, 'that black cat says so. Let's go and reverse the cycle. We'll choose a pukka one. Okay Miss?' she nodded and accepted defeat. But the defeat came in the form of a fortress, a Courtney fortress.

They found one on a main street elevated by stone steps. It was small but the exterior boasted tradition and the smell of garlic and herbs, drew you in. The owner was waiting to greet his customers by the door. Italian lounge music played, making it feel authentic - with red and white checked tablecloths and Chianti bottles, hosting melted red candles; something for Robert to pick at.

'Welcome to Giuseppe's. Can we 'ave a special table for two beyoutiful peeple please,' he said to his waiter, in a smooth Italian accent. He led them to a window seat, where they could look down on the nightlife. Robert couldn't take his eyes off Lillian, pulling the chair out for her; it was the rose motif making a statement on the bright red, accentuating her breasts. The waiter handed them menus and some breadsticks.

'Would you like to see the wine menu, sir?' the waiter asked.

'Uh, Lilly, you drinking?'

'Umm, do you have Mateus? Please?'

The waiter dipped his head, 'just one glass? Or are you partaking as well, sir?'

'Uh, no, not for me thanks. Just water for me please.'

'Of course. Still or sparkling?'

'Still please and one extra for the lady.' He nodded but didn't really understand Robert's accent. He was getting used to the Welsh one, not unlike Italian; having a stab at what he asked for. Lillian looked through the menu, scanning the list for steak. There were Oysters, 'eww', and cannelloni, as expected.

'Mateus? Really? You could have chosen something a bit classier than that,' Robert said as he also scanned what was on offer; the handmade Pizzas did look good.

'Says you, with a black and white canvas of New York on the wall,' she continued reading the menu.

Robert looked up from his 'what else have you seen?!' he asked nervously.

'Enough. Are you saying I'm not classy?'

'Perish the thought. You deserve something a bit better than Portuguese plonk!'

'You sound like Dad. I like Mateus. I don't like red wine; you wake up in the morning feeling like a prune with a mouth like a nomad's sandal.'

Robert sniggered behind the menu, 'you do have a point there, actually. What does your dad drink?'

'Scotch, mostly. Just a little, when, well – on a Sunday. Mum says he's been drinking it on other days lately. Do you drink?'

'No. I don't. But that's for another time.'

'Oh, please, tell me why.'

Robert looked around the restaurant before revealing a scar, just above his heart. 'That's why.'

Lillian gasped, 'what happened?!'

Robert sighed and looked out the window. 'Timing, tree wife, timing. I was stabbed, mistaken identity. I got drunk on a regular basis, wallowing in self-pity – while mum and Helen grieved at home. I came out of a club and this guy thought I was someone else. That's it, really. Luck. Like you and that, thing you had. Few more centimetres and I wouldn't have been sat here looking at your beautiful face. After that, I stayed at home. Never drank a drop since.'

'What sort of timing?'

'What do you mean?'

'Random timing or precision timing?'

'Precision,' he covered his face with the menu, hoping that was the right answer.

Lillian could hear a familiar voice in the restaurant, she turned her head, listening with her eyes. She recognised it.

'I can hear Tim Smith!' she whispered sharply across the table. Robert moved his eyes to locate him, keeping his head still. He spotted him, entertaining customers and a couple of the Tech guys. The waiter returned with the water and Lillian's Mateus; she snatched a gulp.

'Are you ready to order, Sir?'

'Steak. We'll have the steak please, medium rare. With chips,' Robert answered, in a lowered voice.

'Of course. Thank you,' the waiter took the menus and retreated. Lillian revelled in the ambience as she watched the night life pass, giving off electricity as they cavorted under the neon lights; the guitar strumming in the background, adding to the romance of it all. The feel of the city was hostile, diverse but a world away from Coed-y-Ffrind close and Radar. Robert was watching her gazing out the window with contentment. He was beginning to feel at home - Wales grounded him, sheltering the harshness.

'What are you looking at?'

'Humans. Do you ever marvel at what we can build? With just these,' she held up her hands. 'We're just fleshy fragiles, and we did all of this. Or maybe it's done when we sleep.' Robert just smiled, in awe of her.

'Is that your happy face?' he asked.

'Yes, with a hint of hysteria.'

Robert adjusted the cutlery on the table and began to munch on a breadstick.

'Same. How has Phil been?' Lillian also took a breadstick, trying to crunch it without smudging her lipstick. Robert stared at her and the action was a little too provocative as she bit it with red lips. He coughed and brushed imaginary crumbs off the table, her blue eyes, bouncing off the matt rouge. He could feel the charge she emanated, looking out the window at the couples and groups - he didn't want to see what her eyes had to say or if they'd changed colour, she became someone else when they did.

'Do you have a bike?' Lillian asked, afraid of the answer.

Robert faced her, with a puzzled look. 'Bike...do I have a bike? As in, a bicycle, bike?' Lillian nodded.

'Uh...I used to, way back, when I was a kid. Why?'

'Nothing. Just checking,' Lillian was relieved, Robert was perplexed. She would be making sure she told Lisa he didn't have a bike, see what she had to say about that.

'Was there any point to that question?' he sipped his water.

'No. I just wanted to make sure,' he was still none the wiser but loved her randomness.

'Here's a random cliché – what's your favourite film?' he asked.

'Pretty Woman.'

'Meh, I kind of expected that. But yeah, good one. Mine's Jurassic Park. The title music makes me feel all squooshy. You seen it?'

'No. Mum didn't want to see that. Too farfetched, she said.'

'Ha! How ironic! Sorry, just jesting. But you know what I mean. The man's a genius, kids will be begging for all the merchandise. I'll take you to see it. That reminds me, I said I'd call my nephew. No reception in here though. Cardiff hasn't caught up yet, obviously.' She felt herself falling into him, especially now he didn't have a bike – his tenderness for children was also a very big 'tick'.

She studied him, emanated her dark feminine, impressed how he knew how to use a mobile phone so well. He received vibe from her as he did through the mirror, making him perspire.

'Lilly, stop it,' she watched his Adams apple move as he drank and undo a shirt button, the colour blue dancing against his olive skin. He put his glass down, feeling uncomfortable.

'Cut it out!' he said through clenched teeth, 'not in here!' there was a hint of laughter in his voice, but he was trying so hard to be serious to ward her off, for now. Any woman can do it, once she feels appreciated. Lillian located his leg with her foot, making him flinch and bang his knee on the table. 'Lil!'

Tim Smith was on the move, a toilet break. Lillian picked up her glass and held it in front of her face.

'What are you doing now?!' Robert whispered. She looked at him through the peachy liquid, his features distorted. Lillian jabbed her finger at Tim and began to snigger.

'How long is it since you've been out?' he turned around, just catching Tim disappear through a doorway. 'Of all the bloody places to choose, and *he* is here. I mean, what are the chances?' Robert's annoyance made Lillian laugh even more, trying not to choke on her drink.

She couldn't remember the last time she laughed like this, tears appeared, with Robert looking on unimpressed. He wanted a romantic night out and Radar had to go and ruin it. Having visions of holding hands across the table, feeding each other spaghetti, like Lady and the Tramp – fat chance of that now, Lillian was close to laugh-snorting. She let out a very loud Lilly giggle just as Tim was returning to his table. He saw them.

'I don't believe it! Fancy seein' you 'ere!' he was sweating, as always; dressed in jeans and a checked summer shirt.

'Yeah, how about that,' Robert flatly replied. 'You haven't seen us, by the way,' he added.

'Mum's the word,' Tim tapped his nose. 'Tell you what, the bill's on me.'

'No, please Tim, it's fine, I got this. Thanks,' Robert protested.

'How about a bottle then. I insist. You two...err...' he pointed back and forth between them, gesturing with his scruffy eyebrows.

'We're ...'err'...having a break from the tender,' Lillian butted in.

'Ah. I see,' he nudged Robert 'you didn't hang about. Anyway. Better be getting back to the geeks. I'm glad I bumped into you two. Enjoy your night,' he winked a cheeky wink and sauntered back to his table.

The food came; browned steak oozing juices, still sizzling with beautiful chips all crisp and even and quite a nice side salad.

'Buon Appetito,' the waiter said, 'would you like any pepper?'

'Oh! Yes please!' Lillian wanted to see that oversized peppermill, like in the movies, just to see if it was real. She waited and there it was, as real as anything. The waiter turned it, Lillian watching the ground kernels fall on her food. She held her hand up, 'that's it, thank you.' Robert shook his head as it was offered over his side.

They both carved the meat like salivating carnivores.

'I'm taking you to a club after this,' he chewed. 'Get rid of some of that pent up whatsit in there,' he pointed at her with his steak knife. Lillian wasn't sure if that was a good idea, heaven knows what might happen...maybe she would self-combust from all that release.

'Ok. There's Zeus just round the corner.'

'Zeus it is. Although I had a feeling it would be something mythical.'

'Do you dance?' she asked.

'When I'm alone, which is every night basically. Or I seat dance when I'm driving. But we're not going for me, we're going or you. I'll stand on the side and hold your bag.' He winked and shoved in a large morsel of meat in his mouth, smiling as he chewed. They didn't feel embarrassed eating in front of one another. Lillian tried to play footsie again, but Robert had his feet tucked under the seat, on purpose.

There was a long queue outside the nightclub; all walks of life dressed in shimmer and Lycra, ready to enter their escape pod. Lillian gawped, unable to take her eyes off the colourful people. Above the door was a larger than life gold effigy of Zeus; holding up a basket of fire that periodically jetted flames. Red carpet ran from the entrance, in. Either side of the doors were two golden urns and two stocky bouncers holding tally counters, interrogating patrons before letting them enter. They reminded Lillian of the bailiffs that raided Pulse. The building was covered with black, polished granite that sparkled under the streetlights. The boom of the music could be heard, and Lillian's excitement grew.

'They play Ministry of Sound in here!' Lillian whispered, squeezing Robert's arm.

'We're coming out deaf then,' he said, making her smile from her feet. She tried to see inside, going on tiptoe, peering over heads. They reached the ticket box and Lillian could hardly contain herself; the entrance fee was not for the feint hearted or the tight-fisted. They walked up grand stairs that were carpeted in black and gold; laced with tube lighting, the music getting louder. As they reached the top of the stairs, the smell of dry ice and sweat hit them. Lillian's hair stood on end as the dance floor came into view – the DJ inside a raised podium covered in gold discs. Four circular cages were positioned on the edges, each containing a scantily-cladded dancer. The bar stretched along the back of the club, crammed with neatly laid out coloured bottles of all shapes and sizes and over stretched bar staff, showing off their cocktail making skills. Lillian let go of Robert's arm and walked in front of him. She stopped at the barrier and looked down at the mass of raised arms and writhing bodies.

Tables were being served by waiters wearing gold hot pants and white bow ties, with gold Mardi gras masks. Alcoves adorned erotic, gold statues and soft lighting. It was Sodom and Gomorrah, with a touch of class. She felt Robert grab her arm, 'stay close!' he shouted in her ear. The baseline boomed through her torso, taking over her heartbeat. She recognised the music from her darker days of rebellion, overfeeding her ego. Lillian could feel herself getting taller again and the rise of erotica ran up through her neck and flushed her face. Robert caught a glance; he was mesmerised how she could change like that, connecting them in their own realm. She was an open vessel tonight, one that overflowed with the stars. They stood on the edge, embarrassed of being slightly out of place...watching the DJ controlling and seducing his masses, shouting in one another's ears.

She observed the nocturnal life trapped within four black walls, the lights with their own ritual, perfectly timed to the bass. She'd never witnessed it before, enthralled and scared – the uninhibited glowing in the dark. Robert tapped her shoulder, crossing his eyes at her. He was funny, in a sophisticated kind of way and just wanted her attention. Lillian dragged him by the hand onto the dance floor, pushing through people to get to a space she could see; being squeezed by a body mangle. The flashing lights were blinding, the floor pulsated beneath their feet. Lillian's senses reached an all-time high, people in all directions flirted with them, pulling them into the crowd. Her arm was grabbed by a half dressed man who she recognised from one of the cages, with biceps that were obviously his only love. His dark skinned body glistened from the coloured lights illuminating his beads of sweat. Robert watched her being pulled away through the swarm, her arms raised, being twirled in circles – he looked on in adoration as she danced away years of oppressed self-expression; his disdain for Jeffrey, growing. It was that red t-shirt with that big Rose.

Robert fought his way through with a slight panic going on. Feeling inadequate as she was being seduced by a black

Chippendale, with the tightest buttocks he'd ever seen. Her bursting personality was a beacon, animated under the strobe lighting. The track picked up speed and everyone started jumping up and down. Robert winced, pushing through everyone, his eyes homing in on her. He reached for her raised arm, making her turn. They reunited, eyes locked, still, while everything else buzzed around them. The muscle man disappeared into the crowd looking for his next dance partner. She held onto Robert as their space was filling up. Club Anthems were on continuous play, erecting all the hair on their bodies, heating up their fibres. They were being bombarded and forced together – entering personal space, their scents mingled.

The energy from the beat tantalised and hypnotised them into thinking there was no one else around, losing themselves to the psychedelic vice. Robert fought against its temptation but was quickly giving in as Lillian's smile grew and her body moved freely. The beat pumped, replacing their rhythm...he couldn't keep up, she was a good dancer. They were tantalised by the music's manipulation, it felt so good. Lillian screamed with elation and intense excitement - she couldn't be heard but she felt the pressure leave her lungs, releasing the tension of reserve. They danced for over an hour, but the relentless spewing of techno and symbols were starting to take its toll, Robert could no longer tolerate it. He made the 'T' sign with his hands to Lillian, he needed a drink and to get out of this place.

They made their way over to the bar, heaving their way through hand in hand, getting man-handled and groped as they squeezed passed. Robert pushing them aside getting increasingly overprotective. At the bar he ordered two soft drinks, with ice. She drank without pausing for breath, he sipped his like the gentleman he was and didn't take his eyes off her. Nightclubs made him nervous; he clocked far more than she did and was still recovering from her being snatched. She danced around him as he drank. He watched her, his very own Pandora's Box, with the odd squeaky toy. Robert the bodyguard, casing the joint. He was sensitive but exuded a primitive masculinity. Putting his glass down on the bar, he indicated to leave, he was tired of yelling and wary of the clientele.

The cold night air was welcome; their ears ringing, making them lightheaded.

'That was a-maze-zing! Thank you,' Lillian spelt the words out with hand gestures in the sky, still dancing.

'It was and you are welcome. My feet are killing me! Right, where next?' Robert asked. Lillian looked at her watch, 'somewhere quiet and civilised.' Robert immediately thought of the hotel lounge for a coffee.

'Hotel it is.' Lillian agreed, it was a chance to see where he hides out and waits for her mirror contact. 'Tell you what...race you to the car! Last one there is a pig!'

Robert started running and Lillian followed giggling uncontrollably, her feet pounding the concrete, stinging the inflamed muscles. They ran into a crowd of inebriated youths, but Robert kept going, not wanting to lose first position. Lillian was snatched as she ran passed them.

'Oi! Where you running to, love?' stopping her, smothering her. Although he was drunk, he was strong and held on like a boa constrictor. She screamed out to Robert; he stopped and looked around. Where was she? Was she playing? He saw her, doubling back, sprinting and shouting.

'Hey! Leave her! Let her go! Right now! I said, right now!' the guy holding her raised his hands.

'Okay, okay. Blighty,' making fun of his accent, 'just messing, bit of fun,' swaying, trying to focus.

Robert grabbed his shirt and pulled him in with force 'go get a life!'

Lillian tried to release his hand.

'Robert, it's okay, leave him.'

He threw the guy back.

'Ooh! Robert!' they jeered. The gang stumbled together, singing football chants and pointing in his direction, aiming the words at him.

'You all right?!' Robert held Lillian square by the arms, looking her up and down, checking for anything.

'I'm fine, Lancelot,' falling deeper from the rescue. 'But you just lost your position!' She ran, laughing, Robert following, laughing too. He ran across the road to the multi-storey without regard – making Lillian squeal. She lost sight of him as he entered the car park but was determined to get to the car first. She passed him at the ticket machine and kept running.

'Oi! That's cheating!' he called after her, panting. She reached the BMW and leaned on it, as she caught her breath.

'Pig!' she shouted and laughed loud, sniffing and spitting a little, hoping he didn't see that bit.

Robert accepted his defeat. He handed her the keys, 'your prize.' She snatched them off him and got in, adjusting the seat and mirrors.

'You ready? Pig,' Lillian said as Robert got in.

'Is that my new pet name now? After I just rescued you from the grips of broken society?' she turned to him.

'I had a great time. The best in ever. Thank you. I missed you so bad.'

He gulped, getting dizzy from those noises he got in his head when he felt like he was falling into her.

'Don't. Just drive. You'll get us into trouble.'

Thirty-Eight

Lillian looked around the hotel reception discreetly, checking for any Radar employees. But there were just a few strangers talking with brandy and cigars. The pianist played lounge jazz in the background, making it feel expensive. She could feel the butterflies returning.

'What if someone sees us?' she whispered nervously.

'I'll make sure they don't.'

'Tim Smith could be in there for all we know.'

'He won't bring his customers here. Trust me.' The décor was white and turquoise with a large marble fireplace in the centre, which you could see through to the other side of - Lillian made a point of bending and looking. He took her hand, and the sensations came tenfold, choosing a table and waited to be served. 'My ears are still ringing!' Lillian waggled them with her finger.

'My feet are ringing, I don't about my ears.' Robert responded.

'Lightweight!' Lillian sat back and laughed. A member of staff came to the table to take their order.

'Two coffees, please,' Robert asked, wishing he could take off his shoes. The waitress's shift was nearly over, her feet were killing her too. Robert wiped over his mouth and to his chin as he looked at Lillian.

'I didn't know half of the music that was playing in that place. I must be getting old!'

'The DJ was a demi-god.' She unfolded her arms and sat forward. 'We won the tender, didn't we?'

Robert's face drained. 'What? Who told you that?'

The waitress returned with a stainless-steel pot and two white cup and saucers, with complimentary biscuits; stooping to place the tray on the table. Lillian waited for her to leave.

'Phil needs to be more careful having such news on loudspeaker.' Robert poured the coffee, liking it the same as Lillian's. He watched her add the sugar lumps and wondered when she was going to stop.

'You like a bit of coffee with your sugar then?' he said, with Lillian giving him a look.

'Don't change the subject, Courtney.' Maybe a late-night coffee was a bad idea, she wouldn't sleep for weeks. However, the stimulant would be beneficial to her plan.

'Okay. You're right. I didn't think it was *that* loud.' He sat back, the seduction had left abruptly, not knowing what to do with arms.

Lillian slurped the coffee, placing the cup back on the saucer.

'Oh, it wasn't loud,' Lillian tingled all over. Her invasion into the office through her reflection in the window was a first.

'You mean...you, I don't understand, how did you hear?' Lillian added another lump of sugar with the tiny silver tongs, and dropped it in the cup, 'plop'. Just one more should do it.

'I was watching the traffic go by and got lost in the momentum, then I heard the whole conversation, with that man that sounded very public school-ish. I told you it was cheating. We won it because we cheated. *You* cheated!' Robert swallowed nervously, she was onto him. He could hear his mother in his head. 'You don't look like a Robbie, either. But your soul does. Robert is that exterior of yours you carry around, the one that makes me go all weak at the knees,' he felt sick. How foolish to think he could pull the wool over *her* eyes.

'Ok, I'm a bit freaked out right now, but then, what did I expect?' he shifted, looking around, his vision blurring from the panic. He wanted this woman more than anything he dare think about.

'The file. Phil gave to me. The quote I had to get, the one that I was involved in...that guy who works from home...' she finger quoted 'in St. Helier. There aren't any offices in St. Helier, I checked.' She drew on the hot coffee.

Robert ran his fingers through his hair, 'okay, okay. Stop,' he held out his hand, surrendering. 'The guy in Jersey, well, he err, used to work at Sisco. He doesn't work for Radar. Where's that piece paper you sent to him?' He leaned over to her, his palms sweaty, he reached for her hand for comfort, and he was scared.

'Back in the file, why?'

'Get it. Get it out and shred it. As soon as you can. Just get rid of it,' he sat back, chewing his nails.

'What's going on, Robert?' he checked over his shoulder, lowering his voice.

'We didn't win it from that piece of paper, Lil.' Her face, like it had been here before. It put him off what he was saying, it was no use fabricating anything. 'Look, we won it because... I'm a hacker. That's my profession. Phil employs me to win businesses.' Lillian stood, finishing the sweet liquid and began walking out. Robert watched her, fearing she was walking out on him.

She turned, 'come on then' beckoning with her head.

'Where we going?!' Robert waved a ten-pound note in the air at the waitress, gathering himself as he ran after her.

'The woods,' she answered.

'The woods?! Now?! We'll freeze to death!' They both drew in breath as the rush of cold air penetrated the warmth of the lobby.

'Um, did you understand what I just said?' squinting his eyes.

'Yes. We're taking Brutus,' she insisted. The Honda was as cold as the outside on the inside, giving them both goose bumps. Robert laughed to himself at the irony of it, tugging at the seat belt to break it loose.

'What's so funny?!'

'I've been worrying myself sick about this moment, scared to death even,' he paused, 'why are we going to the woods? Are you going to leave me there to die of hypothermia?' Lillian shook her head. He waited for her response, his heart nearly beating out of his chest. She had shooting pains all over her. There was the catch. She pulled the choke out, one click, and started the car.

'So,' she sighed heavily, 'you're a criminal.' Robert never thought about it that way, he wanted to justify it, spin it. But the fact was there, loud and rude, blemishing him. Lillian pulled out of the car park, leaning over the steering to look at the sky, checking there were no clouds.

'We're going to freeze our nuts off, Lil!' Robert's teeth were chattering from nervous energy and the biting dampness of the car.

'I have blankets in the boot,' Lillian flatly replied.

'Blankets?! Is there a bloody picnic basket as well?!'

'Tell me,' she said blankly, with Brutus leading the way. He nervously rubbed his hands together, stumbling over how he should start.

'I used to work as a consultant for a software company. My job was to test new products. I also tested the customers systems to see what their vulnerabilities were, so I could sell them the software. Phil was one of those customers, that's when he approached me and offered me a way out and more money to do the same for him, illegitimately. I hacked into companies and found out what their Achilles heel were, then we tailored contracts to suit, being ahead of the competition. It's also when I got rid of Brutus. Phil offered me a newer model.' he looked down at his writhing hands, his mood solemn. Lillian frowned as she listened, it was all a new language to her.

'Why did you take Phil up on his offer, if you knew it was dodgy?'

'Money and an inflated ego. I was going nowhere, or so I thought. Phil dangled a sparkly carrot in front of my stupid nose, and I took it. It was then we went on to work for Apex. Helen worked there, too. My nephew, he's been asking about you.'

'How is Michael?' Lillian's face altered from her question; her eyes watering - she was glad it was dark so he couldn't see it.

'He's troubled. Phil visits him, y'know, like you visit me.' Robert squeezed his eyes together, pushing out the image of the park. 'I wish I'd had something stronger to drink now!'

'Why? You'll miss all the fun drunk. Continue...'

'I was on a path of self-destruction and I dragged my sister down with it. Phil moved in on her and I didn't stop it, afraid to lose my earnings. I was getting used to living like that.' Robert looked at her with desperation in his eyes, reluctantly continuing with his confession. She looked straight ahead, he couldn't see her reaction clearly in the dark - she concentrated on the road and didn't falter.

'The company needed a cash injection. Phil promised them just that and took me in as his Ace. We were doing very well and living off the fat of the land until we were rumbled. One particular customer had a certified hacker working for them and he sussed it out. I got complacent, left my virtual fingerprints everywhere. The lid was blown off the whole thing. I used Phil's laptop to do most of the work, but my workload ran over on this particular one and I ended up using my own. Phil had dishonest contacts in IT, and he disposed of it, so they only had Phil's to go by,' Robert paused to breathe.

'During the police interview, he covered for me, and bamboozled the inspectors involved. So, the investigation went cold, but Phil was sacked. He told Brian it was down to unfair dismissal, politics, and Brian believed him. There was a long-standing feud between the two companies. So, he got Phil into Radar and then he poached me back. My nose was clean when I left Apex, no one suspected a thing. He is not involved in the tenders, he gets everyone else to deal with it. Keep his hands clean. You would have been caught up in it. Phil would have denied all knowledge of that fax. That's why he just gives the girls the files, without instruction. I'm sorry, Lil, I really am.'

'Girls? You mean, there's been more? And you're the one that butters them up, is it? Buttering me up!' Lillian breathed in to hold her emotion.

'No! Lil, it wasn't like that with you. That was never my intention. Well, maybe, from the start. You know when you said that it was cheating? That's when I knew you were different.' He thought about those other girls that got caught up in the last fiasco, too dumb to know any better. Swooned by his charm and fat wallet.

'So, you have him by the balls and he has yours,' Lillian watched Robert wipe his brow.

'Yes. But Phil has a much bigger hold. That's why I had to go home. I'm not sure what he has up his sleeve in retaliation. Well, that's the catch. I don't want to lose you over it Lilly, none of this changes my commitment to you. But I understand if you want to get out of it, that's something I have to face. If anything, I have to thank you for giving me a conscience.' Robert played with his watch, feeling half the man he was earlier.

'I'm not getting out of anything. You should know by now that I'm just testing your honesty. We're both spies, so to speak.'

He turned away to hide his tears, afraid to come undone in front of her. Another close call, determined to make it his last one.

Thirty-Nine

The woods looked menacing as they arrived in silence; both of them processing the conversation.

'Are you sure you want to do this?' Robert rubbed his arms, looking out to the empty car park.

'Yes. Here, put one drop on your tongue,' she handed him an amber bottle, with a pipette incorporated in the cap.

'What's that?' he asked, sniffing it.

'To relax you. I don't want you having a heart attack.'

He hesitated, 'a heart attack?! What the hell are we doing then?!' He smelt the tincture, wincing at its potency. Then, what the hell, he squeezed the rubber teat, letting out over one drop; his whole body shuddered, leaving an aftertaste of bromide.

'Ugghh! Christ! What *is* this?' he studied it at arm's length, his face screwed up, smacking his lips.

'A little help. Come on,' she opened the boot and took out two tartan blankets, giving one to Robert. He immediately put it around his shoulders, aware of the shadows watching. Lillian's face was lit up by the full moon, the blue hue altering her features.

'You do realise how scared I am?'

Lillian tilted her head, 'scared? Of what?'

'Going in there! It's flippin' pitch black, Lil!'

'Oh, don't be such a wuss! It's exciting in the dark. You're with me, you'll be fine. Here, hold this...' she gave him a large torch. He checked it, flicking the switch on and off, turning it in circles - lighting up creepy sections of the trees. They climbed the stile, Lillian waiting for Robert to find his footing.

'I'm a city boy, make allowances.' She giggled at his clumsy descent off the wooden plank. Holding onto his arm, she led him in. He depended on her, his guide into the unknown. It shrouded them in its cloak as they entered; the smell of dried foliage and warm tree bark hit their senses, an immediate comfort for Lillian - almost as good as the smell of Rose's roast dinners. Their steps split the fallen, echoing as they blindly walked along the dirt path. Lillian quickened her stride, she could sense them; the wise. Robert was sure he could hear faint chimes of some sort. He looked around him, sweeping the torch in all directions. They were all around, disorientating him. He shone the torch on the ground, then ahead of them. 'What is it?' Lillian asked.

'Sssshhhh... I hear something...' his eyes were wide, pupils dilated. 'Bells. Little bells. Can you hear it?'

She pulled on his arm, smirking at him in the dark. He continued to shine the torch on the ground, stopping to watch bluebells appear in the circle of light, pushing up through the mulch and bursting into flower. He blinked several times to clear his vision, questioning his sanity.

'Are they, the same? As before?' he shone the torch in front – their path abundantly lined with a purple carpet. The heavy scent of Parma violets made his mouth water. He stumbled, his head light, kneeling down to inspect the bluebells. They looked incredible, so vivid. He touched them in awe, as if they were a rare species.

'Look Lil, aren't they amazing?' he put his ear close to them 'it's these! They're tinkling! Listen!'

'Come on you, afraid of the dark,' Lillian breathed behind him.

She took him to the clearing, having to pull him along while he stopped at everything to admire its animation - the pile of branches still laying where they left them. The circle was a spotlight lit by the moon, seeming brighter than anywhere else, full of bluebells. The night sky crystal clear and full of stars.

Lillian laid down her blanket and sat, patting it 'will you star gaze with me?' Robert's eyes sparkled and set down his blanket next to hers; their souls illuminated in grey and white. She was an open vessel beneath the portal, her face childlike and full of contentment.

'Wow Lilly, you look like you're home!' He was falling in love, his conscience sharp; this was better than the nightclub. He wanted to hear her voice, read her more and get a sense of who she really was.

'Look,' she said and pointed upwards 'you see? The Big Dipper? There,' she followed the outline with her finger, closing one eye to focus.

'I think it looks more like a saucepan than a dipper, do you?' Robert couldn't take his eyes off her. He wanted to look but was captivated, noticing things about her face he hadn't before; the complex beauty of a flawless creation - her breaths.

'Look!' she demanded. He looked up. The sky was framed by the trees' canopies - the stars twinkled and moved. Or was it his eyes playing tricks?

'Whoa! Lil, look at them! I mean, what tops it? I can see a saucepan, too. Is that your favourite constellation?' she beamed inwardly. She could feel his blood rushing around his veins and the tincture working.

'Yes, but Orion's belt is what I look for. The three sisters, see them?' she shifted his gaze. 'I have them, on my arm,' she showed him her left forearm, turning it over, revealing three moles aligned like the three stars. 'That's my favourite. They are the only constellation like that, in a line. Alnitak, Alnilam and Mintaka,' she tapped them, one by one.

'Wow. How do you know all this stuff? You should write a book. I'm serious!'

'I watch too much TV, I guess. Although I read most of it in the library. They'll be giving me a bed.' Robert touched the three moles in wonderment, checking the stars in comparison; suddenly falling silent around them, his ears buzzing.

'My ears are still ringing from that music, I can still hear it!' He hit them with the palm of his hand. 'I wish I'd known you before, Lil. I feel like I've missed out,' he said, watching a small ball of light float down. He followed it, expecting it to land on the blanket, but it redirected itself and flew upwards – dancing in front of him, teasing. He tried to grab it.

'No! Leave it! Wait!' Lillian whispered sharply, holding down his arm. He saw another, when his eyes focused, there were hundreds! Swooning, bobbing and darting in the moonlight, worshipping the steel rays. He reached out his hand, determined to catch one.

'What are they? Moths?'

'It's them,' she answered, without changing her gaze on the night sky. He looked at again, they weren't balls of light anymore, manifesting into wisps like translucent veils, moving to their ritual, devoting themselves to the Luna.

'I thought 'them' were blue?' His heart beat harder at the realisation. 'Are we dead?' he shivered. Lillian snorted a laugh, humbled by his awe.

'My God, Lil!' Robert whispered, his voice trembling. 'What do they want?' His ego had become non-existent, a transcending unity was taking over.

'These are guardians, of life. The night is their calling.' Robert put his hands up to his mouth, shaking his head, studying the creatures before him. The wisps turning into ethereal figures, materialising from the shadows and beyond, some from the barks, others emerged from the canopies, taking to the air. They weaved through the trunks, their form surrounded by light clothing and iridescent hue; illuminating the woods in greens and yellows. He watched them gather the vegetation. There was music, he was sure - soft and almost inaudible. Their features were blurred, having to squint to decipher them; small noses and thin lips with wide, oval eyes – flesh like vellum. He could hear their whispers in a strange language. They were primitive, intelligent and majestic; grouped together in discussion. Their children hid in the shadows, playing, moving quicker than them, reminding him of Lillian. Others glided, not wanting to be seen, with morphing features similar to ours. He noticed a small group huddled together, looking his way with caution, bringing tears to his eyes as the serene vibration centred his soul. His brain was hurting; the conditioned wires were resynchronising. It was a mesmeric sight that changed his perception, forever. What he witnessed defied all predetermined belief. 'Please, teach me Lil, tell me what they are,' he fell to his knees, feeling an overwhelming desire to submit himself.

'You have a good heart, Robert. That's why we had to come. That's how I know,' a smile played across her face, eyes like crystal pools. Just when he thought he didn't have a heart.

Robert shivered violently. His conscience was shutting down, receiving a spiritual awakening. One that tore at him, baring its teeth. It was revealed to him in a wall of vivid patterns - nebulas forming before his eyes, rushing through his frontal lobe; the divine vision in gold. 'Have you got any pens? Paper?' he asked. Lillian giggled.

'I need to draw what I saw! Quick Lil! Before it goes! Check your bag!' she held his face and kissed him,

'It's not going anywhere. It will always be here,' she placed her hand on his heart.

'Did you, have you, seen it? What I saw? I'm so cold Lil. I feel sick,' his face pallid. She rubbed his arms showing him how to breathe in exaggerated actions, expecting him to faint, wrapping the blanket around tighter, and transferring her calming vibes.

'These won't hurt you. We co-exist, unseen to many. It's not just us, it never was. They've been around longer than we have. We sort of invaded their space, not the other way around.'

Robert looked up, afraid of what else he might see over her shoulder. The subconscious secret behind everything seemingly made up, our fantasies, imagination and longing for the extraordinary.

'Angels?'

'We're not that entitled/ They are keeping the dark ones out, the mimics.' Lillian sat and looked to the stars again, her legs stretched out, waggling her crossed feet back and forth. Her favourite place just got better.

'The dark ones?! Mimics?' Robert turned around, peering into the shadows, shining a shaky torch between the trees. 'Mimics.' he said to himself, 'what do they mimic?' he asked with hesitation in his voice.

'Us, anything. Don't worry, they're not coming.'

'What do they look like, these mimics.'

'It's best you don't know. They look like whatever they want. You'll know it's them, by the way they make you feel. Emptying you, all at once. Things die around them. They have no love, only hate - hate for us. Scaring is their entertainment and defence.'

'Why do they hate us?'

'We are the supreme beings,' she chortled.

Robert regarded the felled trees. 'Do they come here?'

'Yes. They travel anywhere. They're quick, blink and you'll miss them. That's why we perceive them as being cold, it's just big drafts from their movement.'

'How do you know all this?!'

She had changed – was she taller? Something was different about her. One came closer, unafraid. Robert scuffled back as it approached the blanket.

'Uh! Lil! Lil!' It stared curiously at him, clutching its slender hands in front of it, holding foliage. He guessed it was female, she seemed to be, with long, luscious hair; relaxing him, forgetting his surroundings, even Lillian. She was a little shy, handing the gift to him. A tear came to his eye from the saintly offering, a welcome into the realm without judgement. He looked down; a bunch of bluebells and some fern.

'Hello. Uh, thank you, for the uh,' he held up the bouquet, 'this, thank you, for this.'

He felt the sudden urge to run home, hide in the cupboard and put his fingers in his ears. Needing normality to straighten his logic - watch a cartoon to numb his conscience and reload control, reload the establishment. He was petrified but this was a revelation and he had been chosen to be part of this renaissance and unconventional thinking.

The being bowed graciously, turning back into a ball of light, gliding upwards. Robert looked down at Lillian, did he leave? How come she didn't see anything?

'Did you give me something illegal?' he asked her.

'Kind of, well, not exactly. You're kind of standing on it.'

Robert looked down, 'Twigs?!'

'Mushrooms - free your perception a little.'

'Lil! What the hell? And there's me, thinking you were...' he sat, getting the jitters from anything he touched.

'I was what? Innocent?'

'Did you hear what she said? I don't like that whispering stuff they do. Makes me feel ... floaty.'

'How are you feeling now?'

'Trippy, raw and I wish I hadn't married you so soon. I wish I had waited until now.' He ran his ran his fingers through his hair; an intensive sensation this time, feeling every strand and imperfection on his skin - the bunch of foliage still in his hand.

'She did give me this. So, I didn't imagine the bluebells?' he checked his hand again, the plants looked and felt different – they portrayed a new existence.

'Hold me Lil, I'm think I'm about to hyperventilate,' he felt like he was going to burst out of a cocoon, split a skin. She pulled on his hand, laughing. They hugged and reconnected, differently. The smell of him, so familiar and comforting. Touching his skin beneath the shirt, setting off a reaction. Releasing her hold she lay back on her blanket, her eyes opening, beckoning - revealing her soul. They were the brightest blue; she was an opened flower at the zenith of its beauty. All that had been around them suddenly dispersed aware of the privacy required; leaving behind weightless particles, being caught by the moonlight. Robert watched them drift up to the opening, still dancing.

'If we die, here...I'm ready.' He looked down at her, giving him permission to take. That Rose had been luring him in all night. They embraced their fate, absorbing each other and breaking boundaries, feeling part of the universe. Robert entered a zone he had never encountered - entwined with Lillian, part of her bloodstream, pulling at his soul and making him giddy. The fire between them was a yearning fulfilled, becoming the other half of each other. Their cries of release made the woods stop and look, hold its breath. The small orbs that were left, swirled around them in a frenzy as they bonded. Robert was totally aware of the honour he had been bestowed, his sanctification.

Laying on the forest floor, sleepy and blissful; Lillian was listening to Robert's heartbeat as they stared at the stars. The pines swayed and spoke as the nightly breeze rushed through them, accompanied by the distant haunting echoes of an owl, soothing the night.

'Your heart skips a little beat,' she listened again, 'it goes...bump de bump de, de bump,' she looked up at him.

'Well, that's because you're resting on it,' he winked his wink and kissed her head. He was relaxed, his arms folded behind his head leaning against one of the stumps; with a scorched chest.

'I don't think I can slip back into normality or *be* normal, come to that. Makes me feel different about everything. You've given me a special gift. Perspective. Belief! The pursuit of paper money seems all a bit, well, pointless. Think I'll just live out here with you and them. Eat sticks and mushrooms. What d'ya say? Can you fry them?' He didn't want to return to normality, ever. That same feeling you have when holidays are over. He felt saved and lost. A bit spiky, odd, very odd. There was something else. A comparable which dipped its toe in our pond life now and then. Maybe it was magic, maybe it was just Lillian, or that stuff she gave him.

'You didn't know I was calling, did you?' Lillian asked.

'No. It's me you're talking to. My senses are off, well, not anymore. I had to be dragged here by my hair. Did you look at these, every night?'

'Yes, mostly. I knew I had to shift things before it was too late. I guess I should go.'

Robert sat up 'No way! That's it. This was the start of the next chapter. You can get some stuff and we'll blag the rest. He'll smell it on you, trust me, I know.' Lillian sat up holding the blanket around her.

'Smell it?'

Robert smiled affectionately, brushing her hair away from her face. 'Us, he'll smell us. He'll hurt you again Lil, he's already taken the lid off that. I took all what he protects. I know this because I would be the same.'

'You make it sound like you're all just a pack of wolves!'

'We are wolves, stood up straight with skin. Some have good temperaments, others are badly scarred by fights, internal ones. Leaving packs and entering new ones, getting bitten because they don't fit in.'

'So, who's the alpha in all this?'

'Need you ask?' he said, in defeat.

'You're not going to let Phil keep dominating you?!'

'He has me over a barrel, Lil.'

'No, he doesn't! He likes to make you think he has,' she checked her watch; it was 3am.

'We need to go, quick, and I have to be back at some stage.'

'Lil, no! I'm not happy with it. Not after this, all this! How can you leave like that? You got me here eventually, but I never in a million years expected what I'd witnessed. I envisaged being bitten by mosquitos and being uncomfortable...' he stopped. Her face, her eyes again...so open, he feared she might disperse into little balls of light too. He grabbed her hands and squeezed them, 'you're not going back. That's final. Stay with me. Go back in the morning and get your stuff.'

'But my cat.'

'Your cat?! You're leaving me, for a cat?'

'I know how that must sound, I'm sorry. I have to get back to him. Oliver, and we need to get out of here before they come.'

'Who? Does he have a box thing? Can you go to your folks?' He sat down, sulking, picking up dead pine needles and snapping them between his fingers - throwing them to one side.

'I want to talk to you about everything, Lil. I won't sleep tonight! We're not done. Please! Or at least stay with me after this party thing,' he hung his head down, 'party, ha! Celebrating a fraud, celebrating a cheat!'

'Are you ready for the party?' she asked.

'Why have I got to be ready?' Lillian brushed herself off, picking up his blanket and shaking it.

'Robert, we need to go, now!'

'Okay! Okay!'

'Thank you,' she said as she folded it.

'For what?'

'Tonight,' her eyes began to fill with tears.

Robert stood up; it was his duty to wipe them. 'Hey, hey. What is it?'

She lowered her head. 'You stayed.'

He held her and the emotion from her, stung him. 'You're crying because *I* stayed? I'm the one that should be saying that!' Holding her arms, he looked her square in the face.

'Did you really think I was going to walk back through those woods, in the bloody dark, on my own?!' he made her laugh through her soft sobs, wiping them away with his palms. He sighed, reluctantly giving in to her wishes.

'Come on then, Cinderella. I stayed because I am staying. Plant imps and anything else anyone would care to throw at me. I love you, Lil.' She breathed in, choking on it, all she could do was nod and keep nodding. He wasn't expecting it said in return, he didn't need it back. She gave more than words ever could. Just when things were about to hit the fan.

Forty

Phil studied the golden liquid in the cut crystal glass, turning the vessel in his hand, with Lillian occupying his thoughts. A mahogany coffee table adorned strategically placed house magazines and a Criminal Psychology book, which lay untouched. The magazines were for decoration, but the book had been left behind. He felt the presence in the room, but ignored it; there was always something hanging around.

'I know you're here. I'm not listening to your gripes, leave me!' he gulped the scotch, undeterred. Putting the glass down on a porcelain coaster, he picked up the book and fanned through the pages, looking for a suitable article.

'Ah, here's one,' he said aloud, his voice absorbing into the thick, Victorian walls.

'Criminal Psychopaths. You should stick around, might be something interesting,' he began reading the heavy text in a dismissing frame of mind.

"Inflated ego and the need for power and control of a psychopath are the perfect character traits for a lifetime of antisocial, deviant or criminal activity". Phil paused and looked up; the emptiness of the house was deafening- a house where no expense was spared. Paying everyone else to do everything else for him, with no input or personalisation on it. Residing in a dwelling he never laid his hands on.

"The motive of a psychopathic killer will often involve either power and control, or sadistic gratification. Claiming loss of control when caught. Although the killer would have planned carefully and methodically and not impulsively". Phil huffed, closed the book and threw it back on the table. He finished his drink and wiped over his lips, casting his eye on the garden and summer house at the foot of it. Magnolias grew either side which hung over the roof - it was Phil and Janice's retreat. Her favourite season was spring when the breeze blew the petals off in flurries, like confetti. Tastefully furnished by her, memories of laughter and romance still lay within its wooden barricades. Raising a smile he reminisced, looking away, and studying the floors' geometric perfection to divert his shattering emotion. He clenched his fists and breathed in - there was an ache in that stone heart of his, an ache for things to go back the way they were. He wanted to watch their peculiar children running around the grounds, but his coercion with the darker forces had cost him dear; he just needed her temporarily out of the way. Phil wasn't a man who took disappointment lightly, his retaliations were brutal, and his childhood shaped him into the unforgiving man he was.

Michael's angelic persona wasn't what he was expecting in a son. It was unfortunate that Helen was so adamant in breaking all ties, he should have known better, impregnating a Courtney. The financial arrangement kept a hold with intentions to influence the boy as he matured. He had special gifts, planning to manipulate them as his next ace. But for now, Lillian was his greatest mission, to get back what he'd lost. Laughing to himself when he thought of the encounter Robert was about to embark upon and was oblivious to. Every woman succumbs to dominance, eventually. It's what they prefer. A weak man is just something she stands on to reach the top shelf.

Phil rested his head and drifted off into a tipsy, dream filled nap... it was *that* dream, waiting in the window for his father. Hope and trust kept him looking out every night, even though he knew, he was never coming back. Phil frowned and spoke in his sleep as the dream shifted and placed him on the stairs. Listening to his mother's drunken antics, laughing with another strange man, feeling confused and alone. Let down by everyone and the notion that love actually mattered. He blamed himself, becoming distant from his mother when he reached his teens. She turned to drink more often to help numb the pain of desertion, superficial company and a rebellious, strange son. The house became an unpleasant, dirty abode that was just used for her acquaintances, who took advantage of her needy personality and what was in the fridge. She died at fifty-seven from advance stages of hepatitis. Phil stood emotionless at her funeral, his father covertly looked on from behind an Oak tree, battling with his conscience. He had moved on and had his own family to support, letting his vengeful son back into his life may have proven catastrophic. Phil's uncle took him in, but just a year later, at the age of eighteen, they threw him out - making a pact with himself that numero uno was his priority – along with pursuing wealth and revenge for his father. Phil spent the time perfecting his psychic ability, it was all he had to escape reality. The anger in his soul fuelled and intensified it. He realised the potential behind his gift when he started meddling with the unknown, an act of defiance from his let downs. He was born with a heightened intuition but he wanted to perfect it further, turning it into a hidden weapon. As his confidence and book collection grew, he conjured something far more plausible.

'They' never let him down, always willing to please and do what he asked in return for being freed. They gave him the ability to see the unseen and manipulate it. Although his own sixth sense was powerful, he relied on the mimics, snatched from their dwelling.

Annie came in with his coffee on a silver tray, afraid to disturb him.

'Uh. Mitter 'athaway, your coffee.' She shook him gently. His eyes opened, bloodshot from the heavy sleep.

'What? Who came?'

'Nobaddy. Is me. I bring you coffee Mitter 'athaway.'

'Oh right, yes, thank you. I must have dozed off.' He slurped, the caffeine hitting his woozy head and empty stomach.

'I go now Mitter 'athaway. Is late. I see you tomorrow.'

'Yes, of course. Look...' he raised his hip to reach his back pocket, taking out a wad of notes. '... Take a couple of days off,' he fanned out two hundred pounds for her.

'Ok thank you, thank you very much mitter 'athaway,' she left the room backwards, bowing and fussing. The front door closed quietly.

Steadying himself, he idly made his way to the kitchen - feeling astute as he checked the fridge to satisfy his 'munchies'. Camembert, ham, jar of pickle, butter, wilting salad and vegetables; choosing the beer instead. He was confident in making a tidy profit from Helen's house, properties in Guildford were worth twice as much as Wales. The sale would come at a good time, he planned taking Janice on a second honeymoon. Returning to the dining room to continue his night-time rituals – the spell he was trying to make against Lillian wasn't working. A photo of her and a dog and some hair from her brush, wasn't enough. The items just put Lisa back in his good books again.

His Ouija board was lit up by the billiard lamp, noticing the planchette had moved. He'd left it on goodbye, now it was resting on the letter 'L'. He nodded in defiance, picking it up and turning it over.

'You playing tricks with me?!' he called out. There was something watching him from the corner, sneering at this fool, amused by toying with him and making him sweat in his dreams. This human was futile, thinking such a dark force bared any loyalty. It vanished to visit someone else; travelling above, undetected, but on the odd occasion it liked to travel through insensible souls, making them shiver and stumble off balance, casting misfortune on their day. Phil swigged from the bottle before sitting in a plush dining chair. Resting his hands on the table, opening the portal with his Latin recital. His eyes darkened to a muddy green, going into a heavy trance when the connection was made. The room filled with a negative pressure, squeezing his guts; his skin cold and goose bumped. They were refusing to kill the feline, so he would have to do it himself. He used an oval hand mirror, losing himself in the reflection, swiftly entering Lillian's bedroom. He checked the compartment in the wardrobe, looking for the bottle. It was missing, he scowled. Nothing was where it was before. He sensed she had copulated with Courtney but that wasn't his worry, it made for good bait. The bedroom door opened – Oliver sat, glaring at Phil, his bright orange eyes lit up in the dark.

Something had changed; an intimidating pressure and overbearing protection stifled him. The cat started to hiss and warble. Phil waited with a grin, ready. Oliver began to grow in size, standing on his hinds, catching him off-guard – in the blink of an eye, the bedroom door slammed, the print falling off the wall, then the Honda came down the drive. Phil retreated and broke off the connection, pushing the items off the table in a rage. 'That damned cat!' Blowing out the candles one by one; almost spitting at the dancing flames. The room fell into darkness, the lights flickered erratically. He smirked at the arrival of his calling. Which one would it be this time? The dark faced Jinn that stooped in corners, or the shadow figure that lurked in doorways and clung to windows? The anticipation excited him as he meticulously picked out amber remedy bottles from the shelf. Smelling it, squeezing the pipette on his tongue, waiting for the tincture to take effect. The wallpaper moved in repetitive motion, the colours vivid in the room, objects, everyday items, became fascinating, sharp. It was time to make a deeper connection and open a bigger portal. The outside light repeatedly turned on and off, it was usually the offspring of his visitors. Sauntering to the patio doors, he looked out, his stare provoking.

'Come forward!' he called; his stance blasé. The windows began to blacken from the outside; losing his reflection as it penetrated the glass. His smile was wiped off his face as his heart rate increased from the loud footsteps, which vibrated through the floor. He blinked disbelievingly as the large pane flexed and bulged – standing back, ready for it to implode. The entity growled from its belly in retaliation, shaking the frames and whole house. A billowing black mass grew larger, filling the window space. Phil guarded his face with his forearm.

This wasn't the usual visit, 'Zalud?' he questioned with a nervous gulp. Zalud; a large entity, bending its head to fit in the room - ruler of its world and warrior. So sinister, all that was damned came with it. Clinging to him, worshipping the dark magic. It came forward, consuming the room with its nothing – the yellow eyes penetrating the black fog. The form that emerged from the darkness was adorned in black cloth; a material that was indecipherable and bringing an acrid, sulphurous stench with it. The features became clear as the fog dispersed - curdling Phil's blood. One that brought the threat of imminent death, one he thought, he would never see again.

'Stop playing around with me!' the entity tightened its invisible grip around Phil's neck. He gasped and choked, holding his throat. It lifted him off the ground, he struggled, thrashing his legs. The entity was sadistically mesmerised as it watched the human fight for breath, fragile as rotten fruit. It let go, this human was needed. Phil dropped to his knees, coughing and retching as oxygen flooded back into his lungs. 'You're playing with fire!' he strained, red faced, rolling onto his side.

'It is YOU who plays with fire!' the entity's voice was deep; hexafluoride deep, and articulate. The speakers of all languages. Its native tongue, thousands of years old, complicated, mathematical and unfamiliar to this world - but the vital codes into theirs. Phil stumbled to his feet, holding onto the table, feeling vulnerable and terrified. A high-pitched tone pierced his head and dread ran through him. Mercy had

left, there was nothing but damnation. The black mist that billowed below, harboured reflective retinas. He could just make out the pointed joints of mutants that crawled on their bellies, the servers of this devil.

'*You seem surprised to see me,*' its tone gallant, perusing the bookshelves. Phil continued to communicate with darkened eyes, trying to regain any power.

'*You are tiring my servants with your demands*', taking a book from the shelf. Phil lurched forward, trying to snatch it.

'No! Not that one!' It was his favourite book; a rare and expensive find from Egypt - retrieved by his conjures. The entity leafed through it condescendingly - snapping it shut in one hand, sneering at Phil as he watched the book smoulder in its grip.

'*You are crossing a very thin line,*' ousting the book's ashes from its large hand– beginning to take human form; a figure of a man that Phil recognised from one of his books. Confusing, tall and out of shape. Phil quivered.

Zalud pointed to the Ouija board, '*your contraptions are amusing. Considering we are already here, watching over your shoulders, impersonating your dead to uphold deception. You are thrill seekers without sense!*'

Zalud paced, gliding back and forth, twisting his neck.

'*You have been trying to enter forbidden territory. Why did you break the agreement?*'

'I...I want Janice back.'

'What conflicting notions for a malevolent mind. Give us the psychic in exchange. We cannot have such intuition roaming at will. This female talks too much and is unaffected by our consequence. The protection she carries – is of the ancients. From...Al Qayyum.'

The entity flinched, something hit it in the chest, forcing it to bend backwards - flaying out its arms.

Phil stepped back, 'what? What is that?'

The entity stretched upwards and cried out in defiance, raising clenched fists, morphing back into its own form.

'The One existence! Ruler of worlds!' its agony made Phil grimace and cover his ears. The entity roared, bursting the lightbulbs out of their sockets, absorbing the current from the house. Phil felt weak – life, his life, was being sucked out of that room. He used the edge of the table as a guide to reach another light switch. He found it, hitting it with his fist, hoping the entity had left. Alarmed as Zalud stood composed as a taller version of Phil; dressed in black. The eyes were the only feature that remained.

'I... uh...' Phil struggled with the distorted version of himself if that was possible.

'I make a better job as you, don't you think? Bring the psychic to the clearing.' The entity studied its human hands with conceit.

'It's...um...all arranged.' Phil flinched and shrieked as one of the mutants brushed passed his foot.

'If you disappoint me, your inevitability will arrive before its time.' It touched Phil with its long finger, making him contort

from the ice-cold shocks that consumed every nerve ending. Phil cried out, feeling something rupture within. He wiped the corner of his mouth with the back of his hand, scornfully regarding the blood. The entity made a guttural laugh, bearing pointed, yellowing teeth.

'You are weak, humannnnn.' It stared at Phil, draining him. Those eyes were more than just windows to a damned soul; they stood for mankind's' vice and arrogance.

'You cannot replicate your ancestors' methods of communication with us, you are untrustworthy now that you have technology - albeit backward.'

'We are progressing well with our technology' Phil defended.

The entity bellowed again.

'Fool! We have manipulated your species to 'believe' you are making progress; your technologies are impenetrable, for now. But we will return, when it is time - entering through the electronic eyes and ears, and in the minds of your children. Eradicating remembrance of the source. Our presence among you will be rife. Then you will see who controls your constitutions.'

The entity grinned perceptively - releasing a brusque growl from its gut. Phil took a cotton handkerchief from his trouser pocket, shaking out the folds, dabbing the blood flowing from the corner of his mouth; his whole body shaking.

The entity backed away.

'Our greatest capture will be the psychic. She will release what you have imprisoned before her demise. I have redeemed you.'

Phil acknowledged with one nod and Zalud left as it entered. The black vapour escaping in reverse motion, the mutants scurrying behind, squealing.

When normality had resumed, Phil fell to the floor, his muscles in spasm.

'Shit,' he uttered bleakly, hiding under the table; fight or flight had been overwhelmed into numbness. His soul cried out for prayer, but he suppressed it. He didn't do submission – he'd left God on the stairs.

Forty-One

The journey was different today, she'd moved on from the sentimental hold of her hometown. Things were being pushed around the table, causing the magnets to repel. She waited outside before going in. It had all changed, no longer nestling in the bosom of her childhood haven. But the woman she was morphing into would be the one that saves her, still holding the hand of the older version, reluctant to let her go.

'Yoo hoo,' she called out, a little subdued. Benny came rushing, almost wetting himself at her arrival. Martin was in the armchair with a scarf around his neck, holding a mug of honey and lemon, watching the evening news.

'Bluebell,' he said breathlessly, shedding a tear.

'Oh Dad, what's wrong?' kneeling at his feet.

'Been sitting in that garden too long! Got himself a chest infection!' Rose called out, bringing in two teas.

'It's nice of you to turn up, we're honoured,' she said bitterly, kissing Lillian on the cheek.

'Sorry, it's been difficult. Have they given you anti-biotics?' she asked her father, affectionately stroking the back of his hand.

'Yes. Doctor came this morning,' Martin said between wheezes.

'You look really poorly. What about something for your wheeze?' she asked.

Martin held up an inhaler. 'They gave me this thing because they couldn't find what was wrong. Some virus. Huh! that's what they always say when they don't know what it is.'

'So, are we going to know where you've been?' Rose asked.

'I have something to tell you. I've met someone, and well, it's kind of serious. Are you mad at me?' Rose's heart leapt and so did Martin's, and he was close to losing his emotions from relief.

'Well, this is a bit sudden. Is that why you didn't come Sunday?'

'No. I didn't come Sunday, because, well because, I was hurt. I don't know how I'm going to break this engagement off.'

'There's nothing to break!' Rose answered sharply.

'Who is this fine man?' Martin asked.

Lillian smiled shyly. 'Robert. Robert Courtney,' she got a flutter in her stomach just from his name. She swore blind that when she blinked, so did he. 'He looks after me, Dad.'

'Did the BMW belong to him?' Lillian affirmed it with a nod.

'How come it's serious in such a short time?' Rose asked.

'It's him, Mum.'

Rose held her daughters head into her breasts – something Lillian hated, but it was the closest she would feel to her daughter. Her scalp was still painful, but she held in the need to react to the pain. 'I sincerely hope so. I trust you. I have to. There's nothing left to do but that.'

Martin was listening to it all. He needed to stop Jeffrey now; the safety net had arrived.

'Jeffrey keeps harping on about Birmingham.' Lillian said, breaking the silence. Martin clenched his fists. 'I'm not going obviously, not now, anyway.'

Rose continued dusting off her ornaments, 'have you told him you're not going?'

'Yes. But he's not taking no for an answer. I'm actually afraid to sleep, in case he bundles me up and stuffs me in the boot or something.'

Martin coughed, shifting in his seat, sweating, needing air.

'Bluebell, you have to tell him about this Rob. As painful as it is, he has to know.'

'He already knows,' she looked at her father, and felt the bond break a little.

'He knows?! Then why are you still there?!' Rose interrupted. There was a pregnant pause between all of them.

'He came here, to sort out the Honda. I guess that's when he got suspicious and well, it escalated from there, didn't it? I had a word though, about his attitude.'

'It didn't work,' Lillian flatly answered, Martin reading her eyes.

'Has this Rob got one of those, new car phone thingies?'

'Yes, why?'

'Give me the phone, I want to speak to him.'

'No, Dad, It will cost a fortune!'

Martin waved his hand around, 'never mind about that. Just give me the damn thing.' Lillian stretched the phone cable to reach Martin's side table, dialling the number for him, a little nervous.

'*Robert Courtney!*' he announced, giving Lillian a stomach full of hot custard.

'Hey. It's me.'

'*Hello Tree wife. Boy did I need to hear that voice,*' he was in his hotel, reflective, sitting on the bed. '*Let me call you back, it'll cost you an arm and a leg! What's the number?*' Lillian gladly gave him her parent's number and waited for the call back, in anticipation. Martin picked it up when it rang immediately after replacing the receiver.

'Hello? Is that Rob?' he said, with Lillian insisting it was Robert.

'*Uh, yes. Who's that?*' Robert thought it was Jeffrey, getting a stab in his gut, ready for pistols at dawn.

'Ah, jolly good. It's Martin, Lilly's father. I've been meaning to talk to you, I hope you don't mind,' he stopped to cough.

'Oh, right! Of course. Sounds like a nasty cough.'

'Yes, forgive me. I'll try and die quietly.'

Robert chuckled, fretting as to where this conversation was going.

'I understand you and my daughter are an item?'

'Uh, yes, yes we are.'

'Excellent. I mean no malice Rob, you don't mind if I call you that, do you?'

Robert began to warm to his jovial manner, *'not at all. It's good to speak to you, Martin.'*

'You sound like a decent chap, I just wanted to say you have my blessing,' he coughed again, a little too vigorously for Lillian's liking. Robert smiled and breathed a huge sigh of relief, feeling humbled and honoured.

'Thank you. I appreciate it. I will look after her. Don't worry.'

'I have every faith in you. You are welcome in my home anytime. I warn you, she's a force to be reckoned with.'

Robert laughed and started to feel part of the family. *'So I've discovered!'*

'I'll hand you back to her. I'm sure we'll be seeing you soon. Bye for now.'

Lillian took the receiver, feeling a little awkward. 'Okay, well. See you tomorrow night.'

'You bet. In the foyer. Seven. With bells on.' She replaced the receiver, and Robert punched the air, changing the mood

he was in before, his grin almost reaching his ears. It was the confidence and security he needed.

'Thanks Dad.' Lillian said and kissed Martin on the forehead.

'Wasn't that a little overzealous? We hardly know the man!' Rose commented, dusting her favourite ornament.

'It's what a man wants to hear. He sounds like he's got clean hands. Does he put his hand to anything?' Martin asked, closing his eyes and resting his head.

'He said he used to tinker with cars when he was young.' Martin nodded while he was going over the conversation in his head 'it's not everything though, is it?' she asked.

'Well, I guess not. You'll be forever buying houses or paying someone to do the work, with a man that can't put his hand to anything, that's all.'

Lillian wanted to ignore that one. There was more to life than a man that spent half his time outside 'fixing' things. She'd had enough of that. The thought of spending time with Robert, snuggled up on the sofa, made her belly sting.

Martin drank, with a shaking hand. 'I knew a man once. He was as shifty as they come, making money hand over foot. Falling in shit and coming out smelling of roses, you know, those type. Always getting away with it,' he coughed, feeling weary from the effort.

'Martin! You need to rest your lungs!' Rose protested.

'Oh, it's alright. Just let me finish,' he leaned forward, 'but he came a cropper one day, got in with the wrong sort, and everyone was glad of it. He'd hurt a lot of people along the way, even got some of them killed. It was him you see...' he pointed to the ceiling '...up there, waiting for him to hang himself with his own rope. It happens to all of them, eventually. I'm sorry if we ever doubted you, bluebell. You're a fighter and I'm proud of you for that,' he kissed his daughter's hand. She had no words, except for those that stayed in her heart.

'Was there any point to that statement, Dad?'

'Lilly. I need some help in the kitchen please love.' Rose stood by the stove, holding the ornate glass bottle Myriam had given her.

'You know what this is, don't you?' Lillian nodded and held the vessel of protection tightly. 'She gave me this, to go with it. You recite it three times, as you do with the oil.' Lillian took the piece of paper, looking at the passages.

'Uh, how do you say this? I mean, how am I going to remember it?!'

'Myriam said, say it from your heart, not your head.' Lillian looked at the holy words; they were intimidating, like the beamer was when she first got in.

'My brave girl,' she patted Lillian on the back, 'be careful with that mirror and, well, you know what else. This has to be the end of that, okay?'

Lillian kissed her mother. 'I'm scared, mum.'

Rose eyes filled with regretful tears.

'We all are. Myriam said just hold on tight. That's all we can do.'

Forty-Two

She felt awkward surrounded by brass fittings and loud carpet. Her hair was slicked back, her lips the brightest red with peep toe shoes to match. Clutching her rectangle evening bag, wearing the black dress - figure hugging, with a split that ran up her right leg. All that was missing was a semi-auto pistol strapped to her thigh. Everyone looked at her, hardly recognising it was Lillian the new girl; stunning and nervous. Lisa and Brian arrived first, like lord and lady.

'Wow! Lil, you look absolutely gorgeous. This is Brian,' Lisa stood aside so they could get acquainted.

'Great to meet you Lilly, I've heard a lot about you.' Lillian almost curtsied. They shook hands, purposefully. Brian was not like the mental vision she had of him. Greying, wavy hair, a little on the portly side. He didn't look as old as Lisa portrayed him, either.

'Will you be sitting with us? We have the top table.'

'Yes, I'm just waiting for Robert.'

'I see. We'll save your places,' he smiled, like a gentleman. Lisa looked, well, plain and terrified, wearing a blood-red short dress and beige pumps. The reception area was filling up with overdressed staff, all looking completely different in their party attire. She stood on tip toe to keep an eye on the door. It was six fifty-seven and her butterflies were running a mock. Where was he? Suddenly, the crowd parted revealing Robert stood at the entrance, holding a single red rose, turning it between his fingers as he looked for her. She gasped at the Mills and Boon vision. A man in a dinner suit; their ultimate cloak of dominance and seduction. She didn't make herself known just yet, wanting a longer look. His hair was dressed, the waves still visible, the white shirt complimenting the olive skin – or was it the other way around? Lillian gave in and raised her hand to catch his attention. Was he seeing things? He wasn't sure he liked her like that, she looked completely different. He trembled as their eyes met. Who was going to move first? The guests were a blur as they mingled and left. He walked towards her and she knew there would never be another moment like this one, she held onto it before it disappeared. Her memories going back to the patio where she sat looking at the stars, begging for this.

'Hello, tree wife,' he took her hand, he could feel it trembling, raising it to his mouth and kissing the back of it.

'Hello, Cooch.' Whatever it was that resonated between them was staying, in stone. The feelings had changed since the intimacy; they ran deeper. He held out his arm for her, she put hers through.

'You look incredibly hot. New dress?' he said from the corner of his mouth. It looked good on her, a perfect fit but not really Lillian. 'I am officially rescuing you, Miz Lillian. You're too beautiful to be left alone in this over-decorated place.'

There it was, the beginning - she burst out a laugh and took the rose, her eyes moist with the coolness of faint tears and hysteria. They walked up to the Phoenix Suite feeling like they were walking up to their execution. Robert's heart was pounding. Lillian on the other hand, had been preparing all her life for this moment, unbeknown to her. As they got closer, they could hear the entertainment as they climbed the stairs, everyone carrying on as normal while they were running on adrenaline. Lillian held onto Robert's arm tightly as they entered the suite – his nerves were briefly redirected as all heads turned to look at the celebrity couple. Lillian smiled and waved to her peers, Robert acknowledged them politely and the cloak of impending doom lifted a little. A central dance floor surrounded by perfectly laid round tables and mirrored walls either side, the length and height of the room. The ceiling was heavily ornate with a massive chandelier. Hotel staff were dressed in black, on hand to take and bring orders. Lillian leant into Robert and spoke into his ear, making him shiver.

'They have good means of communication in here,' she said, they looked at one another, speaking from their eyes; they did that a lot.

'Don't accept a drink from anyone, except me,' he murmured before they got to the table, reserved for six people with one missing. Tim Smith stood up and pulled a chair out for Lillian.

'Here's the celebrities,' he jovially commented, having a good look at Lilian's exposed leg.

Brian stood to shake Robert's hand, 'Brian Finlay, good to meet you Robert.'

'Likewise,' Robert pulled up the material on his trouser legs before sitting. 'Lisa' he acknowledged her with just a nod; still having his reservations about her. She was already gulping wine with a sour expression on her face - her eyes darting all around the room. There was an awkward moment as everyone pretended to look interested at their surroundings.

'Wow, mirrors,' Lisa commented tersely. Brian cleared his throat, stroking his tie in place.

'Uh, tell me a bit about yourself Robert. I hear you're a bit of a whizz kid with IT.' Tim chuckled deceitfully, puffing on his Havana cigar. Robert pulled at his black tie, undoing the top button of his starched, white collar.

'It has been known,' he smiled forcefully, taking a large gulp of the complimentary water.

'I'm very interested Robert, we have a great opportunity on the cards, our IT Director is moving on, and I feel you'd be the candidate to replace him.' Robert's demeanour changed from shifty to shrewdly confident.

'Oh really? Tell me more,' he turned to face Brian and they became engrossed in detail. Lisa yawned with boredom and gestured to Lillian that they should go and powder their noses. She agreed, telling Robert where she was going. He didn't want to let her out of his sight tonight, the missing table guest was causing tension. They got out of the ball room and passed the busy bar that was quickly filling up.

'You look amazing Lil. Where *did* you get that dress from?'

'Thanks. Where's Phil?'

'Not sure. Anyway, what's been going on? You've been avoiding me. Any juicy gossip?' The women's toilets were just as full.

'You go before me Lil. I'll hold your bag. Christ, what you got in here? Crown jewels?' she jested, shaking it. Lisa put the bags on the sink unit, there was a queue but she let all the others go before her. She checked herself in the mirror, a little conscious that she'd under dressed for the occasion, feeling judgemental eyes on her. But that's how she liked to be, disguising her true intentions. Lillian came out and washed her hands, 'did you bring your mobile with you?'

'Yeah.' Lillian took out her new present, fully charged. 'What's your number?'

'Hey! He bought you one? You kept that quiet!' they exchanged numbers. Lillian was still getting used to it.

'How did you manage to get out tonight? And smuggle that phone in?' Lisa asked, shaking her head, 'you're going to get busted sooner or later, Lil.'

'I've already been busted.'

'Oh, I see. Are we still ok? I feel you're a bit distant tonight.'

'I'm fine,' she dried her hands with a paper towel.

'Don't let me down.' She took her bag from Lisa. Lillian was different; she looked like a despatcher tonight and with no tuition from her on that makeup or outfit either. Lisa half knew what was happening, but Lillian's complete change of personality made her confused and paranoid. Lillian walked ahead of Lisa, everyone getting distracted by her. Robert was relieved when they returned. More bottles of wine had been placed on the table and Brian was about to open some champagne. The cork popped and the fizz overflowed with 'oohs' from everyone. Brian raised his glass, the bubbly frothed and left very little liquid after the bubbles died down.

'Please be upstanding and raise your glasses to another success,' the fluted glasses clinked, with Robert feeling a taint on the celebration. They sat back down, Lillian looked warily at the glass. Robert leaned into her.

'It's ok, you can have some,' he said with an assuring smile. She held the glass up, inwardly making her own toast then downed it; discretely letting the bubbles out through her nose. Robert studied the mirrors inconspicuously and remembered the times Lillian came through to him and the impact that had. Heaven knows the force anything larger than a bedroom mirror would project; the thought of it came with lewd musings. He watched her talking to Tim. She looked incredibly sexy tonight, but he still wasn't sure about it. Maybe it was something she had to do, being trapped and controlled for so long. He smiled at his happy, worrying how this night was going to turn out. He had no idea why he had to be ready, but he was, and also the proudest man.

Mentally drifting out of the room as he people-watched, he thought about the night before, the psychedelic love making and rebirth. He missed the company of the spirits, the real world seemed empty without them, and he had gained a powerful insight that probably no one else knew about, or would even believe. A secret, bigger than all conceivable secrets, seeing everyone and everything differently. Lillian turned to him, catching him in a daydream, seductively caressing his inner thigh under the table. They both became scared as the night they had been pushed into engulfed them, it was finally here and they were on edge, waiting for their predetermined fate.

Forty-Three

11PM. He was having a break sitting on an iron bench, his helmet visor raised, revealing a sweaty and smutty face. The British Aerospace engine towered above him, surrounded by scaffold, keeping a critical eye on his staff. When he was alone, his thoughts went back to the night he saw the entity the garden. Although he never admitted that's what it was. Jeffrey closed his sandwich box and finished off the dregs from his thermos flask. Lillian was heavy on his mind, trying to shake away the tormenting images of her and Robert Courtney. He climbed the metal structure, his limbs heavy with dejection. Reaching the top, he looked out over the factory; massive in size and stretched as far as the eye could see. Cold, lifeless and full of metal, lit by caged, orange lights - no place for the acrophobic. Tutting at the echoed clang of dropped tools, he pulled down his visor. Arc light consumed the electrode, clearing his head as he concentrated on sealing the steel sheets.

It was his fabrication, no one else was qualified. At least up there he wasn't bothered by anyone – with their small talk or brainless banter.

Jeffrey drifted off into autopilot, planning his moonlight flit, it was all set up. Just a matter of persuading Lillian to get in the car. Maybe a deviation would be the best option, like Oliver. He planned to finish early and pick her up from the party. The sweat began to bead and drop onto the shade lens. Turning off the gas, he took the helmet off and wiped it. Suddenly, the siren sounded, startling him- indicating the end of shift. He looked at his watch, puzzled at the error. Other workers were gathering in groups, questioning the alarm. The wail of the apocalyptic defence began unnerving everyone.

'Wass bluddy gowin on now?!' he yelled over the din. The young apprentice looked up, shrugging his shoulders and raising his arms.

'We haven't been near it boss,' it began to slow down to a murmured whir – ushering everyone back to their posts.

'Well, if I find out if any one of ya has been havin' a lark, there'll be trouble. We're on tight deadlines! Right! Let's get back to it, come on! Probably needs cleaning- get some o'that spray on it, would ya?' The young worker didn't have any beef with his boss – he felt sorry for him. Must be a special kind of hell being hated.

Jeffrey checked his watch again; two hours left. The radio played in the background, it was the extra noise that made the work a little lighter. He heard it in bursts when the burner was off. It was playing something, a tune that made his senses home in, echoing and pausing him. That intro made him shiver, he smiled at his favourite song but it also made him feel uneasy. He hunched his shoulders to free the tightened muscles, circling his head, then the whole factory fell into darkness with a 'clunk'.

'What the bluddy 'ell now?!' he kept the burner going for light, 'what the buddy 'ell is going on?!' Jeffrey yelled, annoyed when no one answered. He was sure it was prank night again, at his expense. Pranks came with verbal warning of late, someone nearly lost their life over it. He looked down and couldn't see a good footing, it was too dark. His hair stood on end as a sudden rush of chilled air consumed him.

'Jeffrey!' came a familiar whisper to his left. He froze, swallowing, afraid to move his eyes. Fear gripped him like an icy vice. No one could have got up there that quick, he would have heard their boots.

'Put the bluddy lights back on!' he called out, his voice trembling.

'Boss?!' the young man called out at the foot of the scaffolding, shining a torch in Jeffrey's face.

'Arrgghh! Get it outta me face then!' shielding his eyes, 'what the bluddy 'ell is going on tonight?!'

'I dunno boss– they're just checking the fuse box.'

'Why didn't anyone answer me?!'

'Sorry boss, we were looking for torches,' the boy stood, his overalls a little too big. A fresh face and light features, aiming to please.

'Consider this a final warning if anyone is larking about! It's too bluddy dangerous! Load of idiots!' he feared for his life, it was hanging over him, dread began rising in his gut.

'Not me boss. I swear.'

'Just keep the bluddy torch on that scaffold! I'm coming down!' Jeffrey began his decent charged with anger and fear, ready to sack someone. The young boy held the torch to light the way, following Jeffrey's steps - but then, the torch went out. He hit it against his palm, trying to knock it back on. Shaking it when nothing happened.

'Sorry boss! Uh...just gimme a sec. Come on! Stupid thing!' the civil siren began to sound again, he was relieved when the torch came back on, ignoring the noise. He shone the torch upwards, jumping at a sight that stopped his breathing, stopped his heart. His hand shook when he saw something that would be etched into his soul until his dying day. He couldn't make it out at first, he thought it was one of the bullies but no, it was changing shape, black as night – it's movement like liquid, mesmerising him. The shaking light making it difficult to see it clearly. It darted at a speed that was inconceivable. He tried to follow it and then he saw Jeffrey; hanging upside-down, unconscious - tangled amongst the bars. His head at a funny angle and a thin line of blood ran from one nostril. It was difficult to look at or comprehend.

The boy managed to breathe, he'd been subconsciously holding it in.

'Boss?! Boss?! You, ok?!' the young boy sobbed, 'someone! Someone help! Please!! Over here! Nooowww!' The factory lights came back on, drenching it in orange, the siren stopping abruptly – the radio slurring back into the song, Hotel California. The other workers came running and rushed to Jeffrey's aid but were stopped in their tracks.

'Jesus Christ! How the 'ell did he fall like that?!' the shop floor supervisor exclaimed; in his early sixties, ready to retire and leave this risky job.

'Is he dead? Is he dead?!' the young boy shook, still holding the lit torch.

'I don't know,' it looked like a broken neck to him, it was as if Jeffrey had no bones.

'Someone call an ambulance! Right now!' Two of them ran to the office to make the call.

'What was wrong with the lights?' the young spark asked, his chin quivering.

'Nothing, bloody nothing! They came back on by themselves and that siren works off electric! Something bloody funny going on here. What happened!?'

'I...I don't know! I was holding the torch for him and... It just went out! Then when it came back on, I saw, I saw, the, uh...' he paused, pointing upwards. He saw what? Who would believe him?

'And he...he was like that! It was seconds, I swear!'

'What you still holding that torch for boy? Go and get yourself a cup o' tea or something, calm your nerves, and someone turn that bloody radio off!' The foreman sighed heavily, just when he was looking forward to finishing early and going home to his bed. The young boy went aimlessly to the staff room, putting the torch on the table, it rocked lazily, still lit. Pressing the numbers for his drink, he had to stop himself from losing it, the image of Jeffrey's twisted torso was imprinted on everything he laid his eyes on. He watched out the window to see what was happening, taking some comfort from the heat of his drink. The rest of them were trying to talk to him, they seemed to be like that for ages – shouting his name, scratching their heads – one man had to turn away to suppress his retching. Then he heard sirens, blue light ones this time. The paramedics came in fully equipped. Both medical staff climbed up to where Jeffrey was hanging, looking at each other in disbelief.

'Hello? Jeffrey?' his voice raised, clear 'can you hear me? You've had an accident. We're going to try and move you, okay? Get you to hospital,' there was no response. They proceeded to untangle him, his bones cracking as they were released from the steel structure. Cutting him out would be lengthy option. A couple of the workers joined the young boy in the staff room; they couldn't bear to watch.

'Christ! I've never seen anything like it in all my years! How come he got tangled like that? What did you see, sparky?' they asked the boy, who was sat at the grimy table, still cradling his hot chocolate.

'Torch went out then came back on, and he was like that. Is he dead?'

'I don't think so, but he's pretty messed up. Bet he's broke his bloody neck. That's what you get, I spose.' The young boy just listened in disgust, still shaking, he needed his mother. What was it? What did he see? It made him question his own sanity, even though he believed in stuff like that. He bought those magazines with all the UFO's and pictures of ghosts, but it didn't look like any of them. Should have taken that gardening job he was offered. He hated his job now, maybe he was next.

The paramedics put Jeffrey on a stretcher, his neck in a brace and his limbs strapped and supported, unable to lie him flat.

'He's breathing, just. A big bloke, too. Can you contact next of kin? They need to make their way to A&E as soon as. Is anyone coming with us?'

'Take the young boy with you, he's in shock. I will call his family. I need to stay here.' They put Jeffrey in the ambulance and wired him up. One of them came back to the staff room. The young boy started to whimper when he saw the paramedic, a heroic vision in green.

'Come on, we need to get you checked out too. What's your name, son?'

'Stephen.... Stephen Williams,' he said through sobs.

'Ok Stephen, we'll have a little chat on our way to the hospital.'

'He needs to call his mummy first though, ay,' the other worker jeered, laughing loudly. 'Seen a ghost, he has.'

'We'll sort that out. Thanks lads,' the paramedic took the boy and glared at them over his shoulder. Stephen Williams was traumatised, looking like a rabbit caught in the headlights, snivelling.

The senior worker's thoughts were still on the turn of events as he made his way to the office to call Jeffrey's house. Everyone's contact numbers were typed on a piece of tattered paper, stuck to the wall. Despite Jeffrey's shortcomings, he didn't like what he saw. He'd been in the business since he was sixteen, no one has ever fallen like that. Nearly lost limbs, yes, but tonight was an exception. He dialled the number, not really feeling alive. It just rung out. He checked on Jeffrey's file, there was another contact, but he was reluctant to call it. He returned to the staff room where the burly lads were drinking tea and going over what they saw, morbidly.

'His missus isn't home, where could she be?'

'Playing around I expect, don't blame her, being cooped up with him all day!' their laughter filling the factory.

'That's enough! A bit inappropriate right now, don't you think?!'

'Well, what goes around,' they sniggered in their coffee.

'Be careful what you say, cos it just might come around to you! Right, we need to check the scaffold cos management will be all over this in the morning.' he pressed the drinks machine keypad for a black coffee. Slurping it with the other hand on his hip.

'Me and our Billy put that scaffold up, nothing wrong with it. Solid as a rock!'

'Well, we just need to check it so it's not to blame, otherwise our necks are on the bloody block!'

'Jeffers would have checked it though, you know what he's like.'

'I just think he slipped and fell awkward, and if it turns out you two had anything do to with it, you will be having your notice and your collar felt!'

'Honest, it wasn't us Guv! On me muvers life! I swear! He had us workin' on that unit at the other end! Ask Smithers, he was with us!' the worker spoke with one hand raised and the other placed on his heart. His colleague just nodding in their defence.

'Let's hope so, and I don't wanna hear you two making another sick joke about this! That was someone's son in that mess tonight!' he pointed, arm stretched in the direction of the tragedy. 'Could have been any of us!' he sat down, rubbing his face.

'I doubt if he'll be back to work for a while, maybe never. Best welder we've ever had,' he regarded the strip lighting reflection in the dark liquid, looking at the piece of paper with Celia's number on it, mulling over the decision.

'Thought Jeffers was being transferred to Birmingham?' the burly lad asked.

'He was. Not 'til end of the year though. That'll take some explaining. All the paperwork is done.'

'Means he'll be back 'ere then. Worse luck!'

'I doubt it very much now! That's enough! Not another sordid word, from either of you!'

The phone was ringing. Was it in her sleep, or could she really hear it? Celia moved in her bed; she could still hear it. Groaning, she got up, searching the floor for her slippers with her feet. Her face was screwed up as she made her way downstairs, clutching her lapels. She didn't like phones ringing late at night, it always meant bad news. She found the light switch, it blinded her. She picked up the phone.

'Hello? That you Jeffrey?'

'Uh, hello. Mrs Cunningham?'

'Yes. Who is this?!'

'It's Bob, Bob Scrivener. Jeffrey's supervisor. I'm sorry, but...'

'Ay? What do you want?! I was in me bed! He ain't here. Doesn't live here.'

'Yes, I know, I'm sorry – look, Mrs Cunningham, Jeffrey has had an accident, at work.'

'What do you mean? Nothing wrong with my Jeffrey!' Bob Scrivener wouldn't be forgetting this night in a hurry, he called her the last time.

'He's had an accident...at work. He's gone to hospital my love. I'm so sorry. Are you able to get there?' Celia felt sick, it was the same call she had for her husband. On the same day and at the same time; a call she never thought she'd get again, but always had nightmares about.

'Umm...yes. Just let me uh, get me things. Which one? What ward?'

'The Royal. Intensive care. They're expecting you. We couldn't reach Lillian. Do you know where she is?'

'No! It's all her fault!'

'I see. Are you going to be all right?'

'Yes, yes, of course I am. I'll just get, uh, my shoes, go as I am. Better feed me cat first. Is it, is it serious?'

'We're not sure, Mrs Cunningham. It's best you go now, they'll be able to tell you.'

'Right. Yes. Ok then, well thanks, bye.' She replaced the receiver - life had stopped and she was held somewhere between it. What did God want from her? Celia raised her chin, shrugging off the feeling of helplessness. She put on her shoes, taking the car keys from the kitchen table. Alone in the dark house she felt a compromise materialising.

Forty-Four

The entertainment was loud. Everyone sang along to the cover songs, getting to their feet. They had all eaten a meat and two veg dinner, as small as dolls portions. Tim had been shouting in Lillian's ear telling her about his stories from his Italy trips all night, while she discretely hid her yawns.

They had been dancing together. The tracks were old and not as exhilarating as the ones in Zeus, a little reserved as everyone used their spaces respectfully. Lillian didn't feel like releasing her wild side, although she would have cleared the floor if she did, in that dress.

She looked at her watch, letting out anxious sighs. Robert and Brian had gone to the bar to continue their conversation. Tim moved around to sit next to her.

'Why aren't you drinkin'? How about I get you something?' he yelled.

'Juice, please!' He nodded and swaggered off to get her the drink. Lillian tapped her fingers on the table, hoping no one would want a conversation. The tech guys were eyeing her up. But after seeing her with Robert, they left her alone.

Tim returned, barely making it back on wobbly legs. She drank it without stopping, waiting, the adrenaline made the drug speed around her system faster. Tim watched her, monitoring her body language. The music began to echo in her head, people's laughter loud and close. She stood, steadying herself on the table. The strewn napkins and discarded glasses split and doubled. The room span, tipping her sideways.

'You all right, girl?' Tim asked. Her eyes changed to a vengeful dark, making Tim stumble out of his chair - he was warned this would be the reaction. Seeing his chance, he took her by the arm.

'Come on. We got a surprise for Robert.' He led her out of the noise, her eyes rolling in her head. They stood by the lifts while he looked around, making sure no one saw them. Lillian leaned on the wall, her ears ringing.

'Where you taking me?' she slurred. Tim grabbed her arm and pushed her into the empty carriage. Others wanted to enter, but he stopped them. The doors closed and Lillian's vision was deteriorating. He looked at her with dishonourable intentions.

'I got something to show ya.' She slammed against the walls, her face numbing. Tim was about to move in on her when the lift 'pinged', and the doors opened. He led her out, she flopped about like a rag doll. Managing to hold her up, he found the room. The key card took several positions before it clicked free. He helped her into the bathroom and leaned her against the sink. Her legs couldn't support her, she was silently screaming inside. She tried to look at herself in the mirror, but her face muscles had dropped, unable to focus and losing the sensation in her fingertips. Voices echoed and buzzed in her head. Tim came back in with nothing on but his underpants. Lillian had lost the use of her vocal cords now. She became trapped in her own body, aware of what was happening but unable to do anything about it. Tim pinned her against the wall with this plump, hairy body – gripping her jaw with one hand, fumbling lower with the other. Tears appeared in her eyes as she pleaded in silence; calling for Robert, feeling she was losing him to the incident arising.

'What the hell are you doing?!' Phil came bursting into the bathroom. 'Are you insane?! Just bring her here I said. You idiot!' Phil pulled Tim away and guarded Lillian. 'Get dressed and sort the other one out, Christ!'

'Shame, I fancied a bit of that tonight.'

'Don't be so crass!' he put Lillian's arm around his neck and dragged her out of the room. Looking back at Tim, who raised his middle finger at Phil as he closed the door. He gave her a fireman's lift to down the back stairs which led to the hotel's underground car park; all that working out had paid off.

'I'm sorry. Are you all right? You look ravishing by the way,' he said, his eyes that muddy green. 'I knew that dress would suit you.' He placed her down by fire doors, opening them, checking around. She couldn't catch her breath, afraid she would suffocate, drown in herself, feeling violated and dirty. She just wanted to go back upstairs and pretend it wasn't happening. He stroked her cheek, taking in every feature, continuing down her bare, pulsating, neck.

'You're quite beautiful. I won't hurt you, Lilly. But you should know, I always get what I want.'

She awoke, aware of gentle movement and the angelic voice of Enya. Lillian was sitting in the front seat. Moving her head to the right, a blurry vision of Phil was driving.

'How are you feeling?' he smiled at her, she noticed it didn't carry anything sinister, but a pained affection. The music was haunting, soothing – complimenting his sophistication. Lillian couldn't speak, panicking inwardly, her soul thrashed about in a carcass that had no escape. Everything on the inside worked, but the outside was non-responsive. She looked into the wing mirror hoping for a connection, but it was dark and too difficult to see. Phil had given her something to shut down her ability.

'I know what you're trying to do.' Taking alcohol and narcotics blocked out the feelings of others and 'them', seeing and hearing everything gets exhausting, draining the light. But the psilocybin tincture was the opposite – heightening their senses and allowing them to enter realms, communicate with the interdimensional and regain instinctive consciousness; lost by subliminal control.

Her stomach churned, the car's arrival loud in the gravel. The opening of the door was acute, giving her a headache. Phil helped her out adoring her eyes glinting in the moonlight, like amethyst. Her disappearance into another realm would be permanent and only allowed back in under supervision, once she knew what was behind the truth. Time would not touch her, reflecting on how Janice had been feeling in the same situation. He couldn't wait to see her to live out their lives together - his revenge accomplished. The biting chill of the pensive night air was ineffective on her burning body. Lillian fought hard, getting weak with the battle - giving in, fighting, and then giving in again.

'I've waited a long time for this. I had to move mountains to get you.' He helped her over the stile, like a gentleman. They entered and Lillian tried to pray for her protection, but she couldn't utter one holy word in her heart. She was blocked, silenced. The crushing of the debris beneath their feet and moans from Lillian alerted the night dwellers. The whispers began again, increasing in volume as they walked along the path. She was aware they were being followed on both sides, their grey eyes glowing in the darkness - turning her guts inside out. Her woods felt like it was dying. It had taken on the image of the unwelcome visitors. Everything was perishing, blemished by a sinister erosion. She could hear the barks splitting from it. The mimics were growing in numbers, hissing and calling out their names from within the trees - snarling at the sight of the bewitching humans.

'Do you feel them? I brought them here. Aren't they beautiful?' He stopped, pulling her close. 'You don't belong in this world Lilly – no one understands or appreciates you. Robert doesn't know what he's doing, it won't last. The stars will lose their romance and you will outgrow him. Where you're going, you'll be free, free of all this oppression and judgement. I'm doing this for you, too.'

She was confused how she felt about him, the rescue from Tim and protection changed her feelings. There was another side, perhaps many. They continued, Phil supporting her. She felt them touching her hair and tug the back of her dress - breathing random, desperate words.

Four Five

'What can I get yer?' Tim asked Robert, leafing through a wad of notes, his shirt not properly tucked in. 'C'mon, you haven't touched a drop all night. Let yer 'air down a little,' he puffed on the cigar hanging out of his mouth. Robert waved his hand and shook his head.

'How 'bout a soft drink then? Something fruity, like me!'

'Okay Tim! Just a small one!' Robert yelled over the band.

'Whey!! That's more like it!' he got up, stumbling a little. Swaying as he made his way to the bar. Brian watched his wife dancing with someone else, her body in abandon. He knew she needed younger flesh and stimulation. Perhaps he'd get her that Mercedes she had her eye on. Buying something seemed to pacify her, until the novelty had worn off. She returned to the table out of breath, searching for her glass. Robert looked at his watch, 12.57pm, party was nearing the end. Where *had* Lillian got to? Lisa watched Tim stagger back, sticking her foot out when he got close. He tripped and tipped the drink all over the table.

'Sorry! I'll get you another one!'

'No, Tim, it's fine! Have a seat!' Robert clicked his fingers at Lisa to catch her attention, who had been avoiding eye contact with him all night.

'Lisa? Can you check where Lilly is?'

'She's a big girl now Robert,' she scorned, swaying her wineglass at him, 'toilets are just through there,' she tipping the glass in that direction. He stood – hands on hips, not getting a good feeling in his gut. Focussing on the mirrors, he blinked - sure that one was bending. He looked around the whole room, they were all flexing! Maybe from the music and stomping feet? Receiving a surge from them, a surge of unease.

'What are you looking at?!' Lisa shouted. He gave her a hard stare. Then one of the mirrored panels imploded to smithereens, going off like gunfire. He ducked, but no one had noticed – the music was too loud. Another went, and another, gathering momentum. Lisa had noticed, then Brian. Robert ran onto the dancefloor waving his arms around, going to the band shouting at them to stop. People on tables near the mirrored walls starting screaming and running as more imploded, chaos ensued as realisation swept the room. The band stopped, jumping off the stage, clutching their instruments. Staff came flooding in trying to get people out.

Robert looked at Lisa, 'Lilly!' he shouted, running out of the ballroom. A high-pitched noise in his head suddenly grounded him, watching staff and guests panic in slow motion- their cries muffled and distant. Robert held his head, the piercing pain carried hurried whisperings. Crawling on his hands and knees to the lift, people nearly fell over him. He pressed the button. The lift opened, pulling himself along – the pain squeezing his eyeballs. The doors closed, shutting out chaos, the muzak played Careless Whisper, disturbing him. Robert squinted at the number panel, pressing floor seven – just a hunch. He pulled himself up, watching the numbers flash in sequence. The doors opened onto a silent floor. Looking both ways, his steps clumsy.

'Give me a clue here!' he shouted. Peering down the long corridor, which seemed to stretch away and elude him, the mounted lights buzzed and flickered as he regarded the room numbers.

'Seven hundred and seventy-seven! Wait, how did I know that?' The door was open. He pushed it cautiously.

'Lilly!' he called out, startling the cleaner. 'Sorry. Have you seen a woman, about this high? Black dress, red lipstick?'

The cleaner shook her head.

'No sir. They asked me to clean up. Guests have checked out.'

'Who called? Who called you?!'

'I don't know sir, ask reception.'

'Do you know whose room this is?'

'No sir, they will tell you in reception.' He left, taking the stairs this time, trotting and missing his footing, his hands squeaking on the banister.

People were harassing reception, the beautiful ones were sat on the floor, their diamantes a little dulled. Senior staff organised an evacuation of the suite while paramedics came to treat those for cuts and shock. He stood with his hands on his hips, impatient and unable to keep still. The hotel's phone was going berserk, with guests talking all at once.

'Look, sorry, excuse me!' Robert projected his voice above the hum of raised ones. The receptionist held up their forefinger for him to wait his turn. He paced, setting the automatic doors off. Going back again, slamming his hand down on the desk.

'Listen! This is an emergency! Can you tell me which room Phil Hathaway is in?!'

'Sir! Please! We have an emergency at the moment!'

'I know, but please, I, uh, have something of his, urgent!' The receptionist sighed in frustration, turning to help him – who could resist that puppy-dog face and those teeth? She tapped on the keyboard firmly.

'I'm sorry, we don't have that name booked in.'

'You must have! Check again!'

'No, sorry. When did you say he checked in?'

'Umm, oh! Who reserved room seven, seven, seven?' she tapped the keyboard again.

'I have Tate down for that room. They've left already.'

'Tate? But... they've? What do you mean by they've?' Robert felt sick, his blood light.

'Look, I'm sorry Sir, but we have a bit of a situation here. I can't help any further. Sorry,' gesturing a smile.

Robert was pacing his room close to a panic attack, waiting for Lisa to pick up.

'*Hello!*'

'It's me!'

'*What's happened? Did you find her?*' Lisa had one finger in her ear while she walked around outside the suite.

'No! And you've got some explaining to do!'

'*What? You're not making any sense! Where are you?*'

'In my room. Two, seven, seven,' he hung up.

'*Wait...Robert? Shit!*' she squeezed passed everyone, quickly sobering. Robert waited outside – feeling he should be doing something, be somewhere. Lisa came out of the lift, checking both ways. Her feet stomping down the corridor; he hated the very sight of her.

'If this has got anything to do with you, I'll kill you myself!'

'Bit harsh, Robert,' she pushed passed him to enter the room, knocking his shoulder back. He also looked both ways before shutting the door.

'I wasn't expecting guests, so excuse the mess. I'm all outta tea, but there's a minibar.' Robert's limbs were heavy. 'What's happening down there? I hear the screaming's stopped.'

'People are bleeding. It's a mess, and you should see the glass!' Lisa put all the lights on and gasped, stood with both hands over her mouth.

'Yeah, this. Don't think they cover it under expenses,' Robert said sarcastically.

'It's been vandalised! Who did this? What does it mean?!' Lisa asked, scanning the room, warily regarding the writing all over the walls. The word 'Mandrax' was scrawled in different thicknesses, scrawny, hurried and covering every square inch in black ink.

'I think the hotel is going for an urban look.'

'And what's that smell?' she asked, pinching her nose.

'Yeah, there's that too. Bad drainage?'

'Why would someone write it all over the walls? Your walls?' Robert sifted through the minibar, 'I don't think it was 'a someone' – they'd have to be in here all night to do that.' Lisa gave him a perplexed expression, 'are you taking this seriously, at all?'

He stood up, studying a small bottle of Jack Daniels.

'I'm trying to ignore it,' he sat on the bed, unscrewing the bottle. 'I think Lilly checked out with someone. I went to a room, I don't even know why I went, but I had a gut feeling it was Phil's.' He drank the dark spirit, shivering as it burned his gullet. Lisa sat down on the bed with him, twiddling her fingers.

'Is there any chocolate in there?'

Robert took out a Galaxy bar and threw it on the bed.

'Knock yourself out.' She took it, tearing off the paper and devouring it.

'So, let's have it, and don't spare the horses. Truth Lisa, and you're helping me get her back. We need to go, we're wasting time! I don't even know where!' He opened a packet of Ritz biscuits, tilting his head back and tipping the small portion into his mouth. Then searched the mini fridge for more alcohol. Lisa looked at the writing, sucking the chocolate morsels until they melted in her mouth.

'The writing looks old. Like something from Dickens. You look pathetic, by the way. You're driving, so ease up on the mini bar.' He sniffed a bottle of white wine, shuddering at the acidic bouquet.

'There's isn't enough in here to get a Gnat pissed!'

'Mini bars are expensive.'

'Your chocolate had the biggest price tag, trust me.'

'I think we should call the Police.'

'Oh yeah? And what?' he ran his fingers through his hair. 'This writing...look, I don't want any authorities getting their hands on it. It's a password.'

He took off his tie, looking at himself in the mirror in his suit, another ruined evening...but there was no way he was changing, he was going as he was.

'But why would someone, *something*, write a password on your walls...oh!'

'Yeah, penny dropped, has it? Sherlock. And close your mouth when you're eating chocolate.'

'Are you going like that?' Lisa asked, her cheeks bulging.

'Yeah, why not? You?'

'Well. I need to change my shoes and I don't think I can jump over fences in this dress.'

'Fences? We're jumping over fences?'

'Possibly, maybe. I want to be prepared.'

'This ain't Starsky and bloody Hutch, Lisa. I'm scared. This arsehole has been one step ahead of us the whole time. He knows we're coming.'

'What makes you think he took her under duress? What if she went with him, voluntarily?' Robert frowned, studying Lisa; her stern looks, always like she had a bad smell under her nose.

He shook his head, 'do I detect a little bit of distraction, Lisa? Has she dumped me? Did you see that dress?!' he held down the contents of his stomach '...then tell me now, save me the embarrassment.'

'Don't be so dramatic. Come on,' Lisa took her chocolate, leaving the room.

'Where we going?!'

'To Rose and Martin's.'

Forty-Six

Robert had a lump in his throat turning up to Lillian's family home. She'd described the street perfectly to him. He felt he'd already been there.

He blew hard through his lips.

'I'm not sure I want to do this. Martin trusted me with her. I've let him down.'

Lisa tutted. 'Just get out,' giving him a snide look, unbuckling. Robert noticed a light was on downstairs. It was like walking the green mile as they climbed the steps. Lisa knocked the door lightly. Robert flexed his fingers, wondering what they would look like, feeling petrified and clueless. Rose opened the door, in the middle of putting on a jacket.

'You took your time. I expected you here over an hour ago!' Robert looked at Lisa, his eyebrows almost meeting. She just gave him an 'I told you so' look, she was good at those. Rose wasn't pleased to see Lisa, but her heart leapt a little at the handsome man that must have been Robert.

'You'd better come in,' tilting her head towards the lounge. Benny barked, detecting strangers. The house was small, bright and clean.

Martin was in a plush, red velour chair, standing as they entered the room, his hand held out, 'you must be Rob,' he said with a smile. They shook hands vigorously, Robert feeling reprieved.

'It's good to meet you, Martin. Although I would have preferred under better circumstances.'

Martin wheezed and coughed, slightly bend over. 'Nonsense. You're the missing link.'

'Hello Robert. It's good to meet you,' Rose shook his hand, he kissed her on the cheek. She blushed a little. Such a good-looking man, decent too. Rose had the same effect on him as her daughter; he could feel her stubborn, inner strength.

'I'm sorry,' Lisa said awkwardly.

'Bit late for that now, isn't it?!' Rose looked her up and down.

'Now, now - this is no time for dispute. Time is of the essence.' Martin intervened.

'What's been going on?' Rose asked.

'The mirrors in the hotel exploded, well, sort of imploded – anyway, and there was Mandrax written all over Robert's walls,' Lisa garbled, with Robert glaring at her. Benny ran in when Rose opened the kitchen door, sniffing the air from a distance – 'gruffing' as he took in the mixed messages.

'Why was there an illegal sedative written all over the walls?' Rose asked, fearing the worse.

'A sedative?! I don't get it.'

'Mmm, yes. David Bowie sang about it once, but don't ask me to give you a rendition. Quaaludes is another name they go by.' Rose answered. Robert and Lisa regarded one another.

'A high price would be paid for them now, I would say. I believe South Africa is the place to get them, illegally - but don't quote me on that.' Robert's mind raced and the urgency to leave was increasing.

'So, what's the plan?' Martin asked.

'Forgive me, but how come you were expecting us?' Robert stroked Benny's ears for a distraction; it helped alleviate the awkward moment. Martin and Lisa glanced each other's way.

'Get my coat please, darling.'

'You're in no fit state!' Rose supported him as he caught his breath.

'We'd better get going,' Martin was sweating from the infection, but determined to continue.

'Can I ask what's going on please?' Robert wrung his hands.

'You see, we create our own miseries then blame everybody else for them. We don't listen to our gut often enough, when it was given to us for a very good reason, and not just for digestion, I might add,' he coughed, holding his fist up to his mouth. Robert listened intently.

'We're going to put things right. As they should be.' Rose walked back into the lounge. She stroked his face, her eyes welling up.

'Don't cry darling, we knew this day would come. It's the only way now,' she sniffed, wiping away her tears.

'I just wish you were a little stronger, that's all.'

'Don't worry. It'll all fall into place. You up for it Rob? Bit of cops and robbers?' Rose helped him on with his jacket, the blue one, her favourite.

Robert stood. 'Cops and robbers? I'm confused.'

'I can quite imagine. Let's go get our Lilly, shall we? You can drive.' Lisa felt stupid in her evening dress now, not exactly vigilante gear.

'Right, where are going?' Robert asked. Rose zipped up her red anorak, pushing the collar up around her neck.

'Lilly's house.'

Robert looked straight ahead as he stuck to the wind of the road. He saw things differently since the woods, envisaging there were nocturnal onlookers and urban myths hiding in the hedgerows. He was thinking about every meeting, every conversation he'd ever had with Phil and how he was always in the know about things, ahead of everyone else. There was a point when he actually aspired to it, something he thought he would have to learn. Feeling inferior as he metaphorically walked behind him. Rose sat in the front, he felt so comfortable next to her, if a little afraid. She reminded him of a 1950s film star, but he couldn't put his finger on which one. She gave him directions and was smitten with him too. The silence in the car was filled with Martin's wheeze, all of them needing to open windows from feeling psychologically suffocated.

Lisa held onto the car seat as they picked up speed, watching the rabbits play chicken. Their anxiety risen to get to Lillian. They were exhausted, emotionally and physically, running on cheap alcohol and adrenaline. Robert indicated right onto Coed-y-Ffrind Close, feeling a little strange entering this territory.

'Coydee what?' he asked.

'Coyd 'ee' frind,' Rose spelt out, 'it means, friend of the woods. Not an exact interpretation. It's number seven, just down here on the left,' Robert shook his head at the signs that had laden their path.

'I hope Jeffrey isn't there – I don't think I'll be responsible for my actions.'

Rose took off her seatbelt, smiling evocatively at his words 'he's not here, don't worry.'

'I'll come with you, darling,' she helped Martin out. Robert watched them walk down the drive, it felt surreal; the place he imagined in his head, out of reach.

'I wanted to smell the roses,' Lisa uttered.

'Why are we bloody here?'

'We're taking something to the woods,' Lisa answered, studying the houses with a turned-up nose.

'And we're going there, because?'

'Haven't you been listening?'

'To what? I didn't hear anything about the woods, or why we're going there! Is she there, with him? I mean, seriously, how do you expect me to fathom this?'

'I don't expect your tiny mind to fathom anything.'

'*My* mind isn't tiny! I'm not the one who slept with the enemy!'

'And I'm not the one who got pregnant by it!' there was an edgy pause.

'Ok, you won that one. Tell me, before they get back.'

'I brought Lilly to Radar. You should at least be thanking me for that.'

'Thank you. Why did you bring her?'

'Phil had something to do with the collapse of Pulse, where Lilly used to work. The owner, Simon D'Or, owed Phil money for some other unscrupulous deal. You'd know all about those Robert, wouldn't you?' He pursed his lips, with no come back.

'He told me to get her. She went with an agency, and they wouldn't have put her forward, not enough experience. So, we bypassed it.' Lisa sighed heavily. She was sorry for it all, wanting Brian, her bolthole; she'd overstepped the mark, and needed his grounding protection. She told him she was looking for Lillian. He stayed behind to help with the catastrophe - there would be hefty compensations to fulfil.

'Look, it's me you're talking to. Why was he looking for her and why are we going to the woods? Are the creatures there?'

he regretted saying it, they were his secret – he didn't want Lisa or Phil getting their dirty hands on them.

'Please Robert, just ask Rose – I've already betrayed him. He's probably listening right now. Maybe this will be the last time you see me.'

'Don't worry, I won't cry over it. I am bloody stupid for trusting him, and you! Trying to ward her off me. That bit doesn't make sense!'

'It makes perfect sense! I didn't want Lilly getting hurt! I'm sorry, but we're in it now. I think I'm the stupidest.'

'Is there such a word?' they both laughed and, in that moment, reconciled their grievances with one another.

'Did you have to make Phil a coffee at exactly nine thirty, after you slept with him?'

'That was below the belt Courtney. But I'll take it on the chin, you win.'

'Where's Jeffrey then?' Robert asked.

'Not sure. He was trying to protect her from all this.' They both reflected in silence. Rose and Martin came back, Robert could see his condition was getting worse.

'I don't think that old man can make it.' The opening of the doors made them jump.

'Mirror isn't there. He must already have it. I should have guessed really. Although, I got this damn thing. We should burn it,' Rose held up the leather-bound book. She touched Robert's shirt, pulling it straight. He felt calmed by her action, an overwhelming sense of acceptance.

'I'm sorry we have brought you into this – but I've been waiting for you,' she smiled tenderly at him. 'Whatever happens, I'm glad you showed up and I'm already proud of you. Now, let's get our girl.'

Robert gulped, feeling a rush of love fill his shoes.

'Oh please! Can we go? Before I throw up!' Lisa grouched.

Robert's nausea increased when he saw Phil's car parked by the stile; it looked at home. Martin eased himself out, with Rose rushing to help him out.

'I'm staying here,' Lisa said.

'The fuck you're not! Get the hell out, now!' Robert slammed the door, making her hunch her shoulders and shut her eyes.

'Please, Martin, let me go. Wait here,' Rose pleaded.

He shook his head. 'No, Rose. I'm coming with you.' They all stood by the car, huddled over from the cold night.

'Right, you two...' Rose handed Robert a torch, 'you take this and haven't you got something to give me, Lisa?' holding out her hand towards her. She sheepishly gave Rose the bottle from Lillian's bag.

'What are you doing with it?!' Robert asked. Rose unscrewed the cap and poured some holy water into her palm. She started with Robert.

'I feel you don't really need this. You already have a protection. Open your hands,' he did so.

'I don't think it's a protection, my radar is off! Pardon the pun.'

'Well, that's kind of the same thing. But you need to control your fear. They feed off it. Now, you know what to do with it,' Robert went through the ritual.

'What about me?' Lisa asked.

'I can't protect you. It's too late.'

Robert snapped his head round to look at Lisa. 'What does that mean?!'

'Okay. You both need to listen to me if you want to come out alive.'

Forty-Seven

A chill descended in the clearing, Lillian shivered as she lay on her side – holding onto her forearms to generate some heat; unable to recollect how she got to this point. She could sense the anguish of the dammed as they gathered around the perimeter. Phil crouched beside her and dropped the antidote into her mouth.

'You have to help me, Lilly – before you start your new life, we need to free them,' he circled her, admiring his manicure. Lillian sobered, pushing herself up – she was relieved to be out of the thick cloud, detecting the moving darkness around her woods. The life of the trees waning.

'I need my life back. Now, just open the portal – I have an agreement to fulfil.'

She stood, shivering, her skin blue in places. 'I'm not opening anything.'

'I see. Perhaps a little, persuasion will help?' he raised his left arm, summoning something from the depths of the woods. Her shivering increased – gasping when Dave came out of the dark, levitated and controlled – his back arched, straining and whimpering. Lillian looked between them. Phil laughed, adoring her eyes as they filled with horror, and he'd changed so quickly.

'This one, will do anything for monetary gain.'

'Let him go!'

'Open the portal, Lilly.'

Lillian backed away, shaking her head... she shivered violently.

'You... open...it.' Phil twisted his wrist, contorting Dave – he cried out in agony. Lillian felt pained for him, confused. His beautiful black hair falling down his back.

'I will finish him. Such a pathetic excuse for a human, although I admire his following and choice of idolism.' Lillian mistrusted this newfound power of Phil's, it was an impossibility, even for the highly gifted.

'What are you?' she asked, narrowing her eyes. Phil parted his lips; a dense smoke lazily escaped them. His eyes changed to a deep yellow, as his stature elongated.

'*Opennn the portal, light worker!*' Zalud bellowed.

Lillian gasped and stumbled back; she felt powerless as the demon killed everything beneath its feet. She struggled to recite the verses as Zalud raised his other arm levitating her too, his skin burning in patches as she continued.

Dave cried out from excruciating pain, gurgling from the grip on his body. Lillian was waiting for him to die – she could feel the anguish and pressure on his heart.

'Lil! Help meeee!' She looked into Zalud's goat-like eyes, emptying her, emptying hope.

'*Do it! Psychic! You have the key!*' Lillian choked. She hung there; sure she would freeze to death. He took her arm turning it over to look at the three moles, grinning with delight.

'*Opennn, the portal, star seed! You have been chosen, use it!*' he pressed again. His words deeper, demanding.

She went limp, closing her eyes. 'Forgive me,' she whispered, calling for them, calling for Al-Qayyum. Zalud roared a laugh, ignoring the feeble attempt.

'*Your God has neglected you! You speak with the forbidden! We will make good use of you!*' she knew what they would do to her, testing her pain threshold and experimenting, giving her extra gifts in return. Then dumping her somewhere when they'd finished. Only to be sectioned and imprisoned, for fear of speaking out, branded a nutcase. Zalud produced her mirror from his chest, thrusting it in her face.

'*Open it! Release my prisoners! Free them from human entrapment!*'

'I will free them if you take Phil instead of me. You know he won't stop at his manipulation. I have no intention of using your followers. Surely, you know that. I will protect them.'

Zalud tilted his head from side to side, then bared his teeth with an amused expression. Before she could take a breath, he forced her through the reflection. She was thrown into darkness but feeling warm again. There were no other reflections to choose from this time, she waited, terrified - it was the walkway from her dreams. Zalud released Dave, dropping him to the floor like a concrete pillar, closing his eyes, raising his head up to the stars in glory.

'Christ! It's gone cold!' Robert complained, following Rose struggling with Martin. Lisa lagged behind – hiding her sobs as the dark twisted her innards.

'Let me help you, Rose,' he took Martin's other arm and put it around his shoulders.

'I'm sorry I got us into this,' Martin said breathlessly, needing warmth and his bed.

'You should've stayed in the car!' Rose protested.

'What? And miss all the fun?'

Robert smiled to himself. He shone the torch ahead of them, looking to the floor, walking a little awkward with the extra weight. 'Wait! Look! There! Bluebells! She's here!'

Rose scanned the darker places. 'Where are you?' she pleaded under her breath. 'We're getting close. Remember what I said. Just hang on to all the love you've got and all the belief. Keep hold of it, no matter how much they force you to let it go. Have you got any left, Lisa?' she narrowed her eyes at Rose, her arm wrapped around her waist.

'Do we have to clap three times if we believe, as well?' They ignored her, and everyone went quiet while in survival mode. Martin was getting heavy as he became weaker. His chest rattled, the cold bit his lungs worsening the condition. Rose put her red anorak around him as the ground beneath them crisped.

'Where's this ice coming from?' Robert asked, his teeth chattering, their breaths visible in the darkness. He squinted his eyes at something ahead, 'what's that?' he pointed. As his eyes focussed, his brain received the message - he straightened, his heart pounded, tears broke his voice. 'Dad?' He squeezed his eyes shut, breathing heavy through his nose, controlling his emotions as his father stood before him; wearing that checked shirt and faded jeans.

'Why don't you come here son? Make things up,' the image of his father was holding out his hand – a gesture that Robert ached for. 'Mimics' he murmured, his skin chilling.

'No, Robert! It's not him. Just keep walking!' Rose said, pulling Martin's arm. 'They're trying to stop us!' Robert didn't want to believe it, just one last shake of his hand was all he wanted.

He let go of Martin and walked through the bracken. Every time he got close, the image would move, calling him further.

'Robert! NO! We need you!' Rose set Martin down. 'Wait here. You! Sit here with him,' she instructed Lisa, giving her the torch.

'Robert! Please! I know you're hurting. But it's not him!' she lost sight of him. Standing alone, she could see them, darting from one tree to another: like mischievous children.

'I can see you, and you don't fool me!' releasing their screams, detecting the protection and fearless soul. 'I'll use it, if I have to!' then she heard a baby crying; putting her fingers in her ears, closing her eyes.

'No! It's not you! Leave me! Go! In the name of God, go!' It came again, she couldn't help but follow it. Searching, parting the foliage. Something was moving in a white muslin; it looked like Myriam's hijab. She slapped her hand over her mouth - kneeling down in submission, afraid to touch it. Her hand shook as she caressed the fabric, cold to the touch. 'It's ok. It's ok...shhhh,' she comforted.

'Mummy's here now darling. Mummy's here,' she sobbed, laughing through her tears at the reunion of her loss- one that had severed a large part of her. The baby changed several times, like a bad dream. She knew it wasn't real, but any temporary fulfilment was all she needed to stitch everything back together.

Robert stopped, realising he was alone, it had gone quiet. 'Dad?' there was a growl behind him, he spun. Seeing dark shapes blacker than the night, encircling – disorientating him. Giving him that feeling Lillian described; like they had emptied your soul. He heard Rose calling and ran, fearful of what was following him. There were noises, everywhere, taunting him. 'Rose! No!' Robert clumsily came to her, his Oxford Brogues ruined.

'It's not real!' he took her arm, yanking her back. Her eyes glistening with grief. The cloth went limp, and she watched it being consumed by the forest floor –Rose clawed at the dirt, tearing away the foliage.

'No! No!' She looked at him with a psychotic expression, 'help me, Robert! It's my William!' she said through convulses.

'No, it's not,' he dropped to his knees, 'they're playing tricks!' He saw nothing; just a crazy-looking woman scrabbling in the dirt. Robert stifled his cries, feeling her pain and feeling helpless from the plea in her eyes. He was out of breath, frightened, conscious the woods were alive with something else.

'They're somewhere better than here, Rose. Not out here in the cold, why would he be? We don't lose them twice,' he shook her gently by the shoulders. 'It's just emotion Rose. That's all. That's all these bastards are playing with!' he raised his head and projected his voice – he was ready to confront their torment.

'He's away from here, from all the shit and let downs. That's a blessing, wouldn't y'say?' he understood his mother's ache, after seeing Rose's frailty. She was silent, agreeing with a reluctant nod. Rose wiped her nose on her coat, sniffing.

'I know it's not him. But I was hoping it was for one last hold.'

'You wouldn't be happy with one though, would you? Come on, they're not our responsibility anymore. We have the living to worry about. It's time to face the music.' He pulled Rose up and supported her, taking comfort from her colourful demeanour. That's how he saw his love for Lillian, in deep reds and magentas with no smudge or bleed. They reached Martin and Lisa, their idle chatting halted from the extra guest. Phil was pointing a Colt pistol at Martin - the one that was missing from Lillian's thigh.

'Well, isn't this twee?' He indicated with the pistol for them to get beside Lisa.

'Phil! What are you doing?!'

'Shut up, Courtney. It stops here. Just go back and forget it.' Robert's eyes darted from person to person.

Martin raised his hand towards Phil. 'Please son, there's no need for this.'

Forty-Eight

Phil swallowed his burning resentment, redirecting the gun into Martin's face.

'Son? That slipped off your tongue easy!' his voice trembling. Martin was wrestling with his own emotions and couldn't help but blame himself; a guilt he'd carried around with him that had eventually broke his back.

'Do you know why?'

'Humour me.'

'Your mother needed help and refused to get any. The affairs, and then there was you...' Phil squeezed tighter around the trigger, his eye twitching.

'I can't help the way I am!'

'Oh, but you can. You chose to abuse your ability. It could have been very different.'

'You should've helped me! And my mother!'

'For what? You both took all I had, Phillip. Manipulating innocent creatures for pleasure is twisted! Working all hours to feed her addiction and your odd collections. My girls aren't like that.' Phil's jealously and grudge rose from his stomach and filled his neck.

'Your, *bluebell* is mine now.'

Robert stepped forward 'If you hurt her, I'll....'

'What? You'll do what, Courtney? You have nothing. I gave you everything. I just needed you to warm her up for me,' Robert lurched forward, fists raised, Martin holding him back.

'He's not worth it, Rob. Let me deal with it.' Martin straightened himself. 'What have you done to yourself? Ay? Dragging everyone into your mess!'

'*My* mess? You did this to me! Although, I have to say, I've done very well out of it so far. There's some advantage in being abandoned by your own father!'

'Stop feeling sorry for yourself!' Rose shouted.

'Ah, Rose. Your potions, they're impressive, I'll give you that – but you're too late!' He looked at Lisa, her face streaked with mascara, cowering behind them.

'Siding with the Hill Billies is it?' she glared at him, near to a break down.

'Please...have your grievance with me, not her,' Martin got between them. Looking at his father made everything come flooding back. The stairs, the waiting and loss of all hope, putting his hands over his ears so he couldn't hear his mother and those men - not knowing what to do with his feelings.

They were all part of him, like a life support, breathing it out and back in again. Aiming the pistol, he was ready to fire, to disintegrate the stake firmly buried in his back.

'Kill me, then. If it will make you feel better. I deserve it, I suppose.'

'No! Martin!' Rose protested.

'Bottle!' Lisa shouted behind her. Rose heard, sliding her hand in her pocket and thrusting it in Phil's face.

'That's enough!'

He looked at it and burst into a ridiculing laugh. 'I'm not a Vampire!' Lisa snapped when she heard that – running at him, screaming, knocking him over, the gun firing in mid-air. She punched his chest, his face, his arms raised to protect him from the blows, still laughing. She managed to hit his nose, shocking him, making it bleed. Robert grabbed her arms, dragging her off of him.

Phil saw the opportunity, he raised his arm and shot her in the stomach – then Robert, a lousy aim in the shoulder, and it all fell silent quickly. They both tumbled backwards in an awkward embrace.

'No! *NO!*' Rose screamed, her ears ringing from the shots. She grabbed Martin, covering him with her body.

'What have you DONE!?' Robert held Lisa – blood expanded through her red dress, darker than the material. He looked at the blood on his hands and the splatters on Phil's face. Regarding his shoulder, the crisp, white shirt was getting saturated. The pain hadn't registered yet, but it would once the adrenaline had subsided.

'Of all the people I have known in my life, you have to be the worse!' Robert scorned through gritted teeth, his eyes bulging; his whole body burning.

'Oh, on the contrary Robert. I saved you, remember? Saved you from the pit you were in.' Phil casually got up, brushing himself down.

'You didn't save me - you used me! Look at you, can't even do anything for yourself! Scaring a child half to death is abuse! Keeping everyone quiet with your filthy money! All what you have, is borrowed!' Phil held his gaze, fearing the change in what he once controlled.

'You did very well off of it and you're about to lose it all after that stunt. I'm coming for Michael, once he hasn't got a home to go to – he can come and live with me and Janice – play happy families.'

'Over my dead body!'

'Well, if you insist,' he raised the pistol, grinning, ready to fire randomly if he had to and finish off Robert, finish them all off. They were all getting in the way of his new life. He suddenly felt cold and uneasy, stepping away from them, detecting a presence behind him – he turned; his mother before him, holding a bottle of beer.

'Well, well, well - look what the cat dragged in,' she said, swigging.

Rose was left with a predicament.

'It's okay,' Robert strained, 'I can make it.' He took Lisa, Rose supporting Martin, and they all limped to the clearing.

Phil was left dumbfounded as the vision of his mother took away his attention from them.

'You can't fool me! I know what you are! Think I'm stupid?' The woman stumbled forward, her face grotesque, full of hate and revenge.

'You were never any good,' she slurred, 'look at you – the bad runs right down your middle,' she waved the bottle at him. He began to grimace at this creature before him; resentment even had a smell to it.

'Please, mum, I had no choice, you both left me!'

The thing moved in closer. 'Everyone leaves you, in the end.'

Rose was spurred on when she caught sight of the clearing through the trees, a low bearing mist expanding from it. Robert struggled with Lisa, with blood everywhere, surprised at his primitive instinct to preserve the soul he could feel slipping away, instead of his own. All the hate he harboured for her, dispersed - pulling her along with the strength from his own guilt. He could barely hold the torch out in front, checking behind him, it had gone suspiciously quiet. Lillian and his family immediately came to mind and the realisation of how much they needed him alive, gave him a burst of courage. His vision started to blur as the hormones subsided, then he saw something ahead, shimmering gold. No, perhaps copperish. 'Wait, is that a...*cat*?!' Robert asked.

Rose looked up. 'Yes. It's Oliver.'

Forty-Nine

They followed Oliver – Robert in awe of his unusual coat and regal providence.

'How the hell did he get here?' suddenly stopping as the mist reached their feet. Kneeling on the edge of the clearing, Robert held his breath when he saw Lillian suspended, and the sight of Zalud made him acutely aware of his fragile, skeletal structure; surrounded by its easily penetrable tissue. Fear thickened his blood, staying close to Rose. Oliver continued walking further into the clearing – his tail erect, just visible above the mist.

'What's he doing?! Rose! The cat!' A fierce wind rushed over their heads, reaching the centre and making its way up above the trees, bending and twisting the canopies. Zalud raised a free hand while keeping Lillian where she was - a vertical circle of heat shimmer materialised, opening the gate to their portal, endless beyond.

'I don't feel so good, Rose,' Robert let go of Lisa and passed out.

'Oh my God! Robert? Robert?' she shook him, listening to his breathing. Lisa was losing her colour, holding her stomach, her body in spasm and on fire. Rose searched the trees begging with her eyes - laughing with delight when she saw the small orbs fly out with purpose, bobbing and swirling. She covered Martin with her coat, keeping what little heat he had left, as he drifted in and out of consciousness.

'Martin! No! Stay awake!'

Zalud emanated electrical currents from his torso; hitting the tree trunks and giving energy to the mimics - Rose covered her face from the flying splinters, the noise like tesla coils. She spread her arms over the three people she was trying to protect as they moved in on her. Some passed by, afraid of what she carried and dived into the portal. Others looked on from the perimeter, curious of the human that emanated strength. Salivating at the one that was shrouded in death. Rose was desperate to get to Lillian, her face pale and eyes surrounded by an insipid grey, hung in mid-air, limp and lifeless.

'Lilllyyy!!' her voice faint over the howl. The dress clung to her body, emphasising everything. Lillian could still hear her mother; frantically looking both ways, trapped inside a worm hole. She saw a small window of light, running towards it down a corridor in an abandoned building - tripping over an office chair, stopping her, watching it wheel itself and spin down a walkway she instantly recognised. Their department and everything else was covered in plaster dust, the light fittings hung down from the ceiling, swinging, flickering. She came to Phil's office – the door and glass panel were still intact. This was the parallel where he kept his Jinn, until he wanted them. It was also the place where he kept files, piles of them, including Apex.

'Bal?!' she called out, 'you here?' Something was thrown as a threat, something metal. It was dark, she could barely see. The Jinn looked around the wall by the kitchen; just half of a pale face and oddly shaped eyes. She was used to them, but their presence still gave her the chills.

'You wanna get out?' she asked. Bal hung back, wary of people. It was threatened never to leave otherwise it would be certain death for them and their family. Conditioned to believe all the pious were liars; there was no mercy or Lord of the worlds and only humans were punished - free to kill and do whatever they please, without consequence. Unable to apply logic like us, completely absent of a conscience. The places we leave empty become their torturous dwellings, cast out by their own.

'It's ok, I promise. You can trust me. You know that. I'm setting you free, Bal. I won't be needing you anymore.' Lillian turned the handle to Phil's office, only the chosen could open it from the inside. That's why they're attracted to the special ones - so many to set free. The rest of them heard the door – racing to her; some crawling, others moving swiftly in a blurred manifestation, morphing and agonising. She held on tight to the handle. They tugged at her dress, an icon for their release. Their whispers of insanity and beseech - female, male, child.... pulling at her arms, bearing her down.

Rose could see her choking, straining for breath, writhing in mid-air.

'No! Lilly!' she looked for Oliver - he walked towards her, rubbing up against her face, purring. 'It's time,' she said. The cat blinked with intellect. Oliver stood on his hinds, growing taller, wider – arms, legs, and a head. Rose gawped. A person, but not quite; the image of hair was ginger. The bodice he wore, a transparent armour- in soft shapes, nothing exact, quite indescribable. Light shone from him, making the features and outline hazy. Robert eyes flickered open as Oliver looked down at him. It was one of the beings he saw that night, but very much a male version. Robert smiled at the enveloping vision, then blacked out. Oliver bowed at Rose and was in front of Lillian in the blink of an eye. He smothered her with his light and entered the portal.

They cowered when they saw him, backing away and hiding. He lit up the dismal place with his presence; he was no longer Oliver - his real name was Mintaka, from the arms of Orion.

'You came,' Lillian said with a bittersweet ache in her heart. 'Bal, we need to take him too, please. But he won't come out.' Oliver looked at the timid Jinn, peering around the corner.

'T'aaleh,' he permitted. Bal trusted him, skulking towards them, unsure of his fate, humbled by the reassurance in its own language after being accustomed to threat and torture.

'Take the others, too,' she opened the door, and the light pulled them through. The transition was sharp, opening her eyes and drawing in breath. The mirror shook in her hand and the Jinn poured out of the reflection like a viscous liquid, dispersing amongst the trees. The black mists took to the sky, weaving through the canopies to find a new dwelling, free of human oppression – pleasing Zalud. Bal turned to Lillian and sneered in gratitude, 'go' she said to it, nodding her head towards the trees. 'Go on!' It glided in mist form, reborn out of the dark. She dropped to her feet, relieved to be back.

'Break the mirror!' Rose yelled over the chaos. It flew out of Lillian's hand and into Zalud's - she shrieked in surprise; being dragged by her feet, silenced and restrained. Taking the bottle from inside her coat, Rose couldn't decide who she should choose. Searching for the piece of paper in the other pocket, she took it out, ready to read aloud; trying to hold it as it flapped like a flag. She tried the first line, 'uh, Bismillah...' Zalud increased the wind, and it took the verses from her hand, disappearing into the portal.

'NO!! God damn you! No!' She cradled Lisa, lifting her head up with her arm. 'I hope this works. I'm not sure what else to do!'

'No, Rose. Not me. It's too late. Just say a prayer for me, please. Give it to Robert.' Rose brushed Lisa's blood-stained hair away from her face and caressed her cheek.

'Thank you. I never meant for it to turn out like this, but you were brave enough to help. None of it was your fault. I forgive you.' Lisa's smile quivered, releasing tears that ran from the corners of her eyes.

'Just make sure that arsehole gets what he deserves,' she murmured. No one came for her, no one she knew anyway. Just a little wisp of a thing - with a bright face and wide eyes, pulling her gently. Her mercy came in the form of a bullet.

'Goodbye love, God bless.' Rose tapped her arm and closed her makeup-smudged eyelids. 'Such a waste,' she uttered through tears. Rose lay Lisa down and covered her with the red coat. She tore Robert's shirt open and poured the bottle on the wound. He cried out as the holy water cleansed his flesh and entered his system. The impacted bullet emerged and fell into her palm; pouring the last drops to seal it.

'My, God,' she whispered. Robert coughed and gasped, the burning subsided, looking around him.

He saw Lillian, petrified as she stood before Zalud, with bluebells beneath her feet. He felt numb from the mind-blowing sight before him. The balls of light took form, ready for battle, moving in on Zalud in an effort to restrain his invasion. Limbs long; still practising being human. Their shape, with mesmerising purity and angelic singing, heating his frozen body. He felt solid and protected to be in their presence again. Zalud twisted his wrist, levitating Phil, pulling him towards the portal with extreme effort as he tried to make a quick escape.

'No! Zalud! NO! Our agreement!' Phil looked back for help, but everyone wanted their hate satisfied. The heat shimmer grew, and the wind got stronger. Robert lifted his head, gazing at the portal; hypnotic, gold nebulas within it, like he saw that night – he felt detached from his body, wanting to enter and leave this imprisonment. Rose looked on in horror, holding on tight to Martin as the wind pulled and straightened her hair, she would have to let go to save her daughter.

'Oh, dear God. Please help,' she uttered. A powerful scent filled the area; sandalwood and frankincense, making Rose sniff the air, trying to locate it. Tears filled her smile when she saw her. Myriam - wearing a purple hijab with the same colour clothing - flowing like silk. She clutched her holy book in folded arms - green with gold inscriptions. Her face serene, purposeful. Rose sobbed at her presence.

'Myriam! No!' she came to her, placing her hand on her shoulder.

'I am, Himaya,' she smiled and emanated the purest light from her face, kissing Rose on both cheeks. She nodded her acknowledgement and continued to the centre amongst the fallen trunks. The mimic's faces stretched, almost splitting from their screams when they saw her, fleeing and vomiting. Zalud grinned, ready for the conflict, his black heart glowing like an ember. She knelt and placed the opened book down on the blackened mulch. The pages leafed by the wind – Myriam supplicated. A blue, magnetic vortex rose in the clearing. Verses lifted off the pages and merged with it; speaking for themselves, each as if it were alive – each, a representative of its prophetic phrases. The beautiful recitation filled every gap, bringing Rose to tears. Nearby trees twisted and bent towards its force, worshipping it. More phrases and verses lifted from the pages, imposed onto the swirling mass – calligraphed in Arabic. Zalud held his head and bellowed in their native tongue, his power leaving and the portal shrinking. Robert wanted to jump in before it disappeared completely. It was his imprint, reluctant to let it go. Rose held him down with all her strength.

'No! Robert! Close your eyes! Don't look at it!'

The deities were given energy, bringing snow – a snow without cold, blanketing the dark woods with divine calm, dispersing the dark and preventing further damage. The vortex expanded, lifting and dropping the floor - releasing the network of roots, bursting through the soil, working together. Loud snapping of wood dominated the surrounding noise. Stretching, racing over each other at speed- reaching Zalud and wrapping around him, forming a twisted, iron cage – his creatures panicked and swarmed him; becoming a containment of squirming scarabs. The felled trees levitated as the blue vortex grew, its electrical field resembled cirrus clouds, circling as such. Gravity left and the force pulled.

Robert watched twigs pass his eyes, bugs too, wriggling their little legs while Rose desperately tried to hold them down, crying out from the effort. Lillian stood like a rooted tree. Phil panicked as he felt himself being sucked in, unable to use his ability.

'Lilly! Take my hand!' She looked on, fighting with her feelings. The rescue in the hotel had brought them closer; all she ever wanted was a big brother, pitying him as he hung there – all the bravado that hid another dysfunctional soul. She reached out and the cage burst open - the beetles fell out in a heap, scurrying over each other for safety. Zalud merged with the vortex in a dense, black mist - his portal retracted at warp speed leaving Phil yelling in protest. The mimics left behind, disappeared into the barks to wait for the end-of-days and their leader's return. Phil twisted and grabbed Lillian's arm.

'Don't let go! I'm your brother!' Lillian fought off the tears, her breathing heavy. Robert could see it, but was helpless. Rose lay over him, averting her eyes.

'Martin! Now would be good!' Martin rose to his feet, unaffected by the pull. He could breathe again, the spell had lifted after all these years, suppressing his gift. Walking over to Lillian, he prised Phil's fingers off of her arm.

'Oh no you don't,' he said, as the last finger was released. He grabbed Phil by the wrist before he was consumed, suspended like a kite.

'Dad! Please! I'm sorry! No!' Martin's eyes darkened to a deep purple and Phil's chest began to burn.

'I'm sorry too, son. But this is your consequence. Think of it as starting over, out of everyone's way, where you can't hurt anybody. Count yourself lucky.'

'No! Dad! Wait! I'll change! Please!' Martin inhaled, and let go.

They heard Latin being recited in deep, defensive voices along with the pitiful screaming of Phil, thrust into joining the rest of the quarantined humans. The vortex shrunk and slowed, waiting for its last entry. Myriam stood, looking back at Rose - they smiled at one another, blowing each other kisses, pained from separation – and then, she walked into the blue vortex, her oppression and trials removed. The divine gate closed on in itself, the orbs following. Everything dropped to the floor and a deafening silence prevailed.

Lillian rushed to Rose, and they hugged tightly. She noticed the coat covering Lisa, lifting it from her face, bursting into tears at the pale complexion but one that was at peace. Lillian tidied Lisa's hair and said her goodbyes in silence. Martin held her, comforting the gentle sobs and shocks that ran through her. Oliver waited patiently as himself, ready to join the others and live amongst the organic.

'Bluebell, someone wants to see you,' Martin raised her chin and nodded towards Oliver. He stood there, a vision of a fairy tale; still looking a bit like her pet, perhaps in her mind's eye. Lillian's heart broke, wanting him back in her arms so she could feel his whole body and sumptuous fur; his paws clutched in her hands. The little breaths through that cute snoot, bringing her through it all and the purrs that sent her to sleep.

'I'll come and see you every day, I promise,' she convulsed, her tears dripping in the dirt, adding some life. Mintaka blinked those bright, orange eyes respectfully. His heart had changed, but leaving his person contorted his celestial features – disappearing behind the tree her and Robert got married under, without looking back.

Robert moaned and called her, she knelt beside him, they held hands and kissed; Lillian wiping smears of blood from his face.

'Hey, tree wife. Are we dead?' she burst out a shallow laugh through the flow of grief.

'No. Still here. What is it with you and close calls, eh?'

'I'm just accident prone. You okay? I thought I lost you.' Lillian nodded, closing her eyes and clamping her lips.

'They were just passing through, Lil. Right? To bring us back together.' She cried loud into his shoulder, making him wince, he felt bruised from head to toe. Martin looked upon them; Robert noticed he was different - upright and holy. He seemed younger, fuller. They smiled at each other with no words, just an intuitive nod was exchanged.

'Where's Dave?' Lillian sniffed. He was groaning in a wet and dirty heap and had landed up next to a woman, Janice. Inspector, Janice Tate - curled up, dressed in strange hessian clothing.

'Why didn't you throw the book in?' Martin asked Rose.

'Well, I thought we could keep hold of it, just for a little while. The mother trick worked well, don't you think? But I'm definitely taking that one.' She crawled on her hands and knees to retrieve the Quran Myriam had left behind.

Fifty

5 months later

'Come on Cooch! Time to go!' Robert called up the stairs.

'Coming!'

'Wow. You look positively radiant.' Robert locked up, pulling up his lapels; rubbing his hands together to create some friction.

'You need a coat!'

'I'm too cool for coats.' They got in the Beamer, shivering from the cold.

'What's the craving today then?'

'Feta cheese,' Lillian answered, feeling nauseous.

'What? You just made that up!'

'No, I swear! It's whatever William says he wants.'

'Ok. You're the boss. Feta cheese it is.'

'Do you think Luna will be alright, on her own?'

'She'll be fine, Lil. She's already made herself at home. Someone must be missing her.'

'Well, I asked around and no one seemed to be missing a white cat.'

'She's a beauty, like her mum. Stars after work, is it?'

'Too cloudy. Although the weekend is looking good.'

'Duvets, thermos flasks and hypothermia it is.' Robert smiled and squeezed her knee, then pulled out of the drive and out of Coed-y-Frind Close, content with his new life.

He made an offer on the house that Celia couldn't refuse. She needed the money to look after Jeffrey; spoon-feeding him would take some getting used to, but it was like having her baby back – a very heavy one. At least he couldn't moan about the food anymore, being paralysed. Pushing him around in the wheelchair was an effort through the old house and the wobbly front castors got stuck in the cracks.

Lisa's funeral was a day that carried many feelings, Lillian wasn't sure how she felt - it was someone she did lose twice. Brian was a wreck, but his Italian mistress held him up at her graveside before they moved to Milan. He kept his word and promoted Robert to IT Director and certified hacker. It was downstairs and he missed the light and frivolity upstairs but the different direction he took every day, was his rite of passage.

Lillian still worked in International Sales with a new female boss. It was strange without Lisa, her absence took some getting used to and there were no more belly laughs. Tim was never seen again. No one knew what happened to him either. She wouldn't be staying there that long, deciding to take an extended maternity leave. Funny how things can change at the flip of a coin.

Dave became the new warehouse manager, after a little persuasion and it was great having him back. Although she missed that hair since he'd had a complete change of image and personality - a little quieter than before, no more cocktail sticks or denim jackets - but they still had their 'word of the day.'

Dinner at Rose and Martin's were the best they'd ever been, especially with the new arrival on its way. Rose seemed to have come to life again and so had Martin. He looked 10 years younger and the doctors were baffled how he recovered so quickly –something he tapped his nose and winked about, often.

Michael slept in his own room and his cognitive behaviour subsided making way for a less troubled little man. Contacting Lillian through his new mirror Grandma had bought for him, with racing cars on the back. Helen rented the house from Janice Tate, at a very reasonable price - the lowest in the district. Working again at Apex brought her confidence back, too.

Inspector Janice Tate had a lot of work to do - redecorating the dining room being the first and burning the books, as well as raising Annie's wages. Adrian D'Or was moving in, they'd met in the force. Spraying cars was something he'd left behind. Phil's case had gone cold in the absence of a defendant, and the disappearance would take some explaining and a lot of convincing. But the password written all over Robert's hotel room was a vital lead into illegal transactions of the drug, thanks to Bal. Her experience in the other realm was never spoken about - she was sworn to secrecy or face a return, or worse. Although it was great to be back, it was tough dealing with life in the 90s after being in such an enriched and advanced environment, one which was permanently etched. It took a while to learn how to live like us, all over again. Lillian agreed to help them out with unsolved murder cases, using her new skill of entering rooms. Her gift had become part of her breathing - now that she was loved unconditionally.

Robert blew down his shirt, cooling his scorched chest – he still got a buzz in his stomach from her, especially now he finally knew why she seemed so familiar, slotting all the dèjá vu pieces into place. Helping him remember, with a little bit of magic under the stars. Four-year-old Robbie and his 'imaginary friend' - always waiting for her return in front of his bedroom mirror. Pretty and mischievous, coming through it like a prancing gazelle - bringing a bright haze with her; a bluebell, coloured haze.

If you enjoyed my story, please leave a review, and tell your friends! The best way to help authors progress. You can also copy your review onto goodreads.com. Thank you. For my next book and inspirational posts, head over to Instagram @juliekabouya.writes

Acknowledgements

To list every single person that has provided material for this book, could get me into trouble. So, I would like to thank my beta readers, who gave me the faith to pursue my dream, my family and friends who are my biggest fans, and all that have been a part of this debut journey. Writing is part of my life, made possible by all that have graced my path.

About the Author

Julie Kabouya, an only child, was told that she had too much imagination, a regular comment on school reports. Impatient to be an adult, she left school and made her way through a number of jobs, mainly in the office environment, landing herself in a highly sought-after corporate establishment. That was where she was told she should write a book. Twenty-seven years and three children later, that's what she did – needing to experience life a little first, so she could flourish her gifts. She left the office politics to become a freelance Gardener, being a tree hugger and nature lover at heart. Julie lives in the UK and has pursued and accomplished her dream in becoming a published author.

Julie's stories are influenced by her own extraordinary encounters and beliefs in supernatural phenomena, derived from her faith and interest of paranormal perceptions within Arabic cultures and religious dogmas.

Follow Julie on Instagram for updates on her next books and inspirational posts: @juliekabouya.writes

Printed in Great Britain
by Amazon